THE VELVET TOUCH

NICK VELVET STORIES

EDWARD D. HOCH

Crippen & Landru Publishers
Norfolk, Virginia
2000

Cover painting by Carol Heyer
Cover design by Deborah Miller

Crippen & Landru logo by Eric D. Greene

ISBN: 1-885941-42-0

Second Printing, 2006

Printed in the United States of America

Crippen & Landru Publishers
P. O. Box 9315
Norfolk, VA 23505
USA

Email: CrippenLandru@earthlink.net
Web: www.crippenlandru.com

For Sandi and Doug Greene

CONTENTS

Introduction

I have written elsewhere that the Nick Velvet series started out in 1966 as my answer to James Bond. He was to be a modern, sophisticated thief who used high-tech gadgets to pull off unlikely thefts of valueless objects. Most of the gadgets vanished after the early stories, and Nick has gone on to survive pretty much by his wits. He quickly became the most popular and profitable of my many series characters, widely reprinted overseas and almost constantly under option for films and television.

Like many fictional thieves before him, Nick evolved into an amateur sleuth as well, forced to solve crimes in order to accomplish his mission, free himself from a frame-up, or collect his fee. The series continued like this, without major changes, until I decided in 1983 to introduce a highly skilled antagonist into the mix, a sort of master thief who could top even Nick. If he performed the impossible by stealing valueless objects, his nemesis would perform impossible feats before breakfast, in the manner of the White Queen from *Through the Looking Glass*.

Thus was born Sandra Paris, who has crossed paths with Nick in eight stories so far. Because fictional characters tend to insist on leading their own lives, the relationship between Nick and Sandra has not developed exactly as I'd imagined it would. There has been no romance between them, and they have become admiring adversaries rather than enemies, sometimes helping each other when one of them is in trouble.

When my publisher suggested that this volume might bring together all eight of the White Queen stories published so far, it seemed like a fine idea. One of the stories requires an added word of explanation. In 1991, for the fiftieth anniversary of *Ellery Queen's Mystery Magazine*, editor Eleanor Sullivan suggested I write three stories, each featuring a pair of my series characters. It seemed most likely that Nick Velvet would encounter Captain Leopold, my police detective, and just as likely that Sandra Paris should figure in the plot as well. The result was "The Theft of Leopold's Badge."

I've added six other previously uncollected Velvets to these eight. Two of them were special favorites of well-known anthologists. "The Theft of the Venetian Window" was chosen for Jacques Barzun's & Wendell Hertig Taylor's *Classic Stories of Crime and Detection* (1983), and Martin H. Greenberg included "The Theft of the Four of Spades" in his *Masterpieces of Mystery and Suspense* (1988). Two others, "The Theft of the Sherlockian Slipper" and "The Theft of Nothing at All" have also been anthology favorites. "The Theft of Cinderella's Slipper" and "The Theft of Gloria's Greatcoat" are reprinted here for the first time, the former because it features an impossible disappearance and the latter for those who might have wondered how Nick and his long-time companion Gloria first met. It was written in 1998 to mark my twenty-five years of monthly appearances in *Ellery Queen's Mystery Magazine*.

As I write this at the end of 1999, there have been seventy-six Nick Velvet stories published in all. You'll find a list of the titles at the back of the book. They wouldn't have been possible without the encouragement of the three editors of *EQMM* who have guided the series over the years — Fred Dannay, Eleanor Sullivan and Janet Hutchings.

Since these stories began in 1966, no year has passed without at least one new adventure, and I hope Nick will be around well into the next century.

Edward D. Hoch
Rochester, New York
December 1999

THE VENTURES OF NICK VELVET

The Theft of the Venetian Window

Nick Velvet arrived in Venice on the morning train. It was the first time he'd ever taken a train to an island, unless one counted Manhattan, and there was something just a bit strange about traveling across the long railroad bridge that led into the city. Looking out the window to his right, he could see cars on the highway bridge, the Ponte Della Liberta, racing the train to its destination. Since cars were allowed in such a tiny section of the city itself, he wondered why anyone bothered.

It was Nick's first visit to Italy, though he'd once had a stopover at the Rome Airport. He'd never had the desire of some Italian-Americans to seek out the mountain villages from which their ancestors had come. To Nick home had always been a few square blocks of Greenwich Village where he was born and raised, back in the days when the area was more Italian than bohemian.

No, it was not nostalgia that brought him to Venice — only money. He'd been offered his standard fee of $20,000 to steal a mirror.

"It is the most valuable single object on the face of the earth," Milo Mason had told him a few days earlier in a New York hotel room. There was a time, early in his career, when Nick avoided meetings in hotel rooms on the theory they could be bugged too easily. Now, in a day when even the olive in a martini could conceal a listening device, there seemed little point in his caution.

He'd stared at the fat man with the strange, far-away eyes and answered, "I never steal anything of value, Mr. Mason. I guess the job's not for me."

"You're turning it down?" Mason had asked incredulously.

"A month ago a man wanted me to steal the weather vane from the top of an old New England church. I was ready to do it until I found out that these days antique dealers are offering small fortunes for historic weather vanes. I made a rule years ago to steal only the worthless, the valueless. These days, when everything seems to have value for someone, it's increasingly difficult to live by my rule. But I still try."

"I can assure you no antique dealer wants this mirror, Mr. Velvet. It's a simple rectangle framed in plain wood. No jewels, no gold. It may be old, but the workmanship has no value."

Nick had smiled, trying to kid the man along, trying to relieve the tension he saw in those deep dark eyes. "But it's Venetian glass, isn't it? And that's valuable."

The man shook his head. "It's glass, and it's in Venice. But it's not Venetian glass." The eyes hardened. "If you must know, I will tell you why this mirror is the most valuable object on the face of the earth. Then you can decide whether you dare to steal it!"

"Fine. Tell me."

"Do you believe in an alternate universe, Mr. Velvet? A world in which everything is quite a bit different, in which I might be a king and you might be a priest?"

"I used to read some science fiction," Nick admitted.

"This is not science fiction! This is fact! An alternate universe does exist. As you may not know, these two universes touch at only one point on earth. That mirror in Venice is more than a mirror — it is a window connecting these alternatives. We live in one world, but a step through that mirror would put us in another, far different world!"

Nick nodded. "I think I know the mirror you mean. Fellow named Lewis Carroll used to own it."

"Don't scoff, Mr. Velvet! There's some evidence that the story of this very mirror might have inspired *Through the Looking-Glass*."

"I'm sure."

"Will you do it? I warn you, the mirror is well guarded."

Nick stared at him for just a moment longer. Then he said, "Mr. Mason, you've got yourself a deal."

That had been three days ago in America. Now he was here, approaching Venice, and feeling just a bit guilty about taking $20,000 from a man who was obviously insane. "Your first time in Venice?" a tall man in the next seat asked. He was obviously American, with graying hair and a pleasant smile.

"First time in Italy, really," Nick responded.

"Mine, too. I'm Vincent Cross, here to see a dealer about some tapestry business." He peered out the window as the train came into the station. "Looks like a fascinating city. I wanted to fly in and see it from the air, but the connections weren't right."

Nick agreed. Venice had a small airport in the Lido resort area and the larger Marco Polo Airport on the mainland, but many visitors found it more convenient to take the train up from Bologna. The two men left the train together at the main passenger terminal on the Grand Canal, and Nick told Cross he hoped to see him again.

"Look me up," the tall man urged. "I'll be at the Excelsior."

Nick arranged for his bag to be sent ahead to his hotel, then wandered in a park across from the station, visiting the little booths where souvenirs and trinkets were sold. He had the look of an uncertain tourist, and he wasn't surprised when a raven-haired young woman in a green pants suit approached him.

"Pardon me. Would you like a tour of the city?"

She was American, and quite lovely. "I don't really need one," he replied with a grin, "but it's good to hear a voice from home."

"I thought you might not care for the standard tour of churches."

"Don't I look the type?"

"I offer something more personalized to your interests. My name's Sally Gilbert."

"I'm Nick Velvet. You a student?"

"An overaged one. You're from the New York area, aren't you?"

"How'd you know?"

"I'm studying linguistics. New Yorkers are easy to spot."

"What's this tour business you have?"

She shrugged. "Just a way to make money. I meet the new arrivals and offer personally conducted tours."

He took some lira from his pocket. "I'm game. If I like it I'll buy you a drink as a tip."

"We'll start with a vaporetto trip on the Grand Canal."

The vaporetto proved to be a small steam ferry that operated much like a bus along the canal, stopping first on one side and then on the other to pick up passengers and let them off. Nick gazed up at the drab splendor of the old buildings and said, "It's quite a city. But do the canals always smell this bad?"

"They do in the summer, I'm afraid. Some say the whole city is just rotting away. It's built on 118 islands, divided by 160 canals, and linked by nearly 400 bridges. The Fifth Century Veneti sought refuge here from invaders."

"They picked a good place."

"Because of the high arched bridges and narrow streets, only pedestrian traffic is allowed in most of the city. All other traffic, including police, ambulances, and even funerals, is by water. People phone for a gondola as they would a taxi back home, or else they ride the vaporettos or motorboats."

"You certainly know everything!"

"A guide has to," she replied with a grin. By the pale light reflected off the canal, her face was even prettier than he'd first realized.

"I must confess I'm seeking a specific address on the Calle Lion," he told her. "But perhaps we could meet for that drink later."

Sally Gilbert threw back her head, letting the breeze catch her long black hair. "This is the famed Rialto Bridge," she said as they passed beneath a covered walkway with arched sides. "You must have seen pictures of it." Then she turned her gaze back to his, as if only now hearing his previous words. "I'll take you to the Calle Lion. We should get off at the next stop."

Once on land she led the way through a maze of narrow streets that opened suddenly into the Piazza San Marco. "I recognize this," he admitted, watching a swirl of pigeons take to the air.

"It's a bit out of our way, but I wanted you to see it. This is the heart of the city — the symbol of Venice."

They strolled past the splendor of St. Mark's Basilica and the Doges' Palace, mingling with the noonday tourists. Then she led him deeper into the city, across narrow canals where the odorous water seemed barely to move. "Is it far?" he asked once.

"Not far." They crossed a last canal — and he saw the rusty sign on a corner building. *Calle Lion.*

"This is it," he said, turning to thank her.

"Be careful," she said simply, and she was no longer smiling. He started to speak, to ask where they could meet later, but a group of passing tourists separated them. And then she was gone, back the way they'd come.

The mirror which Milo Mason had described was located in the first building on the left — a weathered stone structure that crowded the narrow street and the canal. Nick climbed the worn staircase to a second-floor apartment and knocked on the door of the dimly lit hall. A small plaque read simply: *Giorgio Lambazi — Tappezzerie.*

He heard a bolt being drawn, and the door opened. "Who is it?"

"My name is Velvet. I'd like to interview you for a news story."

"I grant no interviews," Lambazi said, starting to close the door.

"A man named Milo Mason has made certain statements to the American press."

"Mason? That troublemaker? The man's mad, you know!" But he sighed and reached up to undo the chain. "Very well, come in. I was half expecting him to come in person. I understand he's in Venice. But I can only give you ten minutes. I'm alone here, and there's work to be done."

Nick followed him into a cramped living room that obviously doubled as a study. It was bizarrely decorated with great hanging tapestries, like some sheik's domain. The largest of the tapestries, reaching from floor to ceiling over much of the room's south wall, showed a strange other-worldly scene of American Indians coming ashore from native boats at a European fishing village.

"Do you like it?" Lambazi asked Nick.

"What is it?"

"An Eighteenth Century tapestry titled *The Indian Discovery of Europe.*"

"Oh?"

"Perhaps in an alternate universe it happened that way," Lambazi said. He spoke good English with only a trace of accent, and though he looked close to 70, he moved with the step of a much younger man. He was completely bald, but wore a short pointed beard that went well with his piercing eyes.

Nick sat down opposite him, trying not to look at the conspicuous mirror on the far wall. "Milo Mason mentioned these somewhat wild theories of yours."

"Mason is a writer on occult and paranormal subjects whose work has succeeded in softening his brain. He *believes*, Mr. Velvet, and that is a very dangerous thing."

"Then you don't believe in an alternate universe?"

"I believe only in the money such things can bring me. I have this tapestry, I have that mirror once believed to be a window to another universe, and I have other such trappings of the bizarre. But to say that I believe in them as Milo Mason does . . ."

Nick walked over to examine the mirror, now that Lambazi had brought it into the conversation. It was not large — perhaps 18 inches wide by two feet high — and it was set in a plain wooden frame held flush to the wall by four screws. Nick knew he could have it off the wall and out of the apartment in minutes. It would be the easiest money he ever earned.

"He believes this to be a window to another world," Nick said, but he could see nothing other than his own face in the clouded glass.

"A foolish superstition! I keep the mirror here to amuse people like Milo Mason. It is a mark of his insanity that he believed what I told him."

"He believed it, all right." Nick noted the bolted steel shutters over the room's only window. "Maybe you do too, the way you guard it."

"The window overlooks the Rio di San Lorenzo, one of our dirtier canals. Hardly worth the view. And the precautions are for my tapestries, not the mirror."

"But don't you ever go out?"

"Certainly! I have a shop near here. A friend downstairs, Malamocco, looks after the apartment when I'm away from it."

Nick wondered why he was wasting his time. He knew — as did Lambazi — that Milo Mason was in the city. Nick was to meet him that evening to deliver the mirror. He needed only to tap this man on his bald head, take the mirror, and leave.

"I see the cups," Nick said. "Might I join you in some espresso?"

"Certainly." The old man rose. "Let me make some fresh."

Nick was remembering the sleeping pills he carried in the tool kit around his waist. It might be easier this way. He followed Lambazi into a tiny cluttered kitchen that lacked the baroque grace of the main room. Here, instead of hanging tapestries, there was only a fly-specked calendar that still showed the preceding month.

"You're most hospitable to one who just barged in on you," Nick said.

"When I heard the name of Milo Mason I had no choice but to let you in." He went about the task of preparing the espresso. "Some water, if you please, from the tap there. Be careful — the C is *caldo*, hot."

When the espresso was ready, Nick complimented the old man on its taste. "Fine! Much better than at home!" And when Lambazi turned to unplug the machine, Nick dropped the sleeping pills into Lambazi's cup.

"You must realize," Lambazi said, sipping his coffee, "that Milo Mason is a lunatic. His obsession with my mirror is only one example of it. I don't know what the man might do."

"How did you come by the mirror?" Nick asked, waiting for the pills to take effect.

"It was left in my care by a ship's captain who told me the story I repeated to Mason. The captain thought he saw visions in the mirror, though I suspect they were rum-fogged visions."

Nick shifted in his chair, growing impatient. "It is stuffy in here. Makes one sleepy." He yawned, but it did no good. "Mason said the mirror might have inspired Lewis Carroll."

Giorgio Lambazi merely laughed at that. He seemed as alert as ever, and after a moment he roused himself from his chair. "But I've given you more than ten minutes already. Please be gone now — I have other appointments."

Before Nick knew what was happening, the old man hustled him out the door. Since he'd ruled out the use of violence, there was nothing to do but leave. He heard the bolt and chain fall into place and he stood in the dim hallway considering his next move. Surely the drug would take effect within another fifteen minutes. He'd stay right there, wait till all was quiet, and go to work on the lock.

He pressed his ear against the door and thought he heard the old man's voice. After a time there was the sound of running water from the kitchen, then all was silent again.

After fifteen minutes, Nick set to work on the lock.

It was a simple task with the tools he carried in his belt. Once the bolt had slid free he opened the door far enough to unscrew the mountings for the chain lock. He could see Giorgio Lambazi slumped peacefully in his chair before the mirror.

"Don't worry, old man," he said softly as he entered the apartment and crossed to the mirror. "I won't disturb you a bit!"

He'd taken out his screwdriver to begin work on the mirror when something impelled him to turn and look again at old Lambazi, and that was when he saw the blood.

Giorgio Lambazi's throat had been cut. He was dead . . .

At eight that evening Nick saw Milo Mason enter the lobby of the swank Hotel Excelsior on Venice Lido and head directly for his table in the cocktail lounge. Nick had caught the evening motorship from Riva degli Schiavoni to the Lido, a chain of sandy resort islands between the Lagoon of Venice and the Adriatic. He was glad that Mason was on time for their meeting, because he was very conscious of the hotel's security men eyeing him with curiosity. Perhaps they thought he was a pickpocket, in for the summer resort trade.

"Did you get it?" Mason asked sliding onto the chair opposite Nick.

"No."

"No? What happened? What went wrong?"

"Giorgio Lambazi got himself murdered, that's what."

"Murdered!"

"Keep your voice down! This place is full of security people."

"But who killed him? When?"

"Just a few hours ago, and I don't know who. I don't even know how." He ran over the events quickly for Mason.

"He was dead in the chair? His throat cut?"

"That's right." Nick nodded.

"And you just ran away? You didn't bring the mirror with you?"

"Perhaps I didn't explain it clearly enough. Lambazi was alone in the apartment when he was killed. The only window, overlooking the canal, was shuttered and bolted on the inside. The only door was locked and bolted and I was outside it all the time. I searched the apartment after I reentered and found no one."

"Then how did the killer get in and get out?"

"If I'm to believe you and Lambazi, there's only one way possible — through the mirror."

"Of course!" Mason agreed readily. "*They* killed him!"

"I thought you'd say that," Nick agreed glumly.

"Is that why you didn't take the mirror?"

"In a way. You see, if you've been telling the truth, then the mirror really is of immeasurable value. And if that's the case, I can't steal it."

In truth, that had only been part of Nick's concern. Leaving the building in broad daylight carrying that good-sized mirror would surely be noted and remembered. The police would also notice the empty space on the wall and link Nick to the murder itself. And he had no intention of taking the blame for someone else's crime. It would be easy enough to get the mirror at a later date, if Mason still wanted it.

"Can't steal it!" Mason exploded. "You *agreed* to steal it! I told you at the time that it was the most valuable object on earth!"

"Well, perhaps I didn't quite believe you then."

"And you believe me now?"

"I believe that something — someone — entered Lambazi's apartment on the Calle Lion and cut his throat. And I can tell you they didn't pass through the only door or only window."

"Then the mirror is the only way!"

"Maybe," Nick agreed. "But while I was searching the apartment I noticed something a bit unusual. There were bloodstains on both of the water faucets in the kitchen, indicating the killer got blood on his hands, and perhaps on his clothing, and tried to wash it off. Would that be necessary for your mirror people? A supernatural killer would hardly pause to wash off the bloodstains with cold water."

"But you say there was no way out. Do you claim Lambazi committed suicide?"

"No chance of that. The weapon was missing. And as I say, the killer apparently walked to the kitchen to wash off the blood. I even heard the water running before I worked the lock."

"Did you call the police?"

Nick shook his head. "I was hardly in a position to do that. As it is, when they find the lock picked and the chain removed they'll think it the work of a burglar. I didn't linger to set things right."

"And the mirror?"

"I have to convince myself it's not valuable. And I guess the only way I can do that is by finding out how Giorgio Lambazi was killed."

Malamocco.

Nick remembered the name and wondered what to do about it.

Malamocco was Giorgio Lambazi's friend from downstairs, the one who shared the guarding of the place. If there was any funny business with the apartment — a secret passage or the like — Malamocco would be the most likely one to know about it. Or, Nick quickly told himself, most likely to have used it.

Milo Mason had gone up to his hotel room, leaving Nick to set matters right. As he was debating about taking a motorship or vaporetto back to the main islands, two familiar figures crossed the lobby. One was Vincent Cross, the man on the train that morning. The other was Sally Gilbert.

Still remembering Sally's parting warning to be careful, he crossed the lobby to intercept them. "Hello again!"

"Well," Sally said with a smile, "it's Mr. Velvet."

Vincent Cross looked puzzled for just an instant. Then the frown disappeared. "Of course, on the train this morning! Did you complete your business, Velvet?"

"Not quite yet. And you?" Suddenly he was remembering the nature of Vincent Cross's business.

"No luck. I've just engaged Miss Gilbert here to take me to meet a tapestry dealer."

The American girl nodded. "Would you believe it? Two customers in one day wanting to go to the Calle Lion?"

"I'd believe it," Nick said.

The puzzled look was back on Cross's face. "You were at the Calle Lion today too, Velvet?"

"Perhaps we know the same man — Giorgio Lambazi?"

"Of course! He's a dealer in rare tapestries — the man I mentioned on the train."

"What a coincidence!" Sally Gilbert remarked.

"I rarely believe in coincidences," Nick remarked.

"I didn't know you were in the tapestry business," Cross said.

"I'm not. I deal in many things. Right now it's mirrors."

"Antique mirrors?"

"Let's say valuable mirrors."

Sally glanced at her watch. "It's getting late. An old man like Lambazi no doubt retires early. If you still want to see him tonight we should get started."

Cross agreed. "It's my first time in Italy. I'm afraid I spent more time sightseeing today than getting down to business."

Nick cleared his throat. "You might save yourselves the trouble of making the trip. I just came from there, and Lambazi's apartment is blocked off by the police. It seems something has happened to him."

"Police?"

Nick nodded, but Sally Gilbert said, "There were no police in the Calle Lion this afternoon."

"They are there now," Nick said, hoping he was right. He assumed that someone — perhaps Lambazi's downstairs friend — would have found the open door and the body by now.

Vincent Cross snorted. "Then it's no place for me. I think I'll turn in, Miss Gilbert. Tomorrow morning we can go there and see what's up. Okay?"

"Fine. Should I be here at nine?"

He pursed his lips. "Make it nine thirty. And breakfast with me if you wish."

Nick watched him stroll across the lobby to the elevators, pausing at the newsstand to purchase a copy of an English-language newspaper. "You lost me a job," Sally Gilbert complained.

"So you'll get it tomorrow. Or are your rates higher at night?"

She ignored his implication and said, "The least you can do is buy me a drink."

He ushered her into the bar, to the very table he'd occupied with Milo Mason a short time before. "What'll you have?"

"Scotch and water."

He ordered and turned to her. She'd changed her costume since the afternoon, and now wore a long green skirt topped by a sleeveless jerkin. "I like your outfit."

"Thank you."

"But it's hardly the thing a girl guide wears around Venice by night, is it? Aren't long skirts cumbersome for climbing in and out of gondolas?"

"Gondolas are for tourists and romantics. I'm neither."

"This afternoon you warned me to be careful. Why?"

She sipped her drink before replying. "The streets can be dangerous. I was only expressing concern for a fellow American."

"Bunk! Look, I don't buy coincidences. First, I run into Vincent Cross on the train this morning. Second, I meet you outside the train station. Third, I meet you together tonight. Fourth, it turns out Cross and I both came to Venice to see Lambazi.

Too many coincidences by far."

She let out her breath. "You're into something you don't understand, Nick."

He liked the sound of his first name, but nothing else. "Suppose you try explaining it."

She shook her head. "Not yet. Not till I understand it all myself."

"What's your connection with Cross?"

"The same as with you. I sought him out here. Picked him up, if you prefer that term."

"For Lambazi?"

She hesitated. "Yes. I did some work for him."

"And my meeting with Cross on the train?"

"A true coincidence, as far as I know. Not too unusual for a couple of Americans to strike up a conversation in a foreign country."

"Just what sort of work did you do for that old man? Obviously if you sought us both out, it had to be because of Lambazi."

"I can't talk about that. Not yet."

"Did you know he'd been murdered?"

She hesitated only an instant. "Yes."

"Who told you?"

"Malamocco phoned me an hour ago."

"And just who is this mysterious Malamocco?"

"You'll have to ask him that."

In the morning Nick decided to do just that. Sally Gilbert had left him after the drink, resisting his half-hearted suggestion of a nightcap in his room. Since he'd reached 40, Nick was increasingly aware of the problems of mixing business with pleasure. Where young women like Sally Gilbert were concerned, he was older and wiser — and more faithful to Gloria back home.

So it was not yet nine o'clock when the motorship deposited him back at the Ponte della Pieta, not far from where he'd departed the evening before. The Riva degli Schiavoni stretched along the entire waterfront at this point, running from the Doges' Palace on the Piazza San Marco across several small canals till it merged with the Riva Ca di Dio. He remembered that one of the canals took him directly to the Calle Lion.

When he arrived at the familiar building he saw a police launch on the canal. The men on it seemed to be looking up at the second-floor shutters of Lambazi's apartment. Nick ignored them and went quickly inside, finding the apartment of A. S. Malamocco without difficulty. As Lambazi had told him, it was on the ground floor, directly below the dead man's rooms.

When he answered the knock, Lambazi's friend proved to be a shriveled little man of indeterminate age, younger than Lambazi but obviously suffering from some chronic illness that left his face drawn and haggard. "Who are you?" he asked in passable English. "Another policeman with questions?"

"If you thought I was a policeman, you'd be speaking Italian, wouldn't you? You know very well who I am. And I know who you are, Malamocco."

The directness of his approach caused the man to fall back and let him enter. "Yes, I am Malamocco. And you are the American who visited my friend Giorgio shortly before I found him dead yesterday. Have you come to do the same for me?"

"The prospect doesn't seem to frighten you."

The little man seated himself with obvious pain. "With me death would be a favor. Like Venice I feel I am sinking slowly into the sea."

"I wanted to ask you about Giorgio, and about his mirror."

Malamocco gave a dry chuckle. "I think that mirror was the death of him."

"Then you believe in an alternate universe?"

"Of course not! I believe in the Lord, and very little else. No one believed that rot except Milo Mason, and everyone knows he's crazy! An eccentric author who came to believe his own writings. He started out writing a magazine article about Giorgio and ended up demanding to buy the mirror."

"Is Mason crazy enough to kill for that mirror?"

"Certainly. Or to pay someone else to do his killing for him," Malamocco said pointedly.

"I didn't kill him."

"Giorgio was expecting only three visitors yesterday. He would not have opened his door to anyone else, not even to his young men."

"What young men?"

"Sometimes young men visited him in the evenings," Malamocco answered vaguely, perhaps sorry he brought it up.

"Homosexuals?"

"No, no, nothing like that."

"Who were the three he was expecting?"

"An American tapestry dealer named Vincent Cross and Milo Mason and a young woman named Sally Gilbert."

"What was Sally Gilbert's connection with Lambazi?"

"She came here twice a week, to bring him lists of wealthy tourists visiting the city. She obtained them from hotels and tourist agencies, and Giorgio then contacted the people to offer his tapestries. Sometimes Giorgio asked her to meet people at the station, too."

"That explains her meeting me," Nick said. "And Cross, too. But then Lambazi must have known I was coming."

"Milo Mason would have told him. Otherwise, Giorgio would never have let you into the apartment."

"If Mason was crazy enough to buy the mirror, why didn't Lambazi simply sell it to him?"

The little man shrugged and shifted painfully in his chair. "I think he enjoyed tormenting Mason. He told him once he'd take that mirror to the grave rather than let Mason have it."

Nick turned his attention to the apartment itself. It was laid out exactly like the one above it, with a living room, kitchen, bedroom, and bath. Is there any way of getting up there from here, except by the front stairs?"

"What other way would there be?"

"I don't know," Nick admitted. But he walked across the room to a door in the south wall and yanked it open.

Malamocco chuckled. "Merely a closet full of my dirty clothes. No secret staircase, if that is what you seek. And I assure you the ceiling is quite solid."

Nick closed the door with a smile. "You omitted yourself from your list. Certainly you could have entered Lambazi's apartment at any time."

"Yes," Malamocco agreed. He peered at the ornate wall clock and began shuffling across the room. "Now you must excuse me. I must attend my old friend's funeral."

"This morning?"

"In one hour. The police released the body, and I am seeing to its burial." He put on his raincoat, though the day was warm and sunny. "Now I must go."

"You expecting a storm?"

"The cemetery at San Michele is some distance away by boat. After burying a number of one's friends, one learns that the spray from the water can be very damp."

"I see. He walked with the man to the hallway and peered upstairs at the door.

Malamocco glanced sideways at him. "If you were wondering about the mirror, it's to be buried with him. I placed it in the coffin myself, an hour ago."

"Then he meant it? About taking it to the grave?" Nick stared down at the face of the sick little man, hesitated a moment, then said, "In that case, let me accompany you to the funeral."

The funeral procession, in a trio of specially equipped vaporettos, wound through the canals until it reached the open water opposite the square green island of San Michele. The church was the only dominant structure in view as they headed across the choppy water toward Lambazi's final resting place.

He had no family, and only the priest and Malamocco rode in the first vaporetto with the coffin and the undertaker's assistants. Behind them came a few other people, neighbors perhaps, and Nick saw Sally Gilbert standing among them, gripping a railing against the choppiness of the water. He was surprised to see Vincent Cross there, too, though Cross didn't seem to be with Sally.

Nick was in the third boat, and by the time it deposited him at the dock before the church, the others were far ahead. But that was the way he wanted it. He detached himself from the main funeral procession and headed down one of the wide walks that ran between the rows of ancient graves.

Here, away from the stench of the narrow canals, there was a feeling of openness and peace, a freshness to the air that had eluded him till now. It seemed fitting that those who'd lived their lives on the 118 islands of the city should find peace at last on an island such as this.

When finally he saw the vaporettos leave, Nick made his way to the coffin where it stood beside the family mausoleum, waiting for interment. It took him only a minute or two to unscrew the lid and remove the mirror from atop the old man's corpse. "You won't be needing to see yourself," Nick said softly.

Then he heard a footstep behind him, and turned.

"You saved me the trouble," Vincent Cross said. He held a pistol in his hand, pointed at Nick's chest.

"I'm not surprised to see you," Nick told him. "I've known for some hours that you killed Lambazi."

"A wild guess, but a correct one," Cross said. "Lambazi was standing in the way of a business venture of sorts. I wanted to be cut in, but he wouldn't take partners."

"It was no wild guess," Nick corrected him. "I was baffled by how the killer entered and left Lambazi's apartment, but in truth he was there all the time. Isn't that right? You were there when Lambazi let me in, and you were still there when I returned to find the body. I had only Lambazi's word that he was alone, and there are two good reasons for thinking he lied.

"First, there were espresso cups in the living room, implying more than one drinker. And second, would a man like Lambazi, with double locks on the door and steel shutters on the window, who admitted only certain people to his apartment, allow me to enter when he knew I came from Milo Mason? Certainly not, if he was alone — but he might allow it if he knew someone else was hidden in the apartment to protect him."

"And where was I hidden?" Vincent Cross asked with a smile.

"In the closet in the south wall of the living room. I never looked there because I never saw the door. It was completely hidden by a floor-to-ceiling tapestry of the Indians discovering Europe. But when I visited Malamocco's identical apartment downstairs, I saw it there and realized where you'd hidden. I suppose when you came out and found him falling asleep in his chair it was too good an opportunity to pass up. You figured I'd be blamed for the killing. When you heard me at the door again, you simply returned to your closet behind the tapestry and let me find the body."

"You're so sure it was me?"

Nick nodded. "Malamocco told me Lambazi was expecting three visitors yesterday, and would not have admitted anyone else. They were you, Milo Mason, and Sally Gilbert. If we add Malamocco himself, we have four possible suspects. Certainly Lambazi wouldn't have let a stranger hide in his closet. The girl is ruled out because she was outside the building with me at a time when the killer had to be already with Lambazi. But we can leave her on the list of suspects.

"You see, when the killer cut Lambazi's throat he got blood on his hand, and probably on his sleeve as well. He washed it off at the kitchen faucet. But I found bloodstains on *both* faucets, not just on the cold water faucet that would normally be used for bloodstains. Why did the killer turn on the hot water faucet, too? Because in Italy the faucets are marked C and F instead of the American H and C. And in Italy the C stands for caldo, or hot.

"Certainly Malamocco would know that, and also a frequent Italian visitor like Milo Mason. And so would Sally Gilbert, who knows the city well enough to run tours here. That only leaves you, Cross — the first-time visitor from America."

"Yes." He raised the pistol a bit. "Now please place that mirror very carefully on the ground and step back."

"But I don't know why. Surely you're not a believer in an alternate universe, like Milo Mason."

"I'm a believer in cold cash. Lambazi was using the names he got from Sally Gilbert not to sell tapestries but to rob the hotel rooms of wealthy tourists visiting Venice. He supplied the names to a gang of young thieves who did the actual work, and then Lambazi fenced the stolen goods. Sally Gilbert knew about it, but was afraid to break away."

Nick remembered Malamocco's mention of young male visitors. And Sally's warning to be careful. "She told you of this? And what did she tell you about the mirror?" Nick asked.

"After Mason's fuss about the mirror, Lambazi thought it would be a good joke to use it as a hiding place — for his records of gang members, robberies pulled, the amounts of loot, and where he'd fenced the loot. That's why he left instructions for the mirror to be buried with him. The records are on the mirror's back, beneath this brown paper, and with this information I can take over his organization."

"Why didn't you simply take the records after you killed him?"

"You interrupted me by breaking in. And when you left I feared the police might come at any moment. I planned to return later for the mirror, as you did."

Cross was ripping away the brown paper backing, exposing some white sheets of paper. Suddenly there was a familiar voice from nearby. "My mirror! What are you doing with it?"

Milo Mason sprang out from behind a mausoleum, waving a large revolver. Cross turned quickly and fired a single shot, but Mason fired at the same instant. Both men went down together.

Nick stepped over to the bodies. They were both dead.

He left the papers in the back of the mirror for the police to find, but stopped long enough to remove the balance of his fee from Mason's wallet. He figured he'd earned it. Then he hurried down to catch the next motor launch back to San Marco. He wanted to see Sally Gilbert once more before he left Venice.

The Theft of the Sherlockian Slipper

"Nick Velvet?"

The man who greeted him at the airport in Rome was dressed like Hollywood's idea of an American gangster. He'd been reading a copy of an English-language newspaper published daily in Italy, and he folded this under his arm as Nick approached. Obviously he knew he had the right man.

"That's me," Nick agreed. "Where's your boss?"

"He doesn't meet people at airports. I'll take you to his hotel."

They drove through the crowded Roman streets to a fancy hotel just a bit too Americanized with its plush decor and vague bustle. "I'll bet the boss loves it here," Nick said. "Just like New York."

The man ignored him and motioned toward the elevator. A few minutes later they were entering the suite of Joe Bonoto. "Velvet. Pleasure to meet you."

Nick shook the wrinkled hand. Joe Bonoto was older than he'd expected, an aged man living on memories of the past. Deported from the United States, he ruled a band of faithful followers in the hills of Sicily. To call them Mafia or even bandits was inaccurate. They were dedicated to no cause greater than the welfare of Joe Bonoto.

"I've come a long way," Nick told him.

"But your roots are here. In the old country."

"My roots are in the old Italian section of Greenwich Village. That's as far back as they go."

Joe Bonoto signaled for drinks. "You'll find the trip worthwhile. We want you to steal something."

"That's my business," Nick said, and indeed it was. Nick Velvet stole the unusual, the bizarre, the valueless. Never money or jewelry or objets d'art. "What is it?"

Joe Bonoto smiled. The surface of his face crinkled like a relief map. "A relic of Sherlock Holmes."

"Sherlock Holmes?"

The smile broadened. "There is a new ski resort in Meiringen, Switzerland, overlooking Reichenbach Falls. Naturally it has a Sherlock Holmes room, in honor of the place where Holmes and Moriarty fought to the death. Are you by any chance a Sherlockian, Velvet?"

"I read all of Conan Doyle's stories in my youth, but I haven't looked at them in years. I guess I can't be called a Sherlockian. Just what is this relic you want stolen?"

"Holmes's Persian slipper — the one in which he kept his pipe tobacco. It hangs near the fireplace in the Holmes room they have at Meiringen."

"There are other rooms like that," Nick pointed out. "I've read about one in London, and another somewhere in Switzerland. I'm sure they all have Persian slippers on display. What makes this one so valuable?"

Bonoto spread his hands. "It is not valuable, Mr. Velvet! You do not steal valuable objects, do you?"

"Correct. But you brought me over from New York and you're willing to pay my fee of $20,000. It must be worth that much to you."

"For Sherlockians it has a sentimental value."

"Why not steal it yourself?"

"My men are too well-known to the police. You can catch a plane to New York and never be seen here again."

"All right," Nick agreed. He'd stolen stranger things in his time, with even less explanation. Besides, Switzerland might be a nice place to visit at this time of year.

His first sight of Reichenbach Falls was a breathtaking one, and he wished that Gloria had been there to see it too. A thin stream of white water dropped down from some unseen spot among the trees, hit an outcropping of rock, and changed into a broad cone of foam and mist. He'd expected something like Niagara, but this was utterly different — a fearful, coal-black abyss as sinister now as it had been the day Doctor Watson described it.

Nick remembered the story of Holmes and Moriarty at the falls, and he could well understand the desire of a new ski resort to cash in on the legend. In truth, the resort was some distance from the falls proper, on a hill that faced in the opposite direction. It was still too warm for skiing, and Nick had the place virtually to himself when he checked in.

"Here to see the falls?" a sandy-haired Englishman asked him in the lobby.

"Among other things. I drove up from Italy. Name's Nick Velvet."

"Mine's Cottonwood. Felix Cottonwood. I travel in tobacco."

"Tobacco?"

"My firm supplies tobacco products to many resorts in this area. I come around in the autumn and the spring to take orders."

Nick glanced around the lobby. "I understand they have a Sherlock Holmes room here."

"Right this way. It's a prime tourist attraction."

Cottonwood led him down a short passage to a cluttered sitting room fenced off by a low railing. Here indeed was the famous room at 221B Baker Street, with its bust of Holmes by the window, its bullet-pocked "V.R." on the wall, and — yes — its Persian slipper hanging by the fireplace.

"It seems complete in every detail," Nick said. "I'm surprised that souvenir hunters don't hop the railing and make off with things."

"There's an alarm system," Cottonwood answered casually. "But there's never any trouble like that. Sherlockians are content to come and look. Rooms like this are all they have that's new and exciting, unless someday someone comes up with Watson's fabled dispatch-box of unpublished cases."

They returned to the lobby and Nick excused himself to go to his room. He decided to wait till the following day before attempting to steal the slipper. The thing was too easy, too certain.

And the very simplicity of the assignment is what gave him doubts.

He spent the following day touring the area and getting to know the other off-season guests at the ski resort. He found time after lunch to take another look at the Sherlock Holmes room, this time noting especially the electric-eye alarms that criss-crossed the reconstruction of 221B Baker Street.

That night, when activity had settled down to a table of late drinkers in the resort's rustic bar, Nick made his move. He leaped quickly over the railing and carefully avoided the first of the electric-eye beams, using a misty aerosol spray that pinpointed their path without setting off the alarms. It was a trick he'd learned from a recent film, which proved an occasional Saturday night at the movies with Gloria need not be a total waste.

He crossed the second beam and reached out for the curved Persian slipper on its hook by the fireplace. He wondered if it really was filled with tobacco or if there might be something far more valuable inside — something to tempt a man like Joe Bonoto.

In a moment he would know.

"Hold it right there," a woman's voice said suddenly from behind him. "I have a gun pointed at the back of your neck."

He turned slowly, keeping his hands in sight, and saw that she was only a girl, surely still in her early twenties. She had a tiny automatic pointed at him, but it only added to her beauty — in a way that moviemakers had discovered long ago. She was dark, probably French, but her English had been learned in Britain if he was any judge of accents.

"I'm Nick Velvet," he said with a smile. "Who are you?"

Even against a gun he was more at ease with a beautiful girl than with a goon like Bonoto, and perhaps she sensed this. "My name is Annette — don't move — Annette DuFrois. I followed you here from Rome."

He silently cursed himself. It wasn't like him to travel all that distance without spotting a tail, especially a girl as pretty as Annette DuFrois. "What do you want?" he asked her, feeling just a bit foolish.

"To talk, right now. Come out of the room very carefully, without tripping the alarms. If any bells ring, I'll shoot you."

"But —" He glanced back fondly at Holmes's Persian slipper, then decided it might be safer where it was for the present.

He negotiated the light beams with ease on the return trip, then walked ahead of the girl to the side exit. There was a moment when he might have disarmed her easily, but he was curious now about her reason for following him. He decided to listen before he acted.

"Which way?" he asked when they were outside.

"Straight ahead. I have a car parked down the road."

"Is that it?" he asked, reaching a low-slung white sports car parked among the weeds.

For answer she poked his ribs with the gun. "Inside. The door's unlocked."

Nick bent almost double to fit under the low roof, and the girl followed him into the front seat. He felt the gun nudge him again. "All right, we're here. Now what is all this?"

"You're working for Joe Bonoto," she said. "I saw you at his hotel."

Nick didn't answer at once. A car passed them on the road and its headlights flickered for an instant on her face. "You have lovely eyes, Miss DuFrois."

She raised the gun an inch, otherwise ignoring his remark. "He hired you to steal something from that Sherlock Holmes exhibit, didn't he?"

"Does that concern you?"

"Joe Bonoto concerns me. A long time ago he caused the death of my brother."

The girl was much too young for anything to have happened to her brother too long ago, but Nick said, "Tell me about it."

"There's not much to tell. Richard was running with a bad crowd. He had a job as a courier for Joe Bonoto, and he was paid off in narcotics. Richard became hooked on heroin and died in Paris of an overdose." She stared off into space for a moment, as if remembering it. "I was twelve years old at the time, and I couldn't understand what was happening to him. I was with him when he died."

"That's a reason for you to risk your neck going up against Joe Bonoto?"

"It's reason enough for me. Somebody has to keep the Joe Bonotos of this world from taking over."

Nick wondered if he had ever been that young and idealistic. "You're too pretty to be a philosopher, especially a dead philosopher."

"Are you threatening me?"

"Joe Bonoto will threaten you, if you get in his way."

"I have the gun, remember. You'll do what I say."

"And what's that?"

"Where are you to meet Bonoto after you steal this thing?"

"I'm not. I'll pass it to one of his men." That wasn't strictly true, but he wasn't about to set up his client for a bullet before he'd been paid.

The subterfuge didn't work. Annette raised the gun another few inches, until it was pointed at Nick's chin. "Joe Bonoto doesn't work that way. He never did. He doesn't trust anyone, including you. He'll be close by, ready to show himself and collect the loot personally."

He knew she spoke the truth. "You want to kill him, don't you? I suppose you figure gunning him down up here in Switzerland is a lot easier than shooting up his hotel in Rome or his villa in Sicily."

"Perhaps."

"Well, you won't get any help from me."

"Then I suppose I'll have to shoot you," she said calmly.

"I suppose you will. I've got no great love for Joe Bonoto, but he is paying me. I'm not about to lure him into a trap."

Annette DuFrois smiled. "I'm not asking you to do that. If I kill you now, and hide your body, he'd show up here sooner or later — just to find out what happened to you."

Nick weighed the possibilities and decided it was time to move. They'd talked long enough. He measured the distance between them and decided he could easily reach her before she could fire a shot. There was always an instant's hesitation when an amateur was faced with the need to kill. And that instant was all he needed.

Nick moved.

He was almost on her when the gun exploded in his face, spraying his eyes and face with a stinging cloud of chemical Mace. He'd made one miscalculation — she hadn't planned to shoot him at all.

"You fool," she said, and brought the pistol down on his helpless head.

He woke to awareness slowly, and his first conscious thought was the realization that he was face down in damp grass that tickled his nose. Then he felt something kick him in the ribs and he rolled over. It was just beginning to get light, and he could make out the gangster type who'd met him at the Rome airport. The man was standing over him with a gun, and Joe Bonoto himself hovered in the background, half sitting in the front seat of his car with one hand on the open door.

"Get up, punk," the gangster type growled.

Nick staggered to his feet, still rubbing eyes that felt like burning coals. That damned girl, she'd dumped him from the car and left him by the side of the road!

"We waited for your call," Bonoto said quietly. "When we didn't hear anything we came looking for you. We checked the ski resort and then we spotted you out here."

"I had an accident," Nick mumbled.

"Yeah."

"Besides, I wasn't supposed to call till morning."

Joe Bonoto leaned down. "It was lonely waiting for you. I kept remembering I paid you half your fee already. What happened?"

"A car sideswiped me." His vision was clear at last and he had only a slight headache from the blow of Annette's gun.

"Where is the slipper?"

"Still back at the resort. I didn't have a chance to lift it yet."

"We pay you twenty thousand dollars so we can come up here and get it ourselves?"

"I'll get it," Nick assured them, but Bonoto had made his point. He was on the scene now, and Nick's only payment was likely to come from the barrel of a gun. "Just stay out of sight so you won't be recognized." Or shot, he might have added, remembering Annette.

"Can you get the slipper now, this morning?"

It was still early, and Nick knew the other resort guests wouldn't yet be prowling about. "I can try. Give me a half hour, then drive up the side road and I'll meet you there."

Joe Bonoto nodded. "No tricks."

Nick quickly realized that Annette had driven him some distance from the resort before dumping him out of the car. By the time he walked back, the sun was over the rim of the mountains, but except for a few employees there was still little sign of movement about the place. His car was where he'd left it, and there was no evidence that Annette had returned.

Once more he hurried down the corridor to the Sherlock Holmes room. All was as he remembered it, except for one thing.

The Persian slipper was gone from its hook beside the fireplace.

Nick glanced at his watch. He had twenty minutes before it would be time to meet Bonoto — twenty minutes to explain the slipper's disappearance. Had Annette returned to steal it? He hadn't mentioned what object he was after, but she might have guessed. Or been after it herself from the beginning.

On the other hand, Bonoto might have stolen it and simply saved himself twenty grand.

Nick let his eyes roam over the other objects before him in the Holmes room, but nothing else seemed to have changed. Only the slipper was missing. Someone — Bonoto or Annette or someone else — had negotiated the electric-eye beams and got away with it.

Nick went to the door of the resort and looked down the road. The car belonging to Bonoto had drawn nearer — it was parked just off the road under some trees. Watching it, he was aware of the utter silence of the morning. Only the distant roar of the waterfall — always present and therefore unnoticed — reached his ears.

It was almost as if the spirit of Sherlock Holmes himself had entered the resort and taken down the familiar Persian slipper to fill his calabash pipe.

He went back up to his room to get the gun from his suitcase. Joe Bonoto was not the most stable man on earth, and Nick wanted to be armed when he told him the slipper was missing. Downstairs now there was more activity, as some of the guests had appeared for breakfast. He waved to Felix Cottonwood and a few of the others he'd got to know. Then he went outside and started down the road to Bonoto's waiting car.

The first thing he saw was Bonoto's gunman, sprawled in the weeds to the right of the car. There was little blood, because the dry earth had soaked it up quickly.

Nick drew a deep breath and looked inside the car.

Joe Bonoto was slumped behind a windshield punctured by three spiderwebbed holes. He was an old man, and he hadn't even moved fast enough to die on his feet.

Nick walked away fast without touching anything. His first impulse was to drive to the nearest large airport and book a flight back to New York. The entire assignment had been a bust — the slipper was gone, his client was dead, and the police would surely be looking for him before long.

But then he remembered Annette DuFrois.

Just maybe something could be salvaged from this after all.

It took him till midafternoon to locate her, and long before that some morning strollers came upon the bodies of Bonoto and his bodyguard. Local police cars converged on the scene, with police from more distant points arriving as word of the murdered man's identity became known.

Nick made himself scarce while employees and guests were being questioned, and concentrated on finding Annette. It was her low white sports car that finally revealed her, when he spotted it parked at an inn on one of the winding country roads to the south. He pulled up behind it and slouched down in his seat, waiting.

Presently she appeared, wearing a trim yellow pants suit and carrying a shoulder bag that no doubt held her gun. Nick waited until she had one hand on the door handle and then jumped from his car. Startled, she tried for her purse, but he grabbed it and held it tight. "No more Mace in the face, please."

"How did you find me?"

"It took patience."

"Have you decided to help?"

"You don't need any help. Bonoto and his bodyguard are both dead, back at the resort."

The color drained from her face. "You think I did it?"

"You're a likely suspect. And someone else might have heard you threatening him. The police will surely be looking for your car if somebody remembers seeing it around the place last night."

She gazed into his face. "You're not lying to me? Bonoto is really dead?"

"He's really dead. Isn't it time we talked about your position in all this?"

"I didn't kill him."

"I know that," Nick said.

"You do?" She seemed surprised. "How?"

"It was very quiet just before they were killed — an early morning sort of quiet. At least four shots were fired, one for the bodyguard and three through the car windshield at Bonoto. Yet I heard nothing. That can only mean the killer used a silencer. And a silenced gun isn't the weapon of a woman who announces her intentions in advance, a woman bent on avenging a dead brother. You have a tiny gun that fires Mace, and you probably have one just as tiny for bullets. Bonoto was killed by a professional, someone using a large-caliber silenced weapon."

"Who?"

"Does it matter to you.

"No, I suppose not. But I'm curious."

"I came to steal something for Bonoto, as you know."

"From the Sherlock Holmes exhibit?"

He nodded. "Someone beat me to it. I think that someone must also be the killer. He might have been escaping from the resort when he encountered Bonoto and was recognized."

"What is it that's so valuable?"

"The Persian slipper in which Holmes was said to have kept his tobacco."

"But —"

"Tobacco." He repeated the word slowly, and suddenly he remembered the unusual occupation of Mr. Felix Cottonwood.

Annette was at his side as they sped back up the hill to the resort. He left her car behind because it was too easily identified, and he didn't want the police stopping them now.

"But why would Cottonwood want the slipper?" she asked. "And why would he want to kill Bonoto?"

"That's what I intend to find out."

The police were still very much in evidence when they returned, and a Swiss officer stopped Nick's car at the entrance to the parking lot, allowing it to pass only after they'd identified themselves as guests. He looked first for Cottonwood in the bar, but the sandy-haired Englishman was nowhere in sight.

"He may have skipped already," Nick said, heading for the front desk. But as he was about to ask the clerk, he saw Felix Cottonwood emerge from an elevator.

"Well, it's Mr. Velvet, isn't it? And I don't believe I know the young lady."

Nick didn't bother with introductions. "It's important I talk with you, Cottonwood. I know about the slipper."

"Slipper?"

"The Sherlockian slipper you stole from the Holmes display."

"Now really, Velvet, I think you're going too far. I am a salesman, not a thief."

"And what is it you sell?"

"I told you — tobacco products."

Nick glanced around the lobby, then pointed toward a secluded corner. "Let's go talk."

"If you must talk I prefer the open air. The police around here are quite unnerving."

Nick motioned Annette to wait for him and followed the Englishman outside. Now in the warmth of the afternoon sun there was a grandeur about the place that defied any attempt at description. As they walked together down the path toward Reichenbach Falls, he knew exactly the emotions Arthur Conan Doyle must have felt on seeing this place.

"This should be private enough," Nick said as they strolled.

Felix Cottonwood smiled. "Oh, yes. Even electronic listening devices would be helpless against the roar of those falls."

"Then suppose you tell me about the tobacco business. And especially about the tobacco in the toe of that Persian slipper. I suspect it's hash or hemp at the very least."

Cottonwood allowed himself a chuckle of mirth. "My good man, even if I dealt in drugs, which I do not, the toe of a slipper would hold barely enough for a dozen cigarettes."

They were closer to the falls now, and Nick could feel the spray on his face. Underfoot, the blackish soil was soft with moisture. "But you did steal the slipper, didn't you?"

"Be careful," the Englishman said. "This path is treacherous."

"Didn't you?" Nick repeated.

"Did I?"

"Your mind runs to electronic listening devices, and probably to silenced pistols as well. Why did you kill Bonoto?"

Cottonwood sighed. "You're an exasperating man, Velvet. You chose the right criminal for the wrong reason. Yes, I killed Bonoto and his gunman, but it had nothing to do with narcotics — or even with tobacco, for that matter. It was only the slipper we were after, and what it contained."

"Which is — ?"

Felix Cottonwood drew himself up, becoming for a moment the very model of a British gentleman. "There exists — and has always existed — one item of Sherlockiana more valuable than any other, and more elusive. Today, with the worldwide revival of interest in Holmes, it is not an exaggeration to say this one object could be worth a million dollars."

"Yet it's small enough to be hidden in the toe of a Persian slipper?"

"Quite correct. There was no time to dig it free from the tobacco, so I removed the entire slipper from the room. It is, however, this object that I sought, that I pursued across half of Europe. At last an aged scholar told me where he'd hidden it — but unfortunately he also told others. Bonoto was planning to move in on the Sherlock Holmes business in exactly the manner that the American mob has moved into the distribution of pornography. This I could not allow. He hired you to keep his name out of it, but when I saw him there this morning I knew the truth. And I shot him."

"You're very frank," Nick said.

Felix Cottonwood smiled and turned on the narrow path. There was a mist of spray clinging to his face and eyebrows, and in his right hand he held a silenced pistol. "I'm sorry, Velvet. I was only frank because it didn't matter. I have to kill you, too."

Nick saw death only seconds away as he lunged at the Englishman, then heard the gentle cough of the weapon's discharge. The shot went wild, and he gripped Cottonwood's wrist, forcing the gun into the air. It was no good yelling for the police — the roar of the falls muffled every sound.

They struggled for a moment and then Nick felt his feet sliding on the damp ground. He saw the edge of the chasm looming close.

He felt himself falling.

And then somehow he was clinging to a low bush at the edge of the path, and Felix Cottonwood was tumbling over him, tumbling and screaming into the black depths below.

Nick got unsteadily to his feet and tried to peer into the gorge, but there was nothing to see except the rising mists.

Cottonwood's pistol lay at the edge of the path where it had fallen. Nick picked it up and threw it into the abyss after its owner.

Annette DuFrois was waiting back at the resort. "What happened?" she asked.

"Nothing much. He's gone away."

"And the slipper?"

"It must be in his room. I'm going after it." There was no longer any buyer for the prize, and Nick had no idea what he'd do with it, but he hated unfinished assignments. He had to know what was hidden in the tobacco in that toe.

Finding Cottonwood's room number and opening the door took only a few minutes. Locating the slipper in its hiding place proved to be a bit more difficult. Going through the books and belongings in his suitcase, Nick wondered if he had been a bad man at all — or only a good man with an obsession.

The Persian slipper yielded itself at last, stuffed down inside a bulky climbing boot. Working to empty out the tobacco, Nick could already feel something small and hard in the toe.

Something metallic, with a tiny tag attached.

It was what Bonoto and Cottonwood had died for.

It was the key to a dispatch-box, in the bank of Cox & Company at Charing Cross.

The Theft of Nothing at All

Nothing?" Nick Velvet repeated incredulously.

"Nothing at all," the fat man said, smiling at Nick's reaction.

"Let's get this straight. You'll pay me my usual fee of twenty thousand dollars to simply sit at home and steal nothing at all on next Thursday?"

"Exactly." The fat man, who said his name was Thomas Trotter, lit a cigar. "And if you're successful at it, I may want to hire you again for the following Thursday at the same fee."

"How could I not be successful?"

The fat man smiled again. Nick decided that he liked to smile. Perhaps he'd read somewhere that fat people are supposed to be jolly. "I think we understand each other, Mr. Velvet." He stood up to leave, taking a thick envelope from his inside pocket. "Here is one-half of the money now, in hundred-dollar bills. The rest will be paid on Friday, if you are successful in stealing nothing."

"I'll be successful," Nick assured him.

For the rest of the week, until Thursday, Nick puzzled over it. Thomas Trotter had come to him in the usual way, referred by someone in New York for whom Nick had once performed a service. And he couldn't believe that Trotter didn't want something for his money.

Something. But what?

"It's so good to have you home this week, Nicky," Gloria told him on Thursday evening. "Usually you're chasing off somewhere for the government and we never get to have much time together."

"Next week I'll be getting the boat out of drydock," he decided. "It should be warm enough on the Sound by then."

She glanced at the clock and headed for the television set. "You don't mind if I watch, do you, Nicky?"

"What? One of those crazy cop shows?"

"No, no. Not this early in the evening. It's the state lottery drawing."

Nick grunted and went out to the kitchen for a beer. He was vaguely aware that the state had begun televising the lottery drawings at 7:30 on Thursday evenings. Done up with blinking lights and screaming winners just like a network game show, it had proved to be the most popular Thursday night TV show in the state.

He went back with his beer and settled into a chair opposite the television, watching with mild interest. Gloria had got out her lottery tickets, waiting for the moment when this week's winners would be chosen. This was done by a complicated method involving a previously run horse race, coupled with the choosing and opening of a sealed tin can to reveal two of the digits.

When the grinning announcer finally called out the complete number, Gloria moaned. "Oh, Nicky, I was so close!"

"Better luck next week."

"The weekly winners all get a crack at the million-dollar jackpot drawing in three weeks."

"Hmmm." He picked up the evening paper.

"You're not even watching, Nicky!"

"Sure I am."

By the end of the evening when he went to bed, $20,000 richer, he'd pretty much decided that Thomas Trotter was nothing more than an eccentric millionaire.

He'd also decided to take the money again if it was offered for another Thursday of non-stealing.

"Well," Trotter said, slipping into the booth opposite Nick the following afternoon, "you did very well."

"I did nothing." If he'd been a detective, Nick might have been curious as to why a man who said his name was Thomas Trotter wore gold cuff links initialed *RR*.

"Just what I wanted you to do." Trotter signaled the waiter and ordered a glass of wine. Nick ordered a beer. "Would you like to do the same thing next Thursday?"

"For another twenty thousand?"

"Naturally."

It was Nick's turn to smile. "Sure!"

The fat man nodded and took an envelope from his pocket. "This is the balance on yesterday's assignment." Then a second envelope. "And this is your advance for next Thursday."

"Fine! You keep coming back as long as you want to!"

But by Monday, Nick was beginning to grow irritable. Gloria commented on it after dinner. "Nicky, what's the matter with you lately? You used to enjoy having time off to be around the house. Now everything seems to get on your nerves. And you haven't said any more about taking out the boat."

"I'm all right," he insisted.

But Thomas Trotter was bothering him. Another Thursday was coming — another theftless Thursday — and Trotter's weekly twenty grand was getting to him.

What in hell would he do if Trotter offered him the deal for a third week?

On Tuesday evening a call came. "Mr. Velvet?" the woman's voice asked.

"Speaking."

"I understand you steal things," she said bluntly.

"I don't discuss my business on the telephone.   Perhaps we could meet somewhere."

"Could it be tonight? I'd want to hire you for this week."

"This week?" He thought of Thomas Trotter. "It wouldn't be Thursday, would it?"

"How'd you know?"

"I had a hunch." He gave her directions to a cocktail lounge in a nearby shopping center and arranged to meet her there in an hour.

"Going out, Nicky?" Gloria asked.

"For a while. Maybe it'll improve my mood."

The woman's name was Rona Felix and she was waiting for him alone in a booth near the back of the lounge. The place was very much like the one where he'd met Thomas Trotter, and Nick wondered if maybe some chain supplied suburban cocktail lounges with high-backed booths especially for couples carrying on illicit affairs.

Rona Felix probably wouldn't have been interested in that. Though she was still in her thirties she had the sour look of a woman whom life had passed by. The way she wore her hair, the lack of makeup, the frumpy coat that covered her shoulders — all spread the message that she was a woman who'd stopped caring about her looks.

"It's good to meet you, Mr. Velvet. I've heard a great deal about your exploits."

"Who from?"

"People you've helped. I understand you'll steal anything valueless for a fee of twenty thousand dollars."

"That's correct."

"Could you steal something for me this Thursday?"

"Never on Thursday," he said with a grin.

"What?"

"I'm otherwise occupied this Thursday."

"Oh." She seemed crestfallen. "I was counting on you."

Nick had once been kidnaped by a man to keep him from taking an assignment. He was beginning to wonder if the fat man had been up to the same sort of trick. "Could I ask you a question? Do you know someone named Thomas Trotter?"

"Trotter? I don't believe so."

"All right. Could you tell me what the job involves? Perhaps I could do it tomorrow. Or Friday."

She shook her head. "They only bring it out of the vault on Thursdays. It has to be a Thursday."

"I couldn't steal anything valuable enough to be kept in a vault."

"Could you steal a hundred tin cans?"

"I suppose so. It would depend on what's inside them."

"Just numbered plastic balls. The manufacturing cost is only a few dollars and their value to anyone would be absolutely zero."

"And yet they're kept locked in a vault every day but Thursday?"

"That's correct."

Nick thought about it. "You needn't tell me any more now, since I can't do it this Thursday in any event. But how about a week from Thursday?"

"All right," she agreed after a moment's hesitation.

"Meet me here next Monday night and you can fill me in on the details."

"Fine."

He smiled at her. "Now since you're a prospective client, let me buy you a drink."

"No, thank you. I have to be going."

"Very well. Till next Monday."

Nick went home and found Gloria ironing shirts. "That didn't take long, Nicky."

"I was just arranging for a future assignment." He glanced at the TV set, where a cop was chasing someone down a darkened alley. "Say, I noticed they have a studio audience for that lottery drawing on Thursday nights. If we can get tickets let's take a drive up there and see it."

"You mean it, Nicky? This Thursday?"

"Sure. I'll see about it."

He was beginning to think he should know more about such things.

The weekly drawing of the state lottery was telecast from an elaborate set in the studio of Channel 17 in the state capital. There were about 200 seats for the studio audience, and Nick had to rely on an old political friendship to obtain tickets on such short notice. But as he settled into his tenth-row seat next to Gloria, he saw at once that the journey had not been a vain one.

A short-skirted girl who served as the assistant to the master of ceremonies appeared from the wings, wheeling a cart on which rested 100 vacuum-sealed metal cans. As the show began the M.C. ran quickly through the standard procedure, explaining it to the few new viewers who might have tuned in. The winning number consisted of six digits, the last four of which were determined by a previously run horse race. For the first two digits a member of the studio audience was called on stage to choose one of the 100 sealed cans. The can was opened and a plastic ball bearing a two-digit number from 00 to 99 was extracted.

There it was.

Rona Felix was offering him $20,000 to steal those 100 cans. He was certain of it. And he was just as certain that Thomas Trotter was paying him $20,000 *not* to steal them.

The week's winning number proved to be 450098, and after it was determined, interest shifted to the six finalists from the previous drawing. These were holders of tickets which had five of the six digits correct, and they took part in a game-show type of competition for instant cash prizes.

"Didn't you enjoy it, Nicky?" Gloria asked on the way out.

"The whole thing seemed awfully complicated."

"They have to make it that way so there'll be no cheating," she explained.

"I suppose so."

The master of ceremonies, a toothy young man named Cappy Sloan, was standing at the door saying goodbye to the departing audience. This was his chance to build a show-business career on a lucky job with the state lottery, and he was making the most of it.

"Pardon me," Nick said. "Could I ask you something?"

Cappy Sloan shot him a smile. "Sure, as long as it's not next week's winning number. That I don't know!"

"I do some free-lance articles for our local newspaper downstate, and I was wondering if I might come in sometime and see how things are run backstage. Maybe next Monday or Tuesday I could get some pictures of the equipment —"

"It would have to be Thursday," Cappy informed him. "After the show all the equipment is locked in a special vault here at the studio. We can't have anyone tampering with it, you know. It doesn't come out again till next Thursday, a few hours before showtime."

"Could I call you about it next week?"

"Sure, sure! The state loves the publicity."

They went on their way and Gloria asked, "What was all that about, Nicky? You don't write articles."

"I might take it up," he said with a smile.

The next day was Friday, and Nick kept his appointment with Thomas Trotter. The fat man was waiting in his usual booth, looking uncomfortable. "You're ten minutes late," he told Nick.

"Friday night traffic. Had a good week?"

"Until yesterday."

"What happened yesterday?"

"You were at the state capital, at the lottery telecast."

"Well, yes. We've been watching it on television and thought it might be fun to get tickets."

Trotter looked distasteful. "*Was* it fun?"

"Sure. You know, a night out. I didn't see you there,"

"You were quite visible when the camera panned the audience." He took an envelope from his pocket. "But since you kept your agreement to steal nothing, here's the balance of your money."

"Thanks."

"The offer stands for another week."

"I may have an assignment for next Thursday."

"Cancel it."

"I can't offend a client," Nick said. "Their money is as good as yours."

Thomas Trotter leaned back. "All right, thirty thousand to steal nothing next Thursday. How's that?"

"I only charge thirty thousand for especially dangerous assignments."

"This could be especially dangerous for you if you cross me."

"All right," Nick said with a sigh. "Thirty thousand to steal nothing next Thursday. It's a deal." Whatever Trotter was up to, it was costing him a total of $70,000 to have Nick do nothing.

"And stay away from the state lottery."

"Now wait a minute — that's not part of the agreement."

Trotter waved aside his objection. "All right, so long as I have your word you will steal nothing."

"You have it."

"I have only ten thousand with me. The other twenty will be paid next Friday. Same time, same place."

Nick stood up. "Mr. Trotter, it's a pleasure doing business with you."

On Monday he met Rona Felix as planned. It was a warm spring day and she wore a colorful print dress that made her seem a bit more feminine.

"Well?" she asked him. "Will you do it?"

"Steal one hundred tin cans next Thursday? I'm sorry, but I can't."

She was openly disappointed. "But I thought —"

"Miss Felix, I asked you last week if you knew a man named Thomas Trotter and you said no. Now I must ask you another question. Who knew you were planning to contact me?"

"Why . . . no one."

"Think carefully. Two weeks ago, a full week before you actually contacted me, I was approached by Trotter. Frankly, he's paying me a great deal of money in an obvious attempt to frustrate your plans."

"He is? Why would he do that?"

"I should tell you that I know the assignment involves the state-lottery drawing in some way," Nick said.

This seemed to startle her. "How could you — ? Oh, I suppose you watch it on television. All right, it does concern the lottery. And for that reason the theft must be this Thursday. It's the last week before the grand drawing for the million dollars."

"So you're paying me twenty thousand to make a million."

"Not exactly." Hesitating a moment, she finally asked, "Why should I tell you any of this if you can't help me?"

"I may have some suggestions. And it's not costing you anything to talk."

"All right. If you're familiar with the lottery, you know that the first two digits of the winning number are chosen by opening one of a hundred vacuum-sealed aluminum cans, each containing a numbered plastic ball. The lottery commission has two sets of numbered balls, and the canning is done under guard by a local firm. One of the sets is always in the vault, and when it's removed on Thursday for the show it's immediately replaced with the other set for use the following Thursday. The canner picks up the entire used set each Thursday night for repackaging, though only one of the hundred cans has been opened."

"And you want me to steal the set of cans when it comes out of the vault. Why? What will it gain you?"

"I didn't know you asked so many questions."

Nick smiled. "If you want my help, I have to ask questions."

"Oh, very well! If the cans are stolen just before showtime, they'll be forced to use the set just delivered for the following week. And that's the set I want them to use."

"It's gimmicked."

She nodded. "The final drawing is foolproof, and I can't be sure of winning the million. But each of the weekly winners gets a minimum of $100,000, and that's good enough for me."

"What about the horse race determining the final four digits?"

"That part has been attended to. It needn't concern you. The set of aluminum cans is my problem."

"You wanted to hire me for last week originally. If you'd gimmicked a set of cans at that time, wouldn't they be coming up for use this week?"

She shook her head. "It's not as simple as that. I don't know the number I need until I buy my lottery tickets for the week. Look, I'll give you an example. Suppose I know the horse race numbers are going to be 3456. 1 have to find a ticket to buy that ends in those numbers. It's not as impossible as it sounds in this state, because the numbered tickets are supplied to dealers in consecutive sheets and most places will let you look through the sheets to pick a lucky number. After trying a dozen or so places I'm likely to find a 3456.

"But for the first two digits I have to settle for whatever I get — say 123456. The sealed-up set of balls must be gimmicked to deliver a 12, but at this point the balls are already locked in the vault, immune from any sort of tampering. My only hope is to gimmick the new set of cans containing next week's numbered balls and then force the lottery to use that set a week early. That's where you come in. See?"

"My God!" Nick said with real awe. "How'd you ever dream up this thing?"

"My boy friend at the canning company helped."

Nick's first impression had been wrong. If she'd stopped caring about her looks, it was only because she already had a steady man. "But the person who chooses the can is picked at random, or else he's a guest dignitary. With all the cans unlabeled and identical, how can you possibly gimmick it?"

"The guard they send over with the cans every week is a joke. He sits and drinks coffee."

"Still —"

"And it's easy to substitute a box of a hundred cans for the box he's been watching. All I need is the two-digit number to give my friend a few days before Thursday, so he can prepare the gimmicked set of cans."

"Okay. Suppose you want to open a can and find a ball numbered 12. How do you gimmick it when the can's going to be chosen at random by an unknown person?"

"That should be obvious, Mr. Velvet. In the gimmicked set all hundred cans contain balls with the same number."

"And you think you can get away with this?"

"I'm sure I can. I've been watching the operation for a full year. They never open more than one can. There's no reason to."

"I have to admire your plan," Nick admitted. "I wish I could help."

"But you must! It all depends on you! Someone else might be caught stealing the cans, or might fail to even reach them with the guards and everything. It has to be you!"

Nick thought about it. He thought about the fat man's $50,000, with twenty more to come. And he thought about this bright young woman's fantastic scheme.

There just might be a way . . .

"I'll see what I can do," he told her at last.

"This Thursday?"

"This Thursday."

To steal or not to steal.

Nick pondered the question all the next day, going over assorted plans and possibilities. He still didn't know where Trotter fitted into the picture, and that could be a danger.

On Wednesday afternoon Gloria found him in the kitchen, rummaging through a drawer. "What are you looking for, Nicky?"

"Just something I need. I was hoping we had one the right size, but I guess I'll have to go out and buy one."

She didn't question him further. After a dozen years of living with him she was used to his odd behavior.

On Thursday, Nick drove to the state capital and parked in the lot behind the Channel 17 studio. When the guard at the door stopped him he said he was there to see the lottery M.C., Cappy Sloan. After a five-minute wait Sloan appeared. "Do I know you?" he asked Nick.

"You've probably forgotten. Last Thursday evening, after the telecast, you said I could come over this week and do a story on the lottery."

"Oh, yeah, I remember. Well, we're setting up for tonight. You can come in and watch if you promise not to get in the way."

Nick followed him down a long corridor and onto the large sound stage where the weekly sets and props for the state lottery were being assembled. "A lot of work here," Nick commented.

"Sure is! And especially this week. The Governor himself is coming tonight to lend his support. He'll choose the can containing the first two digits of the winning number."

"Really? I picked a good week to come."

"Yeah," Sloan agreed. "Say, what'd you tell me your name was?"

"Nicholas. Joe Nicholas."

"Well, Joe, back here is the studio's vault. The state had them build it special to store all this lottery paraphernalia between shows. And these are the hundred cans with their numbered balls."

Nick took note of the guard hovering nearby.

"After each show the cans are picked up by a local company that replaces the opened can and returns them all to us next Thursday. They just delivered 'em and we've put them in the vault for next week's show."

"Next week is the million-dollar drawing, right?"

"Sure is!" Cappy Sloan confirmed. "This week's winner is certain of a hundred thousand, but they'll also have a crack at that million-dollar jackpot."

Nick casually lit a cigarette. It tasted strange to him, since he hadn't smoked in years. "I'd like to see the board where you hang the winning number. I've got a little camera here and maybe I can snap a picture of you standing next to it."

Cappy Sloan grinned. "Sure, right over here."

As they passed a large wastebasket full of paper and debris from some previous show, Nick carefully flipped away his cigarette. He spent some time posing Sloan for the picture, and he wasn't at all surprised when he heard a stagehand bellow, "Fire!"

"Damn! That wastebasket's blazing!" Cappy Sloan ran to join the others in fighting the fire.

Nick made certain no eyes were on him and then pushed the cart containing the hundred tin cans behind a convenient curtain. He went at his task, working fast, knowing he'd have only a few minutes at the most. Though the smell of smoke was heavy in the air, the fire was quickly extinguished and he heard Cappy Sloan calling for him.

"Hey, Nicholas! Where'd you go?"

Nick kept working. One more minute . . .

"Nicholas!" Sloan called out.

"Right here," Nick replied. "Just looking around." He finished his task and stepped quickly around the curtain.

"Don't go wandering off," Sloan warned. "The guards don't like it."

"This is a fascinating setup," Nick said, leading Sloan away from the cart. "Where's the light board that flashes when one of the finalists wins?"

"That's over here."

They spent the next twenty minutes looking over the backstage setup. It was risky, Nick knew, because any minute someone might happen to glance at the cart. But he had to arrange for a proper exit.

"Cappy," a voice boomed from the control room, "the Governor's on his way."

"So soon? It's two hours till showtime."

"He's dining with the station executives. They want you there too."

"Damn! All right, I'll be there." He turned to Nick. "That completes the tour. Duty calls. But I'll arrange for a ticket so you can see the show."

"I'd appreciate that."

Cappy Sloan grabbed a tie and jacket he had tossed over the back of a chair and started to put them on. He was heading for the aisle, still knotting his tie, when a girl on stage shouted, "Cappy! What happened to these cans?"

He stopped and turned around. "What do you mean, what happened to them, Phyllis? What does it look like happened to them?"

"It looks like somebody opened them all with a can opener!"

"What!"

He was back on stage in an instant, inspecting the damage while the others clustered around. Nick edged toward the door but made no effort to escape.

"The balls are still inside," the girl said. "Someone just opened them and left them."

Sloan scratched his head. "Now who in hell would want to do that? What for?"

"A joke of some sort."

"Yeah. Only I don't see the humor." He thought about it and finally decided, "Okay, get next week's set of cans out of the safe — we'll have to use them. And put them right out here at stage center where no one can fool with them!" He seemed to have forgotten Nick's absence for those few moments.

"First the fire and now this!" the girl said. "Is somebody sabotaging us?"

"No, no," Cappy Sloan soothed. "Don't you worry, Phyllis. By seven thirty we'll be on the beam. Now get that other set of cans out here. I've got to go eat with the Governor."

Nick decided things were going along better than he could have hoped for. He wandered outside and dropped the can opener down a convenient sewer, then went across the street to a lunch counter for a bite to eat.

He managed to be back in plenty of time for the 7:30 telecast, picking up his ticket and entering the studio just before seven. There was no sign of Rona Felix anywhere, but he was startled to see Thomas Trotter on stage. The fat man was talking earnestly with Cappy Sloan and inspecting the opened tin cans.

Nick spotted Sloan's assistant, Phyllis, and asked, "Do you know the man who's talking to Mr. Sloan?"

She glanced at Nick and then away, intent on more important matters. "That's the Governor's press secretary, Ramsey Reynolds."

Ramsey Reynolds, not Thomas Trotter.

All right, Nick decided, but that still doesn't tell me anything. Was it the Governor who'd really hired him, through Trotter-Reynolds? And what was the connection with Rona Felix and her scheme to fix the state lottery?

When the show began, he sat watching the people on stage go through their motions. Cappy Sloan came out, cracked a couple of bad jokes, and got right to the business at hand. The slip containing the order of finish for a previously run horse race was drawn with much fanfare — Nick wondered if the slips were all the same too — and the last four digits of the winning number were posted.

7821.

Then the Governor made his entrance, to a lengthy ovation. He was popular in the state, and he fed the popularity by public appearances like this one. He said a few words, then stepped over to the cart and selected one of the 100 aluminum cans. Cappy Sloan led him to an electric can opener where the top was removed and the plastic ball revealed. It was number 67.

The next week's winning number, 677821, went up on the board. Nick hoped Rona Felix was holding it. If she wasn't, she'd wasted his $20,000 fee.

Nick was feeling good as he filed out of the studio after the show. He was feeling good right up until the moment when he saw Thomas Trotter standing at the door with two burly State Troopers.

"Arrest that man!" Trotter ordered, pointing at Nick.

They took him to the police station and booked him on a variety of charges relating to tampering with the operation of the state lottery. He used his one phone call to tell Gloria he'd been called away overnight, and then settled down in his cell. It was a new experience for him, and one he hoped would be of short duration.

Late in the evening, close to eleven, Thomas Trotter came to his cell. "I tried to tell you that nobody crosses me, Velvet. I paid you not to steal anything today!"

"And I didn't," Nick answered with a smile.

"No? I checked with Cappy Sloan and he pointed you out in the audience. You're the only one who had the opportunity to open those hundred cans."

"I don' t deny I opened them."

"Good! The District Attorney is outside and you can admit it to him."

"Seems like a minor crime to involve the D.A. in at eleven o'clock at night."

"The Governor asked him to see to it personally."

The District Attorney was a brisk, balding man obviously displeased at being there. "What is this foolishness, Reynolds?"

Nick grinned at the fat man. "I thought your name was Trotter."

"Shut up!" Then, turning to the District Attorney, he said, "Obviously he opened those cans in an attempt to cheat the lottery."

"I don't see how," the D.A. muttered. "What about it, Velvet? Why did you open those cans?"

"I overheard some men talking about a bomb in one of the cans. It was some sort of plot to kill the Governor. I didn't report it to the police because it seemed far-fetched. But I opened the cans myself just to make sure."

"What garbage!" Trotter said with a sneer. "Do you believe that for a minute, sir?"

"It's as good an explanation as any I've heard," the D.A. snapped. "We can't hold this man unless we can show criminous intent!"

"But I —"

"Step outside with me, Reynolds."

Nick relaxed as they left him alone. He was quite certain he wouldn't be spending much more time in this jail.

Presently the fat man returned, looking enraged. "He's dismissing the case against you for lack of evidence."

"I'm glad to hear that."

"But I'm not dismissing my case against you. I'm going to ruin you in this state, Velvet. I'm going to see you never get another job from anyone, and if you do I'm going to have the cops breathing down your neck so close that you'll end up in prison for life!"

"Now wait a minute," Nick protested. "I did exactly what you hired me to do. I stole nothing."

"But you opened those cans —"

"And took nothing from them. Oh, yes, I took *one* thing from them. By opening them I removed the vacuum from each can. I stole a vacuum, Trotter, and as any dictionary will tell you, a vacuum is a space entirely devoid of matter. A vacuum is nothing at all, and that's what I stole by opening those cans — nothing at all!"

The man he knew as Trotter mulled this over. "Who paid you?" he asked finally. "It was that Felix woman, wasn't it?"

"How do you know her?" Nick countered.

"I know her boy friend. He works at the canning plant."

"So you got onto her scheme through him. She said she was going to hire me and you hired me first."

"That's right," Trotter admitted. "It was for the good of the state. I didn't want anyone cheating on the lottery."

"For the good of the state you paid me fifty thousand dollars? That's hard to swallow. It's a lot more likely you've got your own scheme for collecting that million-dollar prize. You're in it with Rona Felix's friend yourself, only poor Rona was going to get left out in the cold. You heard from him that she was planning to hire me, and you thought that the money you paid me was a good investment to keep me away for three weeks till your stooges could win the million. Right?"

"That's ridiculous!"

"Is it? I wonder what your boss the Governor would think."

Trotter was silent for a moment. Finally he opened the door and said, "Get out, Velvet. You're free to go. Get out and never let me see you again."

Nick didn't need to be told twice. He paused only long enough to say, "Remember, you still owe me twenty thousand for stealing nothing today." Then he hurried out.

The steel door slammed behind him.

Nick met Rona Felix the following day and collected his fee. All had gone according to plan and she showed him the winning ticket. "Next Thursday I'll be a hundred thousand — or maybe a million — richer!"

"I'm happy for you," Nick said. "Good luck — I'll be watching."

But as it turned out, he wasn't watching on Thursday night and neither was anyone else. Thursday morning's papers carried the story under bold headlines: *Governor Suspends Lottery Pending Inquiry: Press Secretary Reynolds Resigns.*

"Did you see this, Nicky?" Gloria asked, shaking the paper at him. "The District Attorney became suspicious of this Ramsey Reynolds after Thursday night's drawing and started examining the lottery equipment. He discovered the cans the Governor chose from all contained balls with the same number. And now Reynolds has resigned and last week's drawing has been voided! Isn't that amazing?"

Nick thought about Rona Felix, who was destined to miss her big moment on television. And he thought about the total of $70,000 he'd collected for stealing nothing at all. He'd been the big lottery winner without even buying a ticket!

The Theft of the Four of Spades

Nick Velvet rarely ventured into Manhattan except on business, so he could understand Ron Saturn's surprise at encountering him on West 43rd Street during one of New York's periodic spells of late-summer mugginess.

"Nick!" the little man greeted him. "Nick Velvet! I haven't seen you in a couple of years, and I sure didn't expect to see you in town on a day like this! Isn't this weather terrible?"

"I like to see how you city people live," Nick replied with a smile. Ron Saturn was an aging chorus boy who'd appeared in a few Broadway musicals. But his small stature had kept him from ever hitting it really big and in recent years he'd turned his talents to assorted confidence games involving wealthy, lonely women.

"We're not living well these days, Nick," Ron replied glumly. "All the big money's in Saratoga or the Hamptons this month. And the new musicals don't start rehearsals till October. But what brings you down here?"

"Nothing shady, Ron. Just a bit of shopping for Gloria's birthday."

"How is she? I miss seeing the two of you."

"She's fine. I'll tell her I ran into you."

Ron Saturn scratched his ear in a gesture Nick remembered from the past. "You know, running into you just might be the answer to my prayers."

"I didn't know you ever prayed, Ron."

"Just a figure of speech, Nick. But look — would you be free for a job this evening? It's for a friend."

Nick hesitated, glancing at his watch. "I generally need more time for planning. I don't know if it could be done that fast."

"Come talk to my friend anyway — okay?"

"Sure, Ron. Anything for a friend."

Nick had known Ron Saturn for so many years, off and on, that it was hard to remember how the friendship had come about. It dated from the years following Nick's army service, when he and Ron had worked together at a marina in Westchester County. They'd taken different paths to success after that, but each had always known that at times the other operated outside the law.

Since Nick had been headed back to Grand Central for the train home, they stopped in the lobby of the Biltmore Hotel for a drink while Ron phoned his friend. He was on the phone for some time before he returned, smiling. "He's on his way over. Cary, is — well, difficult at times, but you'll like him."

"Cary?"

"Cary Temple, the actor."

"Oh!" Cary Temple was a vigorous man in his fifties who'd achieved a certain fame in his younger days playing Shakespeare in Central Park and at Jones Beach. He'd even handled the lead in *My Fair Lady*, in one of its road companies. But Nick hadn't heard his name mentioned in years. He had truly fallen on hard times if he'd hooked up with Ron Saturn on a confidence scheme.

They were just starting their second drink when Temple arrived. His face had aged a bit and his fine head of hair was an unnatural shade of brown, but his handshake was vigorous and his eyes had all their old matinee sparkle. "Velvet! Ron has always spoken highly of you! A pleasure to meet you at last!"

"The pleasure is mine," Nick murmured. "I've seen you on stage many times."

"Yes." Cary Temple smiled sadly. "Those were better days, I fear. But Ron tells me you can assist with a little enterprise we have going."

"Possibly. I generally need a little time for preparation. You both know my terms, I'm sure." He paused, making sure there was no one close enough to overhear. Then he asked, "What do you want stolen?"

Cary Temple glanced at Ron and cleared his throat.

"The four of spades from a deck of cards. Possibly from several decks of cards."

"That certainly falls within my province of stealing only valueless objects. Where are these cards located?"

"In the Fifth Avenue apartment of Sarah Wentworth."

Nick thought about that. Sarah Wentworth was a revered widow of the former American ambassador to the United Nations. Long active in social and political circles, she'd become a darling of the media since the death of her husband in a plane crash two years earlier. Columnists constantly linked her with eligible middle-aged men — and some not so eligible. "Her place will be well guarded," he said.

"There's heavy security in the building," Temple agreed, "but I can get you in."

"You mentioned several decks of cards. Are they all in one location?"

The actor hesitated. "No, there's a second location involved. The apartment of one Amanda Jones, on 126th Street."

"Harlem?"

"East Harlem, to be exact. I have the address here. In each case you are to steal the four of spades from all decks of cards you find in the apartments. But take nothing else — only the fours of spades. And leave no signs of a robbery."

"What about new, unopened decks of cards?"

"Those too, if you find any. Can you do it?"

"Not by tonight. It would mean casing two layouts. Give me forty-eight hours." Temple shook his head. "It has to be tonight."

"Sorry." Nick started to rise from the table and Temple turned on Ron Saturn. "I thought you told me he could do it!"

"He can, Cary! Calm down. If anyone in the world can do it, Nick can. Look, Nick, what's your fee now?"

"Twenty-five."

"It's worth thirty to us if you can do it tonight. Right, Cary?"

"That's correct. Thirty thousand."

He moistened his lips as he said it, perhaps remembering better days when he'd earned that much for a week's work on Broadway.

Nick considered the offer. "How would you get me into Sarah Wentworth's apartment?"

"That's the easy part. She's having a cocktail party this afternoon and you could go with me."

"Wouldn't she think that odd?"

"Not at all, dear fellow. I often bring Ron or someone else. But finding and stealing the cards will be your responsibility."

"The other one — Amanda Jones — has to be done tonight too?"

"That's correct. Shall we be on our way?"

Against his better judgment Nick said, "All right."

There was only time for a quick phone call to Gloria, explaining that he might have to stay in town overnight. "Are you working?" she asked, and when he replied in the affirmative she didn't question him further. She knew she'd hear all about it later.

Ron Saturn left them at the hotel and Temple glanced at his watch. "Just after five. If we take a taxi we should arrive just in time for cocktails."

The apartment, a luxury co-op overlooking Central Park, was already crowded by the time they arrived. Nick recognized some familiar types — show-business people, publishing figures, and a sprinkling from the United Nations. Some wore street clothes because they'd come right from work. The show people, between engagements or awaiting the evening curtain, dressed more elaborately. But the star of the party was the hostess, and Sarah Wentworth was as strikingly lovely in person as on the front page of the latest supermarket tabloid. Still in her early forties, she exuded the sort of fashionable sexuality one usually found in models and starlets still in their twenties.

"Nick Velvet?" she repeated, shaking his hand. "I should know you. Are you in the theater?"

"No," he explained. "Cary and I have a mutual friend."

"He's a dear," she confided, patting Temple's cheek as she spoke. "I hope we'll be doing some business together." Then, "Enjoy yourself, Mr. Velvet. I'm so glad you could come."

She moved off to greet other new arrivals and Nick followed Cary Temple through the crowded room to the far end where two bartenders were serving drinks. "You expect me to do the job in a roomful of people?" Nick asked under his breath.

"I'm sure you'll find a way." The actor smiled and accepted a cocktail from the bartender, then went off to join a circle of familiar faces.

Nick stood in the center of the room wondering what to do next.

After a moment Sarah Wentworth approached him again, apparently noticing his hesitation to mingle with the other guests. "What do you do, Mr. Velvet?"

"Card tricks," he answered without really thinking.

"For a living?"

"No, just as a hobby. If you have a deck of cards I can demonstrate."

She smiled just a bit condescendingly. "Perhaps later."

She moved away and mingled with a couple wearing matching pink jackets. They were definitely show-business types, Nick decided. Studying an abstract painting that took up much of one wall, he found his mind wandering to Ron Saturn and Cary Temple, and the sort of scheme they were working. He remembered a movie once where a character under hypnosis was programmed to respond to a certain playing card. But something like that seemed unlikely with Sarah Wentworth. Besides, how would it connect her to a woman in East Harlem, a world away from this Fifth Avenue apartment? He was still puzzling over it as the crowd began to thin out. Obviously the guests were going off to dinner after their cocktails, and soon only a few stragglers remained. The hostess came up to Nick again and said quite surprisingly, "I believe we're ready for your card tricks now, Mr. Velvet."

"Fine. I know a wonderful trick that can be done with six decks of cards. Would you have that many?"

"I doubt it, but I'll go look."

Cary Temple strolled over to Nick. "Going to entertain us a little?"

"I hope so."

Sarah Wentworth returned holding a boxed double deck used for Canasta, two bridge decks, and a pinochle deck. "I'm afraid these are all the cards I have."

Nick knew there was no four of spades in a pinochle deck, so he immediately set that one aside. "These four will do nicely, thanks." If she had produced more than the six requested decks, he would have found a reason to use them all. As it was he ran through some simple tricks he'd known since high school. They were good enough to impress Sarah Wentworth and that was all that mattered. By the time he carefully returned the cards to their boxes and departed with Cary Temple, the four of spades from each of the four decks was in his pocket.

"You're good with your fingers," Temple admitted. "I was watching you and I didn't see a thing."

"I must have shuffled each deck fifteen or twenty times. I'd spot the four of spades on the bottom or when I was cutting, and slip it off the deck. A couple I palmed. One dropped into my lap and one went up my sleeve. It was perfectly safe. Even if someone noticed they'd just think it was part of the trick."

"Give me the cards," Temple said.

"I think I should get half of the money now."

"You'll get all the money when you finish up later tonight. Ron is rounding it up now."

Nick handed over the cards reluctantly. "Sooner or later she's going to know they're gone."

"They only need to be gone temporarily. Next time I'm up there I may be able to slip them back into the decks. But that's my problem, not yours."

"Are you taking me up to East Harlem now?"

The actor smiled and shook his head. "Now *that* is your problem, not mine. My face is too valuable to risk being worked over by some young punks after money for their next fix. Here's Amanda Jones's address. Good luck."

"Where'll I find you?"

"Phone me at this number. Ron and I will meet you with the money."

"It has to be tonight?"

"It has to be tonight."

Nick took the subway uptown. When he emerged from underground to find a gang of leather-jacketed teenagers taunting passersby, he was immediately sorry he didn't have a weapon on him. But they let him pass without incident and he walked the short block to the address on 126th Street.

It was a ground-floor apartment with a light in the window, and for a moment Nick thought he was in luck. A small sign in the window read: *Amanda Jones — Reader — Adviser.* He walked into the dim hallway, past a man sleeping on the stoop, and knocked on the door.

"What you want?" a voice, asked from behind the door.

"A reading. Is Amanda in?"

The door opened a crack. "I'm Amanda."

"Can I come in?"

A brown eye inspected him, then the door opened a bit wider. "Can't be too careful, 'specially at night. Come on in."

Amanda Jones was a fairly young woman with light brown skin and wide eyes that seemed to see everything. Nick thought she could be quite attractive if she dispensed with some of the costume jewelry around her neck and wrists and improved on a hairstyle that could only be called gypsy-wild in its present state. "You want a reading?" she asked. "Is that what you said?"

"Yes."

"Tarot or regular deck?"

That was when Nick realized his luck had run out. There were decks of cards visible everywhere in the small apartment, and many were 78-card tarot decks. How did one steal the four of spades from a deck in which the suits were called, if memory served him, swords, wands, cups, and coins?

"I'm not sure about tarot cards," he admitted. "Does a larger deck make for a more accurate reading?"

"Certainly. Though some customers prefer a reading with an ordinary deck, so they can get the technique and try it at home with their own cards." She smiled ruefully. "I lose more customers that way!"

"Let's try a straight deck first."

She looked him over and said, "That'll be ten dollars. In advance."

"Isn't that a bit steep?" He'd expected to pay twenty.

"Inflation, you know?"

Amanda Jones accepted his money and motioned toward a round table in the center of the room. She dealt out ten cards and arranged them in a careful pattern. After studying it a moment she announced his fate.

"You have a crisis to overcome but you will be successful. I see a great deal of money coming to you — perhaps from your labors or from an inheritance."

"I see. Could you do a tarot reading for me too?"

"That would be another ten dollars."

He laid the bill on the table between them and she rose to get the cards. "Do you get many customers up here?" he asked.

"Off the street, like you? Not too many. A few neighbor women, that's all. But you must be feelin' brave to come up here after dark."

"A friend recommended you."

"Who's that?"

Nick decided to take a chance. "Sarah Wentworth."

"You know Mrs. Wentworth? She's some lady! I'm doing a reading for her tomorrow."

"Don't mention I was here," Nick cautioned. "I'm always kidding her about fortune-telling and I don't want her to know I tried it myself."

"That lady doesn't do a *thing* without a reading from the cards! She used to be my mother's customer and now I've got her."

"Your mother died?"

Amanda Jones shrugged. "She's in jail. Its about the same thing."

As she shuffled the tarot deck Nick asked, "These suits correspond to the regular card suits, don't they?"

"Sure. Cups is hearts, coins is diamonds."

"What about spades?"

"Spades correspond to swords in a tarot deck. Clubs are wands." She began to lay out the cards with their strange, garish illustrations. "I can give you a ten-card spread, a seven-card spread, or a royal spread. Which would you like?"

"Royal, I think."

She removed some cards from the deck, then dealt the remainder after first having him choose a king and four other cards. Her reading this time was longer and more complex, but the conclusion was the same. "See here? The ace of coins means riches and great wealth. It is the same money I saw in the spread from the regular deck."

"I guess I have to believe it, then."

"You'd be wise to." She smiled and scooped up the cards. Then, sensing there might be more money to be made, she added, "For an additional fee I can do you a special spread on your sex life."

"Another time, maybe. You probably want to close up and get home."

"I live right here. You wouldn't catch me out on those streets at night."

Nick had been afraid that was the case. Stealing the four of spades from all those decks without her knowing it would definitely present a problem. He thanked her for the readings and departed, hearing the bolts slam shut on the door behind him. Somehow he had to get her out of that apartment, but he didn't know how.

A gentle rain was falling outside, glistening the pavement and making him sorry he hadn't worn a raincoat. The street was nearly deserted, though he could see activity down on 125th Street. Not surprisingly, the gang of leather-jacketed youths still waited in the subway entrance. There were four of them, and Nick approached them warily. "How'd you like to earn some money?" he asked.

"How, man?" the tallest one asked. "By beatin' on your head?" He smiled and lunged forward as he spoke. Nick sidestepped and sent him spinning against the wall of the subway entrance. Then he grabbed the second one and twisted his arm behind his back.

"Listen, you punks! Do what I say and there's a hundred bucks each in it for you. Otherwise I'll hand out a few broken arms."

It was the sort of talk they understood. Nick took a few bills from his pocket, promising the rest later, and explained what he wanted.

Some twenty minutes later there was a disturbance on the sidewalk outside Amanda Jones's apartment. She came to the window, glanced out, and saw four youths fighting in the rain. She saw the glint of a knife reflecting the glow of street lights, and then one of the youths cried out and slid to the sidewalk. The other three took off running.

The wounded youth gasped and dragged himself up the steps to the door of Amanda's building. He managed to ring her bell before he collapsed again. Amanda had watched it all, and now she unbolted her door and moved cautiously toward the front steps. She opened the street door and knelt beside the bloody youth. "Are you hurt bad?" she asked.

"I — don't think so."

"I'll call an ambulance."

"No! Just get me a bandage for this cut. I'll be okay."

It was dark on the steps and she had trouble examining the wound. "Can you come inside?"

"No. Bring me something out here."

She hurried to do so, forgetting her old fear of the streets at night. She was, after all, only in the doorway of her own apartment house. She came back with a wet cloth and a bandage, washing away the blood as best she could. "It doesn't look too bad. Sure you don't want me to call the police?"

"No, I feel better now. Just let me go."

"I don't know. I'd better report this. Those kids could be waitin' for you again."

"I'll be all right." He got to his feet, a bit shaky and started down the steps.

She watched him for a time but he seemed to be walking all right. In fact, after half a block he broke into a run.

She went back inside and locked the door. She'd only been out of her apartment for seven minutes, but that had been long enough for Nick Velvet.

Nick met the four youths back at the subway entrance and paid them the rest of their money. He gave an extra twenty to the kid who'd played the injured one. "You'd make a great actor," he said. Then he caught the subway back downtown, hoping they'd spend their new riches wisely.

Nick had entered the building on 126th Street by picking the lock on the back door. He had then slipped into Amanda's apartment when she went out to help the apparently wounded youth on the front steps. With the apartment door open, Nick was able to hear their conversation and hide in a closet when she returned for the wet cloth and bandages. Then he'd completed his task, left the apartment, and gone down the hall to the back door, while she treated the boy on the front steps. He'd taken four of spades from seventeen regular decks, and the four of swords from eight tarot decks.

It was after ten when Nick reached Times Square and telephoned Cary Temple. The actor had been waiting for his call, and they arranged a ten-thirty meeting at an Irish bar on Eighth Avenue. The rain had stopped but the pavement was still wet as Nick crossed the street and entered the place. A few customers stood along the bar watching a Friday-night baseball game, but the tables and booths were empty. Nick chose one off in a corner and sat down to wait. He still hoped he could catch a late train and surprise Gloria.

Just after ten-thirty Ron Saturn came in. He was alone.

"Hi, Nick. How'd it go?"

"Fine. Here are the cards."

"Good lord! All from Amanda Jones's place?"

"That's right. I even threw in some fours of swords from various tarot decks she had."

"That's great, Nick!"

"Tomorrow's the big day, eh?"

"What do you mean, Nick?"

"While I was stealing the cards from her I took a second to glance in a couple of books she had on the meaning of the cards. The meaning seems to vary from list to list, but it's generally about the same. The four of spades, or the four of swords in a tarot deck, means *Solitude, exile, retreat*. One book is specific enough to give the meaning as *Have nothing more to do with a certain person about whom you are doubtful*."

"Yes," Ron agreed. "That's correct."

"And Amanda Jones has a session with Sarah Wentworth tomorrow. Obviously Mrs. Wentworth wants to see what the cards say about a possible business deal with Cary Temple. He's still a charmer, and I imagine between the two of you a great deal of money has been removed from wealthy New York ladies. With a target as important as Sarah Wentworth, you couldn't chance anything going wrong at the last minute. You especially couldn't chance the four of spades turning up in that fortune-telling session tomorrow. There are other bad cards in the deck too, of course, but from your standpoint the four of spades would be the very worst. If she believed it, she'd call off the deal with Temple at once. You couldn't be sure if Amanda would bring her own deck or use one of Sarah's, so I had to steal the four of spades from both their decks."

"You're smart, Nick. You always were."

"You and Temple figured one missing card would never be noticed from the deck — not tomorrow, at least. And if Amanda discovered it later it wouldn't matter."

"That's about it."

"What's the con? What is it that Sarah Wentworth is supposed to dump her money into?"

Ron Saturn grew a bit nervous at the question. "You don't need to know that, Nick. In fact, the less you know the better. You know how these things are."

"All right," Nick agreed. "You've got the cards. Give me my money and I can still catch the late train home."

Saturn produced a thick envelope from an inside pocket. "It's not quite all there, Nick."

"What do you mean?"

"We can't raise the rest of it till Sarah comes through with the money Cary's expecting."

Nick felt a growing anger. "You know that's not the way I work, Ron. How much is here?"

"Ten thousand in small bills."

"Ten —"

"I know, I know! I told Cary you'd be angry. But play along with us, Nick. We'll have the rest of it tomorrow for sure."

"I'm not your partner in this, Ron. I have to be paid up front."

"I know, I know! I told Cary that. But we just couldn't raise that much money tonight. You'll have the rest before the banks close tomorrow."

"Was Temple afraid to be here when you told me?"

"No, he's busy working out the final details of his proposal."

"Since I seem to have become an unwilling partner, suppose you tell me about it."

"Like I said, Nick, you don't need —"

"I need to know if I have to wait till tomorrow for the rest of my money."

"All right," Saturn agreed. "I can tell you in a general way that it involves a performing arts center to be built in a city not far from New York. It would be to the arts, what Meadowlands is to sports, drawing people from the entire metropolitan area. Cary approached her for some of the initial financing — a feasibility study to choose the site and determine the method of financing the construction itself. He hopes she'll give him a quarter of a million dollars for a start, with perhaps more later."

"I see. And the study will show the idea isn't feasible at all."

"Who knows? Maybe she'll get back her money and then some. Your thirty comes out of the two-fifty, and we'll spend twenty thousand more on real consultants, to make it look good. Cary and I split the other two hundred thousand. But when she told Cary she had to get a reading first from this Amanda Jones, we knew we couldn't take a chance on it coming out wrong."

"Why didn't you just talk to Amanda and offer her a thousand bucks to give a fake reading?"

"How could we risk approaching her? We didn't even know her. If she went running to Mrs. Wentworth, all Cary's months of preparation would go down the drain."

Nick sighed and ordered another drink. He could see he'd have to spend the night in New York after, all. "You'll give us till tomorrow?" Ron asked.

"What choice do I have?"

Nick took a room at the Biltmore overnight. In the morning he phoned Ron Saturn and learned they were awaiting a call from Sarah Wentworth. The reading was to be at eleven, and they hoped to have the money by noon.

Noon passed and nothing happened.

Nick phoned again as he was checking out of his room at one o'clock. This time Cary Temple answered.

"Don't worry, Velvet. It's just a slight delay. Ron and I are going over there in an hour."

"Good. I'll be waiting for you at the park entrance across the street."

"It might be wiser to remain at your hotel."

"I'm checking out," Nick replied. "I'll be waiting across the street." He hung up before Temple could respond.

Nick reached Sarah Wentworth's apartment building in the mid-sixties just before two o'clock, in time to see Saturn and Temple leave a taxi and walk past the doorman. He found a bench just inside the park entrance and settled down to wait. Though the sky was cloudy there'd been no further rain and he could hear young voices from the children's zoo nearby.

He waited for over an hour but the two men did not reappear. He stood up at last and started across the street. Certainly it didn't take this long to give a final pitch and pick up the check. It was time to investigate the possibility of a rear entrance, and the growing suspicion that his old friend Ron Saturn was pulling a double cross.

He'd crossed the street and was starting to circle the building when he saw them coming out the front door — Saturn and Temple, and two other men. One of the men walked to the curb and signaled a waiting car. Nick kept walking. The men were detectives, and Saturn and Temple were almost certainly under arrest.

He didn't see the other person come out of the apartment building, not until Amanda Jones spoke to him. "Well, don't I know you from somewhere?" she asked with a grin.

"I —"

"Were you waiting for your two friends? They had a previous engagement — with the police."

Nick took a deep breath. "I think I'd better buy you a drink."

They walked South a few blocks to a hotel cocktail lounge and Nick ordered the drinks. "Do you want to tell me what happened back there?"

Amanda Jones smiled again, obviously enjoying herself. "What were you after up at my place last night? You were working with those two, weren't you?"

"I did them a favor, yes."

"That boy who got hurt on my doorstep — it was to get me out of my apartment, wasn't it? Fake blood, wasn't it?"

There was no harm in admitting it. Nick nodded and said, "I took the four of spades from all your decks."

She laughed out loud. "Man, that's the craziest thing I ever did hear!"

"They were afraid if the four turned up in your reading for Mrs. Wentworth it would cool her toward Cary Temple's scheme." He took a drink and lit her cigarette. "Now it's your turn. Tell me what happened up there."

"I did her a ten-card reading with my tarot deck like I always do. I'll admit I didn't notice any missing card. But when I spread the deck, card number two, showing the immediate influence on the questioner, was the moon."

"The moon?"

Amanda Jones nodded. "It's a bad card in the tarot deck, signifying deception, trickery, dishonesty, insincerity, double dealing. Mrs. Wentworth took one look at it and decided to call a friend of hers at police headquarters."

"Are you telling me Temple and Saturn were arrested because of a tarot reading?"

"Not entirely. But the police apparently had two other complaints from wealthy women about Temple collecting money for this arts-center scheme. They sent a couple of detectives up to be present when she gave him the money." She was smiling again. "I guess that's the end of this con game for now."

"I didn't know there'd been others," Nick admitted.

"It was all in the cards. They never fail me. That moon card told it all."

"I'll tell you something — they failed you last night when you did my reading and said I'd receive a great deal of money. Your reading for Mrs. Wentworth *cost* me a great deal of money!"

But Amanda Jones was still basking in her triumph and wasn't about to be shaken. "Your trouble was, you just thought too small," she told him.

"How do you mean?"

"You only stole the four of spades when you should have stolen the moon."

The Theft of Cinderella's Slipper

Gloria had a brother named Arnie who owned a restaurant in Greenwich Village, not far from the street where Nick Velvet had grown up. Nick and Gloria occasionally dined there when they were in Manhattan, but they rarely saw Arnie at other times. He had a wife named Audrey and his own family, and he seemed to make a point of avoiding too much contact with Nick. That was why it came as a special surprise when he phoned Gloria one Tuesday afternoon in June and asked her to bring Nick to the restaurant that evening.

"After all, he is my brother," Gloria argued. "We've got to go. We hardly ever see him."

"Did he say what he wanted?"

"Just that he had a problem and maybe you could help him."

"Well, we'd better see what it's all about," Nick agreed with some reluctance.

The restaurant was located on a corner a few blocks from Washington Square. It had been called *Arnie's* for more than a decade, but after a minor Mafia figure was wounded in a shooting in front of the place Gloria's brother had changed the name to the *Café Venice*. He insisted he wanted nothing to do with hoods or criminals — an insistence which sometimes made Gloria wince when Nick was present.

Arnie was waiting for them when they arrived shortly before seven, and he ushered them into a small private dining room with flocked wallpaper and red velvet drapes. "So good of you to come, Nick," he said, ordering a bottle of French wine from the waiter.

"Gloria said you had a problem."

"I do. I hope you can help."

"It's not your family —"

"No, no, Gloria. Everyone's fine. Frankly, Nick, I need you to steal something for me."

"I don't —"

"There's no need for pretense. I've known about you for years. Some of my best customers have been your clients, and naturally they've mentioned you to me." He had a way of squinting as he spoke that reminded Nick of Gloria. The expression was attractive on her, less so on her brother's craggy features. Arnie was five years older than his sister, in his mid-forties, and was beginning to show signs of middle age. "Naturally I'm prepared to pay your usual fee."

"I have very strict guidelines," Nick said, choosing his words carefully. The idea of having Gloria's brother as a client was not one that appealed to him.

"I know, I know. You never steal anything of value. This is a shoe, a left shoe to be exact. A woman's pump with a pink three-inch heel and pink straps. The pair cost less than twenty-five dollars new, so you can see that one of them alone would be virtually worthless. Hell, she used to wear them in here sometimes."

"Do you have the right one, so I could see exactly what it looks like?"

"The right one is unavailable.'"

The wine arrived and they ceased talking while it was opened. When the waiter had departed, Gloria complimented her brother. "This tastes expensive, Arnie."

"Only the best for you, Sis. What about it, Nick? Is it a deal?"

"Where is this shoe at the present time?"

"In the safe of a lawyer named Frederick Junis. He has an office on the thirty-first floor of the Regal Building on Wall Street."

"Getting into a safe won't be easy. He must think this shoe is pretty valuable."

Arnie shrugged. "He's sentimental. It belonged to a girl he knew."

"What happened to her?"

"She ran away."

"And left her shoe? It sounds like Cinderella."

Arnie's eyebrows lifted a bit. "It does, doesn't it? I hadn't thought of that."

"There's nothing valuable hidden in the shoe? No microfilmed plans of atomic secrets?"

"Nothing of the sort. It's just a shoe, and I'm willing to pay you twenty-five grand to get it back."

"We couldn't take your money," Gloria told him, much to Nick's astonishment.

"I'd insist, if you get me the shoe."

"We can talk about money later," Nick said. "For now, I'll need to know the name of this young woman who ran off without her left shoe."

Arnie hesitated, then replied, "Her name is Sophie Moment. She's done some modeling. You may have seen her on the covers of women's magazines."

"All right." Nick made a note of the name. "How soon do you need this shoe?"

"I need it today. I'll settle for this weekend."

Nick took another sip of his wine. "I won't make any promises."

"I will, Arnie," Gloria assured him. "Nick will get it for you."

"Fine! Now let's have something to eat!"

Nick was silent during much of the drive home. Finally, as their car left the Bronx behind and headed north through Westchester, she asked, "All right, Nicky, what did I do wrong?"

"You promised him I'd deliver by the weekend, and you offered to do it without a fee. Is that enough?"

"It's my brother! Heaven knows we haven't gone out of our way to be friendly toward him these last twenty years. You probably haven't seen him more than a dozen times outside the restaurant."

"I don't like doing jobs for relatives."

"How do you know? You never had one to do before!" Her voice was rising angrily.

"You know the sort of work I do," he replied with a sigh. "Sometimes things don't work out quite right. I've had clients killed, or defrauded of money. Once I collected a double fee, and another time I got no fee at all. I like to keep my options open, and I like to have an escape route if things get hot. Working for your brother ties me down too much."

"Maybe you should stay home and I'll go after that shoe myself."

She sounded as if she might mean it. "All right," he said at last. "I'll do it. I suppose I have no choice."

"He did buy us a nice dinner, Nicky," she said, lowering her voice to a tone of conciliation.

"I suppose so. I just wish he'd been a little more honest about what he wants."

"Honest? What makes you think he wasn't?"

"He described this Sophie Moment as a fairly successful model, appearing on the covers of women's magazines. Is she the sort to wear twenty-five-dollar shoes?"

On Wednesday morning Nick drove back to the city, leaving his car in an expensive midtown garage and taking a subway the rest of the way to Wall Street. The Regal Building was a few blocks from the Stock Exchange, within sight of the twin-towered World Trade Center. Riding the high-speed elevator to the thirty-first floor, he found himself in the company of young men in three-piece suits and women in tailored pinstripes carrying briefcases. It was the world of high finance, and though he'd dressed for it himself he still felt out of place.

The entire thirty-first floor was given over to the law firm of Denton, Blaine & Junis, and Nick stepped from the elevator to find himself already in the reception area, facing a bright-faced young woman behind a kidney-shaped desk. "Can I help you?" she asked.

"Mr. Frederick Junis?"

"Do you have an appointment?"

"Ah, no — but I think he'll see me if you give him this card." He passed over a business card with his name and the phone number of an answering service he sometimes used. In one corner he had written: *Re Miss Sophie Moment.*

The receptionist accepted the card and said, "He's with a client right now. Please have a seat."

Nick sank into a modern foam rubber sofa that ran along one wall of the large reception area. A glass-topped coffee table held a variety of legal publications and the morning edition of *The Wall Street Journal*. Nick chose the latter and engrossed himself in an article about world oil prices. The reception area was a busy place. He watched the comings and goings with half an eye, aware that his card had been passed to a red-haired secretary who disappeared through one of the doors. Presently the receptionist came over to tell him, "Mr. Velvet, Mr. Junis can see you at eleven o'clock, if you care to wait."

He glanced at his watch and decided he could give it another twenty minutes. "That will be fine."

At 10:45 a dark-haired young woman in a white smock emerged from the elevator pushing a large coffee cart piled with doughnuts and paper cups. She rang a little bell and almost at once a line of secretaries began to form, interspersed with a few hardy males who believed in getting their own coffee. There was much chatting and bantering back and forth, giving Nick an opportunity to study the people who worked at Denton, Blaine & Junis. The red-haired woman whom he assumed to be Junis's secretary reappeared toward the end of the line and he watched her buy three cups of coffee which she carried away on a little tray. She didn't glance in his direction.

It was after eleven before everyone had been served and the coffee cart was pushed back onto the elevator, the young woman skillfully wedging the door open with one sneakered foot until she'd accomplished her task. Before Nick could grow impatient with waiting, the redhead reappeared. "Mr. Velvet? I'm Marcia Wilcox, Mr. Junis's secretary. Would you follow me, please?"

She led him into a large office trimmed with warm oak paneling that offered a postcard view of the Statue of Liberty in the harbor. In keeping with the scene, the decor of the office was nautical. Nick's quick gaze took in the framed 19th-century paintings of sailing ships and he wondered if the lawyer's safe might be behind one of them. Frederick Junis himself was a slender dark-haired man in his mid-forties who seemed dwarfed by the office and his massive desk. Perhaps he realized this himself, because he immediately came out from behind it and led Nick to a less formal conversation area at the side of the room.

"I'm sorry I can't give you much time, Mr. Velvet. I have another client arriving soon. Your card mentioned Sophie Moment. Do you know her?"

"Not personally," Nick told the attorney. "I'm a private detective and I've been hired to find her."

"By whom?"

"I'm not at liberty to answer that. Do you have any idea where she's living now?"

Junis eyed him uncertainly, as if weighing just how much information he should reveal. "Sophie is something of a mystery woman, as you may know," he answered carefully. "I don't have an address for her."

"I understood she did some modeling work."

"Off and on. Her agency hasn't been able to reach her either." He was toying nervously with a pencil but suddenly he put it down as if he'd made a decision. "I can confirm that she's missing, however, Mr. Velvet. In fact she disappeared from this very office one week ago today."

"Oh?"

"This is awkward for me to discuss. She'd gotten in here somehow unannounced and I surprised her going through my files. She fled out my private entrance to the hall. I ran after her but she'd disappeared."

"I guess you'll have to tell me more than that," Nick urged. "What was she after in your files?"

"It involved a lawsuit which I'm not at liberty to discuss further. I only mentioned the incident to explain about the last time that I saw her."

"When she ran out of the office did she leave anything behind?"

Frederick Junis's eyes sharpened. "Sophie sent you, didn't she?"

"Certainly not. I don't know the woman and I've never laid eyes on her." Nick believed in telling the truth on occasion. "I just thought she might have dropped her purse or something if she left that quickly."

"To my knowledge she wasn't carrying a purse. And she left nothing which would help to find her."

"What was she wearing at the time?"

"A white dress with a wide pink belt and matching pink shoes."

"Was anything taken from your files?"

"I don't believe so. I saw nothing in her hands as she ran out and slammed the door." His eyes shifted as if he'd been caught in a lie.

Nick felt frustrated. The lawyer wasn't about to admit that a shoe had ever been dropped, much less that he had it hidden away in his office safe. "What about —"

"I really can't give you any more time, Mr. Velvet."

Before he could argue further there was a gentle tap on the door and Marcia Wilcox appeared. "Pardon me, Mr. Junis. Are you free for a conference with Mr. Denton?"

"I can give him a few minutes. Let me check the reception room first. I'm expecting a client."

Marcia smiled sweetly at Nick. "Can you find your way out, Mr. Velvet?"

"I think so.

As he stepped into the elevator Nick saw Junis speaking to the receptionist. No one was waiting on the foam rubber sofa. If there really had been a client, he or she hadn't put in an appearance.

Gloria was anxious to hear all the details but there was little for Nick to tell her. "I can't get a grip on it," he admitted. "This woman Sophie Moment has disappeared, but I don't know why that's important. And I don't know how it involves your brother."

"Do you think Arnie's been cheating on his wife, carrying on an affair with this Sophie?"

"I have no idea. But if I'm going to steal that shoe I have to know a bit more about what's going on."

In the morning he found Arnie at the *Café Venice*. Nick had two shoeboxes under his arm which he placed carefully on the bar. Arnie paused in his task of inventorying the liquor to ask, "Did you get it, Nick?"

"Not yet. I'm no safecracker, Arnie. I have to trick him into opening that box, and so far I haven't succeeded. I need more information about Sophie Moment. All Junis will admit to is that she's missing."

"You spoke with him?"

"Don't worry, it was quite discreet. But right now I need something less discreet from you. That's why I came without Gloria."

Arnie picked up a shot glass and started polishing it absently with a bar rag. "You know, Nick, I was a bartender here before I raised enough money to buy the place."

"I remember."

"Fancy lawyers like Frederick Junis aren't my style."

"How about fancy models like Sophie Moment?"

He shook his head sadly. "There is no Sophie Moment, Nick."

"You'd better explain that."

"It's a long story," he said with a sigh.

"I've got all the time in the world, Arnie."

"Then come on, let's sit down and talk. Want a drink?"

"Just a beer."

Arnie opened two and carried them to a table. "I suppose I'd better start at the beginning. You see, I'm being sued by a man named Thomas Grayson. He was in here drinking one night and he fell and knocked his head on the bar rail. You know how those liability suits are these days. He claims to have suffered permanent damage to his back and is suing me for over a million dollars. That's more than my insurance covers. If I lose I'll have to sell the place."

"Does Gloria know about this?"

"No. Why worry her?"

"And this attorney Frederick Junis is representing Grayson in the lawsuit?"

"You guessed it."

"Strange. A big Wall Street firm like that doesn't usually go in for ambulance chasing."

"That's exactly what I thought. I began to suspect there was something else behind it, especially when Junis and his client refused a quite generous out-of- court settlement by my insurance company."

"Where does Sophie Moment fit in?"

"It's not what you think," Arnie was quick to tell him. "I'm not sleeping with her — though I'd damn well like to! She's a beauty, with long blonde hair halfway down her back. Sophie's like a lot of my customers. People who live in this section of the Village are either on their way up or down. I don't know which she is. She did some acting and modeling but it never amounted to much. Then I think she had a drug problem for a year or so. She's clean now, but not setting the world on fire. Maybe she never will. There's always so much competition in this city. Anyway, I happened to tell her about my troubles with Junis one night and she thought she could help. I don't know what gave her that idea, but I was just about at my wit's end and I accepted her offer."

"Her idea of helping was to sneak into Junis's office and go through his files?"

"Yeah, but I didn't realize that at first. She went to him once or twice posing as a client, to get the layout of his office. Then she sneaked in one morning last week and was looking for my file when he caught her. She managed to escape but lost a shoe doing it."

"The twenty-five dollar shoes. I wondered about that. I guess you were right when you said things weren't going too well for her."

"Junis didn't catch her, but when he saw which file she was after he guessed that I was involved. He phoned me with all sorts of threats, and said he'd have her arrested when he found her. He told me he'd locked her shoe in his safe as evidence to prove his story to the police. Hell, Nick, I couldn't let the girl go to jail on my account."

"So you hired me to steal the shoe. Has Sophie Moment contacted you?"

"Just once. She told me what happened and that's all. I think she's been in hiding since then, and I have no idea how to contact her."

"But you're willing to pay me twenty-five grand for that shoe."

"Like I said, Nick, I can't let her go to jail over this."

Nick reached over and opened the shoe boxes he'd brought along. "You said she used to wear the pink shoes in here sometimes. Take a look at these samples I brought along. They're all cheap pink shoes with three-inch heels."

"I don't know her size."

"Never mind the size. Just look at these four shoes."

Arnie reached out to touch Nick's display. "Not these two . . . and not this one. This is the closest, but I don't know if the shape of the strap is quite right. Hell, Nick, I wasn't on the floor studying her feet."

"All right, it'll have to do for my purpose."

"Which is — ?"

"To earn my money. If Junis thinks I have the shoe, he'll open the safe to check on the one he has. I'll be in touch, Arnie."

When Nick called home that afternoon Gloria had some surprising news. "I checked the answering service and they had a call from Frederick Junis. He wants you to phone him."

"Junis? All right, I'd better see what he wants."

"Is it trouble, Nicky?"

"I hope not."

He called the law office and waited until Junis came on the phone. "I'm glad I was able to reach you, Mr. Velvet. The number on your card is merely an answering service."

"I'm out a lot," Nick explained. "What can I do for you?"

"I've spoken with Mr. Denton and he agrees that we need the services of a private detective. Since you're already involved in the matter of Sophie Moment we'd like to hire you for an auxiliary investigation into her disappearance."

"That could be a conflict of interest," Nick answered carefully.

"I don't think so. Could you come in this afternoon and talk about it?"

He glanced at his watch. It was just past two o'clock. "I could be there around four if that's not too late."

"Fine. We'll look for you then."

Nick wondered what he was getting into, and decided some research was called for. There wasn't much he could do in two hours, but he managed to establish that Sophie Moment was not listed in any of the New York phone books nor in the New York Times Index.

Craig Denton, senior partner of Denton, Blaine.& Junis, was listed, however. The year-old article that Nick found on library microfilm detailed some real estate dealings in lower Manhattan.

He was about to depart when another name came to mind. He checked the phone book for the address of Thomas Grayson and copied down a number on West 17th Street. Frederick Junis's client might be able to shed some light on the whole business.

But first he had the four o'clock appointment with Junis himself. The reception area on the thirty-first floor was empty except for the familiar young woman behind the kidney-shaped desk. "Nick Velvet to see Mr. Junis," he said.

"Oh, yes. You'll be meeting Mr. Junis in Mr. Craig Denton's office."

Marcia Wilcox appeared to escort him down the thickly carpeted corridor. "Nice to see you again," she told him.

"I didn't expect to be back so soon."

"Right in here, please." She closed the door behind him after he entered.

Frederick Junis stood with his hands clasped behind his back, next to a white-haired man who remained seated. "This is Craig Denton, Nick Velvet."

Nick shook the senior partner's firm hand. "I'm pleased you could come," Denton told him. "Fred told me he spoke with you yesterday morning and that you're investigating the disappearance of Miss Sophie Moment."

"That's correct."

Denton turned his head toward Junis and the younger man took up the story. "I wasn't completely frank with you yesterday, Velvet. The truth of the matter is, Sophie Moment disappeared from just outside my office."

"You told me that."

"No — I mean she quite literally vanished. She faded into thin air. I didn't tell you yesterday because I knew you wouldn't have believed me."

"Maybe you'd better go over this slowly," Nick suggested.

"I was in here with Craig. It must have been around eleven, wasn't it?"

"Quarter to," Craig Denton corrected.

"I needed some contracts from my files and I walked down the hall to my office. As soon as I opened the door I saw her bent over the files."

Nick interrupted. "How did you happen to know her?"

"She'd presented herself to me as a client on the previous afternoon. Wanted a will drawn up. I told her one of the junior partners in our estates section could help her, but she asked my advice on some bequests. It was all strictly routine and I realized later that she used it as a sham to learn the exact location of my files."

"What happened after she ran out?"

"I paused only long enough to see that she'd been into the file on a negligence suit we're pursuing — *Grayson versus the Café Venice*. Then I went after her. The private door to my office opens onto a short corridor with just two other doors. One leads to the ladies' room, which was occupied, the other back into the reception area, where a dozen witnesses swear they never saw her. She vanished in that corridor."

"That's hardly possible," Nick said. "Without even looking at the place I can think of a number of answers. She went into the ladies' room, or she hid behind the door as you opened it, or she walked through the reception room without being noticed."

"My own secretary, Marcia, was in the ladies' room and swears no one else entered. When I show you the corridor you'll see there's no room behind the door. And she could hardly have escaped notice by a dozen people in the reception area — especially since she'd have been hobbling on one high heel. She lost her other shoe in the corridor by the ladies' room door."

"A shoe!" Nick said, acting surprised. "Let's have a look at it."

"No need for that," Junis assured him. "It's locked in my safe. I'll produce it when we have a foot to match it to."

"Let me speak to your secretary then."

"Of course." He stepped outside the door and returned in a moment with Marcia Wilcox.

"Could you tell me your version of what happened last week?" Nick asked.

The young woman sat down and crossed her long legs. She seemed to enjoy the attention.

"You mean about that mystery woman? Sure. I was on my coffee break and I slipped into the ladies' room for a second. No one else was there, but then I heard a noise at the door, as if someone started to come in and then changed her mind. I looked out just as Mr. Junis appeared through the private door to his office. There was this pink high-heeled shoe on the floor by the ladies' room door. He picked it up and asked me if she was inside. I said no but he wanted to look anyhow. Then he went through the door to the reception room and asked Jennie — that's our receptionist — if Miss Moment had come out that way. She insisted no one had come out. What's more, she swore Sophie Moment hadn't even come in. She hadn't allowed anyone into Mr. Junis's office, and neither had I."

Nick nodded. "She could have entered the same way she left, through that private door. It's unlocked, isn't it?"

"Well, yes," Junis conceded. But it can only be reached from the reception area, in full view of —"

"What about the stairs to the other floors?"

"This building is very security-conscious. All the fire doors have alarms that ring if they're opened. Nothing rang that day, so she didn't use any stairs."

"If I could see that shoe it might help," Nick suggested.

"Find me the foot it goes on and I'll produce the shoe."

"That's what you said before." Nick decided on a different approach. "What about this file she was so interested in?"

"A routine liability suit. Man injured himself in a bar."

"I didn't know law firms like this one handled routine liability suits."

"There are special circumstances here," Craig Denton said without further explanation.

"Just find Sophie Moment for us," Junis instructed Nick. "We'll take care of the rest of it."

Nick decided to make a final try for the shoe on Friday morning, but first he wanted to call on the plaintiff in the lawsuit, Thomas Grayson. Although he wasn't directly involved in the Cinderella-like flight of the mysterious Sophie Moment, the whole thing was tied together somehow. Nick hated to think that Gloria's brother Arnie was more deeply involved than he admitted, but the possibility had to be seriously considered. And Nick wanted to learn if Grayson was merely an innocent victim of an accident or part of a murkier plot.

It was the evening rush hour by the time he located the apartment building on West 17th Street. Grayson lived on the tenth floor, and Nick had no trouble blending with the building's residents as he rode the elevator up. He hadn't really expected

Grayson to be at home, and when his knock went unanswered he almost gave up the whole thing. Then, as he started to turn away, the door was opened an inch and a woman's voice asked, "What do you want?"

"I'm looking for Thomas Grayson," Nick said. "I'm from the insurance company."

"Please come in. I'll call him."

The door opened wider and Nick stepped inside, congratulating himself on the success of his simple deception. Suddenly he saw a flash of long blonde hair and he was shoved sideways, off balance, into a darkened closet. He shouted as the closet door was slammed shut on him.

Then he heard a television set being turned on, fairly loud, and after a moment the hall door opened and closed. He shouted again, pounding on the closet door, but it did no good. She'd lured him in here and trapped him like an animal. With the TV set smothering his shouts, and given the thick walls of the old building, there was no one to hear him.

Finally he calmed down enough to reach around in the darkness till he found the dangling cord from a ceiling light. He pulled it and now at least he could see the confines of his prison. The small closet, barely three by four feet in size, had only the single thick wooden door. There were no hinges or knob on Nick's side. He tried heaving a shoulder against it, but it didn't budge. A solid kick in the area of the bolt likewise did no good.

He turned his attention to the few garments hanging in the closet — a raincoat, a topcoat, a couple of jackets. There was nothing in the pockets which could be used as a tool, and nothing on the closet shelf except a folded blanket. He took a credit card from his pocket, and tried to work it between the door and the jamb, but the jamb itself was metal, and a metal lip effectively shielded the edge of the door. There was nothing in his own pockets except a few coins and the keys to his car. The keys were of light-weight aluminum which bent when he tried to wedge them between the door and jamb.

He could hear a late-afternoon game show on the television set, and from the street far below came the occasional honking of horns in the city traffic. He tried yelling again, knowing his voice would never carry through the walls. In his car was a jackknife and a set of lock-picks he sometimes used, but they were doing him no good at the moment.

He felt of the wooden bar from which the coats were hung, but it was firmly anchored in the walls. Finally he took one of the wire coathangers, thinking how flimsy it was, and straightened it out the best he could. Using one end as a sort of awl, he rammed it into the wood by the edge of the door, at the place where the bolt should be. A tiny piece of the finish came away, revealing the wood beneath. That was all he needed for encouragement.

He worked on the door with the straightened hanger for forty-five minutes before he'd managed to chip away enough of the wood to reach the bolt. Then he jammed the hanger between the faceplate and the metal door casing and felt the bolt slide open. He was free.

The evening news was on the television, but he gave it only a glance. His eyes were riveted on the middle-aged man slumped near the armchair across the room. A lamp had been smashed over his head. There was no doubt he was dead, and little doubt he was Thomas Grayson.

"It's turned serious," he told Gloria that night. "Arnie may have killed someone and if he did there's no way I can keep him out of prison."

"My God, Nicky, he wouldn't hurt a fly! You've got the wrong person if you think Arnie is involved in anything like that."

"The murdered man was suing him, Gloria. He could have lost his restaurant."

"He still wouldn't kill anyone."

"It might have been a young woman working for him — the same one who lost her shoe at that lawyer's office."

Gloria shook her head. "I don't care what you say. He's not involved in a murder."

Nick remembered the woman's voice as she opened the door, remembered the flash of long blonde hair. His only chance was to find her now, before the police found Grayson's body and linked him with Arnie. But he had a feeling that Sophie Moment, like Cinderella, might be easier to find once he had her lost slipper in hand.

Nick phoned Arnie at the restaurant that evening to ask him one question. "Arnie, when you were telling me about Sophie Moment, at one point you said, *There is no Sophie Moment*. What did you mean by that?"

"Just that it wasn't her real name. She used it for her modeling. It was as phoney as the long blonde hair."

"Yeah," Nick said. "What's her real name?"

"I've got no idea, Nick. She was just Sophie Moment to me."

"You said when you mentioned Junis she thought she could help. Did she say why?"

"No. I got the idea she might know him, though. She was always needing money. Maybe she had some sort of business dealings with him."

"He claims he didn't know her till she came to his office. She hasn't contacted you since the other night?"

"Not a word. Can you get the shoe, Nick?"

"I'll have it tomorrow. Good night, Arnie."

Nick arrived at the Wall Street office of Denton, Blaine & Junis shortly after ten-thirty. Marcia Wilcox escorted him into Junis's office, glancing oddly at the paper bag under his arm. "Did you bring your lunch?" she asked with a smile.

"Just something for your boss."

Frederick Junis did not seem especially pleased to see Nick again. "I think we'd better cancel our arrangement."

But Nick merely smiled. "You must have been watching the morning news. They found Thomas Grayson's body."

"I don't know anything about that."

"He was a client, wasn't he?"

"What have you got in that bag?"

Nick opened it and took out the single pink shoe with its three-inch heel. "This was found at the scene of Grayson's murder."

"By whom?

"By me. I was wondering if it matched the one she left."

"I'll soon find out." He rose from his desk and walked to one of the framed sailing prints on the wall. It swung away on well-oiled hinges, revealing a small wall safe that Junis opened quickly.

Nick saw him produce the shoe, holding it to the light from the window as if it were a rare jewel or a bottle of wine.

"No," Junis decided. "They're not the same. See — the strap is different." He started to return it to the safe.

Then a little bell began ringing in Nick's head. He moved quickly from his chair. He kept moving, even after he realized the bell was not in his head at all but in the reception area. The coffee cart had arrived for the morning break.

"What in hell are you doing?" Junis gasped as Nick wrestled the pink shoe from his grip.

"It's Cinderella time," Nick told him, giving him a stiff-armed shove back into his leather chair.

"Come back with that shoe!"

But Nick was already out of the office, hurrying toward the reception room. There must have been a wild look about him. He saw the receptionist, Jennie, start to stand up. He saw Marcia Wilcox, her eyes on the shoe, trying to block his path. Was Junis yelling something from his office door?

The line of secretaries at the coffee cart parted. Nick Velvet dropped to one knee before the dark-haired young woman pouring the coffee. He looked at her sneakers and her white smock and finally up at her face, and held out the shoe much as the Prince might have done to Cinderella. "Shall we see if it fits?" he asked.

"Damn you!" She was trying to push the urn of coffee over on him when he grabbed her legs out from under her and brought her down.

"There was no time for introductions last night," Nick said. "But I guess you must be Sophie Moment."

Arnie ordered a round of drinks and settled into his chair across the table from Gloria and Nick. "So tell me about it. All I know is that the police arrested Sophie for killing Grayson. I hope they don't think I was involved."

"She made a full statement," Nick explained. "When you mentioned Frederick Junis to her, she realized his office was in the building where she worked with the coffee cart. It's a big building with more than one cart, but it was easy enough for her to switch places with the girl who worked the thirty-first floor. First she called on Junis wearing her blonde wig, posing as a client so she could get the layout of his private office and location of his files. She knew she'd only have a few minutes to find what she wanted. Last week she arrived with her cart as usual and left it in the reception area while she supposedly used the ladies' room. What she really did, once she was out of sight in that back corridor, was to take her wig, a pink belt and pink shoes from beneath her white tunic and put them on. The belt was enough to give her tunic the appearance of a white dress. Her sneakers went under the skirt, where she had a little bag like shoplifters use. I suspect she did some shoplifting too, when times were tough."

"What was she after in those files?" Gloria asked.

Arnie filled her in on the lawsuit and then Nick continued. "In the beginning I think she just wanted to help Arnie and earn a few bucks doing it. But she admitted she found something more valuable in those files — proof that Denton and Junis were using the Grayson lawsuit to force Arnie into bankruptcy so they could get this land for a condominium. When Junis caught her she fled with the papers, doffing her wig, shoes and belt as she ran. Junis wasn't far behind her, though, and she lost a shoe as she slipped her sneakers back on. Of course no one noticed her reappearance in the reception area. Like Chesterton's postman she'd become invisible. It's not too surprising, since without the wig and shoes and belt even Junis didn't recognize her."

"Why did she kill Thomas Grayson?" Arnie asked.

"She decided the document she'd stolen was worth more as blackmail than you'd pay her. She went to Grayson's apartment to demand money, figuring he might be an easier touch than Junis. She was wrong. He tried to rough her up and she hit him with a lamp. She claims she didn't mean to kill him, but a jury can worry about that."

"How'd you know it was her, Nicky?"

"Well, I had a glimpse of her at Grayson's apartment, when she shoved me into the closet. Of course it might have been someone else with long blonde hair or a wig, but I didn't think so. Junis's secretary, Marcia, was in the ladies' room during last week's pilferage from the files, but she was certainly innocent. Of all the people in that office, she'd have the least need of a disguise. She could have removed or copied anything in those files without attracting suspicion. To a lesser extent, the rest of the office employees were cleared too. There were simply easier, safer ways for them to get at the files. Sophie Moment had to be an outsider, but then how had she disappeared?

I remembered the time of the robbery — quarter to eleven, according to Craig Denton. I knew from my own visit to the office that the coffee cart arrives at exactly that time. I remembered the dark-haired young woman wearing the white smock that could double for a dress. Most of all, I remembered Marcia Wilcox saying she'd gone to the ladies' room while on her coffee break — more evidence that the cart was in the reception area at the time of the robbery. Junis told me about all the people out there who hadn't seen Sophie Moment. They were in line at the coffee cart, of course, being served by Sophie after her brief absence."

Arnie ordered another round of drinks. "How can I ever thank you, Nick?"

"That's easy," Nick said. "Here's the shoe you hired me to steal."

The Theft of Gloria's Greatcoat

Friends sometimes ask how I met Nick Velvet, and how I could ever have fallen in love with a professional thief. The second part of that is easy, because for a good many years into our relationship I believed his stories about engaging in secret government work that called for frequent travels to distant cities. The occasional thefts I knew about were only incidental to this, I thought.

As for the first part, how we met, I suppose that's an interesting story. It happened more than thirty years ago, in November of 1965, when I was a girl in my early twenties named Gloria Proctor, just out of a community college in Ohio and determined to make my way in the big city. I'd arrived in New York shortly after graduation and by the fall I had a low-paying job in publishing and a nice apartment down in Stuyvesant Town.

It was a time of increased American involvement in Vietnam. Lyndon Johnson was our president and John Lindsay had just been elected mayor of New York. I was young and the city was an exciting place to be. Actually I'd never planned a career in publishing, preferring the world of art. There was always a sketch pad handy, though I soon learned that I was best with caricatures. There was hardly a market for those unless one was a political cartoonist, an all-male world if there ever was one. So it was publishing for me, at least for the time being.

I decided I couldn't get through the winter season in Manhattan without a good overcoat, something I could wear to work that would also look good at holiday parties. On my budget I couldn't afford too much, but I went searching for something stylish and I found it in a bargain shop on Seventh Avenue. The autumn of '65 was the beginning of a brief Russian craze in fashion, inspired by the film version of Pasternak's novel *Doctor Zhivago* which wasn't even opening until December. I bought a bright red greatcoat that reached to mid-calf, accented by a long knit scarf of red and black stripes. The ornamental frogs on the front of the coat gave it a vaguely czarist look. I couldn't believe my good fortune in finding it at such a reasonable price until I wore it the first time, to the office and to lunch one blustery day. It was still the first week of November but the wind had turned uncommonly chilly. Winter coats were making an early appearance, and at lunch I saw the identical coat on another woman.

"You can't let things like that bother you," Samantha Rodgers told me. She was a friend and co-worker, a brooding brunette in her thirties, a bit taller and ten years older than me, who'd been a friend since my first day at Neptune Books. We were lunching on the lower level of Rockefeller Plaza by the skating rink, about a block from the office. It was a place beyond my budget but Samantha was treating. "Actually, you should feel good about it. That other woman in your coat happens to be Mary Todd, wife of Sam Todd, the record producer. He's got this new British group, the Augers, who could be bigger than the Beatles."

I shook my head sadly. "I'm not into rock music."

"Neither am I, much, but there are certain people around town that you just have to recognize."

"I'm sure she paid a lot more for her coat than I did over at the Seventh Avenue Outlet."

"Maybe not. Wealthy people like bargains too."

That was on a Friday and I spent a quiet weekend around my apartment, enjoying a return of crisp but sunny weather. The park-like area of Stuyvesant Town was especially pleasant in the fall when we didn't have to worry about the lack of air conditioning in our apartments. If nothing else we could watch the antics of the rare black squirrels that made the area their home.

By coincidence I saw Sam Todd on television Sunday night. He appeared on *The Ed Sullivan Show*, chatting with Ed and introducing the Augers to an American audience. Todd was a stocky man in his forties who seemed to be wearing a bad hairpiece. He had a slight accent that I couldn't quite identify, and he made much of the fact that by appearing on *Sullivan* the Augers were following in the footsteps of Elvis Presley and the Beatles. Though I often switched channels when a rock group came on, curiosity kept me watching. There were five Augers and they were lively enough, wearing tight pants and gyrating with their electric guitars. I decided they needed a drummer to carry the beat, but then no one was asking my opinion. When Ed called for an encore I switched to *The F.B.I.* on channel seven.

Monday morning was warm but cloudy and I wore my light raincoat to the office. It was a busy day at Neptune, with first proofs on two spring novels due from the typesetter. I was an editorial assistant to Max Rhinegold, one of their senior editors, a man of great knowledge and a fiery temper. Much as I admired him, I wondered how long I could continue working for him.

"Are the proofs in yet, Gloria?" he called out from his office that morning, shortly after I arrived.

"I don't see them. I'll check the mailroom."

The proofs weren't in, and within minutes he was on the phone to White Plains. I didn't enjoy listening to his familiar shouted vulgarities so I went down to Samantha's office until he'd finished. "You just have to ignore it," she told me. "He'll calm down." She spoke from experience. Of all the editors at Neptune, she worked most closely with him. Now she tried to cheer me up by saying, "I've got a couple of tickets to that new musical *On a Clear Day You Can See Forever*. It's supposed to be pretty good. They're for tomorrow night. If you're free we could have dinner after work and go to the theater."

"Thanks, Samantha, but I'm getting together with one of my neighbors tomorrow. I appreciate your offer, though. I know they're charging $11.90 for those tickets."

She nodded. "It's a new Broadway high. They'll price themselves out of existence pretty soon."

I'd joined Samantha at a Broadway play once before. She'd told me then that her mysterious boyfriend had purchased the tickets but was unable to join her that night. If the same was true of these tickets I wondered if the boyfriend might be married. It wasn't a question I'd ever ask her, though.

Tuesday evening's engagement was with Helen Coin, a young woman about my own age who lived one floor up from me in our Stuyvesant Town building. She made jewelry in her spare time and she invited me up to see some of it, suggesting we might go out to a movie afterward. I suppose she hoped to sell me a piece or two, but it sounded like a pleasant enough evening and I'd told her I'd come around seven. On Tuesday afternoon when Max Rhinegold decided to knock off early I decided to do the same. "Early" at Neptune Books meant 4:30 at best, and that was what time I went out the door. I walked over to Lexington Avenue, enjoying the sunny autumn afternoon. The temperature was 57 degrees according to one of those bank signs, about average for early November, but I knew it was due to turn cold again the following day. I caught the crowded subway down to 14th Street and walked the three blocks east to a corner of Stuyvesant Town. From there it was only minutes to my apartment, and I unlocked the door shortly after five o'clock.

The first thing I saw was the man's smile, because the growing darkness all but obscured his face. I switched on the living room light and asked angrily, "What are you doing here?"

He was by the open closet door, just a few feet away from me. He closed it and said coolly, "I might ask you the same thing. This is my apartment."

That made me hesitate for just an instant, feeling a bit like Alice in Wonderland. Had I entered the wrong building by mistake? Was I in someone else's apartment? Then I saw the familiar furnishings, carefully gathered during my six months in the city. "Like hell it is!" I responded, my voice rising in a mixture of anger and fright. "Who are — ?"

He took a quick step closer to me and clamped a gloved hand over my mouth. That was when I realized I was being robbed.

"Please be quiet," he said softly into my ear, "and you won't be hurt." When he loosened the pressure on my mouth I mumbled, "You're a thief."

"Not exactly."

For the first time I took a moment to study his face, trying to remember it for the police. He was older than me, perhaps in his early thirties, well-dressed with darkly handsome features, liquid brown eyes, a firm jaw and a classic Roman nose. He might have been Italian-American but I couldn't be sure. Tall, just under six feet, and in good physical condition. His body was firm as he pressed against me, holding tight.

"Why don't you let me go?" I asked after a moment.

He grinned at me. "Maybe I like holding you." Our lips were very close together.

A shiver ran through me as I imagined myself being raped and possibly murdered. For the first time since entering my apartment I was terrified.

He must have felt my terror because he relaxed his grip a bit. For a moment I thought he was about to release me but then he pulled a roll of adhesive tape from his jacket pocket. He was going to tie me up!

I kicked out at him then, catching him on the shin, and broke free for an instant. But he shoved me off balance and I tumbled off the side of the sofa, ending up on the floor. "You have nice long legs," he said, ignoring my attempts to kick him again. He pulled a long piece of tape free from the roll.

That was when the lights went out.

I crawled free, out of his reach, seeking safety before the lights went back on. It was my apartment and I knew it like the back of my hand. I tried to crawl as quietly as I could toward the bedroom, knowing I could lock the door once I was inside. Everything was black as pitch and for the first time I realized there were no lights outside either. No lights anywhere that I could see, except on passing cars.

I'd just reached the area of the bedroom door when a small beam of light suddenly targeted me. Of course! No self-respecting burglar would go on a job without a flashlight. "Ah, there you are!" he said.

"Here I am," I conceded. "What are you going to do about it?"

"I don't know. What happened to the lights?"

"Beats me."

"They've been out several minutes, all over town from the looks of it. Do you have a portable radio?"

"In my bedroom," I admitted.

"Let's turn it on."

"You're the damnedest burglar I ever heard of. Why didn't you just run away?"

"Get the radio.," he commanded. "I want to know what's happening."

I found it on my bedside table and turned it on. " . . . the entire northeast and parts of Canada. We're still trying to learn the cause of this massive blackout which has brought subways and elevators to a halt all over the city and may have trapped thousands of rush hour travelers. Only an emergency generator is keeping us on the air."

"You'd better get out of here," I told him.

"On the contrary, I think I'd better stay."

"What?"

"The police are going to be roaming around, looking for possible looters. I might be stopped and questioned."

"That's nonsense! There are lots of people on the streets." I could see the movement of car lights from the bedroom window.

Our conversation was interrupted by the ringing of the telephone. I stared into the flashlight beam, waiting for his reaction. "Answer it," he ordered, "but be careful what you say."

I picked it up and heard the voice of my upstairs neighbor, Helen Coin. "Gloria, are your lights out?"

"They're out all over the northeast, Helen. It's a massive power blackout."

"Then I guess the movie is out for tonight."

"I'm afraid so."

"Want to come up anyway and I'll open a bottle of wine?"

His head was close to mine, listening to the conversation. At her suggestion he shook his head. "I guess not, Helen. The elevators aren't running and I'd probably trip on the stairs in the dark. We'd both better stay put."

I hung up and faced my burglar again. Somehow the phone call had renewed my confidence that I could handle the situation. "If you insist on staying, why don't I get us something to eat? I'm hungry even if you're not."

He was silent for a few seconds, considering my offer. "What have you got?"

"Without my electric stove, it's pretty much sandwiches. Ham or chicken."

"Ham is fine. How about a beer?"

"I can do that. Let me light a few candles."

To this day I don't know what it was that instantly made us trust one another. It certainly wasn't love at first sight when you're trapped in a darkened apartment with a burglar. The glow of the candles, which could have been eerie under the circumstances, was cheerful instead. I made the sandwiches, slicing the bread in half. "Sorry I can't toast it."

He smiled at me. "That's all right."

"Ah, my name is Gloria, by the way."

"I know."

"Yeah, I guess it's on the door." But then I remembered only my last name was in the little slot over the bell. "What's yours?"

He smiled at me, his brown eyes reflecting the candlelight, as he seemed to weigh a decision. "Nick," he answered finally.

"Do you do this sort of thing for a living, Nick?"

"It's not what it seems. I work for the government."

I don't think I ever really believed the big lie, even at the beginning, but just then it was to my advantage to go along with it. He seemed to be using it as a way out, to keep me from calling the police. "Then you must have gotten into the wrong apartment," I said, turning back to my sandwich preparation.

"I guess so."

"How did you open the door?"

Another smile. "I have a way with locks."

We had our sandwiches and beer by candlelight, looking out at the darkened city. Police and emergency vehicles passed frequently on First Avenue, and after a time a giant searchlight lit the sky a mile or so away. "What's that, Nicky?" I asked.

"One of those lights they bring in for movie premieres and store openings. It uses a gasoline engine to generate its own electricity." Presently another appeared in the sky, up toward midtown.

He seemed to like hearing me talk, and I did a lot of it over the next few hours, telling him about growing up back in Ohio. All I got in return were a few vague stories about his Italian-American parents and a boyhood in Greenwich Village. Finally, before I knew it, the time was close to midnight. We'd turned on the radio again and learned that power had been restored to Coney Island. Elsewhere in the city things were going slowly. The federal government was lending what assistance it could, while investigating the remote possibility the outage had been caused by sabotage. It seemed to have begun somewhere in Canada or along the Niagara Frontier in Western New York.

"Well," I told Nick finally, "It looks like the power will be off most of the night. I'm going to bed. You can leave or sleep on the couch."

"How do I know you won't call the police?" he asked.

"You don't. That's why I'd suggest you leave."

He came closer in the flickering candlelight. "What a night this is. I'll bet nine months from today a million women will have babies."

"Not this one," I said, walking into the bedroom.

I closed the door but didn't lock it. Pulling back the bedspread I removed my shoes and slid under the covers fully clothed. I glanced at the phone, knowing I was an idiot not to call the police. Before long I heard a familiar squeak from the living room. I walked to the door and opened it. "Did you open the window?"

"I stuck my head out to see if there are any lights uptown. I can see another searchlight but that's all."

"Close it. There's no screen on that window."

"The bugs have all gone south for the winter."

"I really think you'd better go with them."

He came up close to me. "I've enjoyed the evening, Gloria. I didn't expect you to be here but I'm glad you were. Maybe we can get together some night when the lights are on."

He leaned over and kissed me lightly. I was so startled I drew back as if his lips had been a red-hot poker. Then he was gone out the door.

I locked up and went back to bed, sleeping restlessly for the remainder of the night. Somewhere around four o'clock I became aware that the power had been restored and the living room light was on, but I fell back to sleep without getting up. I awakened around seven as I usually did, and ate breakfast watching television reports of the blackout. The day was cooler, as they'd predicted, and I went to the closet for my raincoat. That was when I noticed something missing.

The bastard had stolen my new Russian greatcoat!

For much of the morning I debated what I should do. Calling the police eighteen hours after I'd discovered Nick in my apartment might take some explaining, and to give a true account of what happened was out of the question. I'd spent half the night chatting with a burglar in the dark, serving him beer and sandwiches which we ate by candlelight. He'd even kissed me as he left. No, he hadn't been carrying the coat at the time.

In fact I could think of only two ways he might have stolen it. Either he'd taken it earlier in the day, returning to my apartment for more loot — which was highly unlikely — or he'd dropped the coat out my window in the middle of the night, retrieving it in the dark after he left the apartment. This seemed more likely, but didn't I have anything more valuable than an inexpensive knock-off of a stylish winter coat? Why would anybody steal it in the first place?

Finally, after much soul-searching, I decided to forget calling the police. I called my insurance company instead, and promptly learned that a police report had to be filed first. In the depths of my frustration Samantha stopped by my cubicle. "Glad to see you survived the blackout," she said.

"Just barely. How was the play?"

"It was canceled."

"Of course! I don't have my wits about me this morning."

"I can turn in the tickets for another performance, but it'll have to be after my vacation."

I remembered she was driving to Virginia Beach with her boyfriend. "When do you leave?"

"After work on Friday. I'll be away all next week. I hope we don't get that cold weather they're predicting."

I decided to tell her about the coat. Not about Nick, just the coat. "You know, I think someone broke into my apartment yesterday. My new winter coat is gone."

"Not that red one! Did they take anything else?"

"Apparently not. I'm going over on my lunch hour to see if I can get another coat in my size."

"I hope you can. It looked good on you that one day you wore it."

"I need a winter coat of some sort."

"How did you survive the blackout?" Samantha asked.

"Fine. The neighbors all got together."

I skipped lunch and went back to the bargain shop on Seventh Avenue. The garment district streets were crowded on this sunny day and I felt certain no one but me would be worrying about a winter coat. I was wrong. When I told the clerk what I wanted she shook her head sadly. "Every one of those coats was gone by Friday. We couldn't keep them in stock. A couple of them turned up on the TV news last week and everybody wanted one. We're expecting more before Christmas, but not at that price."

"Do any other stores carry them?"

"Saks had a more expensive version but I understand they're sold out too."

I phoned Saks from the office and they confirmed that the red czarist greatcoats had been sold out for a week. The clerk suggested a different garment district shop and I called there with the same results. It seemed as if I would have to settle for something else, thanks to that thieving Nick.

The good weather held through the weekend and Samantha went off on her vacation. I though of her that evening when I heard on TV that the new Chesapeake Bay Bridge-Tunnel had been closed by an accident most of the day. On Monday Max was still a bit grumpy about late proofs, but I was used to that. On Tuesday night, one week late, I finally got together with my neighbor Helen Coin to look at her handmade jewelry.

Helen was a short blonde woman with a perky attitude and lots of talent. "I hope there's not another blackout this week," I told her.

"Next time I'll invite everyone in and make a party out of it," she said, laying out some of her recent pieces that I hadn't seen. Later we went out for dinner and then caught the Beatles' new film *Help!* The theater had shown a preview of *Doctor Zhivago*. Helen leaned over and whispered something about my new coat, which I'd shown her the day I bought it. After the movie I decided I should tell her about the robbery.

"That's terrible, Gloria! I thought our building was more secure than that!"

"It happened during the blackout," I murmured.

"Did you actually see this burglar?"

"I might have caught a glimpse of him.

Helen shook her head, unable to grasp it. "This isn't exactly the high rent district. Why would anyone break in just to steal a winter coat?"

"I don't know," I admitted. It was a question that had puzzled me too. If Nick had simply wanted something of mine he could have taken a much smaller object. I was beginning to think he'd entered my apartment simply to steal the coat, but that didn't make any sense. What would a supposed government agent want with my coat?

Two days later, one week before Thanksgiving, the weather turned chilly again.

I almost froze in my thin raincoat walking to work from the subway. Max Rhinegold saw me as I walked in the door. "Don't you have a winter coat for this weather, Gloria?" he asked.

"Somebody stole it," I told him. "The red one. I wore it a couple of weeks ago."

"Sure, I remember. It didn't get stolen in the office, did it?"

"No, in my apartment."

"That's a shame." He seemed to have already lost interest.

My phone was ringing as I walked in the door that evening after work. It was Helen Coin, upstairs. "Your coat's on TV," she said. "Channel four."

I hung up and turned on the TV. A blonde woman in my red coat was being helped into a police car, and I suddenly realized I'd seen her before. In a voice-over, the news anchorman was saying, "Mary Todd, the victim's wife, found her husband's body when she returned from a luncheon meeting. Police are baffled as to how the killer gained entrance to the building, which has a doorman on duty at all times."

They went into a commercial and I flipped channels. On two I caught a file tape of Sam Todd being presented with an award. "Todd, a leading record producer with a string of hit albums to his credit, was believed to have been killed by a burglar. His wife Mary was near collapse after discovering the body. Todd had been working at home recently, completing a book on the current music scene."

I sat staring at the TV screen, trying to fathom what it all meant. Mary Todd had been wearing the coat again, on the first cold day since I'd seen her at lunch in Rockefeller Plaza. And her husband had been murdered. My coat, a virtual duplicate, had been stolen nine days earlier. It certainly meant something, but I didn't know what.

The late news that evening had more details, devoting the first ten minutes of air time to the story. One of the channel four anchors was shown interviewing the doorman at Todd's Park Avenue apartment building. The white-haired man named Samuels insisted he'd been sitting inside the front door reading the morning paper until he was relieved for his lunch break. "Mrs. Todd and a few other tenants went out but no one came in." The younger man who'd relieved him, a former city police officer named Moscowitz, was equally positive. When Mary Todd had returned from lunch with some packages around three o'clock, Samuels had asked Moscowitz to carry them up to her apartment. He'd been there when she unlocked the door and found her husband dead on the floor.

Police officials were saying very little this early in the investigation, though one source confirmed that the position of the body indicated Todd had been shot upon opening his door. That hardly sounded like a burglar to me. Even if he'd heard someone tampering with the lock and surprised a would-be burglar, it was unlikely the man would have had a gun ready to kill him. If no one else had entered the building that morning, might it have been a neighbor who fired the fatal shot?

I puzzled about it as I dropped off to sleep that night. On Friday I picked up one of New York's tabloids on the way to the office and read some of the speculation about the killing. Sam Todd had long been rumored to be a ladies' man, actively courting young female singers in the recording business. Some wondered if a jealous boyfriend or husband might have shot him. The tabloid contained thinly veiled speculation about Mary Todd herself, reporting one rumor that Todd had been about to divorce his wife for another woman, but another report stated that he'd recently broken off the affair and returned to his wife. In the tabloid business they seemed to report every bizarre rumor they heard, letting the reader choose from among them.

Surprisingly, Max was in a grouchy mood about the Todd killing. Going over the schedules with me over coffee that morning, he confided that Neptune had been about to sign Todd to a book contract, a personal overview of the current rock scene. With the success of the Beatles and other groups he was certain it would have been a bestseller.

"I didn't know about that" I told him.

He shrugged. "We'd been working with him for months on an outline, but it was too soon for a formal announcement. Now it doesn't matter."

"Do you know his wife?"

Max Rhinegold shook his head. "I think I was introduced once, but I don't really know her."

"Who do you think killed him?" I couldn't help asking. The possibility that I or my coat was somehow involved had made it extremely important.

"If the police say a burglar, that's good enough for me."

"A burglar," I repeated, and suddenly I knew why the question was so important. The only burglar I knew was Nick and I didn't want it to be him.

That night Sam Todd's murder was still the top story on the TV news. He was one of those semi-celebrities whose real fame had come with the manner of his death. I watched the news until I couldn't take any more, then turned it off and poured myself a drink. I heard a knock at the door and guessed it would be Helen, come down to talk about the murder and my stolen coat. I opened the door without checking the peephole and Nick was standing there.

"Oh!"

"Hello, Gloria."

I stood aside to let him enter. "Hello, Nicky."

He smiled. "Nobody calls me Nicky."

"I do."

He gave me a look through veiled eyes. "Are you going to call the police?"

"I haven't called them yet. I guess I won't start now."

"You know that I stole your coat?"

I nodded. "You dropped it out the window, didn't you? And picked it up outside."

"I swear to God I didn't know it was going to involve murder."

He was confirming my worst fears. "What kind of government agent are you, Nicky?"

"The worst kind, I'm afraid." He slipped his arms easily around me, and I didn't resist.

"Who killed Sam Todd?" I asked. "And why? And what did my coat have to do with it?"

"I can't tell you any of that. It would be dangerous for you to know."

I broke away from him. "But you know."

"I was paid to steal your coat, and I know who paid me."

"The government —"

"Forget the government for now. This was a private individual. People hear about me and they occasionally hire me. So long as the theft is nothing of value, I'll take it on."

I stared into his eyes. "When they want this service, who do they ask for?"

"What do you mean?"

I sighed in exasperation. "What's your name, damn it! Besides Nicky."

"Velvet," he said softly. "Nick Velvet. It used to be something longer but I shortened it."

"Do you live here in the city?"

"Just north of the Bronx, in Westchester. I have a modest house in a working class neighborhood, and if you offered me a beer right now I'd take it."

Somehow we weren't talking about the murder of Sam Todd any longer. This man Nick Velvet had risked arrest to return to me with a sort of apology. I thought that was important to both of us.

I opened two beers.

Samantha Rodgers returned to work on Monday morning. It was a short week because of the long Thanksgiving holiday, and we were both so loaded with work I hardly had time to ask her about Virginia Beach. "Did you have any trouble getting there?" I asked quickly between phone calls.

"No, we went straight down the Jersey Turnpike to route thirteen. That's the fastest way."

I told her we'd talk later. She waved and went back to her office. I'd arranged to take a late lunch hour that day, walking over Park Avenue to the apartment building where Sam Todd and his wife had lived. I wanted to see the doorman, Samuels, and I recognized him at once from his brief interview on TV. He was seated behind a desk with a telephone to announce visitors, his face buried in a newspaper.

"Mr. Samuels?" I said.

He lifted his face from the paper. "That's me. Who are you visiting?"

"No one. I just wanted to ask you about last week."

"Look, lady, I've talked to the police and the press about last week. I got nothing more to say."

"It's not about the people. It's about the coat."

"Huh?"

"I had a red coat stolen a few days before the killing. It's very similar to the one Mrs. Todd was wearing in the TV reports of this tragedy. I wondered if I should go to the police about it."

"I sure can't tell you that, lady." He wrinkled his newspaper impatiently.

"I just want you to answer one question. Are you sure it was Mrs. Todd who was wearing that coat?"

"Who else would it have been? We talked about the weather turning colder. Too cold, really, for the middle of November. Look, nobody gets by me unless I know them. Otherwise I announce 'em on the phone. It was Mrs. Todd both times."

Those were the words I'd been hoping for. "Both times?"

"She went out and came back in about a minute later. Just sailed past me, mumbling something about forgetting her shopping list. She left again about five minutes after that."

"Did you get a good look at her face?"

He folded the paper and put it down on the desk. "I was reading, you know, but I saw the red coat and her blonde hair. That long scarf was wrapped around her mouth and cheeks. The wind was cold that day."

"Thank you, Mr. Samuels. You've been a great help."

Back at the office I took a sketch pad from my filing cabinet. Working from a newspaper photograph of Mary Todd, I did a quick sketch of her face, then drew another one alongside it. I sketched in the scarf on the second figure, then left the pad there when Max called me into his office.

I worked late that night, and when I finally left the office around seven I was surprised to see Samantha just leaving too. "It's hell the first day back from vacation," she muttered. "Want to stop for a drink?"

"I'd better get home, Samantha."

"I'll walk you to the subway."

I laughed. "You live uptown, remember?"

She crowded close to me as a couple of businessmen hurried by, headed for Grand Central. "I saw those sketches on your pad," she said into my ear. I felt a chill down to my toes.

"I thought you would. That's why I left it on top of the desk."

We'd reached the corner of Park Avenue, where the southbound traffic was moving fast. "How did you know it was me?" she asked.

"I was hoping with all my heart that it wasn't."

She tried to shove me then, into the lane of speeding traffic. I don't know what happened next. I closed my eyes and heard her scream. Sometimes even now I still hear that scream.

And then from out of nowhere Nick Velvet was holding me, pulling me away from the curb, letting the gathering crowd wall us out from the scene in the street.

Back at my apartment, he held me for a long time. Once I asked him, "What happened back there?"

"She slipped off the curb. That's all you need to know."

"Samantha." I still couldn't believe what had happened. "She was one of my closest friends here."

He got a couple of beers from the refrigerator. "How did you know? I was very careful not to tell you who hired me."

Instead of answering immediately I asked, "Why were you following me?"

"I was waiting for you outside the office. When I saw Samantha with you I followed along to make sure you were safe. She tried to push you in front of a taxi."

"Did you —?"

He hushed my lips with his fingers. "It doesn't matter what I did. You're alive and unharmed, and that's what matters. Now tell me how you knew."

"Well, you more or less confirmed that the killer had worn my coat and that you'd been hired to steal it. That told me the killer must have seen my coat, and I started counting the people who qualified. It told me also that the killer was most likely a woman. What woman? A clerk in the store where I'd bought the coat? No, because they could have gotten their own off the rack. Someone in my apartment building? My friend Helen Coin saw the coat and she's blonde like Mary Todd, but she's also short. A coat that long on her would have dragged on the floor. Women on the street or in the Rockefeller Plaza restaurant where I had lunch with Samantha wouldn't have known my name or where I lived. You knew both of those things. It narrowed down in my mind to someone at my office. I knew Samantha had seen the coat because we lunched together that day. In fact I told her the store where I'd bought it. She not only saw me in the coat but she saw Mary Todd in her virtually identical coat at the same time. She saw both coats together and that was what gave her the idea. She must have discovered the stores were sold out of the coat and she had to hire you —"

"That part isn't important," he insisted. "Go on."

"How much did she pay you for this?"

"A small amount. I should have charged her much more."

She could see he was uncomfortable with the subject and she went on. "I knew she had a boyfriend she was pretty secretive about. Sometimes he'd buy them show tickets and have to cancel their date. That's when I got to go in his place. She had tickets she'd probably bought herself for the night you robbed me, and she suggested dinner first. You were surprised when I walked in and caught you, just before the blackout, because she was supposed to keep me occupied. As it was, I came home early and caught you in the act."

"How could Samantha even know Sam Todd?"

"That's easy. My boss, Max Rhinegold told me he was close to signing Todd for a book on the rock music scene. Such a book was mentioned on one of the TV reports. Max told me 'we'd' been working with Todd on an outline for some months. When he said 'we' it could only have meant Samantha and him. She worked most closely with Max. Samantha met Todd on the book project and they had an affair. It probably meant nothing to Todd, but when he broke it off Samantha wanted to kill him. And she did. She hired you to steal my coat and pretended to go on vacation to Virginia Beach. Only the tunnel-bridge across the mouth of Chesapeake Bay was closed by an accident that day and she knew nothing about it. She told me they'd driven down that way, on route thirteen, which had to be a lie. She stayed in the city that whole week, waiting for the predicted cold weather, for a day cold enough to bring out Mary Todd's red coat again. Finally it came, as she knew it would. Otherwise I imagine she'd have stretched her vacation by calling in sick."

"She was a bit taller than you, and a brunette, not a blonde like Mary Todd."

"The difference in coat length wouldn't be noticed, and a wig would fix the hair color. She was waiting nearby in my red coat and scarf, watching the building until she saw Mary leave. The doorman barely looked up from his paper when she dashed in and then went out again. She shot Todd as soon as he opened the door, perhaps muffling the sound with my wool scarf."

"And this afternoon?"

"I made some sketches of their two faces side by side on my pad, then left it on my desk. I knew she'd see it because she was always in my office. I didn't know she'd try to kill me, though."

We talked and drank beer for a long time after that. The next morning he asked me to move in with him, to share a crazy life in which he'd often be away. I said no, not yet.

For Christmas Nicky bought me a new red coat and took me to see *Doctor Zhivago*. I moved in with him two days later.

THE WILES OF THE WHITE QUEEN

The Theft of the White Queen's Menu

Nick Velvet first heard the White Queen mentioned as he was dining at one of the flashy Boardwalk casinos in Atlantic City. Across the table from him sat Rooster Vitale, a minor organized-crime figure who'd employed Nick's special talents more than once in the past.

"Have your assignments been falling off lately?" he asked Nick through a mouthful of duck.

"Not especially. I have all the work I want."

Vitale grunted. "I thought maybe the White Queen was cutting in on your territory."

"Who?"

"Sandra Paris. She calls herself the White Queen." Rooster fished into his vest pocket and produced a business card he passed over to Nick. It read simply:

THE WHITE QUEEN
Impossible Things Before Breakfast

There was a New York telephone number printed in the lower left corner.

"This is the first I've heard of her," Nick admitted. "What does she do?"

Rooster Vitale shrugged. "The same sort of impossible things you do, only she doesn't have your scruples about what she steals."

"I'll have to meet her sometime," Nick murmured, finishing his dinner and signaling the waiter for coffee. "Now let's get down to business. What can I do for you this time, Rooster?"

The stout man reached for his wine glass. "I want you to steal a roomful of furniture."

"Stop right there, Rooster. You know I don't steal anything of value."

"Hell, Nick, it's not like it was diamonds or bonds or a shipment of cocaine! This is just furniture! It's in the study of a guy's house down in Maryland. You could —"

"Sorry, Rooster, you know my rule. No money, jewelry, paintings, nothing of value. I've made a reputation, and a good living, stealing only worthless items. I don't intend to change now. A roomful of furniture is out of my line."

"You won't reconsider?"

"I can't."

"All right then," Rooster said sadly. "I'll have to look elsewhere."

"Who will you get?" Nick asked curiously.

"The White Queen, I suppose."

Douglas Shelton was a Baltimore attorney who knew how to live the good life. At fifty-five he was a senior partner in a firm that did a good deal of business with the local and state governments. He lived with his wife Angela in a fine old house near the shore of Chesapeake Bay. Their two children were doing well in college, and with time to themselves Doug and Angela had begun to travel more. She was ten years younger than Doug, a still beautiful woman who took pride in their home and the circle of influential friends in which they moved.

Shelton often worked at home, especially when the winter winds off the Bay brought snow or a chill temperature that made the long drive to his law firm in downtown Baltimore a less than pleasant experience. He'd converted an enclosed back porch into a private study with a desk, bookshelves, and filing cabinets, and made it so handsome that even the woman who'd come through to photograph the house recently for a national magazine and had seen some exquisite rooms had been especially impressed by it.

This morning in April, awakening from a deep sleep, Douglas Shelton's first thought was that he was alone in the wide king-sized bed. That was unusual and it took him a moment to clear his mind of sleep and remember that Angela had gone off to a parents' weekend at their daughter's college. A court appearance had kept Shelton from accompanying her. He opened one eye and could tell from the dim light that it was somewhere just after six. He thought he heard a noise downstairs, but decided it must be his imagination.

He slid out from beneath the covers and stretched, thinking he should fix himself some breakfast before driving into the city for his eleven o'clock court appearance. He went into the bathroom, brushed his teeth, and trod downstairs in his pajamas. Passing the open door of his study, he glanced in at the dim outlines of his furniture in the weak morning light, then continued on to the kitchen. He took some oranges from the refrigerator and started squeezing them.

After a few minutes the telephone rang.

Who would be calling him at 6:15 in the morning? Angela, perhaps? He picked up the wall phone in the kitchen. "Hello?"

"Douglas Shelton?" a woman's soft voice asked.

"Speaking."

"Take a look at your study, Mr. Shelton."

"What?"

The line went dead.

He grunted and replaced the phone, then retraced his steps through the dining and living rooms to the door of the study. Though he'd seen it only a few minutes earlier, it looked different now.

It looked empty!

He snapped on the overhead light and stared with unbelieving eyes. His desk, chair, bookcases, filing cabinet, sofa, and lamps, even the rug on the floor, were gone. The room was completely bare.

In the few minutes while he'd been preparing breakfast, someone had stolen all the furniture from his study.

The robbery at Douglas Shelton's home took place just three weeks after Nick Velvet's luncheon with Rooster Vitale, and when Nick spotted the item in the back pages of the New York newspaper he knew that Rooster had found someone to pull off his theft. Probably it had been the White Queen, and that bothered Nick the way successful competition always bothered a businessman.

"What's the matter, Nicky?" Gloria asked him over breakfast.

"Business. It's been a bit slow this month."

"It'll pick up."

He nodded, finishing his coffee. "Maybe I'll make a few phone calls."

The first person he called was Rooster Vitale in Atlantic City. "What happened with that furniture job you had?"

"It's taken care of, Nick. Sorry."

"I didn't want to do it. I'm just curious."

"The White Queen handled it. She did a neat job too. Maybe you saw it in the papers."

"I think I did."

"She's good, Nick. You better watch yourself or you'll be out of business."

"Thanks, Rooster."

Nick hung up and tried to forget about it. But the nagging memory remained with him. Now he had competition where there had been none before. He spent the following day learning what he could about Sandra Paris. She was a woman in her mid-thirties who'd turned to crime following a brief and unsuccessful career as an actress. Nick hunted out her picture in *The Times* and some show-business publications and was struck by the innocent beauty of her pale face, framed in platinum-blonde hair. Staring hard at the picture, he determined to meet her.

"Where can I find the White Queen?" he asked Rooster Vitale on the telephone.

"Hell, Nick, don't involve me in any feud."

"No feud, Rooster. I just want to meet the lady."

"The only time I ever see her is at breakfast. When she has an assignment she likes to finish it early and eat a big breakfast around ten o clock."

"Impossible things before breakfast."

"What?"

"I was just quoting her motto. Where's her base — that New York phone number?"

"She moves around. That's just an answering service. I happen to know she's back in Atlantic City right now, on another assignment."

"For you?"

He hesitated. "Well, yeah."

"What?"

"You know I can't tell you, Nick. But chances are you'll find her having breakfast at the King's Fountain either tomorrow morning or the day after. Don't say I sent you."

"Thanks, Rooster."

She didn't show on the following morning. Nick managed to drink three cups of coffee while waiting, but by eleven-thirty he gave up and left. He spent the rest of the day gambling away small sums at the blackjack tables and wondering if he was wasting his time by staying over in Atlantic City for another night. A fierce April rainstorm was pelting the city from the ocean, confining his gaming to the mirrored luxury of the King's Fountain casino. He began to speculate about a scheme to cover over the Boardwalk and allow patrons access to other casinos in bad weather. It was a problem Las Vegas never had to face.

A voice he vaguely knew said, "Hello, Nick," and interrupted his thoughts. He turned to see Charlie Weston glaring down at him.

"Hello, Charlie. Long time no see."

Weston was an ex-cop who'd crossed Nick's path two or three times during the past fifteen years. He knew what Nick did for a living, and he was an honest man. The two taken together made him dangerous. He'd sworn on more than one occasion to put Nick behind bars. "What are you after in Atlantic City?" the big man asked, his meaty hand descending on Nick's shoulder.

"Just down for a little gambling. What about you?"

"I'm chief of security at the King's Fountain. My job is to protect the place from people like you, Nick."

"I never turned a crooked card in my life, Charlie. You know that." Nick was seated at a cocktail table for two and motioned toward the empty chair. "Sit down. I'll buy you a drink."

Weston sat down but waved away the offer. "I'm on duty. I suppose you are too."

"I'm not here to steal anything, Charlie. You have my word on that."

"I saw you here last month having dinner with Rooster Vitale. A few weeks later some evidence linking him to a bribery attempt in Maryland was stolen from a man named Shelton. All the furniture in Shelton's study was taken because Vitale wasn't sure where the incriminating papers were hidden. That sounds like your sort of caper, Nick."

"You know I never steal anything of value. Furniture has value."

"There's always a first time. Maybe the recession has forced you to be less fussy."

"It hasn't," Nick replied grimly. "I know nothing about the theft of Douglas Shelton's furniture."

"But you know his first name, don't you? And I hadn't mentioned it."

Nick silently cursed his slip-up. There was something about Charlie Weston that had always unnerved him. "I know nothing about it," he repeated. "I probably saw the name in the newspaper."

"Well, I'll tell you something about it. Rooster Vitale has always operated on the fringes of the organized-crime families. We know he was involved in bribing some Congressmen and state officials both here and in Maryland. Douglas Shelton, an attorney involved in some of the payoffs, had a number of papers that would incriminate Vitale hidden in his study. Since Rooster didn't know exactly where they were hidden, he had every stick of furniture stolen — even the rug on the floor. Shelton claims it was done in about five minutes, while he was squeezing oranges for breakfast."

"I didn't do it," Nick insisted. "It's not my sort of job."

Charlie Weston stood up. "We don't want trouble in our casino, Nick. We don't want Rooster Vitale or Nick Velvet hanging around. Understand?"

"I plan to leave tomorrow," Nick replied. Weston nodded and walked away.

Nick had barely reached the lobby the following morning when he heard the reports of The White Queen's latest escapade. Shortly before four, someone had stolen a roulette wheel from an unused gaming table at the Golden Fleece casino down the Boardwalk. Since the casino was open at the time, no one could imagine how the thieves had struck without being seen. The wheel had simply disappeared from the top of the table, leaving it bare.

She was already eating breakfast when he entered the dining room.

He walked over to her table and asked, "May I join you for coffee?"

She looked up, smiling the same enticing smile as in the newspaper photograph. An innocent beauty, caught between her toast and coffee. "I don't believe we've been introduced."

"My name is Nick Velvet."

"I know your name. I said I don't believe we've been introduced, Mr. Velvet."

"It's time we were," he said, pulling out the chair opposite her to sit down. "I hear you've had an active morning."

She arched an eyebrow at him but did not take the bait. Instead she said simply, "I slept late. Are you in the habit of asking personal questions, Mr. Velvet?"

For just an instant he wondered if Rooster could have steered him wrong. Perhaps she really was as innocent as she acted. Then he decided to plunge on.

"You're cutting into my business, Miss Paris. I thought it was time we talked."

The waiter interrupted to take his order for coffee, and when he faced her again she said, "I understood that you were in a slightly different line of work. I don't bother myself with items of no value, like postcards and teabags."

"You're more familiar with me than I'd supposed. Who paid you to take the wheel this morning? Vitale?"

"Do you really expect me to answer that? You could be wearing a wire and recording every word."

"I don't work for the police."

"You were at a table with Weston, the casino security chief, yesterday."

"My, my — you have been keeping tabs on me. I'm sorry I didn't notice you."

"People rarely do, unless I smile. They think I'm in town for the librarians' convention."

"Tell me about Douglas Shelton's furniture."

"That," she said softly, "is a very sore subject."

"Oh? How well do you know Rooster Vitale?"

"Well enough. I've done some jobs for him." She lowered her voice still further and leaned across the table. "He hasn't paid me yet."

"It's usually cash on delivery," Nick said.

"Yes. Well —" She seemed about to say more, but changed her mind.

"Do you always eat a big breakfast after a job?"

"I suppose it's become my trademark." She passed him one of the cards he'd already seen. *Impossible Things Before Breakfast.* "Remember the White Queen in *Through the Looking Glass?* 'Sometimes I've believed as many as six impossible things before breakfast.' Well, I don't believe them, but I do them."

"Including the wheel this morning?"

She shrugged. "A simple little job."

"I hear it vanished with the casino full of people. You don't walk out the door with a roulette wheel under your arm and not attract attention."

The smile was back. "Someday I'll let you in on the secret, Mr. Velvet, but for now you needn't worry. I hope to be out of here in another day or so, heading for the West Coast. We won't be competitors then."

"I'm glad to hear it. But I admit a fondness for postcards and teabags. Furniture and roulette wheels are a bit out of my line, though I'll venture to say I could duplicate any one of your feats if I had to."

"Is that a challenge?"

"No, no. Let's part friends. I've enjoyed it, Miss Paris."

He rose to leave, but suddenly Sandra Paris seemed to make a decision. "Come stroll on the Boardwalk with me, where we can't be overheard."

"Gladly."

He let her pay for his coffee and then followed her across the hotel lobby to the Boardwalk entrance. The doors slid open automatically as they approached and then they were out in the morning air, breathing in the April warmth. "At least the rain has stopped," she commented. "We might have a decent day for a change."

"Looks like it."

She turned to him suddenly and said, "I need your help."

"Oh?"

"Rooster Vitale won't pay my fee until I deliver some papers he wants."

"That's between you and Rooster."

"But I know they're hidden in that furniture from Shelton's study. All I have to do is find them."

"That shouldn't be hard."

"But it is! I've taken the stuff apart piece by piece!"

"Maybe you've been double-crossed. You must have people working for you. One of them could have found the papers without letting you know."

She shook her head. "No, they've never been alone with the furniture."

"I don't find things," he said. "I steal them."

"What's your fee — twenty-five thousand?"

"That's right."

"I'll pay you that to steal the papers from their hiding place in the furniture and give them to me. It's easy money — no risk involved."

"Do I get to learn how you stole it all while Shelton was squeezing his orange juice?"

"Oh, no. That's not part of the agreement."

"I take a fee only for stealing valueless items. Those papers sound pretty valuable to me."

"Then do it as a professional favor. I'll owe you one, Mr. Velvet."

It was very hard resisting her smile. "You can call me Nick," he said.

They drove in her white Cadillac to a small warehouse west of the city. "I rented space here," Sandra explained. "Two men I've used before helped with the actual theft, but I trust them completely."

They entered the storage area and Nick was startled by the sight. Desk, sofa, chairs, filing cabinets — all but the rug had been reduced to rubble in a futile attempt to find the papers. "What do you think? Where haven't I looked?"

"Behind the pictures on the walls?"

"There were no pictures. The study was on an enclosed porch with big windows on three sides covered with roll-down blinds."

"The papers were rolled up in one of the blinds," he suggested.

"No, we've got them here someplace. And they're not in the filing cabinets. I've looked at every sheet of paper in every drawer."

"Maybe they were never in the study."

She shook her head. "He's frantic to get this stuff back."

"He won't be so frantic when he sees the condition it's in."

"He's not going to see —" She paused and stared at him. "Nick, are we thinking the same thing?"

"Could be," he answered with a grin. He was starting to like Sandra Paris. "If we can't find those papers, maybe Shelton can find them for us."

An hour later, after they'd talked it through, Nick phoned Shelton at his Baltimore law office. "Mr. Shelton, you don't know me but I have some information about your missing furniture."

"What? Where is it?"

"How much is it worth to get it back?"

There was silence for a moment. Then Shelton answered, "Five hundred dollars might be a reasonable reward."

"Double that and we'll talk business."

"Very well," he replied without hesitation. "Where is the furniture?"

"At a warehouse near Atlantic City. Can you drive up here this afternoon?"

"I suppose so. Give me the address."

"No," Nick said. "I'll meet you nearby." He gave the location of a fast-food restaurant in a shopping center on Route 322. "Meet me there at two o'clock with the money."

"How will I know you?"

"Don't worry. I'll know you."

Shelton arrived ten minutes early for the meeting. He was a stout, balding man who looked exactly like his newspaper photos. When Nick was reasonably certain he hadn't been tailed, he stepped up and made the contact. "Mr. Shelton? I'm the man who called you."

Shelton stared at him as if trying to memorize his face. "You're Mr. — ?"

"The name's not important. Did you bring the money?"

"You'll get it when I see the furniture."

"All right," Nick agreed. "Let's go."

As they drove to the warehouse, the lawyer said, "But why? Why steal it in the first place? I never heard of anyone holding a roomful of furniture for ransom."

"I wasn't in on the robbery," Nick admitted. "That was my partner. I just want to get rid of the stuff." He turned into the warehouse parking lot.

"Is this the place?"

"Yeah."

Nick led him through the side door and unlocked the room Sandra had rented. He let the lawyer enter first. "My God!" Shelton gasped as Nick turned on the overhead light.

"Things got a little messed up on the trip."

Shelton hurried to the rug and Nick could see him testing the thick binding at the edge of it with his shoe. Then he looked at Nick seemingly satisfied. "This is all junk. You can't expect me to pay you for this."

"I thought you'd be happy to get your papers back," Nick said.

"Let me gather up a few things and you can take me back to my car. I'll take the rug and some of my files. You can keep the rest and I'll collect on the insurance."

Nick helped him carry the rug out to the car and then waited while the attorney went through his scattered files and pulled out more than a score of fat folders. "You can't expect me to pay for the rest of this," Shelton said again.

"Let's make it five hundred," Nick offered, shifting uneasily.

"Look, I've got your license number. You could be in big trouble," Shelton told him, responding to Nick's tone.

They drove back to the restaurant in silence and Nick helped Shelton move the rolled-up rug and file folders into his own car. As he was about to depart, the lawyer handed him a fifty-dollar bill. "Take this and be glad you're not in jail." Then he slid behind the wheel and drove off without another glance at Nick.

As his car disappeared from view, Sandra came out of the restaurant. "You look pleased with yourself, Nick. How'd it go?"

"Perfect. The papers were on microfilm, hidden in the binding of the rug. I removed it while he was sorting through his files. Here you are." He handed over the small strip of film.

She grinned and kissed him lightly on the cheek. "You know something? We'd make a pretty terrific pair."

They dined together that evening in the plush Guard Room at the King's Fountain. Over coffee she announced, "When I collect my money from Rooster Vitale I'm cutting you in for a share."

"That isn't necessary. I did it as a favor." He returned her smile. "After all, I'm anxious to get the competition out of town."

"You're not interested in teaming up?"

He thought of Gloria, waiting back home. "Not really. I've always worked best alone."

"I'm getting fifty thousand from Vitale," she told him.

"My regular fee is only half that."

"I know." She lit a cigarette. "Maybe I can subcontract some work to you. Do you have any suggestions?"

He shrugged. "I could steal your menu at breakfast some morning. Rob you of your celebration."

"I'll remember that and keep a tight grip on it. You steal it out of my hands and I'll pay you twenty-five thousand."

"It's a deal," he agreed, joining her laughter. They were both being silly, and he enjoyed it immensely. "Have you talked to Rooster yet?"

She nodded. "I'm meeting him after dinner. I told him on the phone I had what he wanted."

"Then I guess you'll be headed west."

"I could be tempted to stay."

"Don't tempt me to tempt you."

As they were leaving she said, "You know my room number, if you want to stop by after I see Vitale."

He spent the next hour randomly playing the casino slot machines. It was a crowded, noisy night, with busloads of evening gamblers down from New York and Philadelphia. After a while he strolled along the Boardwalk to the casino where the roulette wheel had been stolen. The bare table was no longer there. A guard told him it had been removed during the day by a storage company.

Nick had learned a great deal about Sandra Paris in the day he'd known her, but he felt he'd learned very little about her alter ego, The White Queen. He still didn't know how she'd stolen the furniture from Shelton's home or the roulette wheel from a busy casino. Maybe it would be worth teaming up with her just to learn how.

Maybe it would be worth a visit to her room, at least.

Nick strolled back along the Boardwalk to the King's Fountain, knowing he was being drawn to the woman like a fly to a honeyed web.

As he entered the lobby of the hotel, he was intercepted by Rooster Vitale. "Nick, I gotta talk to you."

"Right now?"

"Right now. Let's go have a drink."

Nick ordered a glass of wine and joined Rooster in the lounge. "What's the trouble? You look upset."

"That damned White Queen messed me up on the furniture deal."

"How could that be? I thought she found what you wanted today."

"You know about it, huh? She was supposed to find some papers for me. Instead she comes up with microfilm copies of them."

"Why isn't that good enough?"

"Hell, Nick — the papers are incriminating! I need the originals!"

"I see. Then you haven't paid Sandra her money?"

"Damn right I haven't paid her! She brings me the microfilm and tells me she gave the rest of everything back to Shelton."

"I gave it back, Rooster. I was helping Sandra. Whatever happened is my fault."

"Hell, Nick, I asked you to help me with this and you refused. Now you tell me you're the one that botched the job."

"You'd better explain what's involved. Just what are these papers?"

Rooster Vitale sighed and looked around as if seeking a way out. Finally he lowered his voice and said, "There were several letters and a typed contract. About ten years ago, before gambling was legal in Atlantic City, I was involved in a string of private clubs in Jersey and Maryland. You know what I mean — we had a few games in the back room for high rollers who didn't want to go all the way to Vegas for action. Shelton set up a dummy corporation for us, and those letters and the contract are my only link to it. Now I'm trying to go legit, to get into one of the casino corporations here. But Shelton's been blackmailing me, threatening to tell the State Gaming Commission about my past involvements. The White Queen stole all his study furniture to be sure of getting all the papers, but all she delivered was the microfilm."

"Maybe that's all there was."

Rooster shook his head. "Shelton phoned me an hour ago from home and boasted about getting the papers back."

"That's impossible! All he took back was the rug and a couple of dozen file folders. Sandra had been through every paper in them without finding what you wanted."

"All I know is what he told me, Nick. The problem is, what do I do now?"

"Tell me something, Rooster — did you also hire Sandra to steal the roulette wheel from the Golden Fleece?"

"She told you about that too, huh?"

"No, she didn't. But you told me she was doing another job for you."

"It was a wheel I sold to the Fleece when they first opened up," Rooster mumbled. "They needed equipment in a hurry. I decided I wanted it back. They weren't using it much any more."

"Was it rigged?"

"No. I've never run a crooked wheel, Nick."

"But you needed it stolen. Somehow it tied in with those papers, didn't it?"

"I can't go into all that."

"But you want my help."

"Can you get those letters and the contract?"

"You mean rob Douglas Shelton a second time?"

"Sure. Why not? I'll pay double your usual fee."

"Those papers have value now, Rooster. They're blackmail material. You know I can't take money for that."

"Hell, Nick, come down to earth! Either you're a thief or you're not!"

"Let me think about it, Rooster."

"I got only one alternative, Nick. If you won't do it, I'll send a couple of guys to his house with a firebomb. That'll finish the papers and Shelton both at once."

For some reason the words shocked Nick. He'd known Rooster a long time, and knew what he was, but the idea of murder had never crossed his mind in connection with Rooster. Maybe Shelton didn't deserve saving, but he didn't deserve killing either.

"All right," he said. "But if I do it it's as a favor to you — I'll take no money for it."

"You gotta be paid, Nick."

"Give Sandra her money. I'll settle with her."

"Then I can count on you?"

Nick, who never thought he'd end up robbing a man to save the man's life, replied, "You can count on me."

Douglas Shelton awakened suddenly, wondering if he heard something downstairs. It was still early and his wife Angela was fast asleep at his side. The first faint glow of dawn was just beginning to outline the windows behind their draperies.

Remembering the morning he'd been robbed, he slipped silently out of bed, taking with him the .38-caliber revolver he kept handy now. All was dim and silent downstairs and as he passed the study door he looked in at the shadowed shapes of the new furniture already in place.

"Stand still, please," a voice from the study said. "And hand me that gun."

"What — ?"

"Please. I don't want to shoot you."

A hand reached out of the darkness to grab the gun and Shelton saw the familiar face from the Atlantic City warehouse. "What do you want? How'd you get in here?"

"Getting in was easy. Those study windows are simple to open. And I think you know what I want. The files you took yesterday."

"Those are my private papers."

"Let's not waste time. You may not believe this, but I'm trying to save your life."

"With that gun?"

"Yes."

Shelton hesitated. The man's eyes were hard and businesslike, yet somehow Shelton believed him. "Very well," he said. "Ever since that girl photographed my house for the magazine I've had nothing but robberies. And the pictures haven't even appeared yet."

"Maybe I can do something to have them canceled if you take me to those folders right now."

Shelton sighed and led the way to one of the new filing cabinets. "What makes you think you'll find anything this time when you didn't find anything before?"

"Because this time I know what I'm looking for," Nick Velvet said.

It was nearly ten-thirty when Sandra Paris settled down to breakfast at the King's Fountain. She was still studying the big gray menu when Nick walked in and took the chair opposite her. "Another celebration?" he asked.

She smiled, happy to see him again. "I was expecting you last night."

"I made no promises. And after I saw Rooster I figured you might not be in the mood for visitors."

"That's all settled. He paid me this morning. That's why I'm celebrating. Did you have anything to do with it, Nick?"

"A bit," he admitted.

"Were those papers in the batch I stole?"

"Yes."

"But how could they have been? I looked over every one!"

"I'll tell you that after you let me in on some of your secrets — how you stole the furniture and the roulette wheel, for instance."

"Are we partners, then?" She put down the menu and rested her folded hands on it.

"I'm no good at partners," Nick told her honestly. "And I think I know how you stole the furniture. I happened to see Douglas Shelton again this morning, and he mentioned a woman photographer who took pictures of his house for a national publication. He said the pictures hadn't appeared yet. They haven't appeared because you were the photographer, Sandra. You not only got the layout of the house while posing as a photographer, you also took a wide-angle photo of his study from the doorway. You blew up a print to life size and mounted it, probably on a large window shade, and placed it in the doorway of the study, blocking a view of the room and giving the impression, in dim light, that the furniture was still in place.

"You and some helpers worked quietly through the night, removing the furniture through those big porch windows. When Shelton finally heard something toward morning and came down for breakfast, you'd just about finished. He glanced at the study doorway but noticed nothing wrong. You rolled up the photo and left through the window while he was squeezing his orange juice, then you phoned him from down the road."

"You figured that out all by yourself?" she said, the irony of her tone not quite hiding a hint of admiration.

"Want me to tell you about the roulette wheel next?"

"Don't tell me you've solved that one too!"

"In a way it was one of the cleverest robberies I've come across. You simply walked up to the unused wheel in a casino full of people, waited until no one was looking your way, and pressed a hidden button that made the wheel drop inside the specially constructed table. It remained there until your men picked it up yesterday and took it to the warehouse."

"You're guessing now," she said, but her eyes had turned uncertain.

"It's a guess, but a knowledgeable one. Rooster told me he ran a string of illegal gambling houses in New Jersey some years back and that the roulette wheel at the Golden Fleece came from one of those houses. He needed it stolen so his past wouldn't accidentally come to light now that he's trying to get a legitimate gaming license. If the table came from an illegal house, I have a hunch it was gimmicked to look like an ordinary table when not in use. Of course, anyone could have pressed the hidden button to *hide* the wheel, but he needed your skill in removing the supposedly bare table from the casino later. That's when the real theft took place. Luckily for both of you, the people on duty at the casino never knew it was a gimmicked table. When a couple of workmen showed up with a truck, they let it go."

"All right," she admitted. "Suppose that's all true. It just proves you're a better detective than a thief, Nick."

"I'm still a pretty good thief. I got those papers back from Shelton," he reminded her.

"Are you going to tell me where they were?"

"Sure. You checked through all those papers, looking for the letters and contract Rooster described to you, but naturally you looked only at the front of the sheets. Shelton simply typed other, innocuous memos on the backs of the incriminating letters and contract and put them in his file with the back side up."

"But what did you get out of all this?" she asked, obviously miffed. "Did Rooster pay you?"

Nick shook his head. "The papers had value as blackmail. I don't steal anything of value. I took them to save a life, not for gain. Rooster's not paying me, you are."

"What?"

"Twenty-five thousand for stealing your menu — remember?"

"But my menu is right —" She picked it up and stared at it, then turned it over in her hands. The menu itself was gone. What she held was a blank piece of gray cardboard.

She sighed. "Damn it, Nick, you're always a jump ahead of me. I wish we could be partners." Then she reached for her checkbook.

"Cash would be better," he said quietly. "From the fifty Rooster gave you this morning."

By noon Nick had his suitcase packed and was ready to leave the hotel. When the knock came at his door he thought it might be the bellman. But it was Charlie

Weston.

"You're leaving, are you, Nick?" he asked.

"I told you I would be."

"I thought you might want to know the police just arrested a couple of friends of yours — Rooster Vitale and Sandra Paris."

"I know the names," Nick admitted, trying not to show his surprise. "But I wouldn't exactly call them friends."

"We got them for stealing the roulette wheel out of the Golden Fleece. What do you think of that?"

"A crazy sort of a crime."

"Yeah. For a while I thought it was so crazy we might hang it on you, Nick. But no such luck. Turns out the wheel was hidden inside the table all along. A couple of guys picked it up yesterday at the casino and we traced the truck they were driving to a warehouse out on 322. I worked with the Fleece security men on it. The warehouse room had been rented by a woman we identified as Sandra Paris, and this morning we got films of Rooster Vitale paying her off. That's when we called in the local police."

"How does this concern me?"

Weston chewed nervously at his lower lip. "I don't exactly know. If I did, you'd be in a cell with them. We know you were out of town somewhere overnight, and when you came back early this morning you had a printer run off a copy of our breakfast menu done in disappearing ink that would fade after an hour or so. You slipped the hostess downstairs twenty bucks to give Sandra Paris that menu when she came in. Why'd you do that?"

Nick Velvet shrugged. "A practical joke. Last week was April Fools' Day."

The security man grunted. "Sandra Paris had only twenty-five thousand on her, but Rooster says he paid her fifty. You wouldn't happen to have the balance?"

"If you've got a search warrant you can find out."

They eyed each other until Weston finally looked away. "Go on, get out of here, Nick. Next time you won't be so lucky."

Nick thought about The White Queen all the way home, and he wondered what the penalty was for stealing a roulette wheel in New Jersey.

The Theft of the Overdue Library Book

The man on the telephone was named Fingers O'Toole, and Nick Velvet had done a few jobs for him over the years. "How are you, Fingers? How's business?"

"Frankly, it could be better, Nick. I'm in a bit of a bind."

"Can I help you out?"

There was hesitation on the other end of the line. "Is this phone safe?"

"If your end's safe, my end's safe," Nick assured him.

"Look, I want you to steal a person for me."

"That sounds like kidnaping. I don't do anything like that."

"Come on, Nick, you stole a whole baseball team once! And a jury."

"Groups of people are different," Nick explained. "It doesn't seem like kidnaping when there are a dozen people involved. But tell me a little more. Who do you want stolen?"

"Tony Wilde."

"The restaurant owner?"

"That's him. Can you do it?"

"You're going to hold him for ransom, right?"

"Well, I'm going to hold him till I get something out of him, sure."

"Sorry, Fingers. Count me out. First of all, I don't steal anything of value and Tony Wilde is something of value. Secondly, he's an old friend of mine."

"If you won't do it, someone else will, Nick."

"Tony Wilde can take care of himself. It would be next to impossible to kidnap him."

"I know somebody who specializes in impossible things. Sure you won't give it a try, Nick?"

"Sorry, Fingers," he said and hung up.

It was a warm afternoon in May and Nick went out in the backyard where Gloria was planting some new rose bushes. "Who was on the phone, Nicky?" she asked.

"Business."

"A job?"

"No. I turned him down,"

She stood up, brushing the dirt from her hands. "You look worried."

"Not really. It was just something he said, something about knowing a person who specializes in impossible things. I heard that once before."

Gloria remembered, too. "Sandra Paris, the White Queen."

He nodded. *"Impossible things before breakfast.* That was her motto."

"Do you think she's out of prison?"

"I guess I'd better find out."

Nick telephoned a politician he knew in southern New Jersey. "Marty, this is Nick Velvet. I've got a question for you."

"Good to hear from you, Nick. What's the question?"

"How much time do you get for stealing a roulette wheel in your state?"

Marty chuckled. "Thinking of coming down to Atlantic City?"

"I was already there — last year. Someone I know got into a little trouble."

"Well, a roulette wheel would be grand larceny. It would depend on their previous record, prior convictions and such. Give me a name and I'll check it for you."

"Sandra Paris. Atlantic City, about thirteen months ago."

"I'll call you back, Nick."

Thirty minutes later he phoned to report that Sandra Paris had drawn a one-year sentence and had been paroled after eight months.

"She's out," Nick told Gloria.

"Stay away from her, Nicky. She's trouble."

"I just don't like her taking my clients away."

"You didn't want the job anyway."

"Of course not! Tony Wilde is an old friend. I might even take a run out to see him and drop him a friendly warning."

"He lives in Chicago!"

"I can fly out tomorrow and be back the next day. It would be good to see Tony again."

"Can't you just phone him?"

"Not after all these years, Gloria. I just want to have dinner with him and give him a casual warning about Fingers O'Toole."

"Well, if you're flying to Chicago so am I," she decided. "There's an old school chum in Oak Park I've been dying to visit. She lives in a house designed by Frank Lloyd Wright."

There was no talking her out of it. The following afternoon they were both on a plane to Chicago.

Tony Wilde was delighted to hear Nick's voice and immediately invited him to dinner at his downtown supper club, The Wilde Spot. "Is Gloria with you?" he asked.

"Yes, but she's dining with an old friend."

"Pity. Give her my love, Nick."

Seeing Tony after such a long time brought back memories of Nick's Army days when they were both kids just out of school, catching the tail end of the Korean War and making plans for a future they hoped they'd live to see. It hadn't turned out exactly as planned for either of them, Nick decided, remembering how Tony had wanted to be a lawyer.

He was a stocky man with steel-grey hair. As he greeted Nick at the entrance to The Wilde Spot, he had the familiar twinkle in his eye. "Damn good to see you, Nick! What brings you to Chicago?"

"I thought I'd just stop off and see you after all these years." His gaze took in the lobby fountain and the subdued, candlelit dining room beyond. "I couldn't afford this place if I didn't know the owner."

Tony gave him a friendly pat on the shoulder. "Go on, Nick. I hear you're pretty successful in your line of work." He led the way to a secluded table where a waiter quickly appeared to take their drink order.

Nick motioned toward a piano and microphone. "You have entertainment, too?"

"A singer comes on at eight. It's atmosphere, you know?" He smiled a bit. "Her voice isn't very good, but she looks great."

They chatted over drinks and the meal that followed — an excellent veal concoction that was one of the house specialties. Nick noticed that the couple at the next table had it, too — and cleaned their plates. Tony told Nick about his recent divorce. Finally, when they were relaxing over dessert, Nick asked, "Do you know a fellow named Fingers O'Toole?"

"O'Toole?" Tony's reply was carefully measured. "I may have heard the name. Why do you ask, Nick?"

"I don't want to involve myself in your personal affairs, Tony, but I'd be a little careful these days if I were you. Just call it a tip from an old friend."

"What is it? Did Fingers put out a contract on me?" Wilde asked, apparently deciding to treat Nick's warning as a joke.

"Not exactly, but you're close. Would it be to his advantage if you were to disappear for a time?"

Tony Wilde stopped smiling. "How much do you know, Nick?"

"Very little. Just that O'Toole tried to hire me."

"To steal what?."

"You."

Tony was silent for a time. Nick watched the waiter bring the check and a doggie bag to the couple at the adjoining table. Finally, Wilde said, "Thank you for telling me, Nick. I've often said that old friends are the best."

"I think he'll hire someone else for the job. If I'm right, you might be especially vulnerable in the morning, before breakfast. What's your daily routine?"

"I assure you I'm quite safe before breakfast. I walk my dog in the park across from my apartment. Bruno's a mean German Shepherd who loves to bite people. He's far more effective than a human bodyguard."

"Still —"

"Look, Nick, I appreciate the warning. But I can take care of myself. As a matter of fact, if you and Gloria are free tomorrow morning I'd like to invite you over for breakfast. You can even walk Bruno with me if you'd like."

"I don't —"

"I may have some business to throw your way."

"I deal only in objects without value," Nick reminded him.

Tony Wilde nodded. "Come by in the morning, and bring Gloria. I'd like to see her again."

Later that evening, back at their hotel, Nick told Gloria about the invitation. "I suppose I should go," she agreed. "How was dinner?"

"The food was excellent, and his restaurant is certainly interesting."

"How do you mean interesting, Nicky?"

"It's the only place I ever saw where the customers take home doggie bags even after they've cleaned their plates."

In the morning they took a cab to Tony Wilde's condominium in a swank section of the city not far from The Wilde Spot. The building was across the street from a large park that covered several acres with tree-shaded paths and a small pond. It was here, Wilde explained after meeting Gloria with an affectionate kiss, that he walked Bruno every morning before breakfast.

The dog started to growl deep in his throat at the first sign of Nick and Gloria. Wilde slid his fingers beneath the dog's collar and scratched him soothingly. "There, there, boy. These are friends."

Once on his leash, Bruno calmed down a bit, and as they entered the park Wilde even allowed Gloria to take over and walk with him.

Wilde himself dropped back to talk with Nick. "I told you last night I might have a job for you. Could you steal a library book for me?"

"You hardly need to pay me twenty-five thousand for that, Tony. You just stick it under your coat and walk out of the place. Unless they've got one of these new alarm systems with a magnetic strip inside the book."

"My problem is that the book isn't in the library. It's overdue and I have no way of finding out who has it."

"If it's a valuable first edition or something like that —"

"Lord knows it's not valuable, Nick. It's a cheap hardcover reprint of Hammett's *The Thin Man*, the sort they used to publish back in the 1930s before paperbacks became popular. The paper's beginning to turn brown and I suppose the library will simply discard it before long."

"There are diamonds hidden in the binding," Nick speculated.

"Nothing's hidden in it at all. You can take my word for it. But I need it, and I'll pay you your fee to get it for me."

Gloria and Bruno rounded a curve in the path and the German Shepherd turned his head to make certain his master was still behind him. It was obvious he never let Wilde out of his sight on these morning walks, but Nick decided to test it by pulling Tony off the path and behind a tree. Immediately, the dog broke free from Gloria's grip and bounced back, seeking them out and almost bowling Nick over with the ferocity of his charge. Wilde had to call him off as his powerful jaws were about to settle on Nick's wrist.

"Satisfied?" Tony asked.

"I guess so."

"He's the best bodyguard, I ever had."

"But not much protection against a bullet fired at you from twenty yards away."

"No one wants to kill me, Nick. They just want a piece of my money."

Gloria joined them as Wilde retrieved the dog's leash. "That beast is a *beast!*" she announced.

Wilde chuckled and calmed the dog down once more. "He's just a loyal friend."

"Tell me more about this book," Nick urged.

"It belongs to our neighborhood branch library across the park. They only have one copy, and none of the other branches or the main library have this particular edition. It's more than a month overdue and the library says there's nothing they can do about it except send overdue notices. They have people who go out and collect overdue books, but that's not going to happen with this one for several more months. I need the book now."

"It should be simple enough, once I find out who has it."

"There's the problem. The library records are computerized. It's not as simple as looking in a file drawer." The path had led them to a small cubical building without windows. The sign on the door read MEN. "If this is unlocked, I usually stop here," Wilde explained. Then, turning to the dog, he commanded, "Sit, Bruno!"

"He's a good dog," Nick observed, following Tony into the men's room. The grey cinder-block building contained a single urinal, a toilet stall, and a sink in a space perhaps ten feet square. The walls were marked with the usual graffiti but otherwise the place was reasonably clean.

"I told you so. Man's best friend. He'd wait out there for me all day."

Nick turned on the faucet and washed his hands. "How soon do you need the book?"

"I'd like it by tomorrow night. What do you think?"

"I'll let you know. If I can do it at all I should have it by then."

They emerged to find Gloria and Bruno eyeing each other with mutual distrust.

But as soon as he saw Wilde, the dog was on his feet once more, tagging along at his side. "Is there a ladies' restroom in this park somewhere?" Gloria asked.

"Straight ahead." Wilde pointed, indicating a second cinder-block building about a hundred feet ahead of them on the path.

"Go ahead, we'll wait," Nick told her. He glanced around from where they strolled, noting a single telephone booth at the side of a park road about fifty feet directly behind the men's room. It was a good thing to remember.

When Gloria rejoined them, they circled around and left the park from the point where they'd entered it, across the street from Tony Wilde's condominium. He took them upstairs for breakfast, and over scrambled eggs Nick agreed to go after the overdue book. "I can do it," he said with assurance. "It'll just mean staying here a bit longer than we planned."

"Do you want a retainer now?"

"Your money's good," Nick said. "You can pay me on delivery."

Back at their hotel Gloria said, "You're not staying here just to do the job for him, are you, Nicky? You still think the White Queen's going to turn up."

"I don't know if she is or not, but a job's a job. Stealing things like overdue library books is what people pay me to do."

"Why do you think he wants that book, especially if there's nothing hidden in it?"

"We'll probably find out sooner or later."

"What am I supposed to do while you're out finding that book?"

"I have a job for you," Nick said. "I want you to follow Tony Wilde."

"What for? I'm certainly no bodyguard!"

"I just want to make sure nothing happens to him — because he's an old friend and because he's going to owe us twenty-five thousand dollars very shortly."

"If it's the White Queen, she'll go after him in the morning. Remember? Impossible things before breakfast?"

"I know," Nick agreed. "But I want you to be seen. If there's anyone else watching him I want them to know you're around. It might just be enough to scare them off, at least while we're in town."

Gloria took some persuading, but finally she agreed to keep an eye on Tony. "But what if something *does* happen? What'll I do?"

"Phone me. I'll manage to let you know where I can be reached most of the time."

He spent the rest of the day at the library branch, watching the operation of the computerized checkout system. When he first arrived there shortly before noon, he'd taken the direct approach, asking for the book in the hope it had been returned. But it was still overdue. Next he asked if its location could be traced. It was very important, he insisted, and offered the girl behind the counter a five-dollar tip. She promised to see what she could do, and returned in five minutes with a triumphant smile. "Here you are, sir. We have another edition of *The Thin Man,* in large print. I'm sure it will serve your purpose."

Nick started to protest, then he saw it was hopeless and accepted the book, taking it to a corner of the reading room.

As he studied the library's operations, he learned that each book now carried a barcode, much like those on food items at the supermarket. When a patron checked a book out, it was checked with a light pen, which registered the book's identification number along with the number of the borrower's library card. Nick thought about this for some time, then finally went to the card catalogue to look up the number assigned to *The Thin Man* in the edition he needed. But it was an up-to-date library and instead of a card catalogue he found himself confronted by a microfiche reader.

In a moment, however, he had what he wanted. And he thought he knew how he could discover the location of the book he'd been hired to steal.

That evening, over dinner, Gloria reported that Tony Wilde had gone down to his supper club around noon and stayed till two o'clock, then driven to the Chicago public market, apparently to buy some choice cuts of beef for the restaurant. When he'd returned to The Wilde Spot for the evening, Gloria decided it was safe to abandon the tail.

"So that was my day," she concluded. "Boring. How about you? Did you get the book?"

"Not yet. Tomorrow."'

"Do you still want me to watch him in the morning?"

"Of course. As you said yourself, if it's the White Queen, she'll go after him in the morning."

"While he's walking his dog."

"Exactly." He copied down a phone number from his notebook. "Here's what I want you to do. I'll be at the library at seven-thirty —"

"Do they open that early?"

He ignored the question and went on. "This is their phone number. I want you to call me there from the park. You'll see a pay phone by the road behind the men's restroom where Wilde stopped this morning. Today we reached there at just about seven-thirty, and I assume he walks the dog at the same time every day. Call me whether or not Wilde stops in the restroom, and I'll cross over from the library and meet you in the park."

"Why do I need to phone you if you're so sure of the time I'll be there?"

"Trust me," Nick said.

In the morning he was up early, shaking Gloria awake and reminding her she should be at Wilde's place by seven in case he walked the dog a bit earlier than usual. It was six-thirty when he left the hotel and drove his rented car to an all-night supermarket in one of the residential sections near the library. There he walked quickly up and down a couple of aisles, inspecting the barcode labels on the items until he found three that would serve his purpose. Happily, most barcodes included a digital translation directly beneath. He paid for the items and returned to his car.

It was growing light as he worked, though the dawn sky was cloudy with the threat of rain. The microfiche catalogue-listing for Hammett's *The Thin Man* in the edition Wilde needed gave its number as 4-2222-00003-3522. Nick cut away at the barcodes on the products he'd purchased and taped them together to form the number he needed. Then he drove on to the library.

It was a modern building, open only a few years, and he was stunned that a place with the latest in computers should have such a primitive alarm system. He was inside within five minutes, moving across the familiar carpeting of the main reading room to the book-return desk. He seated himself at the computer terminal and flipped the switch to turn it on. Then he picked up the light pen which served as the machine's optical scanner and passed it over the homemade barcode strip.

At once the terminal screen came alive with the book's author, title, publisher, edition, and publication date, followed by a call number and shelf location. Below this was a list of borrowers, identified by number. Nick studied the final number for some time, wondering what he should do next. He decided he needed help.

In a desk drawer, he found a printed instruction-sheet giving the proper access code for identifying library borrowers. He typed in the necessary words and followed them with the borrower's number. At once the screen supplied the information he needed: Norman Wells, 503 Scott Street.

"What in hell are you doing here?" a gruff voice asked in surprise.

Nick froze at the computer terminal. He'd been so intent on the machine he hadn't heard anyone enter the library. He glanced quickly at his watch as he turned with a smile. It was 7:32. "I'm checking out all the computer terminals for the manufacturer," he explained. "We've had some malfunctions."

The man had a face that went well with his voice. "Nobody told me about it. We're not having any trouble. How'd you get in here, anyway, and what are you doing here at seven-thirty in the morning?"

"I've got a lot of terminals to check today. I had to get an early start. This is the first one."

"A lot of terminals? There are only two branches automated so far in the entire city!"

"Not just libraries. The commodities exchange uses this same model."

"Well, I'd just better check up on this."

"If you'll wait a few minutes, the director's secretary will be phoning me here. You know Miss Fritz, don't you?"

"Who? Yes, yes, I guess I know her," the man answered.

At that moment the telephone rang. Nick scooped it up before the man could reach it. "Nicky? This is Gloria. I'm at the booth in the park. Tony Wilde just went into the men's room and that beast is waiting outside."

"Yes Miss Fritz, I'm glad you phoned."

"What? Nicky, it's me — Gloria!"

"I know, Miss Fritz. I have a gentleman here who wants to speak with you. Can you tell him that I'm authorized to be here, checking the computer terminals for malfunctions?"

"Oh! Sure," she said, finally catching on. Nick passed the receiver to the gruff-voiced man.

He accepted the phone gingerly. "Hello? Miss Fritz? This man — Yes, I see. But it's a bit early in the day — All right, I just want to make sure everything's in order."

He hung up and Nick turned off the terminal. "This machine's perfect. I hope all the rest work as well. Thanks for your cooperation, Mr. —"

"Jennings," the man supplied. "But I still don't understand how you got in here."

"Miss Fritz gave me a key."

"Oh."

"Goodbye now." Nick hurried toward the front door.

"What was she doing at work so early?"

"She came in early to phone me," Nick said, and then he was through the front door and out of there before Jennings could think of another question.

He drove into the park and left his car a short distance from the men's restroom. Even at a distance, he could see Gloria and Bruno eyeing each other again and he wondered why she'd gotten that close. "Where's Tony?" he asked when he joined her.

"Still inside. What was that business on the phone? You almost got caught, didn't you? Is that why you had me call?"

"It was a safety measure in case I needed it. And I did." He glanced at the dog. "How long has Wilde been in there?"

"About ten minutes. He went in just before I phoned you."

"I think I'll see what's keeping him."

The dog glanced up at him as Nick walked past him and opened the door of the cinder-block building. "Tony?" he called out. "Are you in there?"

Silence.

He stepped inside and looked around the tiny space. There was no one at the urinal or sink. He pushed open the door of the toilet stall and that was empty, too. He glanced up at the solid wooden ceiling, as unbroken as the slab of concrete beneath his feet. One door and no windows. Yet Tony Wilde had vanished.

Then he saw the little calling card propped against one of the faucets on the sink. It read simply:

THE WHITE QUEEN

Impossible Things Before Breakfast

It wasn't until Gloria had a look inside the place herself that she was willing to accept Nick's report that Tony Wilde had truly vanished. Then she simply stood there shaking her head. "It's impossible, Nicky, he can't be gone!"

"It's not impossible at all. He probably never entered this place to start with. You were off to one side — you thought he came in here, but he didn't."

"I didn't *think* anything!" she snapped, her temper up. "I was right outside. I saw him tell Bruno to sit, just like yesterday morning, and then push the door open and come in. I saw the door close after him."

"You couldn't be mistaken?"

"Not a chance. I was only on the phone with you for about two minutes, and Tony was in here all that time. Then I went back out and stood not twenty feet from the door. He never came out."

"Well, he certainly didn't get out through the plumbing. And the ceiling, floor, and walls are all solid. There's no place to hide in here, except maybe behind the door of the toilet stall, and he's not there. He wasn't behind the outside door when I entered, either. I felt it hit the wall when I pushed it open. And you were still outside — you would have seen him."

"Should we call the police?" Gloria asked.

"And tell them what? That a lady thief called the White Queen stole a man from a men's room in the park while you and his faithful dog were on guard outside? They'd laugh in our faces, not to mention ask a lot of embarrassing questions about my business with him."

"Then what do we do? What do we do with Bruno, to start with?"

Nick reached out and carefully picked up the German Shepherd's leash. "We'll leave him with the doorman in Tony's building."

The doorman, a white-haired man named Fred, was willing to take the dog when Nick told him they'd found Bruno alone in the park. "He must have gotten separated from his master," Nick said "We saw the name and address on his collar, so we brought him back."

"I can't understand that," Fred told them. "The dog never ran away from him before. What's the matter, Bruno?" He carefully patted the dog's neck. Bruno let out a sudden bark. "Collar too tight?" Fred loosened the dog's collar and Bruno quieted down. "Good dog," the doorman said.

"You'll keep him for Mr. Wilde?" Nick asked. "He's a friend of ours."

"Sure, I remember seeing him with you yesterday. Don't worry, I'll take care of Bruno."

They left him and walked back to where Nick had left the car in the park. "What now?" Gloria asked.

"We look for Sandra Paris. And we look for Fingers O'Toole because that's who she's working for."

"What about the book you're supposed to steal?"

"First I'd better find my client. The book can come later."

They spent the rest of the day checking local hotels, but neither O'Toole nor Sandra Paris were registered under their own names. Every hour Gloria tried calling Wilde at his apartment and at the supper club, but he hadn't returned.

Nick called O'Toole's New York number but there was no answer there, either. "What do you think they want him for?" Gloria wondered.

"I don't know. I don't even know if O'Toole wanted his presence or merely his absence. Maybe Tony was going to do something or be somewhere and they wanted to stop him."

In the afternoon they went back to the park, back to the men's restroom where it had happened. But there was nothing to be found. Nick had Gloria inspect the ladies' restroom as well, though it was some distance down the path. "Are you sure there's nothing you forgot?" he asked her. "Is it possible he came out the roof somehow while you were phoning me?"

"You think I wouldn't have seen him?, You think the dog wouldn't have caused an uproar? Nicky, he walked through the door — that one and only door — and he never came out."

"Come on," Nick said, depressed. "I'll take you out to dinner."

"Where?"

"Where else? The Wilde Spot, of course."

At the restaurant Nick was simply told that Tony Wilde was away. The waiters were as efficient as they had been on the first night, but there was an undertone of uncertainty about the place.

"The food is great," Gloria said, finishing her veal. "Tony must make a fortune here."

"I suspect he does," Nick murmured. He called the waiter over and said, "We'd like a doggie bag, please."

The waiter gestured at their plates. "But you have nothing to put in a doggie bag, sir."

"You know what I mean." Nick winked as he said it.

The waiter hesitated and then said, "You must mean the special dessert menu, sir.

It's not available tonight. You must come when Mr. Wilde himself is here."

"But I'm a close friend of Mr. Wilde. I dined with him here two nights ago. We sat at that corner table."

"I remember you, sir, but —"

"He told me to be sure to ask for the special-dessert menu the next time I was in."

"Well, I suppose it would be all right." The waiter went off and returned after a few moments with a menu. Nick opened it and looked down the list of cakes, pies, and ice creams, thinking for a moment there had been some misunderstanding. Then he found it, on a separate page, in light type, clinging to an end paper:

Not for Consumption on Premises
(Please order by number)
101. Famous marijuana brownies (serves two), $25
102. Hashish cake (full size), $75
103. Apple custard pie, dusted with cocaine, $100
104. Frozen ginger cream with dilute LSD, $80
105. Marijuana mousse, $50
106. Gingerbread with powdered opium, $65

There were twenty-five items on the list in all, and Nick read them with growing astonishment. He had to admit that Tony Wilde had a great imagination when it came to finding new marketing techniques for tried-and-true products. "Just number 101," he told the waiter, handing back the menu.

"Very good, sir."

"What are you getting now?" Gloria asked.

"A take-out surprise for later."

It was eight o'clock, and as Nick accepted the doggie bag and paid the bill, the piano started playing. A slightly husky female voice began singing an old Cole Porter melody. He turned in his chair to look at her. She had platinum-blonde hair and was wearing a sequined evening gown. As Tony had said, her voice wasn't very good but she looked great.

It was Sandra Paris, the White Queen.

Nick gave Gloria the doggie bag and the key to the car. "I'll see you at the hotel," he said. "I have to speak with her."

"Nicky, remember the last time!"

"The last time she went to jail and I collected my fee. I'd like this to be a repeat performance."

"I don't trust any woman who looks like that."

"Don't worry. I'll be back in an hour."

He waited until Sandra Paris took her break and then approached the piano. "Remember me?"

She turned her head just a trifle and he saw again at close range the pale innocence of her face. "Nick Velvet, all the way out here in Chicago!"

"I get around. But then, so do you. I never thought you'd be frequenting men's rooms in public parks."

She smiled as she gathered up her music. "Oh, you found my card."

"Where's Tony Wilde?"

"In a safe place. He won't be harmed."

"How did you do it, Sandra?

"Professional secret, Nick."

"How long is O'Toole holding him?"

She didn't answer right away. Instead she started to walk away and Nick tagged along. "How much do you know?" she asked at last.

"Enough. Fingers wanted me for the Job first."

"I always seem to get your cast-offs, don't I?"

"How was prison, Sandra? Want to go back again?"

She shook her head. "I won't be going back again. I learned a few things since Atlantic City."

"Let me buy you a drink and we'll talk about it."

"I have another set in fifteen minutes."

"That's time enough. How'd you land this job, anyway?"

"The regular girl was persuaded to be sick for a week. I'm filling in."

"Why?"

She shrugged. "To keep an eye on Tony. I figured he'd rather be kidnaped by a familiar face."

They slid onto padded bar stools and she ordered white wine. "You know what he does here?" Nick asked.

"Sure. Have you tried the mousse? It's great."

"O'Toole wants a cut of it, doesn't he?"

"The damn fool wants to franchise the idea! Can you believe it? He says if all his restaurant-owner friends started offering it, with a percentage off the top to him, he could retire."

Nick shook his head. "Fingers is going to end up dead."

"Sure, but I don't question my clients. I just take the money and do the job."

"How much are you getting for this one, Sandra?"

"Fifty, plus my pay for singing here this week. I always wanted to be a singer."

"That's twice as much as I get for a job."

She shrugged her bare shoulders. "I have people to pay out of my share."

"So Fingers is holding him till he agrees to this crazy scheme?"

"Not exactly. Wilde has a big shipment of his raw material coming in any day now. Fingers plans to intercept it. Then it really won't matter if Tony agrees or not."

"Then why did he need to kidnap him?"

"Fingers intercepted a message about the shipment, but it's in some sort of code, he can't read it. That's why he needs Tony — when Tony tells him what it says, he'll be a free man."

Nick was remembering the library book. "I think I might have something you want," he said slowly. "When can we get together?"

"You mean with Tony Wilde?"

Nick nodded. "I want him free."

"That's Fingers' business, not mine."

"Get Fingers and get Wilde, and we'll meet tomorrow morning — around eleven. O.K.?"

"I'm not promising anything, Nick." She finished her wine and stood up. "I have to get back to the piano."

"That was just grandstanding this morning," he said. "You could have taken Tony right off the path, without any impossibilities."

She smiled at him. "I saw you and Gloria with him yesterday morning. I knew one of you would be back today, so I thought I'd show you how the pros do it."

"Call me tomorrow morning, Sandra, or I'll try a bit of grandstanding myself."

She smiled and strolled back to the piano. As he left, she was starting to sing another song.

When he got back to the hotel Gloria was already in bed. "Nicky, what was in those brownies?"

"Go to sleep. I'll tell you in the morning."

Norman Wells lived in a small, single-family house a few blocks from the library. It was shortly after nine o'clock when Nick arrived and rang his bell. A pleasant middle-aged woman answered.

"I'm looking for Norman Wells."'

"That's my son. He's in school. What's he done now?"

"Nothing serious, Mrs. Wells — just kept a library book overdue."

"His room is full of books. I'm surprised it's only one."

"Well, there may be more, but the one I was sent after is *The Thin Man* by Dashiell Hammett. Do you think you could find it for me?"

"Oh, I couldn't find anything in that room of his. You'll have to come back when he's home."

"It's very important. Do you think I could just have a peek in his room to see if I could spot it?"

"Well, I don't know —"

"I'd hate to have the library turn it over to the police."

"The police! Oh, I suppose we could take a look."

His room on the second floor was cluttered with football pennants, old and new sneakers, and an assortment of books from the public and high-school libraries. "He likes mysteries," Nick observed.

She agreed. "Those and horror stories. He reads them all the time, but right now it's the baseball season and he doesn't get so much reading done. That's probably why he forgot to return the books."

A few minutes later, Nick held up the book in triumph. "Here it is!"

"Well, I'm really sorry about this," Mrs. Wells said.

"Don't worry. Just tell him to get any other overdue books back to us as soon as possible."

"He'll have them back tonight, believe me."

At the door, Nick stopped and handed her a ten-dollar bill. "Tell Norman this is for his library fines. I know how it is. I was young once, too."

"Why, what a sweet thing!"

Back at the hotel, Gloria told him, "She called about ten minutes ago. Here's her number."

"Good. We're rolling now."

"Did you get the book?"

"Right here."

"Why do you think it's so valuable to him?"

"Book code. His contacts used a copy of this edition. Something happened to his and he was using the library's one and only copy. Then it got borrowed and never returned, and Tony was in trouble. The other editions have the pages numbered differently, and he couldn't use them to read the message. He was getting desperate because the stuff's due in any day now."

"Drugs?"

Nick grinned at her. "Couldn't you tell from those brownies?" He dialed the number Sandra Paris had left and heard her familiar voice on the other end. "Nick Velvet here. You called?"

"I called, but it's no dice. Fingers won't trade him for anything you have, unless it's the shipment."

"Look, meet me in the park in thirty minutes. By the men's room."

"What for?"

"I still think we can work this out."

When he hung up, Gloria asked, "Where are you going now?"

"To meet the White Queen."

He was at the park in twenty minutes, but Sandra Paris was there ahead of him, seated on a bench halfway between the two restrooms. She looked at the book he carried in one hand. "What's that?"

"The key to the code. Want it?"

Sandra tossed her blonde mane. "It means nothing to me. I've been paid and tonight is my last as a singer, whatever happens."

"Tell me where Fingers is hiding him."

"Not a chance."

"Then tell me how he disappeared from that men's room."

Her eyes twinkled with something like pride in her work. "That's got you bothered, hasn't it? He walked through that door, the only door, and Gloria and his faithful pet waited outside. He never came out and yet there's nowhere he could have gone."

"Suppose I could figure out how you did it. Then would you tell me where he was?"

"Forget it. You'll never figure this one out in a hundred years."

"I thought you were a gambler after Atlantic City, Sandra. Give me a crack at solving it. If I'm right, you take me to him. If I'm wrong, I give you this book and you can sell it to Fingers for another fifty."

Her eyes dropped to the book, weighing the possibilities. His mention of cash had obviously interested her. "How much time would I have to give you?"

"Ten seconds.

She laughed and slapped his hand to seal the bet. "You're on! All right, ten seconds — how did I do it?"

Nick smiled and said five words . . .

When Fingers O'Toole turned, startled at his sudden entrance, Nick held up his hand.

"No gunplay, Fingers. I don't want trouble."

"How the hell did you find me? Did Sandra — ?"

Nick could see Fingers was determined to make trouble. He crossed the room quickly and hit him on the jaw, sending him backward over a low coffee table. He knelt to remove the holstered revolver on Fingers' belt, then went into the back bedroom to find Tony Wilde handcuffed to a brass bed. "Hello, Tony," Nick said. "Sorry to have taken so long. I'll get the key to those cuffs."

That evening, Nick was once again Tony's guest at The Wilde Spot. Gloria was with them, demanding explanations. "How did you disappear from that restroom when I was outside watching?" she asked Tony.

He smiled. "Since the White Queen isn't here to tell you, I think Nick should explain."

"I told Sandra I could solve it — and I did, in just five words. We had a sort of bet — the book against Tony's hiding place. She was quite gracious about it — took me right to the door of O'Toole's house before she headed for the airport."

"What were the five words?" Gloria asked.

"It was a different dog."

"What?"

"It was a different dog. The first time we saw Tony with Bruno, I remember he calmed the dog by sliding his fingers beneath the collar and rubbing him. But yesterday, after Tony's disappearance, the doorman wondered if his collar was too tight. Had Bruno's neck gotten bigger in a single night? No, Sandra Paris saw the dog with Tony, probably even took instant photographs of him, and obtained an identical German Shepherd with the same coloring."

"But Tony must have known the difference," Gloria insisted.

"It was still Bruno when Tony left the house with him. It was still Bruno when Tony told him to wait outside the restroom. But then Tony stepped through the door and found the White Queen waiting for him, dressed as a man in case someone else entered. She knocked him out with a quick injection and then opened the door, firing a tranquilizer dart into Bruno. A couple of hired cohorts brought in the substitute German Shepherd to take Bruno's place and carried Tony and Bruno away.

"You were on the phone to me. Remember, the booth was directly behind the restroom and so for two minutes you couldn't see what was happening out front. That was all the time they needed. Sandra removed Bruno's collar and put it on the new dog, getting it a bit tight rather than risk buckling it into a different hole that might be noticed. Then they all vanished into the trees while you came back to wait with the dog."

"What if I hadn't phoned you, Nicky?"

"I asked Sandra that. She was prepared to kidnap you, too, if necessary — along with any other early-morning strollers who happened along. But the whole thing went off exactly as she'd hoped, creating a nice impossible disappearance. We should have realized it wasn't the same dog, of course. Bruno was far less aggressive than he'd been the previous day."

"What happened to Fingers O'Toole?"

"I told Nick to let him go," Wilde said. "He's made a lot of enemies in organized crime, and this caper won't help him any."

"What about the book?" Gloria asked.

"My contacts telegraphed me about shipments using a book code from this edition of *The Thin Man*," Wilde explained. "My copy got left with my ex-wife when we divorced, and I was temporarily using the library copy. I wish Nick hadn't been so generous in offering it to Sandra Paris as a gambling stake."

Nick chuckled. I put the library jacket on the bible from our hotel room. Sandra might have gotten religion, but she wouldn't have gotten the message."

"I decoded it just in time. The shipment's due tomorrow."

"Watch yourself, Tony. You're in a dangerous business."

He waved away the words of advice. "Anyway, you've earned your fee, Nick. More than earned it! You stole the book, rescued me, and even rescued Bruno from O'Toole's basement."

"Give him a bone for me."

"I'll do that," Wilde said with a smile. "Now how about some dessert?"

The Theft of the Cardboard Castle

During the summer months Nick Velvet sometimes arranged to meet prospective clients at the yacht club on Long Island Sound where he maintained a membership. This day, seated on the new cocktail terrace overlooking the club's marina, he regretted that he hadn't chosen to meet Tommy Traylor at the corner bar. He was a bulky man who moved awkwardly and managed to upset his beer before they'd even begun to talk.

"I guess I'm nervous," he admitted. "It's not every day I hire a criminal to steal something."

"I've never regarded myself as a criminal," Nick responded. "Everything I steal is valueless. I think of myself as being in a service business."

A waiter had appeared from inside to sweep up the broken glass and bring another beer for Traylor. When they were settled down again, he told Nick, "Whatever you do, I want to hire you. They tell me your fee is twenty-five grand."

"It is if I take the assignment. What do you want stolen?"

"A cardboard castle, like children play with."

"Where is it?"

"In the children's play room at a home on the north shore of Long Island." He squinted into the afternoon sun. "Near Glen Cove — probably just about opposite where we are now. You can sail across and do the job in an afternoon."

"What's so valuable about a cardboard castle?"

"Let's just say I want it for sentimental reasons."

"Is the house guarded?"

"Alarm systems. Possibly a guard. The family's away right now."

Nick nodded. "How soon do you need it?"

"This week, before Saturday. I think the castle might be flying to England over the weekend." He passed a thick envelope to Nick across the table. "There's the address and a floor plan of the house, plus what little I know about the alarm system. And half your fee in advance. Agreed?"

Nick flipped through the contents of the envelope while Tommy Traylor sipped his beer. "Agreed," he said at last.

They reached across the table to shake hands.

It was the sort of thing Nick Velvet had done a hundred times before, and he barely mentioned it to Gloria when he returned home. "It's a job across the Sound. I might even take the boat."

"Can I come with you?" she asked.

Gloria and Nick had lived together for over eighteen years, and for the first twelve or thirteen she'd had no real idea of how he made his living. Telling her the truth about what he did had brought them closer for a time, but then, a year or so back, they'd had a brief separation. Gloria had gone off with someone else. There'd been a woman in Nick's life too, in a way. Her name was Sandra Paris, and like Nick she was a professional thief. She liked to call herself the White Queen, and used a quote from Lewis Carroll, *Impossible Things Before Breakfast*, for her motto. She'd wanted to team up with Nick, but he'd rejected the idea. Gloria knew about Sandra Paris, and he sometimes wondered if she was the cause of the occasional tension between them.

It's a fairly routine job," he assured Gloria. "I'll simply sail across the Sound and back. I won't even be gone overnight."

That seemed to satisfy her and she said no more about joining him. On Wednesday afternoon, when he kissed her and left for the marina, she merely said, "Be careful, Nicky."

The trip across was easy enough. He'd been sailing the Sound for years and the sight of him on the water attracted no undue attention from other boaters. The idea of a thief arriving by boat amused him. With the house standing empty he had no reason to believe the theft of a child's toy castle would be soon discovered or reported, but even if it was, escape by water seemed the most inconspicuous route possible on this sunny August afternoon.

He docked at the pier shown on Traylor's map and approached the house with a studied nonchalance. The grounds seemed deserted, as he'd expected. An in-ground swimming pool — a conspicuous luxury this close to the Sound — was drained of water and served only as a resting place for a few dead leaves from the previous autumn. The burglar alarm, still in place on the windows of the big house, proved no problem for Nick. Within ten minutes he stood inside the living room, surveying the rolled-up rugs and the furniture covered with plastic sheets.

The children's playroom was at the rear of the second floor, according to the floor plan. Nick quickly mounted the stairs, moving quietly on his cork-soled shoes in the unlikely event that he was not alone in the house. He opened the door at the end of the hall and saw more plastic-covered chairs, along with children's bunk beds, a toy chest and a table. Assembled on the table was the cardboard castle he sought, garishly printed in red and green and gray, with its pointed turrets rising toward the ceiling. Though it was fairly big, it came apart easily and folded into sections no larger than 8 ½ by 14 inches.

Somewhere in the back of Nick's mind a troubling thought began to take shape. If everything in the house was packed away and wrapped up for a long absence, why was this single item — the very object he sought — not only out and fully assembled but virtually on display for him? It was too easy, somehow, and when things were too easy he started to worry.

He finished folding the cardboard pieces and started out of the room. Then he froze, staring at one of the plastic-covered chairs. It looked as though there was a person sitting in it, his face pressed against the wrinkled plastic sheeting. A man—

Nick took a step closer and lifted the plastic sheet. The man was staring directly at him, but Nick knew he wasn't seeing anything. A cord had been pulled tight and knotted around his neck.

"Freeze!" a voice from the hallway suddenly shouted. "I'm a police officer and you're under arrest!"

The detective was a tall granite-faced man named George Lowndes who handcuffed Nick and read him his rights in a monotone. "You're making a mistake," Nick tried to tell him. "I came in looking for the owner, Mr. McGruder."

"That's Tim McGruder dead in the chair, as you well know. Come on, downstairs with you!"

"I know nothing about his death. I just found him a moment before you arrived."

"You'll have plenty of time to tell your story." He checked the telephone at the bottom of the stairs and found it working. In a moment he was speaking with the local police headquarters. "Detective Lowndes here. I'm out at the McGruder place. Tim McGruder's been murdered and I have an intruder in custody."

It had been a long time since Nick had been arrested, since he'd felt the cold, unyielding pressure of handcuffs on his wrists. He still couldn't quite believe it. They'd realize their mistake soon and release him. But as more police arrived, as lab technicians and the medical examiner went about their tasks, he began to have a sinking feeling.

It all made terrible sense in a way, and the more Nick thought about it the more obvious it became. He heard Detective Lowndes telling his superior he'd received an anonymous call saying a robbery was in progress at the McGruder home. He'd found the window with its cut pane and disabled alarm, entered the house and discovered Nick with the dead man.

"You can see I didn't kill him!" Nick insisted. "He'd probably been dead for hours."

The other detective, Sergeant Steinmitz, shrugged. "The M.E. will tell us about that, but not till tomorrow. Meanwhile, you'll be held for arraignment. You're allowed one telephone call when we get to headquarters, and then you'll be mugged and fingerprinted. Let's go."

There was an efficiency about them that made Nick feel he'd be in a cell before he knew quite what had happened. They took him to the sheriff's office and the adjoining county jail where he'd be held, and he used the offer of a phone call to contact Gloria.

"I've been arrested," he told her.

"Oh, Nicky!"

"There was a dead man in the house. They think I killed him. Can you get over here with a good lawyer? I'm in the county jail out on Long Island."

"I'll be there as soon as I can."

After the formalities were over, Lowndes asked, "Do you wish to make a statement?"

"I have a lawyer on the way," Nick told him, scrubbing the fingerprint ink from his hands.

It took an hour for Gloria to drive down from Westchester, and when she arrived she was alone. "I called Ralph Aarons. He's the best lawyer I could think of. He said he'd meet us here."

"Thanks," Nick said glumly.

"What happened?"

Though they were alone in the room, Nick was all too aware that the place might be bugged. "I was set up. Tommy Traylor tipped them off that I'd be there."

"What about the thing you went to . . . pick up?"

"It was sitting out for me. The whole thing was just too easy. I should have realized it was a trap."

"But why?"

"To frame me for the murder, I suppose. I don't think it'll stand up in court, but I'm going to be stuck here until I'm arraigned and the judge sets bail."

Ralph Aarons arrived a few minutes later and joined them. He was a dapper Manhattan attorney whom Nick and Gloria had consulted about business matters. Nick knew he had a criminal practice, and he had a reputation of smooth-talking many a felon out of what seemed like a certain conviction.

He sat down at the table opposite Nick and looked at him, a little smile playing about his lips. "I told you one day you'd go too far, Nick."

"I didn't kill McGruder. I never touched him. He was dead and in storage, covered with a plastic sheet."

"I'll check the autopsy report as soon as it's ready. If you're telling the truth we shouldn't have too much trouble beating the murder charge. I assume you'd have an alibi for this morning and last night?"

"He was with me all the time," Gloria confirmed.

Aarons opened his briefcase and took out a legal-sized pad. The sight of it stirred something in Nick's memory, but he couldn't quite bring it to the surface. "Your problem, Nick, is that they caught you inside the house. You're going to have trouble explaining that away. They're going to dig into your past and discover a number of embarrassing facts. You can't run an operation like yours for nearly nineteen years without a great many people knowing about it. Sergeant Steinmitz and Detective

Lowndes might never have heard the name Nick Velvet, but other people have."

"Can you get me bail?"

"They won't arraign you till tomorrow when they can see the autopsy report. If they decide not to press the murder charge I should be able to get you released on bail. You have a home and a permanent address. You're a solid citizen, most of the time."

Steinmitz knocked and entered the room. "Is your client ready to make a statement?"

Aarons glanced at Nick, who answered, "I'm ready any time. I have nothing to hide."

Gloria was sent out of the room and Steinmetz and Lowndes entered with a stenographer. Ralph Aarons moved his chair around the table to sit at Nick's side. When everyone was ready, the sergeant turned to Detective Lowndes. "Let the record show that the arresting officer is Detective first-grade George Lowndes."

The granite-faced detective took over at that point. "Shortly after four I received an anonymous telephone call telling me that a robbery was in progress at the north shore home of Tim McGruder. I was familiar with the house since my wife and I have been there socially on occasion."

Sergeant Steinmitz interrupted. "How recently was that?"

"We were there one afternoon in June to go swimming in the pool. Shortly after that we learned McGruder's wife Michelle was leaving him and taking their son with her."

Nick felt a sudden chill at his words. There had been dead leaves in the swimming pool from last autumn. Lowndes hadn't gone swimming there in June. He was lying, and if he lied about the reason for his visit to the house he might be lying about the rest of it.

As Lowndes finished his account of finding Nick in the house, the detective sergeant asked, "Just what were you doing there, Velvet?"

Nick figured he could outlie Lowndes any time. "I'd been sailing on the Sound when I was suddenly taken ill, probably from some seafood I'd eaten for lunch. I docked the boat and went up to the house to phone my wife. No one answered the bell, and when I noticed the broken window I went inside. I went upstairs to lie down for a few minutes until the nausea passed. Just as I discovered the body, Detective Lowndes appeared, scaring me half to death with his gun."

"You entered the house to rob it," Lowndes barked. "Tim caught you and you strangled him."

It went on like that for another hour before they grew tired of Nick's denials. "Take him to his cell," Sergeant Steinmitz said. "He'll be arraigned in the morning."

"On what charges?" Aarons demanded.

"If the autopsy confirms the time of death as shortly before the arrest, the District Attorney will ask for second-degree murder."

Before they took him away, Nick met briefly with Gloria. "Aarons will get you out," she assured him.

"Sure, if they settle for breaking and entering. Murder is something else." He realized he knew nothing about Tim McGruder, or Tommy Traylor or Detective Lowndes. "Look," he told Gloria, "I need some information." He outlined what he wanted.

"I'll take care of it," she assured him.

They locked Nick in a holding cell for the night.

In the morning there was more bad news. Ralph Aarons arrived shortly after ten to inform Nick that the autopsy report placed the time of death at between three and four o'clock. Lowndes had arrested Nick at the scene shortly before four-thirty.

"Our argument will be that the killer phoned Lowndes himself after strangling McGruder," the lawyer told Nick. "But the D.A.'s position is that you could have killed McGruder, searched the house for valuables, and then returned to the body at the time Lowndes caught you."

Nick shook his head. "Lowndes is lying. I'm sure of it. He never went swimming at McGruder's. He went there for some other purpose, and I think he killed McGruder. He probably strangled him just before I arrived. When he heard me downstairs, he covered the body with that wrinkled plastic sheet in hopes it would go unnoticed. When I did discover it, he appeared with his gun to arrest me."

"That's all conjecture, Nick. You can't accuse a police officer of murder without good solid proof."

"What about that phone call? They must keep a log of calls. I'll bet there wasn't one to Lowndes around four o'clock. I'll bet he wasn't even here at four, because he was out at that house killing McGruder."

"I'll check on that with Sergeant Steinmitz. Meanwhile, I don't believe we should volunteer any information about your somewhat dubious career. The less they know, the better for you."

"Where do I stand, then?"

"You'll be arraigned before the judge this afternoon and held for grand jury action. I may not be able to get you free on bail quite yet."

"So I stay in jail?"

"You stay in jail. But only for the moment. I'm working on it."

"Thanks," he mumbled as the lawyer rose and left the room.

Gloria arrived an hour later. "I talked to Aarons," she said. "If he can't get you out I'll find somebody better."

"Don't worry about it."

"I want you home, Nicky."

"I will be. They'll never make this murder charge stick. Tell me what you found out about McGruder."

"It wasn't hard to do. The morning papers are full of his murder. It seems he was the president of a medium-sized Long Island bank that was recently investigated by the government. They were making large transfers of cash to Swiss banks without reporting it as required by government regulations. There was a suspicion the bank was laundering money for drug dealers or organized crime. Anyway, the board of directors dismissed McGruder as president a few months back and that's when his wife left him. The newspaper theory is that he might have been killed by a hit man for the mob."

"They think I'm a hit man?"

"Maybe that's why Aarons couldn't get you released on bail right away. Don't worry — the truth will come out."

"That's what I'm afraid of. By the time they decide I'm innocent of the murder charge, they might find out too many other things about me."

His court appearance was postponed one more day, till Friday, and he went to bed that night feeling more depressed than at any time since his arrest. Aarons had sent word they could not expect bail to be granted before the following week at the earliest. Gloria had been unable to get a line on Tommy Traylor, and Nick knew it was doubtful that his erstwhile client would suddenly decide to come forward. He began to consider the real possibility of serving a lengthy prison sentence, no matter what happened.

Nick was awake again at dawn, listening to the depressing sounds of his fellow prisoners preparing for another day. There was a toilet and wash basin in his cell, and he washed up the best he could. Gloria had brought a suit from home for his courtroom appearance, but for now he dressed in the faded gray shirt and trousers that were the prison costume.

A matron wearing slacks, shirt and a peaked cap intercepted him on his way to breakfast with the other prisoners. "Velvet!" she called out. "Which one is Nick Velvet?"

"That's me," he acknowledged.

"Come with me. Your lawyer wants to see you."

"I haven't had breakfast yet," he protested.

"That'll have to wait. Come along."

He left the line of prisoners and walked down the corridor at her side, then turned left with her down an empty corridor that led to the stairs. They were passing the door to a women's rest room when suddenly the matron slammed him hard on the shoulder, pushing him through.

"What the hell —?"

"Quick — get into these clothes!" she ordered.

For the first time his eyes focused on her face. "Sandra Paris!" he gasped. "What are you doing here?"

"Helping you escape from jail. *Impossible things before breakfast,* you know."

In their two previous encounters, Nick Velvet and the White Queen had been more or less on opposite sides of the fence,.each pursuing their own goals. It was difficult for Nick to accept her help now, but he did because it was his only way out. He didn't bother to consider the consequences of a jailbreak. He just wanted to be gone from there. Quickly he dressed in the guard's uniform Sandra had supplied, then followed her once more into the corridor.

Five minutes later they had passed through the gate and were in her car, heading west toward New York City. "How did you pull that off?" he asked in amazement.

"A little bribery and lots of luck. Don't you worry about it."

She'd taken off the ugly peaked cap and he had an opportunity once again to admire her long blonde hair as it fell around her shoulders. "You amaze me," he admitted. "I was just about resigned to spending the next few years in a prison cell."

"I wouldn't let you do that, would I? Don't you remember, I suggested that we team up as partners once."

"I remember."

"So what were you working on when you got grabbed? I know darn well you didn't go there to kill McGruder."

"Did you know him?"

"Mostly by reputation. A wealthy banker who was making money on the side. I met him last summer out in the Hamptons, at a fancy champagne brunch one Sunday."

Nick smiled and shook his head. "I travel in the wrong circles. I never meet people like that."

"We operate in different ways," she told him. "Sometimes I think it's just a game with you, the crazy things you steal! It's not a game with me. I'm in it for the money."

"The mention of money reminds me that I was hired to steal something from McGruder's house."

"What was it?"

"A cardboard castle. A plaything probably abandoned by his son after McGruder and his wife split up."

"I met her briefly at that brunch," Sandra Paris said. "A handsome woman, much younger than he was. I think her name was Michelle. Maybe she had a hand in his death."

"I've got my own suspect for that."

"Who?"

"The detective that arrested me — Lowndes. He lied about his reason for visiting McGruder earlier in the summer. They might have had a business deal involving some laundered drug money." He stared out at the morning rush-hour traffic along

Queens Boulevard. "I just wonder where Tommy Traylor fits in."

"Who's Traylor?"

"The man that hired me. He knows why that castle is valuable, and at first I thought he might have set me up to take the rap for the murder."

"You don't think so any more?" Sandra asked.

"I need to see him again."

"I have an apartment in Manhattan. That's where we're headed, so you can get out of that guard's uniform and into something a bit less noticeable. You can try calling him from there if you want."

"Good idea," Nick decided.

The number Tommy Traylor had given Nick was connected to a telephone answering machine. As he listened to the recorded message, Nick glanced around at the small but expensively furnished apartment overlooking the East River. Business must be good for the White Queen, he decided, and then spoke into the phone to leave a message. "This is Nick, the fellow you hired for that dredging work on the Sound. I'm calling to —"

Traylor's voice broke in. "I'm here, Nick. I just wasn't taking calls. I heard about you on the news."

"I have to see you. I've got a lot of questions."

"Do you have the merchandise?"

"Not yet."

"Look, Nick, you're a bit hot right now. I can't risk meeting you. Can't we do this over the phone?"

"Not if you're recording it."

"Hell, the machine's off and the phone's not tapped. Speak up. Did you kill McGruder?"

"No," Nick answered. "Did you?"

"Wise guy! I had nothing against the guy. I just want the money."

"What money is that?"

"The stuff in the Swiss bank account. McGruder transferred it for me. It's my own money. I'm not trying to steal it."

"You'd better explain."

"There are legal documents involved with Swiss bank accounts, especially when there's a transfer of funds from an American bank. McGruder's bank was laundering a little money for me and some of my friends. The government finally caught on and started investigating. The bank's board of directors fired McGruder a couple of months back and when that happened this last batch of money got caught in the pipeline. McGruder claimed there was nothing he could do because he was no longer with the bank, but I knew better. He was planning to fly to Zurich this weekend with the necessary documents, withdraw the money, and live comfortably somewhere in Europe or South America until the statute of limitations ran out."

It was all falling into place for Nick. He remembered Ralph Aaron's legal pad and what it had almost triggered in his mind. Legal pads, and legal documents, were 8½ by 14 inches — the same size as the largest pieces of the disassembled cardboard castle. "The documents are printed in invisible ink on the backs of those cardboard pieces," Nick said, as if he'd known it all along.

"Sure — the secret account numbers and everything. All that's needed to withdraw the money. Tim McGruder was a great talker. Once after a few drinks he told me about it. He and his wife made the flight to Zurich two or three times a year."

"His wife. Michelle?"

"Yeah. They split up after he got fired."

"How'd you know he was flying to Zurich this weekend?"

"His old secretary tipped me off. He had her make two reservations for Friday night, with a stopover in London. That's tonight."

"Two? Who was he planning to take?"

"Beats me. When you're on your way to empty out a Swiss bank account, I suppose there's no lack of traveling companions."

"When I got there, the cardboard castle was sitting out," Nick said, "as if I was expected to steal it."

"He was expecting someone else — the guy who killed him. You just walked in at the wrong time."

"Yeah," Nick agreed. There was no arguing with that.

"What're you going to do now?"

"Do? I'm going to finish stealing that cardboard castle for you."

The White Queen sat regally in a big armchair, her back to the river, and listened to Nick talk. "I'm more certain than ever that McGruder was killed by George Lowndes, the detective who arrested me. I think he's flying to Zurich in McGruder's place, to empty that bank account."

"You do jump to conclusions, Nick."

"I know how we can prove it. Do you have any connections with the airlines? Traylor said McGruder was planning to fly there tonight, with a stopover in London. He'd booked two seats. There can't be more than a dozen or so overnight flights from New York to London. If we could learn his flight number, and whether the tickets have been canceled —"

"Why would Lowndes take his place?"

"If he stole the cardboard castle himself, he'll be anxious to get his hands on the money."

"He's probably anxious to get his hands on you, after you broke out of jail. He won't go running off while you're at large."

"That's exactly what he would do, before I'm recaptured and they need his testimony for the grand jury."

Sandra Paris nodded "I'll get busy on it."

"Got any food in this place? I never did eat breakfast."

"Look in the refrigerator while I make a few calls."

He had a sudden thought. "I'd better phone Gloria."

"No. If the police are tapping anything it'll be her line."

Nick settled for a sandwich and a bottle of beer. By the time he'd finished it, Sandra had completed her calls. She came into the kitchen smiling, tossing her long hair. "I played a dumb secretary and called till I hit the right flight. Mr. and Mrs. McGruder are still booked on the 8:30 departure from Kennedy to London, continuing to Zurich on Monday morning."

"When the banks open."

"Exactly." She opened a beer for herself. "If your Detective Lowndes is leaving on that flight, he must be making preparations."

"I was just thinking the same thing," Nick said. "I was thinking there might be a way to steal that cardboard castle at the airport."

"From his luggage?"

"He wouldn't risk checking it through, not after he committed murder for it. He'll have it with him, in a brief case or carry-on bag." He had an idea. "Do you have an instant camera of some sort?"

"I've got an old Polaroid I use occasionally."

"Perfect! I want you to go out to Long Island and get a picture of Lowndes, preferably with whatever kind of case or bag he'll be carrying on the plane. We may want to duplicate it if we can."

"You're really thinking, Nick. But how will I know which is the right one?"

He thought about that. "It has to hold 8½ by 14-inch pieces of cardboard. That rules out most airline flight bags. Look for something with hard sides, like an attache case."

She was back by four o'clock, flushed with triumph. "This time I posed as a reporter. I called and asked him for an interview on Monday, but he told me he'd be away next week. He left headquarters early, carrying a black attache case, just as you predicted. Here's a picture of it."

Nick studied the instant photo of George Lowndes unlocking his car door, carrying the case. It was an inexpensive imitation leather one that wouldn't be too hard to locate in New York. "A fine job, Sandra."

"One problem — his initials are on the top, in those stick-down metallic letters. GPL. You can barely see it in the photo."

"That shouldn't be hard to duplicate."

"You're going to bump into him and exchange cases'?"

"Hardly! He'd recognize me and yell for the nearest security man."

"Then how — ?"

"I'll explain later. Let's find this case first."

They tried three stores in midtown Manhattan before they located the identical attache case. The metallic letters were easy, but Sandra Paris raised another question. "What about the weight? If we do a switch he's sure to notice it's heavier or lighter."

"We'll put a couple of newspapers in it and hope for the best. We know he wouldn't try to board the plane with anything really heavy, like a gun. Chances are it'll contain nothing but the cardboard castle and some reading matter for the trip. Even if it feels odd, the initials on the top should reassure him."

Back at her apartment, Sandra asked, "How do we make the switch?"

"There's only one place at the airport where the attache case will be out of Lowndes's grasp — passing through the x-ray machine at the security check. If you could get a uniform and take the place of the girl operating the machine, you could make the switch as the case passes through. There's a narrow space inside the machine, on either side of the conveyor belt, where the duplicate case could be stored until Lowndes appears."

Sandra Paris was dubious. "There are usually two girls on the machine, plus a security guard not far away. It would be tricky to make the switch without being seen. Besides, I couldn't make a quick getaway with the case while there was a line of people waiting. If he discovered the switch before the plane left the gate, I'd still be there, waiting to be caught."

He had to admit she was right. Too many things could go wrong. "It's nearly five o'clock. Not much time to come up with a better scheme."

"I might have something here," she said, going to a closet. She returned with a medium-sized suitcase. "This is a booster bag, a device popular with professional shoplifters. See, the bottom is hinged, in two sections. You set it down directly over the object you want to boost, and then pick it up with the stolen goods inside. I've modified this one to make exactly the sort of switch you have in mind. I used it once to steal the blueprints of a new auto plant from an architect's office. By the time they discovered the substitution I was on a plane back to New York."

"It might work," Nick agreed, "if he ever takes his hands off the case."

He'd always admired Sandra Paris's resourcefulness, and as they drove to Kennedy Airport he was confident she could bring it off. "He doesn't know me," she reasoned. "I can stand or sit next to him in the lounge and wait for my opportunity."

"If you bring this off, you'll get a share of the money from Traylor."

"Of course. I told you I don't work for free."

At the airline's departure building, the waiting began. As six-thirty passed, and then seven o'clock, Nick began to worry. "I don't think he's coming."

"There's still over an hour till flight time."

"They like passengers to be here an hour early for overseas departures."

It was Sandra who finally spotted him, getting his seat assignment. "There he is. That's Lowndes!"

The detective turned from the counter carrying the black attache case. He was immediately joined by an attractive auburn-haired woman who took his arm. "Who's that?" Nick asked.

Sandra gave a little gasp. "McGruder's widow, Michelle."

"That explains a lot. Lowndes visited the house to see her. She must be the one who tipped him off about the cardboard castle. Maybe it was even Lowndes who caused the breakup of her marriage. She sent him there to steal the castle and probably to kill McGruder while he was at it. Maybe she's the one who made the plane reservations in the first place, through her husband's old secretary."

"You're great on theories, Nick, but you'd better get practical. I met Michelle McGruder at that party I told you about. She might recognize me and start talking. Then how do I make the switch?"

"Try it and see. If she does recognize you, I'll create some sort of diversion."

He watched from behind a convenient pillar as Sandra approached the row of seats where Lowndes and Mrs. McGruder waited. Just before she reached them, another passenger took the only vacant seat by their side. He could feel Sandra's frustration, especially when a voice over the public address system suddenly announced, "Flight 223, eight-thirty departure for London's Heathrow Airport, will begin boarding in five minutes. Please have your boarding passes and passports ready for inspection."

Five minutes, and the castle would be beyond Nick's reach.

He saw Sandra switch tactics and walk right up to them, carrying her trick suitcase. She said a few words to Michelle McGruder and the auburn-haired woman's face brightened. She smiled, extending her hand, as George Lowndes got politely to his feet. The black attache case was on the floor between his legs.

Nick turned away, almost afraid to watch. When he looked back a few seconds later Sandra had maneuvered Lowndes away from the attache case and lowered her suitcase into position. Ten minutes later she joined him. "You got it?"

"Of course I got it," she answered with a smile. "Right in here. They didn't suspect a thing, once I reminded Michelle that we'd met in the Hamptons. I had to stay around until they boarded the flight, but Lowndes picked up the attache case without noticing a thing."

"Good thing you didn't have to go through security with that suitcase of yours. It might have looked odd on the x-ray machine." He took it from her as they started toward the exit.

And found Sergeant Steinmitz blocking their path.

It was the sergeant who recovered first from his surprise. "What are you doing here, Velvet? Are you trying to flee the country too?"

At Nick's side, Sandra Paris had frozen, waiting for an indication of their next move. Nick was ready to knock the man aside and make a run for it, but something in Steinmitz's attitude made him hesitate. "Hello, Sergeant. Good to see you again."

"There's a warrant out for you. Jail-breaking, unlawful flight to avoid prosecution. We'd better settle those as soon as I take care of George Lowndes. If you're smart you'll come see me in the morning."

"Lowndes." Then it dawned on Nick. "You came here looking for Lowndes! He's on that plane to London."

"I know. The control tower caught it before takeoff and it's returning to the gate."

"You know he killed McGruder?"

Steinmitz nodded. "We've got a pretty good case against him. Evidence of an affair with McGruder's wife. She's on the plane with him. And he made a sloppy attempt to change the log of phone calls at headquarters to back up his story of that anonymous call reporting the burglary. There was no call, and he wouldn't have been there to receive it anyway. We have a witness who saw him leave headquarters at three, and one of McGruder's neighbors saw him arrive out there at three-thirty. He killed McGruder and when you entered the house he figured he could frame you for the murder."

"Then I'm off the hook?" Nick asked.

"Not completely, but I think we can get the escape charges dropped if you sign a paper promising not to sue for false arrest. There's no evidence you took anything from that house."

They stayed long enough to see Lowndes and Mrs. McGruder being escorted from the plane. Then they left quickly and headed back to Sandra's car. For the first time in days, Nick could relax. "I'm in the clear and we've got the cardboard castle for Traylor. I guess Steinmitz never knew about that part of it."

"I told you we'd make a great team."

"I won't forget what you did, rescuing me from jail."

She headed north on the Van Wyck Expressway, toward the bridge that would take him back home. "There's something I should have told you sooner, Nick."

"What's that?"

"You know it's not a game with me. I'm only in it for the money. I never pull off a caper except for good hard cash."

"So?"

"Gloria decided your lawyer wasn't doing enough to get you out. She hired me to spring you. I'm taking you there now, to collect my fee."

The Theft of the Faded Flag

The embassy of the tiny Caribbean nation of Coronado was situated on Massachusetts Avenue in Washington, not far from the Naval Observatory and the Vice-President's house. It was in one of several aging mansions that had found new life in the world of international diplomacy and each morning at sunrise early-rising neighbors were sure to see the rainbow-colored flag of the nation being raised to the end of the pole which protruded from the center window of the top floor.

This particular morning in September seemed no different from any other. The flag of Coronado, looking just a bit faded from the sun, was run up to the top of the pole promptly at seven a.m. by the First Secretary of the delegation, a slick-haired man named Leon Oeste. He stood for a moment in the window as he always did, offering a salute, as traffic passed below and a newsboy delivered his morning papers. Then he closed it and went down for breakfast with the ambassador.

Across the street at the entrance to Normanstone Park, Nick Velvet sat in the passenger seat of a compact car driven by a man named Art Schraeder. "That's the flag," Schraeder told him. "I want you to steal it."

"It looks faded. They could use a new one."

"They're replacing it with a new one the first of October. That's why I need it stolen before then."

"No value?" Nick asked. He was extremely particular about what he stole.

"No value. What's a faded flag worth?"

"Twenty-five thousand dollars to you, if that's what you're willing to pay me."

"I need the flag, and embassies are tricky things. They're well protected. I figured I needed to hire the best in the business."

"You've got him," Nick said, a bit immodestly.

"Right! And up there —" He stopped in mid-sentence.

"What is it?"

Art Schraeder was craning his neck out the car window. "Where's the flag? The damn flag is gone!"

"Maybe they took it in for something."

"They never take it in till sunset. Besides, we were watching it every minute."

"Not the minute it was taken down, obviously."

"Suppose somebody beat us to it. Suppose somebody else stole it."

Nick tried to reassure him. "It's only seven in the morning. Who'd steal a flag from under our eyes before breakfast?"

But even as he said the words a possible answer came to him. There was one person, a woman whose path he'd crossed more than once before, who always committed her crimes before breakfast. Her name was Sandra Paris but she was better known in criminal circles as the White Queen.

"*Impossible things before breakfast,*" Nick repeated to Gloria back home that evening. "That was always her motto."

"You haven't heard anything from Sandra Paris in two years," Gloria objected. "You have no reason to think she's connected with this."

"It's just a feeling I have."

"The flag was really stolen?"

"Yes indeed. When that fellow Oeste discovered it was missing he was out in the street with a couple of security guards looking all over for it. Somebody even climbed out on the roof in case it had blown up there somehow. They didn't find it."

"But you were down in the street when it happened."

"Apparently."

"So you're out the twenty-five thousand?"

"Maybe not. Schraeder tells me there's another flag in existence at the Coronado consulate in New York. He says that one will do just as well."

"Couldn't he just go out and buy a flag?"

"He's very specific about wanting one of these old, faded ones. I don't question him. I've had far stranger requests in my time."

"When does he want it?"

"I'm planning to scout the place tomorrow. It's on upper Madison Avenue, in the 70s."

"Don't lose any sleep about Sandra Paris," Gloria cautioned him. "I'm sure she's not involved."

The following day Nick took the train into New York and rode the Lexington Avenue subway to 77th Street. Walking briskly over to Madison, he observed that no police were on duty in front of the Coronado consulate as they were at some of the other diplomatic missions around Manhattan. The familiar rainbow flag with its obscure seal in the center was in place on the flagpole at the third-floor window.

At first he barely noticed the well-dressed gray-haired woman who strolled by at one point trailing an eager little poodle on a leash. He might have taken no notice the second time either if the poodle hadn't leaped up on him, as if intent on calling attention to its mistress. As soon as he saw the gray-haired woman's eyes, he knew.

"Hello, Sandra."

"Hello, Nick. It's good to see you again."

"What brings you here?"

"I'm living just a few blocks away now." Then, to the poodle, "Get down, Bon

Bon! Behave yourself!"

"Your hair has gone completely gray in just two years," Nick said with a trace of irony. "Such a shame for a woman your age!"

She arched an eyebrow at him, a familiar gesture he remembered from their earlier meetings. "Suppose you buy me a cup of coffee. The place across the street is nice."

"It would be a pleasure, Sandra."

Over coffee she came to the point. "What are you up to, Nick? What are you doing here?"

"You mean outside the Coronado consulate? I might ask the same question of you. At least I'm not here wearing a wig and walking my dog."

"It's business," she said simply.

"Was it business yesterday morning in Washington too?"

She lowered her eyelids and dipped her head to take a sip of coffee. "You were there?"

"Yes. Just a bit too late."

"Then it appears we're after the same thing."

"The faded flags of the nation of Coronado."

She smiled. The time for pretense was past. "Correct."

"How did you get that flag off the pole yesterday?"

"That's my secret."

"Who are you working for?"

"Another secret. Obviously not the same person who hired you."

"What makes these old flags so valuable all of a sudden?"

She shrugged. "I don't ask questions."

"Are we going to have a fight over that flag?"

"Not at all," she said with a smug expression. "I'm taking it tomorrow morning. If you want it you'll have to beat me to it."

"How did you manage it yesterday, Sandra?"

"Want to see it again? Come by tomorrow morning. I don't mind playing to an audience."

Nick knew it would be virtually impossible for him to steal the Coronado flag once it had been stored away for the night. Prowling around a strange building in the dark, with no idea of his goal, was out of the question. That only left the time when the flag was taken down, around seven p.m. if they did it at sundown.

It was obvious that the flagpole couldn't be reached from the street, not without a crane and bucket sure to attract attention. The flag had to be stolen from inside the building. When the door opened for a visitor he could see a formidable-looking guard seated just inside. If there was any sort of back entrance to the consulate it was completely blocked from the street. A narrow alleyway running between the buildings had a firmly locked iron gate.

Nick took a chance and entered the building next door. It housed a small dress shop and the woman clerk was surprised and bit apprehensive at the sight of him. "Health Inspector," he explained, showing a badge and ID that he carried for such occasions. "We've had a report of a foul odor that seems to be coming from the back of your store."

"What?" The young woman wrinkled her brow in disbelief. "You've got to be kidding!"

"All I know is what they tell me. Have you a back door to the shop?"

She seemed a bit dubious. "The owner's not here right now. I shouldn't —"

"If there's no odor I'll be finished in a minute," he assured her.

"All right," she decided. "Follow me."

He noticed a little name plate on her blouse identifying her as Miss Shepherd. Her green and white dress was casual but smart.

They walked through the stock room and she opened a side door. Nick saw at once that it led onto the same narrow passageway he'd observed from the street. "See? There's no odor."

"Is there a back door?"

"This is it."

Nick sniffed the air. "You're right. There's no odor. Sorry to have troubled you."

A bell sounded from inside the shop. "I have a customer, if you're finished here."

"Sure. Thank you." She closed and bolted the side door, then escorted him back into the shop where a middle-aged woman was glancing through a rack of dresses.

Out on the street Nick walked away quickly without a glance at the Coronado consulate. Miss Shepherd had provided him with everything he needed.

The dress shop closed promptly at six, a full hour before sundown, and Nick was waiting across the street when Miss Shepherd locked the front door and headed home. During his few minutes in the shop he'd managed to check the lock on the front door and slice through a key wire on the alarm system.

Now it took him only a moment to cross Madison Avenue and walk up to the door as if he belonged there. He had it unlocked in less than ten seconds and was inside without the alarm sounding. Passersby on the street paid no attention. He walked through the shop to the side door, disconnected the alarm there, and opened it. Once in the alley separating the two buildings he walked to the rear. There had to be a reason for the alley and the most likely one was to provide access to the consulate kitchen for deliveries and rubbish removal. He found the door to the kitchen standing open behind an unlocked screen door. The cooks were busy with dinner preparation and only one bare-chested dishwasher noticed him. "Who are you?" the man asked in Spanish.

"Health Inspector," Nick answered, flashing his badge. "Put a shirt on or I'll have to write you up for a violation."

The man quickly reached for his shirt and Nick continued on his way. He passed through the kitchen and out the swinging doors that led to the dining area. A few people were already seated at tables but none of them challenged him. Coming from the kitchen seemed to provide him with the necessary authority.

The interior of the consulate was garishly decorated with bright colors and murals depicting various events in the nation's history. Nick recognized one that was in the process of being repainted. It depicted three sailing ships at anchor in a little cove and the same scene was repeated in a simplified form in the seal on the rainbow flag.

At that moment Nick spotted a white-haired man in a business suit descending the staircase with a folded flag in his hand. "Pardon me," he said, approaching the man. "Are you Señor Montanya?"

The man frowned at him. "Jose Montanya returned to Coronado three months ago. I am Christopher Onza, the acting envoy."

Nick silently cursed the outdated reference book he'd consulted. He dredged his mind for another name and came up with one. "Sorry, I was mistaken. Leon Oeste, the First Secretary at the Washington embassy, sent me here to pick up the flag you've been flying from the consulate. He said you've been informed and would be expecting me."

"I knew there was to be a change, but my instructions were merely to burn the old flag."

"No, no. He sent me to pick it up. Is that it in your hand?"

The man hesitated only an instant. "Yes. I just took it down. Do you wish to give me a receipt for it?"

"Certainly." Nick took a notebook from his pocket and scrawled a few words, signing it with an alias. Then he tucked the flag under his arm and headed for the front door.

"You have to sign out," the guard told him.

He showed the badge one more time. "Health Inspector. I came in through the kitchen."

"I don't care if you came down the chimney. You still have to sign out."

Nick signed out.

That evening in a Times Square hotel room, he delivered the flag to Art Schraeder. The balding man smiled as he accepted it. "That was good work, Velvet. Faster than I'd expected." He opened his briefcase to remove an envelope containing the remainder of Nick's fee but then paused in mid-motion. "However it doesn't seem as faded as I'd expected." He unfolded the flag until it was fully revealed, spread across one of the room's twin beds.

"He told me that was the flag —" Nick began.

"Well, it isn't! This flag is new. It's never been flown anywhere."

"Does it matter that much?" Nick asked lamely.

"Of course it matters! I hired you to steal a faded flag from the Coronado government, not one of these new ones."

"It looks exactly the same to me — a rainbow background with the nation's official seal in the center."

"I need a faded one," Schraeder insisted. "Whoever gave you this tricked you."

Nick had already realized that. The man on the stairs hadn't been the easy mark he appeared to be. By now the real faded flag was tucked safely away till morning. "I'll get it tomorrow," he assured the man.

He tried not to think of what else could go wrong. He especially tried not to think of Sandra Paris.

In the morning he was on upper Madison Avenue before dawn, standing in a doorway next to a homeless man who slept bundled inside a shabby overcoat. Precisely at seven, as the first rays of sun appeared over the East River, the man who had given him the false flag on the previous day appeared at the third-floor window. He unwrapped the halyard from the pole and attached the flag to it, then unfurled it as he raised it to the top.

The flag hung out over the sidewalk below, at what Nick estimated was an angle of about forty-five degrees. He watched as Christopher Onza finished his task. Then Nick left his doorway and prepared to go into action. During the night he'd arranged to hire a truck with a moveable boom, having a bucket at the top, a cherry picker used by an outdoor advertising firm to change its billboards. He saw it coming along Madison now and waved to the driver. He'd have the flag off its pole before anyone knew what had happened.

"All right," Nick told the driver when the truck pulled up to him. "Take me up there, to that flag. When we're close enough I'll take over the controls in the bucket myself."

The driver looked blank. "What flag is that?"

Nick Velvet had a sinking feeling as he turned his head and glanced up at the consulate window. The flagpole was empty, its halyard flapping gently in the breeze.

Across the street he noticed that the sleeping man was no longer in his doorway. Only the shabby overcoat remained. Its wearer had vanished as neatly as the flag.

Nick crossed the street and picked up the coat. A little white card fell free and he knew what it would say before he bent to pick it up.

Impossible things before breakfast.

"I've never seen you so upset, Nicky," Gloria told him as she poured a second cup of coffee.

"Sandra Paris beat me twice in three days. She stole both of those flags from under my nose and I don't even know how she did it. The only flag I managed to steal was the wrong one."

"What does Mr. Schraeder say?"

"I haven't told him yet."

When he took the train back to Manhattan that afternoon, Nick fully expected his meeting with Art Schraeder to be a total disaster. He was prepared for the first real failure in his long career, prepared for the news to travel quickly among the people who were most likely to hire him.

He was not prepared for Schraeder to grant him one more chance. The balding man listened to his story with a sour expression on his face and finally said, "I would have done better hiring this Sandra Paris, apparently. There is one more opportunity to steal the flag before the old ones are destroyed at the end of the month, but you'd have to fly to Coronado to do it. What do you think?"

Nick would have traveled to the South Pole to redeem himself at that point. "Of course I'll go. Where is the flag?"

"In front of the presidential palace in Coronado City. The place is well guarded, of course. Stealing that one won't be nearly as easy as the first two."

"Those first two were pretty difficult for me. Things can't be any worse in Coronado City."

He arrived there the following Monday morning and took a taxi to the presidential palace. His confidence eroded a bit when he saw the military guards surrounding the place, and for the first time he realized that he knew very little about the island nation of Coronado. He picked up a guidebook for tourists and took it along to his hotel room to read. The hotel itself was a white stucco structure of vaguely Spanish architecture, with balconies overlooking the palace across the square. Around the back was a patio lined with palm trees surrounding a large, inviting swimming pool. Nick changed into his trunks and relaxed there while he read the tourist's guide to Coronado.

The island had been discovered by Columbus on his second voyage, which accounted for the three sailing ships at anchor on the nation's seal — even though, as the book explained, there had really been seventeen ships on that second voyage. The exact point of their anchorage was unknown. Coronado had been a Spanish possession until the late 19th century when it won its independence. And independent was the right word for Coronado. Nick knew from recent newspaper headlines that both the United States and Cuba were actively courting the tiny nation in an attempt to win rights to a naval base there.

Nick's reading was interrupted by a gentle tap on his shoulder. "It seems we're fated to keep meeting like this," a voice above him said.

He looked up into the pale blue eyes of Sandra Paris.

She was wearing a one-piece black bathing suit, cut fashionably high on her hips, and she might have been any young American tourist spending a few days away from the bustle of her job. Her smile was both teasing and tempting as she enjoyed the surprise of her sudden appearance.

"What are you doing here?" he asked, rising to his feet.

"Can't a working woman relax once in a while?"

"You're not here to relax. You're here to steal another flag."

"My, my! You have a terrible opinion of me, Nick. Let's go for a swim and cool off." Without another word she dove into the pool.

Nick followed reluctantly, diving deep and then surfacing next to her. "How did you do it?" he asked, treading water. "You were the bum in the doorway, weren't you?"

"Of course! I wanted to reach out and grab your ankle but I was afraid you might have a heart attack."

"Still, you were in the doorway and the flag was on the pole. How did you get it without my seeing anything?"

"The same way I did it in Washington. The same way I'll do it here."

"The flag at the presidential palace is a lot larger, and there are armed guards all over the place."

"No problem!" She did a skillful backflip and disappeared from view.

When she surfaced again, some distance away, Nick swam over to her. "This feuding between us is damned foolish. In a sense we're both on the same side. Why don't we team up and split the fees?"

Her pale eyes twinkled. "How would we split the flag?"

"You've got two already. Let me have this one."

"My client needs all three."

"What for? They're just like the new ones."

"No, not quite."

"Tell me who you're working for."

"That's against the rules." She swam effortlessly to the ladder and pulled herself up. He followed along and when he reached her side she was toweling droplets of water from her long legs. "But the least I can do is tell you why the flags are important, since your own client obviously failed to do so. Want to come up to my room, or would that compromise you?"

"I'll take my chances," he said, watching while she slipped into a short terry cloth robe.

She was on the eighth floor, two levels above Nick's own room, with a perfect view across the park to the presidential palace. He settled into a chair by the balcony and watched while she removed two carefully folded flags from her luggage. Both were the familiar rainbow banners of Coronado, but one was clearly faded, with a tattered edge from constant flapping in the breeze. "This is from the Washington embassy," she explained. "I bought the other one at a flag shop in Manhattan, just for comparison."

Sandra Paris unfolded the two flags on the bed where Nick could examine them. "They look alike to me, except for the fading."

"Look at the seal in the middle."

"Three sailing ships at anchor. What's — ? Oh, I see what you mean. The shape of the coastline is a little bit different. On the old seal they're in a sort of cove. The new flag shows them just along a shoreline."

"That's it."

"That's what? Why would that make the old flags so important to anyone?"

"Certain factions must want to preserve them. They don't want them burned."

"But flags are printed in full color in most almanacs and dictionaries. Anyone could see the old design without stealing the flag itself."

"Not in this much detail. That seal would only be a tiny spot of color in reproductions. Even a printed description, *three sailing ships at anchor*, wouldn't tell the whole story. The ships are still there. It's the coastline that's changed."

"You may be right," Nick admitted, remembering how the mural on the wall of the New York consulate was being altered when he paid them an uninvited visit.

"Of course I'm right! There are two factions involved. One faction wants to keep the change secret, so it hired me to steal the remaining three flags. The other faction wants to reveal the change for its own purpose, so it only needs one of the flags."

"What's so important about the shape of the coastline?"

"That's what I don't know," she admitted.

Nick watched her fold the flags and return them to her suitcase. "Where's the one from the New York consulate?"

"That's already been delivered to my client."

Her bedside telephone rang and she scooped it up with a quick motion. "Hello ... Yes ... Yes ... I can't talk now. Tomorrow, that's right ... Bye-bye."

"Your client?" Nick asked.

She merely smiled. "I'll have to ask you to leave now. I'm sure we both have a great deal to do."

"I have a feeling I'll see you tomorrow," he said as he departed.

Nick wandered over to the palace at sundown and watched while the flag was lowered and folded by an honor guard of four soldiers. He knew that Sandra Paris would make her move the following morning, true to the White Queen's motto of impossible things before breakfast. If he hoped to steal the flag himself he would have to act first.

He was just starting away from the palace steps when he spotted a familiar face. It was Christopher Onza, the white-haired gentleman he'd encountered on the stairway of the Coronado consulate in New York. "Pardon me, Señor Onza. You may remember that we met in New York last week."

Onza frowned at him for just an instant. "Oh, yes. You were the man collecting flags."

"I received the wrong one from you. I'll have to return it."

"Don't worry about it."

He started to continue on his way but Nick said, "I understand the flag was stolen from your consulate the following morning."

"Stolen? I doubt that. It did disappear mysteriously. Apparently it came loose from the pole and was blown away by the wind. We replaced it, as we had planned to do anyway."

"There's no value in old flags," Nick said by way of agreement.

Christopher Onza nodded and continued walking. Nick couldn't help wondering if it was the missing flag that had brought him back home to Coronado.

Nick had a number of tasks to carry out before morning, and he was awake much of the night. At three a.m. he stood on the balcony of his room gazing out at the moonlit square and the palace beyond. He felt good about his plans. This time the White Queen would not be quite so impossible before breakfast.

He arrived at the palace guardhouse well before sunrise, dressed in a colonel's uniform he'd managed to obtain at some expense. An earlier phone call had informed the captain of the guard — convincingly, he hoped — that the president wished a new flag to be flown that day. A colonel would arrive with it before sunrise. The man who met Nick at the door checked his identification and then admitted him. The captain of the guard, a young man with a neat mustache and brooding eyes, produced the old flag with some reluctance.

"I understood it was not to be burned until the first of the month," he said.

"You can see how faded it is," Nick told him. "There will be special visitors at the palace today and the president wants everything perfect."

"Certainly." The captain passed over the flag without further question.

Nick returned his salute and was gone, leaving the new flag in its place. It had been as simple as that. The palace flag was much larger than the embassy ones, but he knew it would fit in his suitcase for the flight back to New York. The sun was rising beyond the palm trees by the time he completed his walk to the hotel. He turned and stood for a moment, watching the honor guard march out to raise the flag of the nation.

He saw the white puffs of two exploding smoke bombs, quite near the soldiers, and he knew Sandra Paris was at work. Just a bit too late this time, Sandra, he said to himself.

He hurried through the lobby and took the elevator to his room. The few guests and employees who were in the lobby at that hour rushed outside to see what was happening, paying scant attention to him. Unlocking the door, he stepped inside and tossed the folded flag on the bed, then began to shed his uniform.

Then he heard a sound from the bathroom but before he could turn a harsh voice rasped, "Stand very still, Mr. Velvet. I have a pistol pointed at the back of your spine, and in this country they would award me a medal for shooting you."

He recognized the voice at once. It was Christopher Onza.

"Don't I deserve an explanation before you shoot me?" Nick asked, keeping his hands carefully raised.

"Of course. Since I am known to have an interest in the matter of the flags, the captain of the guard telephoned me after he received your call. I told him to give you the flag, but then I arranged to be here when you returned. I will kill you, take the flag and avoid having to pay that foolish woman I hired."

"If you mean Sandra Paris, she's over there risking her life for you right now."

"Life is cheap in these parts. Lie down on the floor, please."

Nick turned instead to face him. "I knew you were the one who hired her."

"Did she tell you?"

"She didn't have to. When I met you in the New York consulate you knew enough to give me a new flag instead of the old one. That told me you were involved somehow in the conspiracy, whatever it was. Sandra still has the flag from Washington, although she told me the New York one was already delivered. That told me two things — how it was stolen and who hired her."

"You are a wise man, Mr. Velvet."

"She didn't have to deliver the consulate flag to you because you stole it yourself. I assumed all along that somehow she stole it from the doorway across the street where she sat watching, but in truth she was only making certain her device worked properly. It's the same trick stage magicians use to vanish a small object from their hands. You ran the flag out to the end of the pole with a heavy elastic band attached. Instead of hooking it to the halyard as usual, you merely secured it with tape. After a few minutes, when the pull of the elastic overcame the resistance of the tape, the flag came free and was yanked — not up the magician's sleeve, but down the pole and into the open window. Right into your hands. Of course the purpose of the entire charade was in case someone other than Sandra was watching, someone like me, so it would appear the flag had been truly stolen."

"You should have been a detective instead of a thief, Velvet."

"I've been told that before. Just how did you know my name?"

"We had a report that you had been hired by a private group with ties to the American government."

"Oh?" Nick thought about Art Schraeder and decided it was possible.

"Enough talk — lie down on the floor!"

"Don't I have a right to know the flags' big secret? I already know it involves the shape of the coastline on the seal in the center."

Christopher Onza seemed surprised. "One more reason why I can't leave you alive. National flags and seals have changed the course of history more than once, and we don't intend to let it happen again. If you remember your Central American history you know that Nicaragua lost the canal to Panama because the seal of the country showed an active volcano, which frightened members of the American Congress. In Coronado's case both our seal and flag show three sailing ships from the second voyage of Columbus at anchor in Coronado Bay, a place we have insisted to both the Americans and Cubans is too shallow to serve as a naval base. We now contend that Columbus landed at some uncertain place along the coast rather than in the bay. Our seal has been changed, and the flags were being changed too. Reproductions of the flag are too tiny to show the critical details, and our government thought that all of the flags themselves had been safely replaced. However when it became known the Americans were after one of them, I hired this woman Sandra Paris to steal the last three in use, before they got to them."

"What does your president think of all this? You're acting without his knowledge, certainly, or you wouldn't have needed to steal the flags. He could have ordered them withdrawn at once."

"Our president —" Onza began. He never finished the sentence.

The door burst open and the room was full of uniformed men with automatic weapons pointed at both of them.

Nick Velvet was an hour early for his flight back to New York that afternoon. He saw Sandra Paris seated in the private lounge of the airline club and went over to join her. "Going back to New York?" he asked.

She shook her head. "Los Angeles. I hope I have better luck there. I heard they found the flag in your room."

Nick nodded glumly. "It was right on the bed when the security police burst in. At least I'm alive. Your friend Onza was about to kill me."

"He's no friend of mine. He denies now that he ever hired me."

Nick ordered a couple of drinks for them. "How did your smoke bombs work? I saw them go off."

"They worked fine, and in the confusion I got the flag away from the honor guard. When I realized it was a new one I hesitated just long enough for them to capture me.

I figured if I was having a failed mission you might as well join me, so I gave them your room number. I do hope you didn't mind."

"As I say, it probably saved my life, even if it did cost me my twenty-five thousand dollar fee."

"Onza says you were working indirectly for the government."

"Apparently. I didn't know it till he told me. I suspect it was some sort of international pressure that got us freed so quickly. They wanted a flag to use as evidence of that deep harbor. Maybe our Secretary of State was planning to drop it on the table in front of their president. Onza was acting on his own, without the president's knowledge, which is why he had to hire you to steal the flags rather than simply take them himself. I suspect he was working out his own deal with Cuba for a naval base, and perhaps even planning a coup. He had to remove the flags before they fell into the wrong hands, and before the president learned of his special interest in them."

"Did Onza tell you how we stole the flag in New York?"

"Yes, but how did you work the theft in Washington? Was Leon Oeste an accomplice too?"

"No." She sipped her drink and smiled at him. "I hired an embassy maid to cut through the halyard in two places and glue the rope ends lightly together. The weight of the flag pulled them apart after a few minutes and the flag simply fell to the sidewalk, still attached to a section of the halyard. I picked it up and walked away. I was a newsboy that morning and the flag went into my sack of papers. You didn't see me."

"I saw you but I didn't recognize you."

She glanced at her watch. "My flight's boarding. It's been fun."

He walked her to the gate and watched while she boarded the plane. Once it was off the ground he sent a telegram to her at the Los Angeles airport, to be delivered upon her arrival.

Sandra: I only needed one flag so I removed the Washington embassy one from your suitcase last night while you slept. Climbing up two stories to your balcony wasn't easy, but it was worth it to see you so peacefully asleep in the moonlight. Nick.

The Theft of Leopold's Badge

On what was to be the most exciting and memorable day of her young life, Rita Mulroney arrived early at the Parker Museum of Fine Art. She'd been up before dawn in the hotel room she was sharing with Christina Black, checking her costume and reviewing the plan for the day's events. She'd moved heaven and earth with the casting director in Manhattan to win a spot as one of the nine muses in the day-long pageant, and she wasn't going to miss her big opportunity.

It was, in reality, an elaborate fund-raising activity for the benefit of the Parker Museum, beginning with "Breakfast with the Muses" at eight a.m. It was designed mainly to attract the community's business and financial leaders, who would be entertained by dancing girls while they breakfasted on eggs Benedict and hopefully pledged a generous sum for the museum's expansion. This would be followed by luncheon and dinner performances by the muses for other community and social leaders, all in the museum's Grand Atrium, surrounded by ten centuries of art treasures.

The nine muses, mostly modern dance students recruited in New York, had been in town for two nights already, and had held a dress rehearsal at the museum the previous evening, running through the simple dance numbers they'd be performing during each of the meals. Rita Mulroney had been cast as Erato, the muse of erotic poetry.

Leaving the hotel room at six-thirty, she shook Christina awake and told her the time. Then she hurried downstairs and found a taxi. She was at the back door of the Parker Museum before seven, and it was the director himself, Samuel Pearlman, who admitted her. He recognized her at once from the previous night's rehearsal. "It's Rita, isn't it? You're early. Sorry about this rain but I think it's stopped."

"I thought I'd change into my costume here and limber up a bit. The others should be along soon."

Pearlman was a balding, paunchy man in his early fifties who looked more like an old-style banker than the director of an art museum. He smiled at her a bit mechanically and directed her down the basement hall to the makeshift dressing room by the employees' lockers.

Rita's costume, which she carried in a tubular canvas tote bag, consisted of a flesh-colored body stocking, together with a toga-like garment whose color provided the dancers with their only individuality. Hers was saffron and her hotel roommate Christina would be wearing a pale blue. Rita unzipped her bag and quickly shed her street clothes. She'd barely gotten into her body stocking when the dressing room door opened to admit another woman. She was older than Rita, perhaps in her mid-thirties, but still quite attractive, with platinum-blonde hair framing a pale face.

"Hello, there," the woman said by way of greeting. "Are you one of the muses?" She was about Rita's size, with good legs.

"That's right." Rita was busy slipping into her saffron-colored toga. "Rita Mulroney."

The young woman smiled pleasantly. "Me too."

"You're a muse? I didn't see you at rehearsal last night."

"I'm filling in for one of the girls that's sick. My name is Sandra Paris." She started unbuttoning her dark blue raincoat.

Rita still wasn't quite convinced. "Where's your costume?"

"You're wearing it," Sandra Paris said, and her fist shot out to clip Rita on the jaw.

By the time Rita Mulroney came to, a few minutes later, Sandra was busy tying her hands and feet. The younger woman tried to scream but there was already a gag in her mouth, held in place with adhesive tape. "Now," Sandra said, hoisting her to her feet, "I'm going to put you in the maintenance closet across the hall. Just don't be too noisy, though, or something worse might happen to you. Understand me?"

Rita nodded, her eyes above the gag wide and terrified. Working fast, Sandra Paris checked the hallway to make sure it was still deserted, then carried the girl across to the closet, leaving her on the floor on a pile of rags. She returned quickly to the dressing room and came back with Rita's street clothes and her tote bag, throwing the coat over the girl and the rest on the floor beside her. "I wouldn't want you to catch cold on my account," she laughed.

She was back in the dressing room slipping into Rita's saffron toga as two other young women arrived.

They looked at her a bit uncertainly, and one of them asked, "Do you have the right costume?"

Sandra acted uncertain. "I think so."

"I'm Christina Black. At rehearsal last evening my roommate, Rita, was wearing that."

Sandra relaxed a bit. "That explains it! She was taken ill as soon as she arrived here and the director pressed me into service as a last-minute replacement."

Christina, a tall dark-haired girl with deep brown eyes, seemed uncertain. "Where is she? Did they take her to the hospital?"

"No, just back to her hotel. It's nothing serious."

The other dancers were drifting in, and Sandra introduced herself to them. "What about the routines?" Christina Black asked, still bothered. "Do you know them?"

Sandra passed it off easily. "Oh, sure. We did the same sort of thing up in Boston last month. These museum gigs are a cinch. The key is to look sexy without smiling. The muses never smile."

One or two of the dancers stared at her a bit distastefully, but all seemed to accept her for what she professed to be — a last-minute replacement. The nine girls were barely into their costumes when Samuel Pearlman, the museum director, appeared with the show's director and choreographer, a slim young man named Harvey Tort.

"Make it good," Pearlman told them. "We have to give these people something for being here at eight in the morning."

Harvey Tort gave them last-minute instructions as he herded them up the stairs to the Grand Atrium. A dozen large tables had been set up in this area, and breakfast was being served to the assembled business leaders. They were mostly male, Sandra noted, with only a scattering of middle-aged women in business suits. The other eight dancers quickly went into their act, but Sandra lingered by the sidelines, faking a few basic dance steps. Almost at once Harvey Tort spotted her and frowned. He started moving through the tables toward her side of the dance area.

Sandra spun around on her toes, out of the performance area, toward the near wall of the atrium, where an early van Gogh, one of the museum's prize acquisitions, hung in a place of honor. From beneath her saffron toga she pulled a small roadside flare. Yanking off the cap, she ignited it, and suddenly every eye in the room was on her. She gave them her best smile as she tossed the flare at the center of the van Gogh and watched it erupt in a flash of vivid flame.

Captain Leopold had visited the Parker Museum only once before, in the company of his wife Molly. By nature he was not a museum-goer, though he was secretly pleased when Molly made an effort to broaden his horizons. On that Tuesday morning in late September, the urgent call from Samuel Pearlman had brought both Leopold and Lieutenant Fletcher to the museum, where they found a police car, two fire engines and a chief's car already blocking the street in front of the building.

"We're all clear," the fire chief called out to Leopold. "The rest of it's your job."

"Thanks, Chief." Leopold went up the marble steps to the museum entrance with Fletcher at his side.

An overweight man with thin hair was waiting at the door for them. "I'm Samuel Pearlman, Inspector —"

"Captain. Captain Leopold. This is Lieutenant Fletcher. What's been going on here, sir?"

"A madwoman has destroyed one of our most valuable paintings — a van Gogh worth millions!"

Leopold followed him inside. "Who are all these people?"

"We were having a fund-raising breakfast as part of our expansion drive. Nearly a hundred business and civic leaders were invited."

Leopold recognized several of them now — a judge, some lawyers, a prominent real estate developer, a couple of bankers. But his attention was diverted at once to a scorched section of the atrium wall, where an empty frame about eighteen by twenty-four inches hung as a bleak reminder of the outrage. "Was the woman apprehended?" he asked the director.

"No. Somehow she escaped in all the smoke and confusion. She left this card stuck to the wall beneath the painting."

Leopold stared at it, uncomprehending:

THE WHITE QUEEN

Impossible Things Before Breakfast

"Check this out," he said, handing it to Fletcher. "See if anyone has a record on this person."

"She tied up one of the muses and took her place," Pearlman was explaining. "Luckily our choreographer found her."

"What muses?" Leopold asked.

"The show, the entertainment! We hired this fellow Harvey Tort to put on an entertainment while breakfast was served. He does this sort of thing for conventions and trade shows all the time. He hired nine dancers in New York to represent the nine muses. Thought it'd be appropriate with the museum setting."

"And this madwoman, as you call her, substituted herself for a muse?"

"Exactly! She hurled a lighted flare at the van Gogh painting and completely destroyed it."

Leopold stepped closer to the damage, running his forefinger over the inside of the slightly charred frame. The police photographer and fingerprint man had arrived, and after another moment's examination he turned it over to them. "Let's go talk to this muse she tied up," he suggested to the director.

Pearlman led the way to the basement room where a pale young woman wearing a body stocking and a raincoat sat huddled on a chair. A slender man and a dark-haired girl of about twenty were with her, trying to comfort her. The man proved to be Harvey Tort, who'd staged the dance of the muses. "You found her?" Leopold asked him.

He nodded. "After the trouble upstairs I realized that Rita hadn't been ill as that woman claimed. I came down to look for her and found her tied and gagged in a closet across the hall. I was calling her name when I heard a pail overturned in there. The door was unlocked and she was inside."

Leopold smiled at the young woman. She was a few years older than the dark-haired one, though still in her early twenties. Her eyes were red from her ordeal. "Could you tell me your name, Miss?"

"Rita Mulroney."

"I'm her roommate at the hotel," the dark-haired girl volunteered. "Christina Black. She left before me this morning."

Rita Mulroney nodded. "I was the first one here. Mr. Pearlman let me in. I was changing into my costume when this woman came in, older than the other muses."

"Can you describe her?"

"Good-looking, platinum-blonde hair, about my height, maybe in her mid-thirties."

Leopold made a few notes. "Now tell me just what happened."

"I was in here early, changing into my costume. When she arrived she said she was one of the muses, though she hadn't been at rehearsal. I asked where her costume was and she said I was wearing it. Then she socked me in the jaw." She worked her mouth a little. "It's still sore. She knocked me out for a minute or two, and the next thing I knew she had me tightly gagged and was tying my hands and feet. She must have known the others would be arriving any minute, because she carried me across the hall to that maintenance closet and left me there."

"Then what happened?"

"I struggled with my bonds for what seemed like an hour. I could hear sirens and a lot of commotion upstairs. Finally I was beginning to loosen the ropes around my hands when I heard Harvey calling my name. I was still gagged but I kicked my tote bag with my feet and managed to hit a metal pail. He heard the noise and found me."

"You didn't see this woman again after she tied you up?"

Rita shook her head. "But she told me her name. She said it was Sandra Paris."

"Probably fake, but we'll check it."

The dressing room the girls had used obviously served as a locker room for the museum's employees and security staff. A line of metal lockers stretched along one wall, with benches in front of them. Leopold opened some and saw the muses' street clothes hanging neatly. "Which was your locker?" he asked. Rita showed him and he opened the door. There was only a blue raincoat inside. "Is this yours?"

Rita frowned. "I think that belonged to Sandra Paris. You know, now that I think of it I don't believe she was wearing anything but underwear beneath it."

Leopold went quickly through the pockets, certain they'd be empty. What he found surprised him. It was an empty match flap on which had been written: 135YYZ.

He was still pondering this when Fletcher hurried in. "Captain, we've got trouble."

"This White Queen business?"

"No word on that yet, but Pearlman has found two more valuable paintings missing, cut from their frames."

"All right, I'll come look."

"That's not all."

"What else?"

"There's a dead man in the parking lot."

The body was slumped behind the wheel of a mini-van parked in the museum lot. One of Fletcher's men had spotted it while checking out the escape route this woman Sandra Paris must have used. The victim was a white male, and his driver's license gave them the rest of the information. "Name: Frederick Farley," Leopold read. "Thirty-one years old and lives in Rye, over in Westchester County. Has this car got New York plates?"

"Yeah," Fletcher confirmed, "I'll run a check on it."

"Shot once in the right temple. Powder burns. The killer was probably sitting next to him. Small caliber weapon. With the windows closed like this the sound wouldn't have carried far."

"You're thinking of a gang hit?" Fletcher asked.

"More likely a falling-out among thieves. Maybe this was meant to be her getaway car. But if that's the case, how did she get away?"

"The medical examiner's on his way. Maybe he can tell us the time of death."

Leopold studied the spots of blood on the dashboard. "Not too long. More than a couple of hours and this blood would be dried." He went around and glanced at the car's license number. It was nothing like *135YYZ*. He handed the match flap to Fletcher. "While you're checking out the car, run a check on this number too."

"License plate?"

"I don't know. Maybe."

The police photographer, finished inside the museum, had been summoned to the parking lot. Samuel Pearlman was right behind him. "What's this I hear about a murder?"

"Looks like it," Leopold confirmed. "Did you ever see this man before? His driver's license says he's Frederick Farley."

"No, the name means nothing to me."

"Take a look at him. A former employee, perhaps? One of your guards?"

Pearlman made a distasteful face as he peered through the window at the body. "No. Never saw him before."

Some of the others had come out too, led by Harvey Tort and a few of the muses. Tort also failed to identify the man and Leopold wasn't about to parade the city's business leaders past the body. Judge Wilbur did come forward, however. "How are you, Captain?"

"Good morning, Judge. Sorry your breakfast was interrupted."

Wilbur had a mane of white hair and the manner of a judge. Leopold often wished that he lived up to his appearance in the decisions and sentences he handed down from the bench. "I understand that madwoman killed someone in addition to destroying a painting."

Leopold didn't answer. Instead he said, "Excuse me, Judge," and moved away. "Mr. Pearlman, if you could show me where those paintings were stolen —"

"Right this way." The museum director led him through a side entrance and up a short flight of stairs. Halfway down the wall was an empty frame about eight by thirteen inches — smaller than the van Gogh. One of the uniformed museum guards stood by it.

The card beneath the empty frame identified the missing painting as a Matisse. "Worth how much?" Leopold asked.

"You're talking in the millions, just like the van Gogh that was destroyed. Here's the other one." On the opposite wall, further down the gallery, was another empty frame. "This was a Manet."

"Three of your most valuable paintings?"

"They certainly were. The French are bringing fabulous sums at art auctions these days."

"This one is twenty-one by seventeen inches." Leopold examined the frame. "Both cut out with a razor blade, I would guess. Where were your guards while this was happening?"

"When the fire alarm went off everyone hurried to the atrium. That woman destroyed the painting as a diversion so her partner, the man in the car, could get in and steal these two paintings."

"We've found no paintings in the car."

"Of course not! She killed him and took them herself."

"Possibly," Leopold conceded.

He ordered the fingerprint team to dust the area, but he already suspected they'd find nothing — just as he was certain in his own mind that there'd be no record of anyone called Sandra Paris or the White Queen.

On that he was wrong. As the body was being removed shortly before eleven o'clock, Fletcher hurried up to him. "The van belonged to the dead man. He's a small-time crook with a small-time record. This hardly seems like his type of job."

"Maybe someone hired him as a driver."

"Just what I was thinking, Captain. How about Sandra Paris?"

"Did you find anything under that name?"

"Sandra Paris, alias the White Queen. Several arrests, suspicion of robbery and grand theft, but only one conviction. She served eight months in New Jersey for stealing a roulette wheel from an Atlantic city casino."

"A roulette wheel?"

"Apparently she goes in for unusual or difficult thefts, always committed in the early morning, before breakfast. That *Impossible things before breakfast* is something the White Queen said in *Through the Looking Glass*. It's sort of a trademark with her."

"What about *135YYZ?*"

"No idea, Captain."

"At least we're not dealing with a madwoman, or with someone who would destroy a valuable painting simply to divert attention from the theft of two others."

"Everyone saw her destroy the painting," Fletcher pointed out.

"Then the impossible thing would be if she *didn't* destroy it."

The blue raincoat Sandra Paris had left behind was sent to the police lab, though Leopold doubted they'd find anything useful. It seemed inexpensive and newly purchased for the occasion.

At noon he noticed a number of cars driving up to the museum doors. "What's going on?" he asked Harvey Tort.

"Mr. Pearlman thinks we should proceed with the other fund-raisers. The dancers are here and the food is ordered. Even though the paintings are insured, he feels this morning's events make the necessity for expansion and tighter security more important than ever."

Leopold nodded. "I'll come up and watch," he decided.

The invited guests at the luncheon were mainly female — women who would consider themselves the social and artistic leaders of the community. Leopold watched them dine on elaborate-looking salads while being entertained by the nine dancing muses. The pitch for money would come at the end, and Samuel Pearlman stood at Leopold's side during the performance, waiting for the proper moment.

As the applause died down at the conclusion of the dance, Leopold asked him, "What would a thief do with those paintings? They're hardly something you take to the local fence."

"I imagine she'd try to get them out of the country. There are art collectors in Europe and the Far East who would pay vast sums with no questions asked."

"Out of the country," Leopold repeated, and glanced at his watch. It was five minutes to one.

As the girls ran by on their way down to the makeshift dressing room, he caught Rita Mulroney by the arm. "Come with me," he said.

"Where to'?"

Leopold chuckled. "Don't worry, you're not under arrest. I may need your help in identifying someone."

"Who?

"Sandra Paris." On the way out of the parking lot he yelled to Fletcher to follow him.

"Where to, Captain?"

"The airport. We've got to hurry."

Sandra Paris gave a final tug on her black wig and was satisfied with her appearance in the ladies' room mirror. She picked up the oversized briefcase and walked out just as her flight was being called. "Now boarding, Flight 348 to Toronto, Canada, with a 1:35 departure."

She paused at the security checkpoint while the uniformed woman eyed the briefcase. "That's too big for our x-ray. You'll have to open it."

"Gladly," Sandra said, unzipping the top and sides. "It's advertising art, for a client in Toronto."

"You'll have to show that to customs over there."

"No problem."

Sandra rezipped her case and started walking toward the line at her gate. There was a young woman standing with an older man and somehow she looked familiar. The woman was staring at her, and Sandra Paris suddenly remembered where she'd see her before, only six hours earlier.

"I think that's her," Rita Mulroney said. "Her hair is different, but —"

The older man — he must have been close to sixty — smiled and asked politely, "Sandra Paris?"

"You must be mistaken. My name is —"

"I'm Captain Leopold," he said, showing his badge. "I'll have to ask you to come with me for questioning."

She was thinking she could outrun this man any day of the week, and he wasn't likely to use his gun in an airport crowded with passengers. She started to turn and Leopold shouted, "Grab her, Fletcher," and suddenly there was another man pinning her arms.

They took her down to police headquarters and sat her on a hard wooden chair in the squad room while the one named Fletcher carefully read off her rights from a printed card. When he was finished, Leopold came out of his office holding one of the big advertising layouts from her briefcase, carefully matted, mounted and easeled. "You do advertising for the First Bank of Toronto?" he asked.

"That's one of my clients. It's for a full-page newspaper ad."

He stripped away the backing cardboard and carefully lifted out an oil painting of some farmers working in a wheat field. "I'm sure Mr. Pearlman will be delighted to recover the van Gogh he thought you destroyed this morning, Miss Paris. Where are the other two?"

"The other two what?"

"The paintings you stole along with this one."

"I don't know what you're talking about."

"We found Mr. Farley's body, Sandra," he said, switching to her first name. "We're talking about murder."

She sat for a full minute in silence. "Well?" Leopold asked.

Sandra Paris moistened her lips. "Do I get one phone call?"

"Certainly. Do you wish to call your lawyer?"

"No," she answered. "A friend over in Westchester. His name is Nick Velvet."

It had been a busy Tuesday afternoon for Nick Velvet. He and Gloria had decided the sailing season was over, and they'd been at the yacht club arranging winter storage for the boat. Then there were some calls to return on his answering machine, and some mail to read. He'd just opened a beer and settled down to relax when the phone rang again. He let the answering machine handle it until he heard a woman's voice saying, "Nick, this is Sandra Paris — " Then he picked up the receiver.

"Sandra! How are you?"

"Thank God you're there! I'm having a bad day."

"Where are you?"

"At the moment? In jail about fifteen miles east of you."

"Jail! What happened?"

"Can you come here? I got you out of jail once, and I was wondering if you might return the favor."

"Tell me where you are. I'll be there."

Nick explained to Gloria that Sandra Paris was in trouble. They hadn't seen her in a couple of years, but she had indeed rescued Nick from prison once, at Gloria's behest. "You'd better go see what you can do," Gloria agreed.

"It's right over the state line. I'll try to be back tonight."

He drove immediately to police headquarters where a man with graying hair and piercing blue eyes introduced himself as Captain Leopold. Nick had a feeling he wasn't the sort of cop you'd want on your tail. "I'm Nick Velvet. I've come to see Sandra Paris."

"Are you acting as her attorney?" Leopold asked.

"No, just a friend. I hope to get her out of here."

"Bail won't be set till morning, and there may be no bail in a capital case. She did tell you she's being held on suspicion of murder, didn't she?"

Nick didn't answer directly. "I'd like to speak with her."

"I suppose that's allowed, since she seems to have chosen you over a lawyer. Just what is your occupation, Mr. Velvet?"

"I'm a free-lance consultant."

Leopold led him to a private room used by lawyers. "I'll have Miss Paris brought in."

Nick waited only a few minutes before she appeared, opening the door and striding into the small, almost bare room as if in her own home. "Good to see you again, Nick."

His first thought was that she was still a very attractive woman. He'd sometimes fantasized about the two of them teaming up, using their combined talents, but Nick had been a loner for too long. Besides that, it was difficult to imagine, after all these years, a woman other than Gloria in his life. If there ever was one, though, it would be Sandra Paris.

"How did you end up here?" he asked.

She glanced around at the room. "Do you want the whole story? I imagine the walls have ears in this place."

"Tell me what you can."

"There's a fund-raiser going on today at the Parker Museum of Fine Art. They imported some dancers from New York to perform as the nine muses while about a hundred business leaders had breakfast in the gallery's main atrium. One of the girls claims I slugged her in the downstairs dressing room, and hid her in a broom closet, then took her place in the dance."

Nick smiled at the thought. "You've added dancing to your other talents?"

"Enough to get by. Anyway, then they say I lit a flare and tossed it at a van Gogh painting worth several million dollars, utterly destroying it."

Nick grinned again. "Up in flames. I'll bet not a shred of canvas remained."

"You've got it. Of course I escaped during the uproar, but here's the complication. While escaping, they have me cutting two more valuable paintings from their frames and then pausing in the parking lot to put a bullet through the head of my boyfriend and getaway driver."

"I thought you worked alone, like me."

"Of course I do! The whole thing is ridiculous, but how do I prove it? How do I get myself out of this mess?"

"It seems as if someone took advantage of your presence to do a little work of their own."

"But who was the man in the car and why was he killed? I certainly didn't need him. I had my own rental car."

"How did they catch you?"

She bowed her head. "I'm embarrassed to tell you, Nick. So I could change fast into the muse costume, I left my dress in the car and just wore a cheap raincoat over my underwear. I abandoned it there and left a match flap in the pocket with my flight time and destination on it. *135YYZ.* That was 1:35, and I used the airport code for Toronto, YYZ, the way some people refer to Los Angeles as LAX for its airport code. Even after I realized I'd left it in the pocket I wasn't worried. I didn't think there wasn't a cop in town smart enough to figure it out before my plane left."

"And?"

"There was one. His name is Leopold."

Nick Velvet nodded. "I met him."

"But I've talked enough."

Maybe too much, Nick was thinking, if they had the room bugged. "What do you want me to do?"

"Get me out of here."

"That might not be too easy. You've got to tell me the truth, Sandra. Do you have any idea who killed the man in the car?"

"No."

"Or who stole those other two paintings?"

"No."

"But they did find the van Gogh in your possession. That one's going to be hard to deny."

"I'm depending on you, Nick. I did the same for you once."

What she'd done for him was to pose as a matron and help him escape from jail. He didn't feel up to duplicating her feat, though he'd come prepared for something similar. Still, perhaps there was another way. "Let me talk to this Captain Leopold and see what he's got. Meanwhile, write out for me every detail of what you did in there."

She wrote for about ten minutes on a lined legal pad, then tore off the sheets and handed them to him in silence. Nick glanced over them, reading the details of her entering the museum, substituting the color reproduction for the real van Gogh, hiding the van Gogh in the basement near the door to the parking lot, and then attacking Rita Mulroney. *I couldn't risk a guard stopping me on the way out with the van Gogh under my coat,* she'd written. *I had to divert them with the flare and the resulting fire. I was able to retrieve the painting and make my escape. The apparent destruction of the van Gogh served another purpose too. I knew they'd discover soon enough it wasn't canvas that burned, but it would give me a few hours to be on a plane out of the country before they realized the painting was stolen and not destroyed.*

Nick read the whole thing once more, carefully, and then hid it away in an inside pocket.

He found Leopold waiting for him in a little glass-enclosed office off the squad room. The detective captain was having a cup of coffee and Nick joined him, though at the moment he felt more in need of a cold beer. "Have you finished speaking with your client?" Leopold asked with a smile that was more ironic than friendly.

"I'm not really an attorney, Captain. I'm sure Miss Paris explained that to you."

"She did. I don't quite understand why you're here, Mr. Velvet, but of course we ran a check on you." He held up several sheets of paper. "These fax machines are great little gadgets. I don't know how we ever managed without ours. I had a report on Sandra Paris earlier in the day, and now I have one on you." He raised his eyes from the papers. "Yours is longer than hers."

Nick smiled slightly. "I'm older. More years on the job."

"Do people really hire you to steal items of little or no value?"

"There have been stories to that effect."

"Quite a few arrests here, but no convictions. Isn't that strange?"

"I'm no criminal, Captain. I perform a service. Today I'm here to see about obtaining the release of Sandra Paris."

"There isn't any possibility of that at this stage. The district attorney is requesting she be held without bail."

"The painting was recovered," Nick reminded him.

"The other two haven't been, and there's the murder charge as well."

"You have no evidence implicating her in that or anything else."

"We have Rita Mulroney's statement of what happened. Here it is."

Nick read it over. "Has the fax machine identified the dead man?"

"His driver's license did that. Fellow named Frederick Farley, from Rye, New York. You come from over that way, don't you?"

"I do, but I never heard of Farley."

Leopold picked up another sheet of paper. "Small-time hood. Handsome, though. The sort someone like Sandra Paris might have teamed up with."

"She didn't. She works alone."

"You're telling me she pulled off that museum stunt alone? I don't believe that."

"I could pull it off alone," Nick said. "I could duplicate it."

"And destroy another painting? Not a chance!"

"You're still convinced the van Gogh was destroyed? Then what did you find in her briefcase?"

"I don't know," Leopold admitted. "Maybe a copy. It's being examined right now by the museum's director, Mr. Pearlman."

"If I stole something other than a painting in exactly the same manner would you believe it could be done?"

"What would that prove about the killing?"

"You believe that Sandra's destruction of the van Gogh was merely a diversion so she could steal the other two paintings and kill her partner. Is that a fair statement?"

"I'm leaning toward that theory," Leopold admitted, "but I'm not committed to it. When I examined the van Gogh frame, after the fire, it seemed to me that the painting might have been cut out of it. I just don't know how she managed it in full view of a hundred people."

"I'll show you," Nick promised.

"What are you going to steal?"

He leaned back on his chair, watching the captain's eyes. "As you know, it has to be of little or no value. I'm not giving you an excuse to arrest me too." He thought for just a second and said, "How about your badge?"

"No, you're not pulling anything like that."

"Come on, it's something personal that I can't duplicate on the spot. I have no idea what the number on it is, so you can easily verify that I stole the real thing. And I promise to return it immediately after the demonstration."

"If you don't succeed?"

"Then I go back home and leave Sandra Paris to you and the courts. If I do convince you that her actions were completely separate from the other crimes, then we take it from there."

Leopold thought about it. Finally he nodded. "All right, where do you intend your theft to take place?"

"At the Parker Museum of Fine Art, of course. Where else? All I need from you are the sizes of the other two missing paintings."

Nick took his own car and made just one quick stop on the way. He pulled into the surprisingly full parking lot only moments after Leopold, who was still standing by his unmarked car. A younger man was with him, and Leopold introduced him as Lieutenant Fletcher.

"This seems like a busy place," Nick commented, carrying a flat thin package. "I thought it would close up after a robbery."

"Ordinarily I imagine they would, but they're launching a fund-raising campaign," Leopold explained. "They scheduled breakfast, luncheon and dinner events today for prospective donors. The dinner guests should be arriving within the hour. That man walking toward us is Harvey Tort, who handled the muses' choreography."

Tort seemed upset to find the police back on the scene. "What is it now, Captain? I hope you're not going to question my girls again. Some of them are very nervous. The robbery was bad enough. When they learned of the murder they were ready to head back to New York."

"Will they be going back tonight?"

Tort nodded, "As soon as we finish this performance."

Nick glanced at his watch. "What time do you start?"

"Our performance is at seven."

"Plenty of time, but I think we might avoid the crowd by using another part of the museum. Lead the way, Captain."

They entered the side door off the parking lot and immediately encountered two of the costumed muses. Leopold spoke to them both and introduced Nick. "This has been a terrible day," the tall, dark-haired girl insisted. "Only one more dance and we're out of here! I've never been so frightened in my life."

Nick smiled at her. "Are you the one who was knocked out by the woman thief?"

"No, I'm Christina. That was Rita here."

The other young woman stepped forward with a hesitant smile. "I'm Rita Mulroney. Do I have to answer more questions?"

"If you could run quickly through what happened —"

"She popped me on the jaw and when I woke up she had me bound and gagged, very tight. She hauled me across the hall to a closet and dumped me on the floor, and my things after me." Nick nodded. Sandra's written account has been truthful "Later when I heard fire engines and all the commotion I managed to kick out with my feet and make some noise. Harvey found me and untied me."

The choreographer nodded. "By that time the damage had been done. One painting destroyed and two others stolen, plus a man shot to death in the parking lot." He took out his car keys. "If you'll excuse me, Captain, I have to get clean togas for the dancers."

Nick watched the three of them till they reached a blue van at the side of the lot. It reminded him of something. "How did Sandra get from here to the airport?" he asked Leopold.

"The same way she got here in the first place. A rental car. We found the papers for it in her purse, and the car had been returned to the agent at the airport."

Nick grunted.

"What does that mean?"

"Well, I just assumed you thought the dead man in the parking lot was her accomplice and getaway driver. But she didn't need one, did she?"

"We're still working on their relationship," Leopold admitted. "But what about stealing my badge? Have you given up on that?"

"Not at all. Let's go take a look at where those other two paintings were stolen."

They reentered the wing of the building off the parking lot, one level below the Grand Atrium where the dinner and performance were to be held. Nick was aware that Lieutenant Fletcher's eyes never left him, and he knew he was in grave danger of ending up in a cell next to Sandra's. He followed Leopold along a corridor lined with paintings on both walls, until the gray-haired detective stopped before an empty frame.

"Here's one, the other is over there."

Nick peered closely at the frame. There was no damage to it at all, only a few strands of canvas along the inner edges where a sharp razor blade had done its work well. "Was the painting you found in Sandra's possession cut out in the same manner?"

"It seemed to be. Only the witnesses all swear she couldn't have done it. They saw the painting burnt up."

"Well, I think I can duplicate anything Sandra Paris comes up with." He took a piece of stiff paper from the flat package he'd been carrying. "I stopped at an art supply store on the way over and had this cut to the exact size we need to fit the frame — eight by thirteen inches." He quickly secured it to the frame with bits of tape. "Now if you'll take your badge, Captain, and pin it to this stiff paper, exactly in the center —"

Leopold and Fletcher exchanged glances. Then, with some reluctance, he removed his leather identification holder from an inside coat pocket and unpinned the badge. He walked up to the frame and attached it to the center of the stiff white paper.

"I'll have to ask both you and the lieutenant to move back," Nick told them. "I'm going to use a flare just like she did upstairs, and I don't want anyone injured."

"I don't know about this," Leopold said, having second thoughts.

"Have Lieutenant Fletcher get a fire extinguisher from the wall down there. I'm sure the fire won't spread, but he can keep it ready if that'll ease your mind."

"You'd better do it, Fletcher, just in case. Pearlman would have our hides if anything else is damaged."

Fletcher went down to retrieve the fire extinguisher while Nick stepped up to the frame and made a final adjustment. "There! That's just right. Both of you stand back, now. A little further. I don't want any accidents." He took a highway flare from his jacket pocket.

"Where'd you get that?" Leopold demanded.

"From my car. Most auto first aid kits are equipped with them."

They were standing about twenty-five feet from the frame where Leopold's badge was on display. Nick tore off the end of the flare, igniting it, and tossed it with a sure aim right at the badge.

There was a sudden flash of light and flame, and Fletcher lifted the nozzle of the fire extinguisher. "Wait!" Leopold cautioned, holding up his hand. The flare fell harmlessly to the floor.

The fire burned down to some charred paper, barely scorching the frame. Leopold's badge was nowhere to be seen. It wasn't in the frame, or on the floor beneath it. The badge was simply gone.

"A good trick, Mr. Velvet," Leopold commented. "You should go on the stage. Now where is it?"

Nick Velvet smiled. He dropped a hand into his pocket and took out Leopold's badge, handing it to him. "Now are you convinced that Sandra Paris could have done it too?"

The first thing Leopold checked was the badge number — 946. It was his, all right. No mistake about that. His immediate reactions were mixed. The man was nothing but a clever criminal, and yet Leopold had to admire the way he'd brought it off, with Fletcher and him both watching.

"How'd he do that, Captain?" Fletcher asked.

"The only time he came in contact with the badge at all was while you were getting the fire extinguisher. He made the switch then, when he walked up to the frame to adjust the badge. His back blocked it from my view, just for an instant."

"That's all I needed," Nick said. He was smiling, enjoying himself.

"Switched it for what?" Fletcher wanted to know. "If he switched it for another badge, what happened to that one?"

Leopold turned to Nick Velvet. "Do you want to answer?"

"Not just yet. I think we have to reach an agreement on Sandra Paris first."

"Let's go sit down," Leopold suggested. "This might take a while." The music was beginning upstairs, and Fletcher decided it might be wise to keep an eye on things up there.

"We've had enough surprises for one day," he said.

There were a pair of chairs at the end of the corridor, and though they looked like antiques Leopold could see no warning that they couldn't be sat upon. He took one and motioned Velvet to the other. "I'm not as good on my feet as I used to be," he explained. "Just a year from retirement and some days my wife doesn't think I should wait that long. But then people like Sandra Paris and Nick Velvet come to town, and it makes the whole thing worth while."

"I'm glad of that," Nick replied.

"Tell me your theory of what happened."

"Well, you're investigating three different crimes here — the theft of the van Gogh that Sandra pretended to burn, the theft of the other two paintings from this lower corridor, and the death by shooting of the man in the car."

"Frederick Farley."

"Yes, Farley. I believe your mistake was in trying to hang all three crimes around Sandra's pretty neck." He shifted in his seat. "I think I can show you how unlikely it is that Sandra committed either of the other crimes. First of all, the other two paintings. Your original theory was that she threw the flare at the van Gogh as a diversion while Farley cut the other two paintings from their frames. Then she went out to the parking lot, killed Farley and took them."

"What's wrong with that?"

"Several things. First, if Sandra stole the other two paintings, where are they? Why weren't they with the van Gogh when you grabbed her at the airport? Second, assuming Farley was an accomplice and getaway driver, why did she need him when she had a rental car waiting for her?"

"I told you she needed him to steal the other paintings," Leopold replied, exasperated.

Nick shook his head. "That would make sense if the van Gogh business was merely a diversion, but it wasn't. She was after that painting and she got it. She entered the museum early, posing as one of the dancers, and sliced it from its frame while the guards weren't looking. A skillful person can do it in seconds, as museum directors are discovering to their sorrow. Then she went downstairs and attacked Rita Mulroney."

"But the painting was still there when the muses began their performance," Leopold objected.

"What people saw, if they bothered to glance in that direction at all with so much else going on, was a full-color reproduction of the van Gogh, actual size, no doubt cut from a poster or a coffee table art book. It wouldn't fool anyone for a minute, unless they were twenty feet away with their minds on something else. That's what burned up so quickly, no doubt aided by a sheet or two of flash paper. You should know that an oil painting on canvas wouldn't burn that fast, and a thrown flare probably wouldn't even ignite it."

"Flash paper?" Leopold repeated.

"Chemically treated tissue paper that magicians often use. It disappears instantly with a bright flash when set afire."

Leopold began to see it then. "That's the same thing you used just now."

"Yes," Nick Velvet admitted. "It helped the trick."

"But the badge —"

"I happened to have a detective's badge like yours with me. On the way here, when I stopped at that art supply shop, I was able to use a color copying machine. Nearly flat objects like badges reproduce quite well on sheets of paper. The effect is almost three-dimensional. Of course the badge number was different from yours, but I knew you'd be too far away to see that. I had to keep you both away so it would still look like a real badge to you."

"You substituted that color copy when you went to adjust the badge."

"It was behind the top sheet all the time, with flash paper behind it. I simply loosened the tape and slid the sheet of heavy paper with your badge under my jacket. When I stepped away the badge — or its double — was still there. If the position was off by half an inch you didn't notice it."

"And you just happened to have that duplicate badge with you." Then Nick grinned, and Leopold knew there was still something being held back. He decided not to press it, but said instead, "You gave me two reasons why Sandra only stole the van Gogh. Any others?"

Nick nodded. "Yes, she was dancing with the others when you say the paintings were stolen and Farley was shot. Farley may have stolen the paintings, but when did she have time to shoot him? After she threw the flare? She was lucky to escape in the confusion. She certainly wouldn't have lingered to shoot her partner and search for the paintings. She'd have hopped in the van with him and waited till later to kill him. Besides, where could she conceal a gun in that skimpy costume?"

"Maybe he had the gun and she got it away from him."

"More *time*, Captain! Don't you see, she didn't have the time!"

"You make a pretty good case," Leopold had to admit. "But if Sandra Paris didn't kill him and take those other pictures, who did?"

"Someone who took advantage of Sandra's caper to do a little thieving of their own. The trouble is, that theory doesn't explain the dead man in the parking lot."

Samuel Pearlman came down the stairs at that moment and saw them seated there. "Please, gentlemen, those chairs are not to be sat upon."

"Sorry," Leopold said, rising at once. Nick Velvet moved a bit slower. "How about the painting we recovered? Is it the real van Gogh?"

"Yes, thank, God! The muses are just completing their dance. After the main course is served I'll unveil it for the guests."

"Is Harvey Tort taking the dancers back to New York in his van?" Leopold asked.

"No, just to the train station. Ten people in the van would be a bit uncomfortable for a long ride. They'll pick up their gear in the locker room and head for the station."

He went off by himself, leaving Leopold and Nick standing next to the chairs. "Everyone has a van these days," Leopold observed. "Tort has one, and the murdered man had one."

"I wonder if they looked anything alike," Nick said.

They went up to the parking lot where the first girls were arriving with their totes and raincoats. The evening had turned pleasant and the coats were no longer needed. "Bad guess," Leopold said at once. "Tort's van has windows in the side and it's dark blue. Farley's was small and a light gray color. It was a mini-van."

But Nick wasn't even looking at the van. He was staring at something else, at Christina Black's tote bag as she handed it to Harvey Tort. "Captain, if I give you the murderer, and the missing paintings, can Sandra Paris go free?"

"I don't know about that. There are still the charges —"

"Hurry up! Yes or no!"

Leopold took a deep breath. "Yes, I'd see what could be done."

"Good." Nick stepped up to the line of dancers and tapped one of them on the shoulder. "Excuse me, could I inspect your tote, please?"

Leopold saw the little pistol appear from nowhere — saw it come up fast to aim at Nick. He moved more quickly than he had in months, knocking the girl to the parking-lot pavement as the gun slid away across the asphalt. Then he had her in his grasp, pinning her to the ground, as Fletcher ran up from somewhere to lend a hand, turning the twisted, angry face toward them.

It was the face of Rita Mulroney.

Fletcher had handcuffed her, read her rights from the printed card he carried, and taken her to their car. Nick was left with Captain Leopold. "I guess I have to thank you," he told the detective. "It looks like you saved my life back there."

"I don't quite understand what I did," Leopold admitted, "but when you asked to see her tote bag she went for her gun. I'll admit it surprised me. Rita Mulroney was the only person who couldn't have stolen those paintings and killed Farley. She was bound and gagged in a closet the entire time."

Nick shook his head. "You're looking at it wrong, Captain. She's the only one who could have done it. Maybe it's the sort of case that needed a criminal mind to solve it. You see, I was convinced, for the reasons I outlined earlier, that Sandra Paris was not responsible for the theft of the other two paintings or the killing of Farley. Yet the paintings were stolen, and Farley, with his criminal record, certainly seemed involved. I had to face the fact that two separate thieves chose today to rob the Parker Museum. Coincidence? Of course — but not as major a one as you might think. The fund-raising events had been well-publicized, and gaining access to the museum by posing as one of the dancers must have appealed equally to Rita Mulroney and Sandra. They went about it in different ways, with Rita managing to get herself hired as one of the muses in New York."

"What about Farley?"

"At that point she thought she needed a getaway driver. She'd arrived with the other dancers, but she planned to escape as soon as she had the paintings. That meant someone had to be there with a car for her. And Farley's presence was the clue that pointed to her."

Harvey Tort came up and asked when the rest of them would be allowed to leave. It was growing dark in the parking lot, and the lights had been turned on. "A few more minutes," Leopold told him. "Go on, Nick."

"Of all the people in the museum, who would have needed a getaway car? Certainly not the guests or any of the staff or guards. Not the director, Samuel Pearlman. These people would have branded themselves as guilty if they'd fled the scene. Also, of course, the staff people wouldn't need the fund-raising event to gain access to the place. They worked there every day. If Farley was the getaway driver, he had to have been working with one of ten people — Harvey Tort, or one of the nine muses."

"I'll buy that," Leopold agreed. "If Pearlman stole the Manet and Matisse painting on the spur of the moment, after Sandra's theft, he wouldn't have had Farley on the scene."

"Which of the ten could have done it? Tort was upstairs with the dancers the whole time. You told me Sandra only danced a few steps before hurling the flare. So he wouldn't have had time to slip away unnoticed. Christina Black and the other seven legitimate muses were in full view of all the guests. Only Rita Mulroney was missing. Only she could have used that brief time to slice the paintings from their frames. More important, only Rita knew that another robbery was afoot. With Sandra Paris to take the blame, Rita no longer needed her getaway driver. She had a perfect alibi, and could safely return to New York with the other dancers. Better yet, the stolen paintings were all hers, with no need to cut Farley in on the proceeds. She took a small pistol from her tote bag, slipped into her coat, and shot him in his car, stopping to steal the paintings before or after. Then she returned to the maintenance closet, retied herself the best she could, and when she heard the sirens and uproar she made some noise so she'd be found. Sandra would be blamed for the killing."

"Wait a minute!" Leopold protested. "You're forgetting that Sandra Paris left her tied tightly hand and foot, wearing only a dancer's body stocking. How did she get free in the first place?"

"I said it was the sort of case that needed a criminal mind to solve it, Captain. Rita came to the museum to steal those paintings, to slice them from their frames with a razor blade after she finished her dance. The razor blade — probably more than one — had to be taped to her body where she could reach it when she needed it. She reached it after Sandra left her tied hand and foot, and used it to slice through one of the ropes, enough to get free."

"And she put on her raincoat and got out and cut the paintings from the frames. So where are the canvases?"

Nick had been holding Rita Mulroney's tote bag. He bent and unzipped it. "They're here, curved to fit inside a special pocket in the bag's outer lining."

He pulled them free and handed them over. "The larger painting is only twenty-one by seventeen inches — they both fit easily into the tubular side of this bag."

Leopold sighed and held out his hand. "I have to thank you, Velvet. You should have been a detective."

"Now what about Sandra Paris?"

At ten o'clock the following morning, Sandra was led into the courtroom. Nick had already spoken to her and told her everything had been explained to Judge Wilbur.

The judge himself peered down at her from the bench, and she remembered him from the breakfast performance the previous morning. "Sandra Paris, the charge against you has been reduced to malicious mischief. How do you plead?"

"Guilty, your honor."

"I'm sentencing you to thirty days in jail, but I'm suspending the sentence due to extenuating circumstances. You are also fined five hundred dollars." He banged his gavel. "Next case!"

In the car Nick told her everything that had happened. "Well," she said as he concluded, "I asked you to get me out of jail and you did it. But I still don't understand how you happened to have a detective's badge from this police department in your pocket."

Nick smiled as he turned onto the Turnpike toward Westchester County. "You got me out of jail once by posing as a prison matron. I'd planned to impersonate a detective to get you out. As it happened, the badge came in handy in a different way."

"That Leopold's no dope."

Nick agreed. "I think we'd both better stay out of his city in the future."

The Theft of the Bald Man's Comb

It had been more than a year since Nick Velvet's last encounter with Sandra Paris, a thief who some found more audacious than Nick himself. Using the name of the White Queen, and the Wonderland motto *Impossible things before breakfast*, she had carved a niche for herself in the world of bizarre crime. The rivalry between Sandra Paris and Nick had settled down to an amiable understanding, with a conscious effort to avoid each other's territory. Thus it was a bit of a surprise when she invited him to join her for breakfast at the Waffle House on route 22.

"Good morning, Sandra," Nick greeted her, sliding into the red plastic booth. "You're looking as charming as ever."

She smiled in return. "A compliment, this early in the morning!"

"That's when you're at your best, isn't it? Before breakfast?" He glanced at the menu and then tossed it aside. "What've you been doing with yourself? I haven't seen any mention in the papers lately."

"In our profession we work best without publicity. You know that, Nick." They ordered breakfast from a pert waitress and over orange juice she continued, "I want to hire you for a job."

"That's a bit unusual, isn't it? After you called me in on that museum business —"

"This is different. A woman has approached me with a very good offer. I find I cannot fulfill the commission, yet I hate to turn down the money and admit to failure."

"Suppose you tell me the whole story, Sandra, from the beginning."

"This is in a southern state, back in the hills. You'll get the exact location if you agree to take on the assignment. The woman who contacted me hired me to steal a comb —"

"Something valuable?"

"No, just an ordinary pocket comb that a man carries around with him."

"Who is the man?"

"His name is Willie Franklin. He and his two brothers live in the remotest part of the hill country. He rarely ventures into town at all. Some say he operates a still and that's why he stays out of sight."

"Do they have illegal stills these days? It sounds like something from thirty or forty years ago."

"Whatever he's doing, he stays out of sight. He and his brothers are said to live in an abandoned water mill on the Casaqueek River. I drove down there last week, Nick." She leaned forward across the table, more lovely and intense than he'd ever seen her before. "That's a man's country. The women — well, maybe they're not barefoot and pregnant but they might as well be. As soon as I drove into town the word was all over the county. I went up to the mill to look around early one morning —"

"Before breakfast."

"Sure, before breakfast! All I got for my trouble was a couple of rifle shots that came so close I could feel the breeze. Back in town someone let the air out of my tires, and the next morning I found a dead dog in the back seat of my car. That was enough for me!"

"So you want to subcontract the job."

"I never thought I'd say this, Nick, but it takes a man. There's no way I could pull it off, even if I went down there wearing a beard and a peg leg."

"How much?"

"Your regular fee."

"How much are *you* getting, Sandra?"

She pressed her lips together. "Fifty," she said quietly.

"I'll take forty."

"What? Your usual fee is only —"

"You need me, don't you?"

"I need you," she admitted. "Forty it is."

"Now tell me about the man with the comb. What's he look like?"

"Willie Franklin. He's the oldest of the brothers. All I saw was a group photo of the boys taken at their mother's seventieth birthday party last year. I have it here."

She passed Nick a color snapshot of three men in patterned shirts and jeans, squinting into the sun. The one in the middle was completely bald, with no facial hair. The one on the right wore a neatly trimmed mustache, while the other had a full beard that obscured much of his face. "The bearded one is the youngest," Sandra explained. "He's Jud Franklin, in his late twenties. On the right is Jessie. He's maybe thirty-five. Willie is in the middle."

"The bald one?" Nick asked incredulously.

Sandra Paris sighed. "That's right. I want you to steal a comb from a bald man."

Two days later Nick Velvet flew south to the area of the Casaqueek Hills, renting a car at the airport for the final portion of the journey. He'd considered making the entire trip by car, but decided his New York license plates would attract too much attention in the southern hill country.

West Alum, the place he sought, was little more than a crossroads by the Casaqueek River, with a bar, a general store, a volunteer fire company and a small church occupying the four corners. Nick assumed there'd been an East Alum at one time across the rickety wooden bridge, but there was no sign of it now. He parked in the cinder lot next to the bar and went inside. It was as good a place to start as any.

The bartender was a middle-aged man named Andre whom Nick suspected might have drifted up to West Alum from the Cajun country to the south. "Just passing through?" he asked, setting a glass and a bottle of beer in front of Nick.

"Looking for the Franklin family, actually. Drove over from the state capital to settle an insurance claim they've had outstanding."

"The old lady lives up the Post Road. Take the first right over the bridge. It's on the left, about a half-mile up the road."

"Are the sons up there too?"

"Sometimes. Mostly not. They're up in the hills somewhere. The old lady has a black handyman stays with her."

"Mr. Franklin is deceased?"

"Died of cancer a long time ago."

Nick finished his beer and went back to the car. Down the road a bit he could see the sign for the motel where Sandra Paris had stayed. At the risk of getting a dead dog in his car too, he drove down and took a room for the night. Then he returned to the bridge and headed up to the Franklin place.

It proved to be a few acres on the side of a hill, with a tethered German shepherd that started growling as soon as he pulled up in front of the farmhouse. A short white-haired woman came to the door and called him off, then asked Nick, "What you want?"

"I'm looking for a . . . Willie Franklin," Nick told her, pretending to consult some papers from a briefcase he was carrying. "It's about an insurance claim."

"That's my son Willie. My oldest. Don't know anything about no insurance claim, though."

"Mrs. Franklin —"

"I'm Cassy. Everyone calls me Cassy." She smiled when she said it, and he could see the remnants of beauty there, even at the age of seventy-one.

"Well, Cassy, is your son at home?"

"Willie don't live here. He has a place over the hill with his brothers."

"Could you give me directions?"

"He's not friendly toward visitors. I never been there myself."

"He'll be friendly toward me. I have a check covering storm damage to his mill."

"Damage to the mill?" She frowned at that, trying to understand. "He never mentioned anything to me." A strand of white hair drifted over her face and she pushed it away.

"It was fairly minor. He probably didn't want to bother you. Is this mill on your property?"

"No, it's —" She waved her hand toward the crest of the hill. "— over there someplace."

"You see, I need his signature before I can deliver the check. That's why I couldn't simply mail it."

"Maybe Gus can help you," She suggested, waving toward a tall black man who'd just appeared around the corner of the house. "Gus, this gentleman is looking for Willie. See if you can help him. I have to take Lucky inside."

Gus's hair was almost as white as hers, though Nick judged his age to be no more than sixty. His skin was relatively light, but the hair, lips and general features left no doubt as to his race. He appeared to have spent a lifetime working outdoors. "What can I do for you?" he asked.

"I'm Nicholas, from State Liability and Life Insurance. I have a check for Willie Franklin, but I need his signature. Could you show me the way to his place?"

"The boys don't like visitors."

"Oh, they'll like me!"

Gus thought about that. "They've been known to shoot at strangers."

"Not if you're along." He reached for his wallet. "Look, I'm so anxious to get this matter settled that it's worth ten bucks if you can take me up there."

He shrugged. "I'll take you. Leave the car here. The shortest way is up over the hill."

Nick locked the car and set off on foot with the tall black man, climbing up the hill to a point where they could gaze on the meandering route of the river through two counties. "It's quite a sight," Nick agreed.

"It's nice like this in the spring, with all the new growth on the trees."

"You've probably seen a lot of springs here."

Gus turned to him. "Been with Mr. and Mrs. Franklin most of my life. They only had the one child when I came."

"What happened to Mr. Franklin?"

"Died of cancer about fifteen years back. She's been alone since then. I do what I can, but the boys don't help much."

"She never had a daughter?"

The black man shook his head. "There was another son, Tom, but he took off when he was seventeen. Went out west somewhere, I hear."

"When was that?"

"Twelve years, maybe. He's between Jessie and Jud in age. Yeah, I've seen them all."

"But the boys don't come home much any more."

"They like livin' up at the old mill. Willie and his mother don't get along, and none of them ever got married."

"It happens in the best of families."

They hiked a bit further in silence, until another bend in the river became visible far below. "There it is," Gus said, pointing a bony finger. Nick could see a large building constructed of brown timbers, set at the edge of the water. The window frames were painted white and an unmoving mill wheel was orange. Though the building belonged to another era, some effort had been made to brighten it up. As they started down the hill through a stand of trees, Nick glimpsed a figure moving out the door of the mill. Almost at once they heard the crack of a rifle being fired.

Nick dropped to the ground but Gus merely laughed. "You're not used to country ways. If he was shootin' at us he'd have come a lot closer than that. It was just a warning because he don't know who we are."

He went out to the edge of the trees, shouting and waving his hands. Nick could see the bearded man with the rifle now — that would be Jud, the youngest — putting down his weapon and going back inside. If they weren't to be shot, they weren't exactly being greeted, either.

It took them another ten minutes to make their way down the steep hillside to the mill. Up close the building was more dilapidated than Nick had thought earlier. He could see bits of light showing through gaps in the side walls, and even the paint around the windows was chipped and peeling.

Two of the brothers came out to greet them. Jud reclaimed his rifle, leaning against the wall, but said nothing. The other, with a mustache and bright blue eyes like his mother, asked, "Who's this you've brought us, Gus?"

"He's an insurance man with a check for Willie. For damage to the mill."

The brothers exchanged puzzled looks. "There's no damage to the mill."

"Storm damage," Nick added quickly. "A claim was filed. Perhaps your mother filed it and doesn't remember. I'm Mr. Nicholas from State Liability and Life —"

"See if Willie knows about this," Jessie told his younger brother. Jud went off, taking the rifle with him.

Gus was shifting uneasily from one foot to the other. "I gotta get back to your mom," he told Jessie. "She'll wonder where I am."

Jessie turned his pale blue eyes toward Nick. "Can you find your way back, Mr. Nicholas?"

"I think so."

"Go ahead then, Gus. We'll see you around."

As the black man started doggedly up the hill, Jessie smiled. "Moves damn well for his age. Gettin' toward seventy, Gus is."

"He looks younger."

"Handsome man in his day. We always thought he was on the run from something, else why spend his life up here?"

"It's nice country," Nick observed. There was a slight odor in the air that he couldn't quite place. He wondered what an illegal still smelled like.

Jud came back then, still carrying the rifle. "He don't know anything about insurance, and there hasn't been any damage. He says it's a mistake."

Nick took the check from his briefcase. "Here it is, all signed and legal. Three hundred and fifty-four dollars in full payment of the claim. All I need is his signature."

Jessie reached out his hand. "I'll take that up to Willie and get him to sign for it. He can't leave his job right now."

"What's he doing that's so important?"

"Business. We all have our business, don't we?"

"I'm sorry, but the release has to be signed in my presence. I have to verify his signature."

They seemed to have reached an impasse. The brothers stepped inside the door and did some whispering. Finally the older one, Jessie, came out and said, "Follow me."

Nick entered the building, with the younger brother bringing up the rear. The main floor of the mill had been converted into reasonably comfortable living quarters, with a television set and a rack of rifles and shotguns for hunting. The windows overlooked the river, with a convenient kitchen and dining area at the other end of the big room. There was no indication of any female presence.

Jessie led the way up an open wooden stairway to the second floor. Nick could see doorways to separate bedrooms and a bath that occupied one side of the building. The other side was occupied by some sort of large storeroom, and Nick caught only a glimpse of it as Jessie opened the door. "Willie, you got a second?"

A beefy bald man came out to join them. He glanced at Nick with something close to contempt. "Why'd you bring him up here?"

"He has to see you sign for the check. He just wouldn't go away."

The big man grunted and extended his hand. "Willie Franklin. You got business with me?"

Nick shook hands and extended a business card. "A claim was filed for storm damage —"

"There's no damage."

"Perhaps your mother filed it and forgot."

"This ain't her property."

"Look, I just need your signature and the money's yours. I want to be on my way."

Nick guessed the bald man to be around forty, though his size and appearance added years. He took the check and the release form and studied them carefully. Nick didn't believe in cheating people while he was robbing them. The check was drawn on an account that had exactly three hundred and fifty-four dollars in it.

"We'll have to ask Mom about it," Jessie suggested.

Willie Franklin's face broadened into a smile. "Hell, can't look a gift horse in the mouth, as they say. Who's got a pen?" Nick purposely refrained from offering his own, and Willie finally reached into his pocket. He was wearing an old pair of army fatigue pants with the deep patch pockets and his meaty hand came out like a claw machine holding a number of objects. Nick caught a quick glimpse of a small black pocket comb before it dropped back out of sight. Franklin held a cheap ballpoint with which he carefully signed his name. "That satisfy you?"

"Fine, fine." Nick handed over the check. "I'll be on my way, then."

"Not so fast," the youngest brother said. "How do we know he's not a cop, come to look over the place?"

Willie Franklin frowned. "Sheriff Garvey's got no reason to bug us."

"I'm just an insurance man," Nick tried to reassure them. "If you fellows are making a little home brew on the side, it's nothing to me."

They all laughed at that and Willie waved his hand. "Go on, get out. Don't try to come back, though. We keep watch day and night. Hate to mistake you for a deer."

As Nick clambered over the rough terrain on his way back to Cassy Franklin's house, he heard the crack of a shot and the snipping of branches far overhead. The bullet hadn't been meant to hit him. It was just the good old boys sending him on his way.

The first thing Nick did upon reaching his motel was to phone Sandra Paris back in New York. When her voice came on the line he said, "I'm having difficulties. Nothing serious, but it would help a great deal if I could speak with the woman who hired you."

"Why is that necessary?"

"I went over to the mill today. The experience was about as you described it. Those boys are fast with a gun, and I'd like to know how serious they are."

"I got the impression from my client that they're damned serious. That's why I backed off. You know it takes more than a gun to scare me off, Nick, but I guess I operate better in an urban atmosphere."

"Can you give me her number?"

"Not without her permission."

"Get it and call me back." He gave her the phone number of the motel.

In less than ten minutes she was on the line with the answer. "The woman's name is Dusty Wayne. She sings country and western songs at a bar over in Gunnerville. That's about twenty miles away. You can see her there tonight, any time after eight. I described you as an attractive older man." He could detect the trace of humor in her voice.

"Thanks," he said dryly.

"Don't mention it. The name of the bar is Hardy's. It's right on the main road. You can't miss it."

"I'll be in touch," he promised.

That evening Nick found the town of Gunnerville without difficulty. Hardy's proved to be more of an old-fashioned roadhouse than a bar, with a large parking lot and flashing neon signs on all sides. The lot was about half full, which struck him as a fairly good crowd for a weeknight.

Inside there were little tables and a dance floor, but Nick ordered a beer and stood at the bar, listening to the sweet-voiced country singer who wore fringed buckskin and strummed her guitar like someone left over from the Sixties. He sent a note to her via one of the waiters and presently she took a break, resting the guitar atop the stool she'd used while singing.

She came up to him and asked, "You're Nick Velvet?"

"That's right."

"I'm Dusty Wayne." Up close she was attractive in a tomboyish way, probably in her mid-thirties, with black bangs that reached almost to her eyelids. The buckskin pants fit with just the right degree of snugness.

"I enjoyed your songs. They reminded me of Loretta Lynn."

"Thank you." Dimples appeared as she gave him a slow smile. "Sandra said you were nice."

"How did you come to know her?"

"That goes way back to our school days. We were classmates at college for a year, but I dropped out and went on the road with my guitar."

"You know what I'm here for."

She glanced sideways at the bartender. "Let's get a table where we can talk privately." Nick followed her to one against the far wall. She sat down and lit a cigarette apologetically. "I was off these things until I heard about that damn comb."

"Tell me about it. Why is it so valuable to you?"

"I won't know if it's valuable at all till I see it. Back when I first started singing I fell in love with one of the Franklin boys — Tom Franklin. He was six years younger than me, just seventeen, but he was the best-looking of them all. Very dark, with curly black hair and eyes that could look into your soul. We were going to run off together and travel around the land singing country music. Then one day he just . . . disappeared. His brother Willie told me he ran away, went out west."

"What about the comb?"

"I'm getting to it. Tom was always fussing with his hair. I think he wanted to look like Elvis, but his hair was too curly for that. Anyway, I gave him a comb that he always carried, with his initials on it, *TF*. He treated it like some sort of lucky charm. He never went anywhere without it, and he certainly wouldn't have gone out west without it. He might have left me, but he'd never leave that comb. A couple of months back someone from West Alum told me they ran into Willie Franklin at a pharmaceutical supply house over in Casper Hill and he had a comb in his pocket. He dropped it when he was getting out some money."

"That's true," Nick confirmed. "I saw it too."

"My friend thought it was funny for a bald man like Willie Franklin to need a comb, and I thought it was funny too." She took another drag on the cigarette. "Then I got thinking about Tom one night, and about his comb. I never really believed that he just ran away twelve years ago, without even a word or a note to me."

"What do you think happened?"

Dusty Wayne took a deep breath. "I think his brother might have killed him and buried the body somewhere. There was always bad blood between them. I'll probably never be able to prove it now, but I just want to know. If he's carrying Tom's comb around, that'll be proof enough for me."

"You're paying a great deal of money to find out."

"I've done well on a couple of CDs, and I've appeared in Nashville a few times. I'm married now, but sometimes I still dream of Tom Franklin and what happened to him. I want to know the truth. It's worth that much to find out."

"I'll do what I can," Nick promised.

The next morning Nick drove a few miles up-river from West Alum and rented a rowboat, speaking vaguely about doing some fishing. He went out in the gently flowing Casaqueek, getting the feel of the current, and finally rowed to shore about a mile up from the old mill. Approaching the place by night might be dangerous. He wasn't a woodsman but he'd read enough to know that the mere breaking of a twig could be fatal in the dark with an armed man nearby. An arrival by water should be safer.

He had some other tasks that day. First he found an almanac at the county library and checked out the time for the rising of the moon. Happily it was only in its first quarter and shouldn't give too much light. Then he went searching for a stray cat. He'd noticed a couple on the prowl around the town, and before too long he managed to entice one to him with some catnip purchased at the store near the library.

Just before midnight he set off in his rowboat with the cat in a convenient bag. He kept the boat toward shore, avoiding the more visible center of the river. Before long the mill came into sight, but he saw that there was still a light burning downstairs. He couldn't be sure if they left it on every night or if it was a sign that someone was still up and about. Nick grounded the rowboat in the shadows near the mill wheel and waited.

He was rewarded about fifteen minutes later when Jud Franklin strolled to the door and stared out at the night. He had a beer bottle in one hand and drained it as Nick watched. Then he closed the door and turned out the light. Presently a light went on in one of the upstairs bedrooms, stayed lit for about ten minutes, and then was extinguished. Nick waited another half-hour before he left the rowboat carrying his bagged cat.

He had no trouble with the door, entering silently and closing it behind him. Remembering the downstairs room as well as he could, he crossed to a table and picked up a lamp, then thought better of it and chose an empty beer bottle instead. He carried bottle and sack silently up the staircase to the second floor. "Now you come out, kitty," he whispered, leaning over the staircase to drop the cat onto a main floor sofa some eight feet below. He followed it with the beer bottle, but this landed on the bare floor, shattering with a satisfying crash.

Nick ran quickly into the workroom where Willie had been and hid behind the door. Already he could hear the Franklin brothers shouting and jumping out of bed. "What was it?" one of them called out. "Get your gun!"

They ran to the top of the stairs, and he saw the glow of lights from the main floor. Willie, his bald head gleaming, grabbed the rifle from his brother and led the way. As soon as they were all downstairs, Nick left his hiding place and hurried silently into the nearest bedroom. He was pretty certain it was the one from which Willie had emerged, and a sweep of his tiny flashlight across the nightstand next to the bed proved he was correct. There was the comb, along with coins, a pocket knife and a handkerchief. He turned it over and saw the initials: *TF*.

"A cat!" someone downstairs exploded. "It's a damned cat!"

"Jud, you were the last one up. Did you let a cat in?"

"There was no cat here when I went to bed," Jud insisted.

"Well, he's here now. Toss him outside or I'll put a bullet in him." Nick could recognize Willie's voice now, ordering his brothers about. He stayed in his hiding place, reasonably certain that if they decided on a search it wouldn't include the upper floor.

Presently the cat was exiled to the outer darkness and the brothers came upstairs to bed. "I still say I didn't let the damned cat in!" Jud insisted.

After a time they settled down, but Nick remained where he was for another thirty minutes. When he finally tiptoed across the floor to the stairs, something on the bottom of his sneakers made a scraping sound. He pried it off and dropped it in his pocket, but Jessie Franklin had heard something. "That you, Jud?"

From the next room Willie shouted, "Shut up, damn it! I'm trying to sleep."

"I think somebody's out there, Willie."

Nick heard the bed squeak and knew he had to hurry. He went down the stairs and out the door, just as the light went on. Slipping down the river bank toward his hidden boat, he saw Willie outlined in the lighted doorway as Jud had been earlier. "He got away," Jessie said.

"It don't matter," Willie's voice spoke calmly. "I know who it was. He'll be dead by morning."

Nick returned the rented boat in the morning and then phoned Sandra Paris. "How'd you make out?" she asked.

"You owe me forty."

"Good. I'll fly down and you can meet me at the airport in Atlanta. You'll get paid and I'll continue on my way to make delivery to Dusty."

"Sounds agreeable to me. Name the time."

"I'll check the flights. Call me back in two hours and I'll let you know. It'll be either late this evening or tomorrow morning."

Nick was just leaving the phone booth when a sheriff's car pulled up next to his. "Mr. Nicholas?" the deputy asked as he slipped out from behind the wheel.

Nick had a sinking feeling in his stomach. If they knew the name he was using, it meant they wanted him for something. "That's me."

"You were at the Franklin home day before yesterday?"

"That's right. I went there to settle a claim —"

"Come along with me, sir. The sheriff would like to speak with you."

"What about?"

"There's been a killing. Black man named Gus Adams who worked for Mrs. Franklin."

On the way to the sheriff's office, following the deputy's car, all Nick could think of was that Willie hadn't known who it was after all.

The sheriff was a small man who spoke in a soft voice and seemed completely out of place in West Alum and the Casaqueek Hills. His name was Garvey and his first statement was, "Mr. Nicholas, I find no record of the State Casualty and Life Insurance Company. Isn't that the name of your employer?"

"It is indeed. They sometimes do business under the names of subsidiaries."

The sheriff grunted. "Mrs. Franklin says you came to her place on Tuesday with a check for her son."

"That's correct."

"And Gus Adams took you to the mill where her three sons live."

"That's right. I only knew him as Gus."

"Too bad you didn't know him better. He was a fine man, much liked around these parts."

"He seemed friendly enough."

"Someone killed him this morning."

"That's what your deputy said."

Sheriff Garvey leaned back in his chair. "Shot him with a rifle through the window of his cabin on the Franklin place. Killed him at the kitchen table. Any idea who could have done it, Mr. Nicholas?"

"None. What would I know about it?"

"A man like Gus don't make many enemies. Hell, he was almost seventy years old."

"Maybe he was killed accidently by a hunter," Nick suggested.

"It's not hunting season. Did he say anything to you about any threats to his life?"

"He wouldn't be likely to talk to a stranger about it."

The sheriff played with a pencil and studied Nick carefully before speaking. "I think you'd better stay around here for a day or so till I can check on you."

"I'll certainly want to pay my respects to the Franklins before I leave." As Nick stood up another thought came to him. "When I was out to that old mill it looked like the Franklin boys were doing something illegal, maybe operating a still."

Sheriff Garvey chuckled. "That's Willie's idea of humor. I went out and took a look once, but there's no still. He's got a couple of old lab machines of some sort, but there's no moonshine in sight."

Nick hadn't noticed the humorous side of the bald man in their brief meeting, but he let that pass. "I'll be around if you want me," he said, trying to sound sincere.

There were several cars parked in front of the Franklin home when he paid a visit after lunch. Inside Cassy Franklin was in a state of near collapse, being tended to by neighbors and friends. Her three sons were nowhere in evidence. "Mr. Nicholas," she said, recognizing him at once.

"I was still in the area when I heard about your tragedy," he said. "Gus was a real gentleman. I'm sorry his life ended in such a terrible way."

"He worked for me nearly forty years, " she said. "Don't know what I'll do without him."

"When is the funeral?"

"Saturday. He'll be laid out tomorrow at the funeral parlor in town."

"I'll try to come by if I'm still in the area." That was the least he could do for the man who had died in his place.

He went back to the phone booth by the gas station that he'd used before. It was probably the only phone booth in the county. Back in New York, Sandra Paris was waiting for his call. "It's been more than two hours, Nick. Closer to three."

"I'm sorry, there's been a complication here. A man was killed and in a way I'm partly responsible. They thought he broke in and stole the comb."

"Why is that?"

"I don't know," Nick admitted. "But I should stay around till tomorrow, anyway, if only to keep the sheriff happy."

"Don't get arrested, Nick. I can't be springing you from jail again."

"I'll be careful."

"I'd better phone Dusty and tell her what's happened. Who was it got killed?"

"An old black man named Gus Adams who worked for Mrs. Hamilton."

"You think the sons did it?"

"One son — Willie. Damned if I can prove it, though."

"Be careful," she said again as she hung up.

Nick left the booth again and headed for his car. This time, happily, there was no sheriff's car waiting. He put his hand in his jacket pocket, reaching for his keys, and felt a little piece of something. It was a flattened gelatin capsule of the sort used for medication. He remembered prying it from his sneaker in the dark the previous night. He remembered something else, too. A friend of Dusty Wayne's had run into Willie Franklin at a pharmaceutical supply house.

Nick decided it was time he paid a return visit to Sheriff Garvey.

The sheriff needed some convincing. He listened to Nick's story and shook his head. "You may be right about Willie Franklin, Mr. Nicholas, but I need some evidence to arrest him."

"Then arrest his brothers. Bring them in and see if they'll talk."

"On what charges?"

Nick sighed, feeling frustrated by his attempt to work within the law. "Look, Sheriff, Willie may not have an illegal still up at that old mill, but he's got something illegal. Why else do they take shots at people who approach too closely. He's filling these capsules with an illegal substance, a drug of some kind."

"Prove it and I'll have them locked up within an hour."

"I'd prove it if I could get back inside that mill."

The sheriff smiled at him. "Right this minute all three of the Franklin boys are at their mother's house."

Nick Velvet returned the smile. They understood one another.

The mill was quiet when he reached it a half-hour later. The door was even easier to open by daylight, and he wasted no time. He took samples of all the capsules he could find, along with loose powder that was in barrels labeled *flour*. When he left he went along the river bank, careful not to encounter the brothers on their way back.

Sheriff Garvey studied the samples that Nick delivered to him late that afternoon. "The state police can analyze these for me overnight if I put a rush on it."

Nick smiled. "You don't like the Franklin boys any better than I do."

"Maybe even less, Mr. Nicholas."

Nick went back to his motel and found a visitor waiting in the parking lot. It was Dusty Wayne, sitting behind the wheel of her little sports car. "I'll bet you're looking for me," he said, leaning in the open window on the passenger side.

"Get in. We have to talk."

Nick slid in beside her. "You've talked to Sandra?"

She nodded. "That's why I'm here. Do you have the comb with you?"

He showed it to her. She took it, barely able to breath, and turned it over in her hands. He saw a tear start to run down her cheek. "That's it?" he asked, knowing the answer.

"That's it. Tom's own brother killed him."

"But why? A man killing his brother —"

"It's been happening a long time, Mr. Velvet. Let me tell you about Cain and Abel sometime."

"He might have dropped the comb, or given it to Willie when he left."

"No. This was the first gift I ever gave him. He'd have kept it. He might have thrown it away at thirty-five, but not at seventeen."

"I have an appointment with the sheriff in the morning. Come there with me."

"Nobody listened to me before."

"I think they will now."

They were at the sheriff's office before nine. He shook hands with Dusty Wayne and pulled out a chair for her. "A pleasure to meet you, Miss Wayne. I like your music."

"Thank you!" She gave him a broad but brief smile. "I wish we were meeting under more pleasant circumstances."

His gaze shifted to Nick. "You're a bit early, Mr. Nicholas. The state police haven't phoned in with the lab report yet."

"Can't you call them?"

"I suppose so," he agreed, reaching for the phone. After a few moments' wait he was connected to someone in the lab, and made several quick notes as they conversed. When he finally hung up he was smiling.

"An illegal drug of some sort," Nick guessed.

Sheriff Garvey shook his head. "No, it's quite legal. A common, though expensive, prescription heart medication."

"What?

The sheriff smiled at Nick's surprise. "But it's been cut to fifty percent its normal strength with flour — the flour from that barrel you sampled. Willie and his brothers are doctoring prescription drugs, repackaging them in their own capsules, and selling them at a big profit."

"Isn't that dangerous to the user?"

"Damn right it's dangerous! In some cases it could kill them."

"What are you going to do?"

"The state police want to move in today. We can't admit that you broke into the place to get the evidence, so they'll request a search warrant for an illegal still. We have to shut down their operation and discover whether they were selling the stuff in large lots or to individual pharmacies."

"Try to question Jud and Jessie separately," Dusty suggested. "Offer them a plea bargain if they tell you about the murders."

"Young lady, I don't need instructions from you." He narrowed his eyes. "What murders? Gus Adams and who else?"

"Their brother Tom. He disappeared twelve years ago. He was supposed to have run away but I never believed it."

As it turned out, Willie Franklin was not at the mill when the state police moved in. Jud and Jessie denied everything, but it was immediately obvious they weren't about to take the fall for Willie. By late afternoon they'd both signed statements implicating Willie in the shooting of Gus Adams.

Nick listened as Jud's confession was tape-recorded.

"Why did your brother want Gus dead?"

"He thought Gus had broken into the mill and stolen a comb."

"What comb?"

"It belonged to our brother Tom. Willie kept it, carried it with him all the time. Crazy thing to do."

"What happened to Tom?"

"Willie killed him a long time ago. Twelve years ago."

"Do you expect us to believe that?"

"I can show you where he buried the body. You'll find it in the river bank just behind the mill wheel — what's left of it."

"Where's Willie now?"

"Gone to the pharmaceutical house for supplies. He'll be at the funeral parlor tonight."

Listening to the confession with Nick, Sheriff Garvey nodded. "We'll take him there," he said.

Nick phoned Sandra Paris and told her he'd delivered the comb to Dusty. "She's pleased. The local police are wrapping it up tonight."

"Good! I've made arrangements with her about the money. She'll pay me with a draft and I'll pay you."

"I only want my usual twenty-five. Give her back the rest."

"What's this — a charity case?"

"She was paying the money for love — love of a kid who's been dead twelve years."

"Suit yourself, Nick."

They drove to the funeral parlor just as it was opening for its evening hours. Gus Adams didn't have any family, and Cassy Franklin was the closest thing to it. She stood by the open casket, greeting everyone who came to pay their respects. He knew she hadn't been told about the arrest of Jud and Jessie.

Willie Franklin was seated in a far corner of the room. He got up when he recognized Nick and started toward him. Then he got another surprise as Dusty

Wayne entered, wearing a plain black dress.

"Hello, Willie," she said.

"What — ? Dusty, is that you? It's been a long time." The top of his head was growing moist with sweat.

It was Sheriff Garvey who spoke the words. "Willie, I'm going to have to arrest you on suspicion of murder."

"Murder? What murder?"

"Two, actually. Gus Adams and your brother Tom."

He tried to break through them then, heading for the door or perhaps just away from the casket behind him. The state police had him before he got more than a few feet, and his hands were quickly cuffed. Nick hoped his mother hadn't noticed the brief scuffle.

It was Nick who said to him, as he was being led away, "Willie, we know about Gus, but why did you kill your brother?"

He stared at Nick as if seeing him for the first time. Perhaps he thought Nick was a state cop too, and was cursing his brothers for ever letting him into the mill.

But he turned and looked back at the black man in his coffin, and in that instant Nick remembered the descriptions he'd heard of Tom Franklin — the dark complexion, the curly black hair. "He was seventeen years old," Willie said quietly. "He was starting to look too much like his father."

The Theft of the Snake Charmer's Basket

Sandra Paris, a specialist in the commission of bizarre crimes who was sometimes known as the White Queen, had been in Marrakesh only a few hours when the two men started following her. She noticed them first as she entered the Place Djemaa el Fna, a vast open square of shops crowded with fruit and spice sellers, ironmongers and barbers, musicians and snake charmers.

Sandra was a tall attractive American in her thirties with an angelic face framed by platinum-blonde hair. Moving among the Moroccan natives and overweight tourists, she knew she was the focus of attention. It was something that couldn't be helped unless she'd chosen to wear a dark wig and native garb. Even in a city of more than a half-million people someone like Sandra Paris stood out.

She knew little of the official Arabic language but one shop had a sign posted in French and English. She entered and asked, "Which way to the snake charmers?"

The little shopkeeper shrugged. "They come and go. Look for a story- teller named Gulez at the far end of the square."

Sandra Paris returned to the sweltering, sun-baked square and made her way through the crowd to the other end. Almost at once she was aware of the two men following her, tracking her through the swarm of shoppers and camera-toting tourists. They were dirty and ragged, not the sort who would be looking for a date.

She found the story-teller as promised, seated cross-legged on a bale of hemp. He was a bearded man wearing a belted-tunic and a turban, enchanting listeners with what might have been a tale of the Arabian Nights for all she knew. When he noticed her standing there among his audience he switched to passable, accented English for her benefit. It was a story about how the camel got its hump, and she thought she remembered it from Kipling. She waited until the story ended, then joined the others in dropping a few dirham coins into the story-teller's bowl.

"Are you Gulez?" she asked.

"That I am," he replied with a smile, showing a few fruit-stained teeth.

"I was told to ask you about the snake charmers," she said as he gathered up his meager earnings from the bowl. "Will they be coming today?"

"Why would you desire to watch a cobra being charmed when I can enchant you with another story, good lady?" She saw now that he was younger than she'd first supposed, certainly under forty. The beard had deceived her.

"I want a picture," she told him, producing a small camera from her purse. "To show my friends back home."

"Then I am glad to oblige." He hopped down as Sandra moved closer for a better view. Gulez produced a large woven basket about a foot high and two feet across. He removed the lid and glanced inside, then picked up a reeded cane flute with holes along one side.

"You are a snake charmer too?" she asked, amazed.

"In Marrakesh many talents are needed to earn a living, good lady." He placed the flute in his mouth and began to play, resuming his seat on the bale of hemp. As the hypnotic music flowed from the flute his relaxed body began to sway slightly.

Sandra watched as the hooded head of the cobra emerged slowly from the basket, raising higher and higher as if about to strike. She was transfixed by the sight, and when Gulez stopped playing for an instant he had to tell her, "Remember to take your picture."

"What? Oh, thanks!" She raised her camera and snapped the picture.

When he'd finished his performance and returned the serpent to its basket he explained, "This is an Egyptian cobra. It is both aggressive and dangerous, but it has one overriding advantage for snake charming — it does not spit like some other African cobras. There is no danger of spectators being hit by venom."

"That's a relief," Sandra told him, eyeing the creature with distaste. "Where do you keep it at night?"

"Usually in a cage. You take no chances with an Egyptian cobra." He replaced the lid on the basket and picked up his flute.

"You speak English quite well," she told him.

He shrugged. "I pick it up from the tourists."

As he started out of the square Sandra fell into step beside him. The two men were still following and she pretended this performer with his snake offered a degree of protection. "Do you live nearby?" she asked.

"Nearby, yes."

"This is my first visit to Marrakesh."

"I supposed it was. Tourists rarely pay return visits."

"Why is that?"

"Everything may be seen in two days. And the climate does not encourage lingering." He shifted the basket to get a better grip on it.

"Does the snake weigh much?"

He smiled at her through the beard. "It is my snake. It is not too heavy to carry."

They'd left the Place Djemaa el Fna, passing now through an area of tents that housed merchants who had journeyed here to sell their products. Beyond the tents, still well within the city's ramparts, was a run-down residential district.

Sandra knew the men were still following her and she hoped he'd notice them. "Where did you learn all those stories?" she asked.

"I steal them from books I read," he admitted. Then, "Do you know we are being followed?"

She nodded. "Two men. They were after me in the square."

"We must do something about that. Come in with me for a moment while I put away the cobra."

He led the way up a flight of stone steps to a dingy two-room apartment. In the main room was a wire mesh cage. Gulez carefully removed the serpent from its basket, holding it just below the head so it could not strike at him. He dropped it into the cage and locked the lid. The room was drab and sparsely furnished. Sandra could see the corner of a bed in the next room but had no desire to investigate further.

"I must be going," she decided suddenly. She'd seen what she came for.

"Who are those men?" he asked.

"I never saw them before."

He considered the situation for a moment. "There's a back way out of here. Come with me."

She followed him down a narrow passage to the back stairs. They led to a little alleyway and he stayed with her for a few blocks until they were sure it was safe. "Thank you," she said. "I'll be all right now."

"Attractive American women are always a target. Be careful. If those men reappear, call the police."

"I will," Sandra promised. She shook his hand. "I enjoyed meeting you."

They parted a few blocks from her hotel. She covered the distance quickly, without looking back. When she reached the lobby Hashim Bey was seated in an oversized cane chair against the far wall. She walked directly to him. "Two men have been following me all afternoon."

"We must be careful. There are others after the basket." He handed her a slim envelope of money from his inside pocket. "The rest when you deliver it."

"What if something goes wrong?"

"Then, you are on your own, Miss Paris. I will be on the first plane out of here." He made a little bow as they parted.

Sandra Paris went up to her room, showered and changed for dinner. She ate lightly at the hotel, already plotting her moves for morning. She'd always been an early riser, which accounted for her motto: *Impossible things before breakfast*. The following morning she was up before the sun, dressed in a black catsuit which she knew was highly inappropriate for a woman in a Moslem country. With luck she'd be back before dawn.

The Hotel les Almoravides was the closest to the square, and she'd chosen it for that reason. When Hashim Bey hired her to steal the basket she supposed the snake charmer would live near the square, possibly in one of the tents. He would not want to transport the serpent long distances every day. Actually, the two men who'd followed her had helped her accomplish the first part of the mission, giving her the location and layout of his apartment. She could find her way back in the dark, which was exactly what she was doing now.

When she reached the building where Gulez lived she pulled a black hood over her head and moved soundlessly up the back steps to his apartment. The locked room presented no obstacle. She was inside within seconds. A gentle snoring from the bedroom told her that the snake charmer was peacefully asleep. She moved to the wicker basket and lifted the lid, shining her penlight inside. She saw only a cluster of dead leaves at the bottom. Sandra doused her light and stuck her gloved hand down among them, searching for something of value.

The fangs were instant, the pain indescribable. She screamed in spite of herself and fell back as the great Egyptian cobra reared up from the basket, its deadly teeth sunk deep into her arm. Oddly, in the instant before she lost consciousness, her final thought was of Nick Velvet.

Gloria came into the kitchen carrying a sheet of paper. Nick looked up from his morning toast and coffee as she said, "This came in on your fax machine during the night."

Only a handful of business associates knew his fax number. He accepted the sheet and read the brief handwritten words. *Recovering from cobra bite at Marrakesh Hospital. I need you! Sandra.*

"Sandra Paris," Gloria said. They knew no other Sandra.

"It's not her handwriting."

"The snake probably bit her on the right hand so she dictated the note to a nurse." He smiled. "You should have been a detective."

She poured him more coffee. "Are you going?"

"To Marrakesh? It's halfway around the world."

"Just North Africa. You could probably get a connecting flight in London or Paris."

"You want me to go?"

Gloria smiled sadly. "She's helped you once or twice. If she really needs you —"

Nick had to admit he'd never had such an appeal from Sandra Paris before. A cobra bite wasn't exactly an everyday event, even for the White Queen. There was a story behind it, perhaps one he'd be interested in hearing. With Gloria's urging he caught a night flight to London, changing there for Marrakesh. Under a hot Moroccan sun the following afternoon he arrived at his destination.

Menarsa Airport was a brief four miles from the walled city. Nick checked in at his hotel and then took a taxi to the nearby hospital. He knew nothing of Arabic, and he was relieved to hear some French being spoken. A nurse led him down the corridor to Sandra's room. "Only ten minutes," she warned. "The patient is still very weak."

Sandra Paris was sitting propped up on pillows, her right arm encased in bandages. "God, Nick!" she almost yelled. "It's great to see a friendly face!" The color was drained from her flesh and he could see she was far from recovered.

"What happened, Sandra? What are you doing here?" He bent to kiss her on the cheek, something he'd never imagined himself doing before.

"I got bitten by a cobra — an Egyptian cobra. They don't spit but they sure do bite!"

"When did this happen?"

"What day is it — Thursday?"

"That's right. Thursday afternoon."

"It was early Tuesday morning."

"Before breakfast."

"Of course!" She shifted painfully on the pillows and he tried to help. "No, no — I can manage. It's just this arm. They cut away a chunk of it around the wound."

"You're lucky you're not dead."

Sandra regarded him through half-closed eyes. "*You're* lucky I'm not dead! It would take half the fun out of your life."

He didn't deny it. "Where did this happen, at the zoo?"

"I doubt if they even have a zoo. Why should they, when you have camels and cobras loose on the streets?" She changed her position again. "It happened in a snake charmer's apartment. I had my hand in his basket."

"I'll bet." Nick pulled up a chair and sat down. "Suppose you tell me about it from the beginning."

"It's a pretty dull story."

He smiled at her. "I just spent the better part of twelve hours on planes. It better not be too dull!"

"The man is a storyteller and snake charmer who works the crowd in the Place Djemaa el Fna. It's a square at the center of the city, full of merchants and street performers. I went there to meet him and found I was followed by a couple of local goons. He took me home with him till we could shake them. I checked the lock and got the layout of the place. He took the cobra from its basket and put it in a cage. Only when I went there before dawn the snake was back in the basket under some leaves."

"It's a wonder you're not dead."

"I almost was! The doctor says the only thing that saved me was that the snake had been fed a rat the night before and used some of its venom on that. It wasn't back up to full strength when I made my move."

"What were you trying to steal?" Nick asked.

The smile disappeared. "I don't know. I was being foolish, Nick, and I suppose I got what I deserved."

"Tell me."

She sighed. "I did some work in Rome for a man named Mazolli. Apparently it involved a Mafia double cross of some kind. Mazolli was dead before I could collect my fee and I was left with a briefcase full of travel folders sent from a man named Hashim Bey."

"Bey's in the travel business?"

"As a front for other things. He'd mentioned once that there was a pipeline through Marrakesh for some sort of contraband. In Mazolli's papers Bey and I found a recent travel folder with pictures of the Place Djemaa el Fna. One showed a snake charmer with his flute in a typical pose, with the cobra coming up out of the basket. The basket itself — not the snake — had been circled in ink, apparently by Mazolli."

"So you went after the basket?"

Sandra nodded. "I wanted to recover some payment for my work and Bey paid me to steal it. The other morning when I peered into it with my penlight all I saw were some dead leaves. The snake was under them."

"Did this snake charmer —"

"His name is Gulez."

"— Gulez get you to the hospital?"

"I was unconscious by then, but he apparently called for help. I haven't seen him since. And Bey apparently skipped town. I needed you."

Nick nodded. "I'll get a ticket so you can fly back home with me."

"Not without that basket!" she insisted.

"Be reasonable, Sandra. There's nothing in the basket except a cobra."

She reached out to touch his arm. "Get it for me, Nick. That's the least I deserve after losing a piece of my arm to that creature."

"I value my life more than that. Snakes and I don't get along. When are they letting you out of this place?"

"Probably Saturday, the doctor said. Two more days. He wants to be sure I don't get an infection."

She told him everything and Nick finally agreed to seek out the snake charmer, Gulez. "I haven't agreed to steal the basket, though," he insisted.

"I know you'll do what you can, Nick."

When he left the hospital he planned to head directly to the Place Djemaa el Fna. His plans changed abruptly when a slender bearded man approached him near the front entrance. "You are the friend of Sandra Paris?"

"I know her, yes," Nick admitted.

"I am Gulez. It was in my apartment where the cobra bit her."

Nick nodded and introduced himself. "Have you been to see her?"

The bearded man shook his head. "It was a terrible accident and naturally she blames me for it. I could not face her, but I come daily to learn of her condition. The nurse told me today that an American friend was with her. How is she?"

"Coming along. Tell me how it happened."

Gulez answered in hushed tones. "She came to see the snake charmers. After my performance she seemed frightened by two men who were following her. I walked with her and finally took her to my apartment to avoid them. Later in the night, she must have gotten too close to the basket and my cobra bit her."

"She stayed there with you?"

"In all innocence! She feared the men who were following her."

It wasn't exactly the story Sandra had told, but Nick let that pass for the moment. "I'd like to see your performance. Are you in the Place Djemaa el Fna every day?"

"Every day that shops are open. "Come in the morning and I will give a special performance with my cobra."

Nick promised to be there. The man seemed open and friendly enough. If there was a secret involving his basket perhaps he didn't even know about it. The two men parted and Nick continued on to his hotel. He found someone else waiting in the lobby.

"Are you Nick Velvet?" the man asked. He wore a rumpled white suit. and could have used a shave, but his accents were American. Nick guessed his age to be around forty, based mainly on the thinning brown hair that was flat against his head.

"That's me." There was no sense denying the obvious.

"I'm Morgan Herty. I don't suppose you've heard of me."

"The name—" Nick began uncertainly.

"I'm a novelist. Largely unread but I keep trying. Been coming to Marrakesh for ten years now. Could we have a drink and talk?"

"I suppose so." Nick followed the man into the hotel lounge and they sat facing each other at a little circular table. Both ordered glasses of the local wine, which Herty assured Nick was quite good. After a few sips Nick decided anything might taste good if one drank it for ten years.

"You're here because of what happened to Sandra Paris?"

Nick shrugged. "She's an old friend. There's something a bit frightening about being hospitalized in a strange country when you're alone. She needed me and I came."

"She's a lucky woman. The bite of an Egyptian cobra can be quite deadly. The best thing you could do would be to get her back home as quickly as possible."

"That's just what I told her," Nick agreed, risking another sip of wine and wondering why Sandra's departure should interest this man. "I hope she'll be on her way home by the weekend. Are you a friend of hers?"

"No. I'm just interested in the story, as a writer. Even in Marrakesh it's not often someone is bitten by a cobra. Perhaps you could tell me how it happened."

"Sandra wasn't too talkative. They've still got her drugged up. You probably know as much as I do."

"I'd like to interview her briefly before she leaves the city."

Nick frowned at the suggestion, as he knew Sandra would. "I don't know if that's going to be possible."

"Ask her about it. See what she thinks." The man finished his wine and stood up. "Nice meeting you, Mr. Velvet. I'll be in touch."

Nick shook his hand. "A pleasure, Mr. Herty."

He sat at the table for a time after the man in the rumpled white suit had departed, wondering what that was all about.

Nick had lost a night's sleep on the flight from New York so he retired early, rising in the morning with a clear head and an empty stomach. After a hotel breakfast he decided to visit the square where Gulez and his cobra performed. Perhaps he'd have something to report to Sandra, though he wasn't betting on it.

Already by nine o'clock the Place Djemaa el Fna was beginning to fill with people. The merchants from the various shops were open for business and the fruit and spice sellers were unloading their wares. Basket sellers displayed great woven towers of their product, while men with leather water bottles and tin drinking cups circulated through the crowd selling a cool drink for a couple dirham. Nick heard the sound of a flute and that led him to Gulez, practicing a few notes while he waited for a crowd to gather.

Tall and thin and bearded, not too old. He could have been Moroccan or Sudanese or even French behind those whiskers. Here in the city square he seemed much more sure of himself than he had outside the hospital the previous afternoon. He smiled and nodded when he saw Nick. Presently, as enough people gathered round, he stopped playing and went over to lift the lid on the basket. Children crowded in to see the coiled serpent and one teenager, braver than the rest, threw gravel into the basket to annoy the sleeping cobra.

"Go on!" Gulez shouted at them. "Go away! My cobra has bitten one person already this week. Do you want to be next?"

His words drove them back and they settled down with the others to watch the show. The bearded man picked up his flute and started to play the ancient melodies of his people. After a moment the cobra's head raised up, flattening into its familiar hood, its weaving motion seeming to follow Gulez's own swaying movements.

Nick watched the whole thing from a distance, fascinated by the spectacle. When Gulez had finished, replacing the lid on the snake's basket and circling through the crowd for donations, Nick commented, "That's quite a performance."

Gulez smiled. "To some extent it's a trick. The music is mainly for effect. The cobra follows the gentle swaying of my body as I play. But the crowd enjoys it. Snake charming is even more popular in India. You should go there if you are truly interested."

"I heard you tell the children your cobra had bitten someone."

"Sandra, of course. Have you been to see her this morning?"

"Not yet."

"I take the cobra home now and return this afternoon. Perhaps we can go to see her together."

Nick had no objection so he accompanied the bearded man back to his apartment. "Do you just perform twice a day?" he asked as they made their way through the narrow sweltering alleys, retracing the route Sandra Paris had no doubt traveled earlier.

"I am a story-teller too. In the early afternoon, when the sun is at its hottest, I tell stories while the serpent sleeps. Come — up these stairs is my apartment."

Nick observed that the lock on the door was a simple one. It would have given Sandra no trouble at all. Gulez led the way into the apartment, carrying the basket carefully in both arms. It was much cooler here, out of the morning sun, and for that Nick was thankful. He never saw the two young men in Arab robes who lay in wait for them, and he had no chance to defend himself before the heavy knob of a walking stick caught him across the left temple.

N ick Velvet fell to the floor, stunned but not unconscious. Through the slit of one open eye he saw them grab onto Gulez and pin him against the wall. "Remove the snake," one of them ordered in English.

"He will do you no good," the charmer insisted. "He performs only for me."

Nick thought he saw the glint of a native dagger. He tried to move but his head seemed bursting with pain. "Take the snake from the basket," one of them ordered.

Gulez did as he was told, with a firm grip just below the cobra's head as he lifted it from the basket. "What's in it?" the man with the knobby walking stick asked.

"Only dried leaves," Gulez responded, the knife at his throat.

The first man reached in with his stick, poking around to make certain no second cobra lurked there. Then he pulled out the leaves by the handful, shaking them in the snake charmer's face. "Are these leaves of Indian hemp, for hashish?"

Gulez ignored the blade at his throat and spat on the floor. "They are leaves of the Moroccan cork oak. They have no use, except as bedding for my cobra."

"What else is in there?"

The man with the knife peered into the basket. "Nothing. It's empty."

The first one leaned his stick against the wall and bent to examine it personally. That was the moment Nick had hoped for. With one foot he kicked at the stick, sending it toppling to the floor within easy reach. He grabbed and twisted it, catching the ankles of the closest man and bringing him down. The one with the knife loosened his grip on Gulez as he swung around to face Nick. Gulez seized the moment and twisted the blade from his fingers as the assailant yelped with pain.

"Thank you," the snake charmer told Nick.

"What will we do with them?" The one who'd held the knife was sobbing with pain and he suspected the man's fingers were broken.

"I will kill them and dispose of the bodies," Gulez said.

The two men were still young enough to be frightened. "No!" the one who'd hit Nick pleaded. "We're only doing our job!"

"Who do you work for?" Nick asked.

"The Afrikaner," he answered, before the other ordered him to shut up.

"What's his name?" Nick wanted to know.

But now both of them were silent.

"I'll handle them," Gulez assured him.

Nick's head was still throbbing, but he was in no mood to see murder done. "Let them go," he said. "We know what they look like if they come around again."

An hour later Nick was at the hospital, waiting outside Sandra's door while a nurse checked her vital signs. When he finally entered she was in a chair next to the bed. Her color was better and he could see she was nearly recovered.

"What happened to your face?" she asked as he came in.

"A stupid accident. I bumped into a door."

"The whole side of your head is bruised! It looks recent. You'd better let a doctor see it while you're here."

"I'll be all right," he assured her, perching on the edge of the bed.

"Come on, Nick — what really happened?"

"A couple of goons jumped us at Gulez's apartment. They were after the basket. I suppose they were the same ones that followed you."

"Did they get it?"

"No, and I hope they learned a lesson. I told Gulez to let them go. It was either that or kill them."

She shook her head. "Seems like everyone's striking out trying to steal that basket."

"Not everyone," Nick reminded her. "I haven't had my try yet."

"Did you find out what's in it?"

He shrugged. "A cobra and some dead leaves. Listen, did you ever hear of someone called the Afrikaner?"

She shook her head. "It's a South African of European descent. I don"t know any of those."

"Neither do I. What would someone like that be doing in Morocco?"

"I thought things were relatively peaceful down there these days, since the elections. Of course there are always troublemakers everywhere."

"Anything to connect your Mafia friends with an Afrikaner?"

She shook her head. "No."

"What about the basket itself? You've seen it. Could the wicker be valuable somehow?"

"No way," she insisted. "It was just a cheap basket with a lid. They're sold everywhere in the bazaars."

"All right," he decided. "I'm going after it tonight. I'll have it by the time you're released from here tomorrow."

Sandra Paris smiled at him. "Good luck, Nick. Be careful."

He was halfway out the door when he remembered Morgan Herty. "One other thing. There was a writer at my hotel yesterday. He wanted to know if he could interview you. He seemed interested in when you'd be getting out of the hospital."

"What'd you tell him?"

"Not much. You don't want to see him, do you?"

"Not a chance. My business isn't one that craves publicity."

"I'll tell Mr. Herty you're still weak from your experience. Too weak for an interview."

By the time Nick returned to the Place Djemaa el Fna, Gulez had finished his story-telling and removed the lid from the wicker basket. He showed no sign of the morning's ordeal, and their two assailants were nowhere in sight. Nick watched from a distance as the beggar boys tormented the snake again and the bearded charmer tried a few notes on his flute. Then he began playing, and after a moment the cobra's hooded head appeared above the rim of the basket.

"An amazing sight, isn't it?" a voice behind Nick asked. He turned and recognized Morgan Herty, still in his white suit. The pungent odor of his cigarette told Nick he was smoking kif, a form of local marijuana.

"Snakes have always fascinated me," Nick admitted.

"And how is our patient today?"

"Miss Paris? She's coming along."

"Did she agree to see me?"

"I'm afraid not. She just isn't up to it."

"Too bad." He dropped the cigarette in the dust and ground it underfoot. Before them the Egyptian cobra had risen to its full height, its body matching the gentle swaying of the flute player. "I'm sorry about your face," the man in the white suit added.

"So am I. Did you have something to do with it?"

"Not directly." He glanced around the square. "Can we talk, Mr. Velvet?"

They made their way to a little outdoor café in one corner of the square, avoiding the entertainers with their performing monkeys and the dancers who gyrated to native music.

Morgan Herty ordered mint tea and Nick did likewise. "You are the man known as the Afrikaner, aren't you?"

Herty smiled slightly. "Those two that I hired may have referred to me that way." He removed a leather case from the inner pocket of his white suit and opened it for Nick. "These are my credentials."

"Police?" Nick asked with a frown.

"South African Special Branch. I'm up here on assignment."

"To steal a snake charmer's basket?"

He lit another cigarette. "I'll be frank, Mr. Velvet, because I need your help. Certainly you've read about the state of things in the former Soviet Union. You know that large quantities of plutonium are unaccounted for, and some has been offered for sale to terrorists in the west. Some of these terrorists, sadly, are in my country."

"I thought —"

"That things had settled down after the election? Hardly! There are white supremacists still bent on seizing back control of the country. A supply of plutonium and some small tactical nuclear bombs are just the weapons they need."

"Those things must cost a fortune."

"There are men in South Africa who have several fortunes, and would willingly spend them to see the nation restored to white rule."

"Surely you can watch these people, keep them from sending money out of the country."

"We can and we do. Our currency laws are very strict. Still, we know they are getting money out somehow. A Mafia figure named Mazolli had established contact with some renegade Russian physicists. He told them there was money coming from South Africa by a devious route through the continent to Morocco. After Mazolli died —"

"How did he die?"

"That's no concern of ours. The Americans are as interested in this as we are. Sometimes one helps one's friends. Anyway, Mazolli died and it came to light that his contact in the money pipeline was this man Gulez. We expected a Marrakesh banker at the very least. What we found was an itinerant snake charmer. He's been watched day and night for weeks. There's been no contact with any stranger. As you may know, Morocco's currency regulations are even stricter than ours. The local dirham cannot be exchanged for foreign currency and cannot be taken out of the country. This is one of the worst places in the world for a pipeline of illegal currency."

Nick Velvet smiled. "Which is exactly why they chose it. An impossible country with a snake charmer as money pipeline. Who would ever suspect it?"

"The two men who attacked you were hired to watch Gulez in the square every day. The only money he ever received were small donations following his act. He met with no one at night, and he usually dined alone. Still, before he died Mazolli indicated the money was being transferred somehow in that wicker basket. The woman, Sandra Paris, is after it. We're after it. And I suppose now that you are too."

"There's nothing in the basket but a cobra."

"Perhaps the cobra is fed a diet of currency," Herty said, allowing himself a slight chuckle that turned into a cough. He tossed away the cigarette. "What about it, Mr. Velvet? Can you do what those men failed at — steal the basket?"

"I'm only a tourist."

"We both know better than that. I asked the Americans to run a check on you. They have quite a dossier. You're a thief who steals valueless things."

"A basket full of money is hardly valueless."

"But you say it's empty!" the South African reminded him. "We don't want the cobra, only the basket."

"Did the dossier tell you my fee?"

"Twenty-five thousand plus expenses."

"That'll do."

"When can you steal it?"

"Is today soon enough?"

Later that afternoon Nick returned to the square and visited one of the workshops selling baskets. He purchased a dozen that were nearly identical to Gulez's basket. Then he rounded up thirteen children who were playing in the area. He gave them careful instructions and presented each with half of a fifty-dirham banknote. "You get the rest when it's finished," he promised. It was only a bit over five dollars each, but for these children it was enough.

As Gulez was finishing his act a while later, a peculiar thing happened. One of the children ran up and grabbed the empty basket while the snake-charmer held up his cobra for a final bow. He shouted at the youth and tried to pursue him, but that was difficult with the snake in hand. Almost at once the running boy was surrounded by a dozen others, all carrying identical wicker baskets. For a few minutes the square seemed filled with running children. Gulez bellowed helplessly and waved his cobra.

Nick Velvet stepped into the midst of the madness and grabbed one of the running boys by the shoulder. He took the basket from him and delivered it to Gulez. "Here — you can put the snake in this."

"It's not my basket!"

"It is now. They're all the same, aren't they?"

"You did this, Velvet!"

But Nick had moved on. The children would be waiting for their money.

It was toward evening when he met with Morgan Herty in the South African's hotel room. Herty accepted the basket and handed over payment in American dollars. He removed the cork-oak leaves that had served as the snake's bedding and carefully examined the interior. "There must be a false bottom to this thing."

"No, I already checked for that. It's just a wicker basket."

"But the money has to be here!"

"It is. Gulez used it as a collection basket as surely as the ones they pass in church."

"Then where —?"

"If you want me to explain it to you there might be an additional fee."

There was a knock on the door and Herty got to his feet. "That's probably the night maid to turn down the bed."

He opened the door and was shoved backward immediately by an angry Gulez. "Don't move, Velvet," he ordered, aiming a Walther pistol at Nick. "I've come for the basket."

He entered the room, closing the door behind him. "It's good to see you again," Nick greeted him blandly. "How'd you find us?"

"You don't work for free," the snake charmer replied, his accent subtly changed from North African to something more European. "I figured Herty must have hired you. Now hand me the basket."

Before Nick could decide what to do there was a second knock on the door. Gulez leveled the pistol and called out, "Who is it?"

"Night maid," a woman's muffled voice replied.

"I don't need you."

"We have to check all the rooms, sir."

"Go away."

"Is something wrong in there?" she persisted.

Gulez kept the gun level as he unlocked the door. "Come in and see, if you insist."

The unlocked door slammed against him, knocking him off balance. Then Sandra Paris was inside, bringing him to the floor and kicking the weapon from his hand.

"Sandra!" Nick could only shake his head in amazement. "What are you doing here?"

She gestured toward the man on the floor. "I was following him. They let me out of the hospital a day early."

They tied the snake charmer's wrists and ankles with a torn bedsheet while Nick explained the situation to Sandra. "Mr. Herty here has paid me to steal the basket you and others have tried to get. Now that he has it, he doesn't know where the money is."

"Do you?"

"I do, and I'll tell him for an additional twenty-five thousand."

"You're mad!" Herty said with an angry growl.

"Then you're never going to know, are you? I'm sure Gulez here isn't about to tell you."

For a moment it seemed they were at an impasse. Then Morgan Herty sighed and threw up his hands. "It's the government's money, not mine." He opened his shirt and removed some currency from a money belt.

"All right," Nick said, giving it to Sandra to count. "It goes back to Sandra's story of her visit to his apartment the other day, before she was bitten by the cobra. Gulez removed the snake and placed it in a separate cage. This would have made sense except for the fact that when Sandra returned to search the basket that night the cobra was back there and bit her arm. Why had Gulez removed it? To clean it and change the leafy bedding, perhaps, but it also seemed likely he wanted to remove the money he'd collected during the day."

"There was no money," Herty insisted. "My men found nothing yesterday, and I find nothing now. Are you telling me these leaves are pieces of currency?"

"No, but there had to be something else in the basket. Twice today I saw boys pestering the snake, trying to get a rise out of it. I saw a teen-age boy throwing pebbles into the basket."

"Pebbles?"

Nick upended the basket and shook it. Six or eight small pebbles were dislodged and scattered onto the hotel rug. "Bring me a glass of water from the bathroom, Sandra."

Morgan Herty's mouth dropped open. "Are you telling me — ?"

Nick dunked the pebbles in the water and carefully washed off the coating of dried mud. "A South African, of all people, should know there are more forms of currency than mere paper money. These are small but perfect diamonds, straight from the Kimberley mines, I imagine. They were smuggled here to Marrakesh where that teen-ager was given the task of throwing them, a few at a time, into the cobra's basket. Gulez collected them at the end of the day and passed them on along their route. Soon they would be changed into currency with which to buy the plutonium the terrorists wanted."

"That's all I need," the South African said grimly. "This man will be turned over to the Moroccan police. Their laws are quite strict. I'll deal with the people who supplied these diamonds in the first place."

With the double fee safely in hand, Nick decided he and Sandra should be on their way. Outside, he asked, "How are you feeling?"

"Fine. It takes more than a cobra bite to keep me down."

"I'll fly back with you tomorrow."

"I'm just sorry I came all this way for nothing."

"It wasn't for nothing," he said. "I'm giving you half the money. After all, you did rescue me."

"You're a good man, Nick Velvet." She started to walk away, then turned to add, "And a smart one, too."

The Theft of the Birthday Candles

Sandra Paris, known in some circles as the White Queen, moved silently across the marble lobby of the Pan Pacific Hotel in Vancouver like a patient lynx stalking her prey. She was a woman in her late thirties with a face of innocent beauty framed by striking platinum-blonde hair. Some might have guessed her to be in show business, and indeed she'd had a brief career as an actress before turning to more profitable ventures.

As soon as she spotted Raymond Della Ventura leaving the elevator she pounced, intercepting him on the way to the dining room. "Hello there," she greeted him in her coyest voice. "I'm Sandra Paris. You probably don't remember me."

Though she was a tall woman, Della Ventura still towered above her by several inches. He grinned and seemed about to pat her on the head, then said, "On the contrary. I believe we met at Monte Carlo last spring. If you're free would you join me for breakfast?"

She dazzled him with a smile. "My favorite meal!"

"Yes, it would be."

As with Lewis Carroll's White Queen, Sandra prided herself on accomplishing impossible things before breakfast. Nothing pleased her more than settling down to a morning feast following some particularly brazen endeavor. "They have a fine buffet here," Della Ventura pointed out, "or you can order from the menu."

"What brings you to Vancouver?" she asked after they'd grazed at the buffet and settled down with their food. "I seem to remember you were an arms dealer when we met at Monte Carlo."

"I still am," he said with a smile. "But it is a terrible trade to be in these days. The larger nations all talk peace, so I'm left in bidding wars for small contracts that aren't worth the effort."

Sandra tasted a strip of bacon. "There are times when I've been able to help out in such matters."

"How? By seducing my rivals?"

"I was thinking more of stealing their plane."

Raymond Della Ventura's face froze for just an instant and then relaxed into uncertain laughter. "Surely you jest!"

She shrugged and buttered a piece of toast. "Whether or not I jest depends entirely upon you."

He glanced around at the other tables and lowered his voice. "We can't talk about this here."

"After breakfast perhaps we could go for a stroll along the harbor."

At about the same time, a thousand miles south in Reno, Nick Velvet was having breakfast with a potential client named Beth Blanchard. He was explaining to her the exact nature of his business. "My usual fee is thirty thousand dollars plus any unusual expenses. I steal only objects of little or no value."

"I understand that, Mr. Velvet." Beth Blanchard was old California money, which usually meant oil or water. Nick's first glance at her stylish hairdo, carefully sculpted face and a large diamond ring had almost made him double his fee. She was probably in her forties, trying to look younger and pretty much succeeding. "I am prepared to pay half your fee in advance."

"Just what is it you want stolen?"

She took a sip of wine. "The candles off a birthday cake."

"I once stole an entire birthday cake, but — just the candles?"

"Just the candles."

"Nothing special about them? No diamond rings attached or anything like that?"

His question made her cover her own ring with her right hand. "So far as I know they're ordinary candles, a few inches long, sold in boxes of a dozen for a dollar or less. Nothing is attached."

"And where are they now?"

"More important is where they'll be tomorrow evening. I'm giving a birthday party for my step-daughter Tess at the Friars' Inn. She's turning twenty-five and I've invited nearly a hundred of her friends. There'll be an orchestra and dancing after dinner, and that's when the cake will be served."

"She's your husband's daughter by a previous marriage?"

Beth Blanchard nodded. "Ralph died five years ago, swept overboard during a yacht race on Lake Tahoe, and I made a vow to look after Tess as if she were my very own. I think I've done that."

"It must have been terrible for her, losing her father like that."

"Worse for me. He left a pile of debts. Tess is all right because her grandfather set up a trust for her many years back, but I had to do battle with the IRS."

"Where's her real mother?"

"Back in New York. She's been out to see Tess once or twice, though not recently. Tess asked me to invite her tomorrow night."

"Why do you want me to steal the candles from the birthday cake?"

"I understood that you asked no questions involving motives."

"I don't. Sometimes I just get curious."

She passed him an envelope across the table. "Here's half your fee. That should satisfy your curiosity."

"It does." He produced a small notebook. "This party will be held tomorrow at

Friars' Inn. Where's that located?"

"Right by the airport. You can do the job and catch the red eye back to New York."

"Sounds good to me," Nick agreed. "About what time will the cake be brought in?"

"After dinner, around eight-thirty. Tess's birth-mother has requested that she do the honors. She'll wheel the cake out of the kitchen into the party room at the inn."

"And that's when the candles will have to be stolen. It doesn't leave me much time."

"One other thing — no one should know about the theft."

Nick stopped writing. "How do I steal them without anyone knowing they're gone?"

"That's what I'm paying you for."

It was a cool, misty morning in Vancouver, typically April, as Sandra Paris and Raymond Della Ventura strolled slowly along the harbor walk toward the ferry dock. "I know you're running guns to various groups in Latin America and the Far East," Sandra told him. "And I also know that your business is threatened by a man named Murkum, who appeared out of nowhere a few years back and is trying to monopolize the small arms trade in those areas."

"You know a great deal."

Sandra watched an elderly man lingering nearby. When she was certain he was harmless she continued. "Murkum is well named. His past is murky indeed, and even his nationality is not known with any degree of certainty. What is known is that he arranged to purchase a used Russian cargo plane, an Antonov 26, in Latvia this week for $30,000."

Della Ventura smiled slightly. "Your information is accurate but outdated. The sale has been completed and Murkum took delivery of the plane yesterday morning."

Sandra glanced at her watch, calculating the time difference in her head. "Do you want the plane?"

The tall man snickered. "I want it with its cargo. It's no good to me empty."

"The cargo is small arms?"

He nodded. "Seventy-seven cases of Bulgarian-made weapons including 300 Kalashnikov assault rifles with 20,000 rounds of ammunition, fifteen 9-millimeter pistols with 4,000 rounds of ammunition, two sniper rifles with night vision sights, ten rocket launchers with 200 rocket grenades, and 100 hand grenades."

"You know those figures by heart!" she said with some amazement.

"A copy of the real bill of lading, not the fake one showing machine parts, was faxed to my hotel by an associate in Sofia this morning. That's enough to start a small war, or to keep one going. The cargo was picked up yesterday afternoon and is now on its way across the Pacific by the great circle route. The plane will refuel here overnight and take off before breakfast on the flight south. I believe the cases of arms will be parachuted to members of the guerrilla movement in southern Mexico, though one can never be too certain with Murkum."

"The fact that you're here tells me you plan some action during that refueling stop."

The tall man shrugged. "My associate tells me Murkum himself is on board the plane. I am planning to suggest a partnership to him."

The idea of it made Sandra laugh. "A partnership! This man has purchased the plane and the shipment of arms, as well as hiring a pilot and crew. Why should he want a partner at this stage of things?"

"Because he is very short of working capital. The arms cost him $65,000 in American money. I understand he has been paid $165,000 for it. Out of that $100,000 profit must come the cost of the plane, the cost of parachute rigging from South Africa, and payments to the pilot and crew. That doesn't leave much profit considering the risk of the enterprise."

Sandra did some silent calculations. "How much would the plane and its cargo be worth to you?"

"The plane plus cargo cost Murkum $95,000. Forget the parachute riggings. You can have them if you want. I'd give $50,000 for the plane and cargo."

They walked along a little further, reaching the ferry dock just as the boat sounded its horn and slipped away toward North Vancouver. Sandra watched its crossing through the morning mist for a few moments and then said, "One hundred thousand."

"Are you crazy? I could buy the whole thing for ninety-five!"

"Maybe you could, maybe you couldn't. Obviously you want the shipment for another buyer, one who'll pay more than the $165,000 Murkum received from the Mexican guerrillas."

He scowled down at her. "Why is that so obvious?"

"Because, for one thing, you don't want or need the parachute rigging. You're not planning a parachute drop for those weapons. You're going to land the plane somewhere, and certainly not in the Mexican jungle. And since Murkum already collected his money, what would you gain at this point by hijacking the plane and delivering the guns to the original buyers? No, the guns are going somewhere else, where there are bigger bucks and some sort of airport or landing strip. That's the deal you'd offer Murkum for a partnership and that's the deal I'm cutting in on. Pay me one hundred grand and the plane, with its cargo, is yours before breakfast tomorrow."

Raymond Della Ventura held out his hand. "Lady, you drive a hard bargain. A word of warning. Murkum is probably armed. You may want a gun. I have one."

"I won't need it," Sandra answered. "Guns just get you in trouble."

When Nick Velvet learned that Tess's birth-mother would be presenting her daughter with the cake, he asked Beth Blanchard to arrange a meeting with her. "I'll do better than that," Tess's step-mother told him. "Her name is Irma Fine and her plane arrives from New York at four this afternoon. You can come with me to meet her. We'll leave a little early and I'll show you the Friars' Inn."

After phoning Gloria at home to assure her all was going well, Nick picked up Mrs. Blanchard at two o'clock and drove her in his rental car out to the Friars' Inn. Designed like a mission church complete with bell tower, it was an up-scale restaurant with a party room in back that could accommodate two hundred people. "We'll only be using half of it," Beth Blanchard explained after she'd told the banquet manager they wanted to have another look at the room. "Cocktails will be served at six-thirty, followed by dinner an hour later. The cake will be a large sheet with *Happy Birthday Tess* written on it in pink icing. Irma asked if she could do the candles and wheel the cake in, and I had to agree. It will be nice for Tess. She hasn't seen her mom in nearly ten years."

Nick glanced into the kitchen, noting the location of a back door to the parking lot. A small serving table on wheels sat next to the swinging doors to the party room itself, and he assumed that would be used to transport the cake once the candles were lit. Back in the car he had a question for his client. "Is it those specific candles you want stolen? The only way to keep the theft a secret is to substitute other candles for them. That way there'll still be candles on the cake."

She considered the suggestion. "Would you have time to remove the candles and put in new ones?"

"I have a method. I'll have the candles positioned in a frame. I'll push them into the frosting, release the frame and lift it off. They won't be in exactly the same holes as the original candles, but with thick, soft birthday cake frosting no one is likely to notice. On sheet cakes the candles can be almost anywhere."

"How will you remove the original candles? How will you have time to light the new ones?"

"Let me worry about that. We'd better get on to the airport. These transcontinental flights are often a few minutes early."

They arrived at the Reno/Tahos International Airport just as the flight from New York reached the gate. Irma Fine was the third passenger off the plane, which told Nick she'd almost certainly flown first class. She was a handsome woman in her fifties, not quite as flashy as Beth Blanchard but with a quick intelligent gaze that took in Nick and Beth in an instant and formed some conclusion about their relationship.

Beth must have seen it too, because she introduced them with a throwaway phrase. "Irma, this is Nick Velvet. He does some work for me."

"Hello, Nick," Irma Fine said, shaking hands with an extra squeeze reserved for those who were more than hired help. "Nice to meet you."

"Likewise." She was carrying a shopping bag with a gift-wrapped package inside, obviously a birthday present for her daughter. Nick took it from her and led the way to the baggage claim area. Beth and Irma walked behind him, their conversation friendly but a bit forced.

"How's my daughter?" Irma Fine asked.

"Fine. She likes her job and she's dating a nice young man. We may be hearing marriage plans soon."

"That's good news. I hope I'll get to meet him."

"He should be at the house with Tess now."

The Blanchard house was an expensive one with a panoramic view, and as he drove up a servant hurried out to assist with the luggage. Once inside Nick was introduced to the birthday girl herself. Tess Blanchard was a slim blue-eyed beauty with a statuesque grace that reminded him just a bit of Sandra Paris, the White Queen, a rival and occasional partner in their shady world of larceny for hire.

At her side was a young man named Frank Duvout. Both were wearing white tennis outfits and it was obvious they were a couple. Tess gave her mother a hug and a kiss on the cheek, as if they'd seen each other only a few days earlier, then quickly introduced Duvout. "I'm so glad you're getting to meet Frank, Mom. I was beginning to think we'd have to fly to New York to get you two together."

"I've heard a great many wonderful things about you, Mrs. Fine," the young man said.

"It's been like having two mothers," Tess agreed. "I'm a lucky woman, even though I see far too little of Mom here." She gave Irma a little hug.

"Is there anything I can do to help with tomorrow's party?" Nick asked.

"I believe the restaurant is handling everything," Tess said.

"Except the cake," her mother interjected. "I'm handling that."

"Well," Nick told them, "I'll be there if you need anything."

He decided to retreat then, allowing Irma to become acquainted with Frank Duvout. Beth walked him to the door. "That went well. At tomorrow's party you can intrude a bit on her cake preparations."

"I intend to," Nick said.

She opened the front door for him and froze. A gray-haired man with a briefcase stood there, about to ring the bell. "Mr. Perkins! I wasn't expecting you!"

He cleared his throat, peering at her through tinted half-glasses. "I was in the neighborhood, Mrs. Blanchard, and took a chance that you might be home."

Beth Blanchard, obviously flustered, managed the introductions. "Nick Velvet, this is my attorney, Rich Perkins."

The attorney squinted, shook hands, and returned his attention to Nick's client. "I wanted to go over tomorrow's formalities with you, Mrs. Blanchard. If this is a bad time, perhaps we could —"

"Yes," she readily agreed. "This is a very bad time. My step-daughter is inside with her mother."

"I'm sorry. My secretary will phone you in the morning."

He quickly retreated down the front steps to his car. Beth muttered something under her breath that sounded like, "Pompous ass."

Driving back to his hotel, Nick wondered what business had brought the attorney to the Blanchard home, and why Beth had been so reluctant to see him in the presence of Irma Fine. It gave Nick something else to think about as he mulled over the best method of stealing birthday candles from a cake.

Early the following morning, with the April mist still hanging heavy in the air, the man known as Murkum strode quickly across the tarmac at Vancouver International Airport. He had the look of a vigorous outdoorsman, perhaps in his fifties, though his weathered face made age uncertain. He slowed his pace as he neared the Russian cargo plane that had carried him across the Pacific, recognizing the tall man waiting there for him.

"Ah, Della Ventura, isn't it?"

"That's right, Mr. Murkum."

"This is a surprising place to encounter you."

"I came here to talk about our business partnership."

Murkum snorted. "We have no partnership. I barely know you."

"I'm aware of the contents of that cargo plane. In fact I have a bill of lading in my pocket."

"That would be of interest only at my final destination. Planes are not searched during routine refueling stops."

Della Ventura shook his head. "You don't understand. I'm not threatening you with the authorities. I understand you're in bad financial straits at the moment and perhaps I can help."

"My finances will be improving very shortly. Excuse me, here's my pilot now. What is it, Androv?"

A man who might have been Russian, wearing a pilot's gold-braided cap along with a flight jacket, came up to them. "My co-pilot's been taken ill. I think he had some bad food. We'll have to hire another lad." He motioned toward a fellow with shaggy black hair and the shadow of a beard on his jaw. "This is Kyle Hendrix."

Murkum stared at the co-pilot. "How much flying time do you have?"

"Eight hundred hours."

"Ever flown an Antonov 26 before?"

"No," the young man admitted, "But I've been co-pilot on cargo planes a lot like it."

Murkum turned back to his pilot. "I'd rather have your other guy."

"That means waiting at least a day till he's well enough. He can't fly like he is."

"We can't wait." Murkum looked the new man up and down. "All right, Hendrix, you're hired."

"I'm going too," Della Ventura said.

"Like hell you are!"

The tall man waited until the pilots were out of earshot and then said, "If you won't agree to a partnership, I'll buy the plane and cargo from you on the spot for one hundred thousand American dollars. That's more than you paid, and you'll have the money from the Mexicans besides."

Murkum squinted at him, facing the rising sun to the east. "You must have another buyer in mind."

"That's right."

"The Mexicans wouldn't like being double-crossed. They'd come after me."

"It's a big world."

Murkum considered it for a moment. "Who's your buyer?"

"I can't tell you that, not yet."

"But he's paying how much — two hundred grand?"

"In that neighborhood. About three times what the Mexicans paid you."

"Get on the plane," Murkum said with a sigh. "We'll talk on the way. My time is getting short."

There was another man already on board, one whom Raymond Della Ventura had not yet met. He was introduced simply as Quinen. He was along to handle the cargo, Murkum said, and his broad shoulders certainly seemed capable of that. The seventy-seven cases of arms and ammunition were held in place by cargo webbing, their parachute harnesses not yet attached. That was fine with Della Ventura. It would save him the trouble of removing them again.

"Are we ready for takeoff?" Murkum asked the pilot.

"Five minutes. I'm having some breakfast brought on board for Hendrix and myself. Want anything?"

Murkum glanced at Della Ventura who shook his head. "No, we ate already."

"We'd better get this deal worked out," Della Ventura said. "I have a cashier's check in my pocket, drawn on a Swiss account."

"Wait till we're in the air."

Della Ventura was growing nervous. Even after the boxed breakfasts from the airport's food vendor arrived he paced the plane's interior until the pilot told him to take one of the crew seats along the side and fasten his belt. Then the engines turned over and came to life. The big plane coasted onto the runway and within minutes they were airborne.

Della Ventura had expected Sandra to make her move then, but nothing happened. The cockpit door was closed and he couldn't see what might be going on.

He moistened his lips and stared at Murkum and the broad-shouldered Quinen. "How long is the flight to Mexico?" he asked.

Murkum managed a pasty smile. "There's been a change of plan. We're flying to Utah instead, and then to Nevada."

That was when Della Ventura noticed the gun coming up in Quinen's hand. He was fast reaching his own weapon, and in the instant they both fired it was dead even.

The guests gathered early that evening at the Friars' Inn for Tess Blanchard's birthday party. Nick Velvet was somewhat surprised to find himself seated next to the stuffy Blanchard lawyer, Rich Perkins. His tinted glasses reflected the overhead lights as he turned toward Nick and said, "I know we met yesterday at the Blanchard home, but I missed your connection with the family. Are you Tess's uncle?"

"An unofficial uncle. I couldn't miss her twenty-fifth birthday party."

"It's a big day for the young lady," the attorney agreed. "I've only known the family a few years, but Mrs. Blanchard and her step-daughter have been very close, especially since the tragic accident to her father on Lake Tahoe."

Waiters had begun serving the food, and Nick let his gaze move around the room, observing Tess and young Frank Duvout snuggling at the head table. Beth Blanchard and Tess's mother Irma Fine were both seated there too, along with a few other relatives Nick didn't know. After the salad had been served he took the opportunity to continue the conversation. "The boating accident was five years ago, wasn't it?"

"That's right. Of course I didn't know the family then but I remember the newspaper accounts. They searched the lake for weeks. They even found a body, but DNA tests proved it wasn't Ralph Blanchard."

"I understand Tess has a trust fund from her grandfather."

Perkins nodded as he ate his salad. "I never knew him but he was quite well off. The trust fund is a lucky break for her. If the money had gone to her father it would still be tied up."

As the dinner guests were finishing the main course, Nick spotted Irma Fine heading for the kitchen. It was nearing cake time. He quickly followed and found her opening two small boxes of candles. They seemed ordinary enough, hardly anything that might prove lethal to the guest of honor. As he'd guessed, they were pink for a girl. Irma arranged them in uneven rows across the top of the sheet cake. Nick offered to help but she waved him away. "This is a mother's job."

She threw away the two empty boxes of candles and lit a match, passing the flame from one wick to the next. One of the chefs casually watched the operation before turning back to his stove. Then, when all seemed ready for the presentation, a snag suddenly developed. "Where's the little cart?" Irma demanded. The chef came over to look around and confirmed that it was missing from its usual place. They went in search of it together, exactly as Nick had planned.

Quickly he wet his fingers in the sink and pulled the candles from the cake, dousing the flames as he did so. He knew it would only be moments before they located the cart where he'd hidden it earlier in the storage room. Then, working as fast as he could, he dropped the stolen candles into his pocket and produced the frame he'd left in the kitchen on a high shelf. It held twenty-five new pink candles, which he turned upside down, pressing the accelerant-treated wicks against a hot stove until they all caught fire at once. Then he pushed the candles into the top of the cake, releasing and removing the frame.

Nick's candles covered a smaller area of the cake than Irma's had, but by the time she returned a moment later with the cart she was too hurried to notice. He lifted the cake onto the cart for her, positioning it in the center, and she gave him a quick thank-you smile. Then he held open the kitchen door while she wheeled the cake into the party room to a chorus of *Happy Birthday!*

Tess Blanchard beamed with pleasure. It was her big moment.

The Antonov 26 cargo plane had touched down at the Reno/Tahos International Airport just before noon that morning. The pilot reported an emergency on board and requested permission to land. The story he told was that two members of the five-man crew had gotten into an argument and shot each other. Both were dead. The men were identified as Raymond Della Ventura and Abel Quinen. Although jurisdiction was unclear at that point, the Reno police were summoned and Detective Sergeant Ritter arrived shortly to take charge of the investigation.

Ritter was a handsome young man who wore his dark hair cut short. He had a way of squinting when he spoke, which Sandra Paris found attractive. If he'd been ten years older she might have taken off her wig and makeup and revealed herself to be a woman. As it was, she simply answered his questions as the co-pilot, Kyle Hendrix. "Where did the flight originate, Mr. Hendrix?" the detective asked.

"Somewhere in eastern Europe, Latvia or Bulgaria I think. I didn't hire on as co-pilot until Vancouver, when their regular man got sick." She was using her best bass voice, one that had fooled plenty of men in the past.

"What was your cargo?"

"Machine parts of some sort."

"The cargo bay is empty now."

"After the shooting the plane began losing altitude. Mr. Murkum was afraid a stray bullet might have damaged the controls. We had to jettison the cargo over a lake."

"Tell me about the shooting."

"I didn't see what happened. I was in the cockpit with the pilot. We heard shots and Androv gave me the controls while he checked on them. When he came back he said Della Ventura and Quinen had killed each other."

Ritter flipped back a few pages in his notebook. "Let's see now. Murkum says you were headed for Mexico, right?"

"That's correct."

"From Vancouver?"

"Yes."

His eyes studied her carefully, as if seeking out some deep secret just below the surface. "I see." He made a notation in his book and asked a few more routine questions. Finally he said, "All right, Mr. Hendrix. You may go. But please wait outside until I'm finished with the pilot and Mr. Murkum. I may have some follow-up questions."

Sandra waited impatiently in the customs lounge at the airport until the questioning ended some hours later. Androv and Murkum both emerged around eight o'clock. They were free to go, but the pilot felt he should check over the plane first before they thought about continuing their journey. Murkum and Sandra both carried American passports, hers in the name of Kyle Hendrix, and they passed through customs together. He made a quick phone call and then joined her. "Where are you headed now?" she asked, still in her deep voice. With her client dead and the cargo she'd been hired to steal now resting at the bottom of Eagle Lake, she was at loose ends. She only knew she wouldn't be returning to that plane.

"I have to see a man named Nick Velvet," he told her. "I owe him some money."

Sandra froze at the sound of the name. What was Nick doing in Reno? Certainly he wasn't involved in stealing a shipment of small arms. "Maybe I'll go with you," she said casually.

He considered it for a moment and then said, "Fine. I might need some extra muscle."

Beth Blanchard slipped away from the head table when the dancing began, and met Nick in the hallway near the back entrance of the restaurant. She led him outside to the parking lot where they were alone. It was almost dark and across the field he could see the lights of planes landing and taking off. Nick handed over the candles with bits of frosting still adhering to them. "Here they are, as promised."

She accepted them with a smile. "Was it difficult?"

"Should I say it was a piece of cake?"

"I expect the balance of your money to arrive shortly. There was an unexpected delay at the airport."

"Is my fee so high that you have to fly it in?"

"I have a partner." She glanced toward the door. "And here he is now."

Two men walked in from the airport road at that moment. The taller of the two had the weathered face of an outdoorsman. The other, wearing a worn leather flight jacket, looked like a boy despite a shadow of beard along his jaw. When a passing light caught his face he seemed familiar to Nick. "Hello, Beth," the older man said.

"What happened at the airport?"

"It's a long story. I'll tell you sometime. Is this Velvet?"

"It is," she answered, "but who's the kid?"

"My co-pilot, Hendrix." Then he motioned toward Nick. "Did he do the job?" She showed him the candles. "It went well. No one noticed, not even Irma."

Murkum nodded and took a thick envelope from his pocket. "Here's my share."

Nick's fingers reached for the envelope, seconds away from finishing the job, when the back door of the Friars' Inn opened and a woman stepped out to join them. "What's going on?" she asked. "I came out to have a cigarette." It was Irma Fine.

"This is private, Irma," Beth Blanchard said, trying to step in front of Murkum.

But she wasn't fast enough, and Irma got a good look at Murkum. "My God, Ralph!" she exclaimed in surprise. "You're alive!"

Murkum gave an animal growl of frustration and pulled out his pistol. "You're through messing up my life," he told her.

Then the co-pilot, Hendrix, grabbed his wrist and flipped him to the ground like a baby. Nick had seen that trick before. Now, even in the fading light, he recognized Sandra Paris.

It was sometime later when Nick and Sandra finally had a chance to talk in a booth at the Friars' bar. She had removed some of the makeup to retrieve her feminine image, and Nick gave a sigh of relief when he saw her emerge from the ladies' room. "Now you're starting to look like yourself again. What were you doing on a Russian cargo plane disguised as a man?"

"Trying to do an impossible thing before breakfast, but today it proved too impossible. One of Murkum's man drew a gun and my client was foolish enough to shoot it out with him while we were in the air. It's a wonder we weren't all killed,"

"How did they get all these guns on a plane? Murkum must have had one too."

"They don't check transport crews like they do commercial airline passengers. But with my client dead I was in one heck of a scrape. If I revealed who I was and what I was there for, Murkum might have killed me. As it was, I had to sit there while he and the pilot argued over what to do next. Murkum wanted to fly over a lake and dump the bodies out. The pilot wanted to dump the guns and keep the bodies. He argued that if someone happened to see us dumping the bodies and they were later recovered, we might face murder charges. He said it was safer to land in Reno with the bodies and an empty plane, and tell the truth about the shooting."

"So that's what you did," Nick said. "But where were those guns bound for?"

"Della Ventura thought they were headed for Mexican rebels, but in truth

Murkum planned to land the plane on a dry lake bed in Utah and deliver them to a group of right-wing militants. My client had a similar customer in a different state. There seem to be a lot of crazy people around."

"So Murkum always planned to be in Reno tonight, after delivering the arms?"

"I guess so," Sandra agreed. "But you know more about that part than I do."

Nick Velvet sighed. In retrospect it all seemed unreal. "I was hired to steal the candles off a birthday cake, but I wasn't told why. Beth Blanchard said it was her stepdaughter Tess's 25th birthday. Her father had supposedly drowned in Lake Tahoe five years ago, though apparently his body was never found. He had a great many debts at the time. As we now know, he didn't drown, though he may have arranged for a body to be found in the lake so he'd be declared dead. That didn't happen because the DNA wasn't right. But Ralph Blanchard escaped to Europe and started a new life, parlaying a little money into a hit and miss business of buying and selling small arms."

"What happened tonight? Why did you need to steal those candles?"

"Tess's real mother, Irma Fine, was Blanchard's first wife. Somehow she heard about the birthday party for her daughter and insisted on attending. Not only that, she insisted on providing the birthday cake. She wanted to light the candles in the restaurant kitchen and wheel the cake in herself. There was no way Beth could stop her, other than hiring me to steal the candles."

"But why?"

"A lawyer told me Tess was due to inherit a large trust fund from her late grandfather. Since she hadn't received it at age 21, it was a pretty safe guess that she would get it at 25. The lawyer even remarked that it was a big day for her."

"She'd receive the trust fund tonight!"

Nick smiled. "That's what everyone was supposed to think. Except Irma Fine. If anyone knew Tess Blanchard's correct age, it was her mother. I watched her put those candles on the cake. She opened two small boxes, arranged the candles, and threw the empty boxes away. Those boxes almost always hold twelve candles each. But say it was an odd manufacturer who packed thirteen to the box. If that was the case, what happened to the 26th candle? No, there had to be twelve candles in each box, 24 candles in all. What does that tell us, from the hands of Tess's mother herself? That Tess was not 25 tonight, despite what her stepmother said, but only 24. I was hired to steal the candles so no one would notice and question the number. Tess's inheritance from her grandfather had become very important to her stepmother, and to her father."

"So they made her a year older, but how?"

"It's not as difficult as you might think. Tess went along with it, of course, even though her father and stepmother would have taken part of the inheritance. They had a new lawyer who hadn't known the grandfather or drawn up his original will. They only had to change one figure on a copy of her birth certificate and one figure on the copies of the grandfather's trust papers. A small bribe to a paralegal at the law office could have handled the whole thing. I imagine the original plan called for Ralph Blanchard faking his own death so that Beth could collect his insurance. But without a body the insurance payment had to wait for a legal presumption of death, which is seven years in Nevada and California. With things closing in on him, he couldn't wait another two years."

"Couldn't you or the stepmother simply have added a candle to the cake?"

"If it didn't match the others it would have stood out like a firecracker. My replacements didn't match exactly, but at least they were pink and all alike."

"What'll Tess's father do now?"

"Answer a great many questions. Irma was calling the police before we left. They'll want to ask him about that other body in the lake, and about pulling a gun on his ex-wife. Irma will also accuse him of attempted fraud in changing his daughter's birth date. Even if he talks his way out of all that, those militants in Utah are going to want their money back."

Sandra Paris gave a sigh. "At least I hope Tess Blanchard had a happy birthday. Maybe she'll invite you back next year for her real 25th."

A Nick Velvet Checklist

COLLECTIONS

The Spy and the Thief. New York: Davis Publications, 1971. Contains seven stories about Nick Velvet and seven about Jeffrey Rand.

The Thefts of Nick Velvet. New York: The Mysterious Press, 1978. Contains thirteen stories about Nick Velvet. The limited edition includes a fourteenth story in a separate pamphlet.

The Velvet Touch. Norfolk: Crippen & Landru Publishers, 2000. Contains fourteen stories about Nick Velvet.

FIRST PUBLICATION OF EACH STORY

1. "The Theft of the Clouded Tiger," *Ellery Queen's Mystery Magazine* [hereafter, *EQMM*], September 1966. Collected in *The Spy and the Thief* and *The Thefts of Nick Velvet*.
2. "The Theft from the Onyx Pool," *EQMM*, June 1967. Collected in *The Spy and the Thief* and *The Thefts of Nick Velvet*.
3. "The Theft of the Toy Mouse," *EQMM*, June 1968. Collected in *The Thefts of Nick Velvet*.
4. "The Theft of the Brazen Letters," *EQMM*, November 1968. Collected in *The Spy and the Thief*.
5. "The Theft of the Wicked Tickets," *EQMM*, September 1969. Collected in *The Spy and the Thief*.
6. "The Theft of the Sacred Music," *Mike Shayne Mystery Magazine* (as "Dead Man's Song"), September 1969.
7. "The Theft of the Meager Beavers," *EQMM*, December 1969. Collected in *The Thefts of Nick Velvet*.
8. "The Theft of the Silver Lake Serpent," *Argosy* (British), January 1970. Collected in *The Thefts of Nick Velvet*.
9. "The Theft of the Laughing Lions," *EQMM*, February 1970. Collected in *The Spy and the Thief*.
10. "The Theft of the Coco Loot," *EQMM*, September 1970. Collected in *The Spy and the Thief*.

11. "The Theft of the Blue Horse," *EQMM*, November 1970. Collected in *The Spy and the Thief*.
12. "The Theft of the Dinosaur's Tail," *EQMM*, March 1971.
13. "The Theft of the Satin Jury," *EQMM*, June 1971.
14. "The Theft of the Leather Coffin," *EQMM*, November 1971.
15. "The Theft of the Seven Ravens," *EQMM*, January 1972. Collected in *The Thefts of Nick Velvet*.
16. "The Theft of the Mafia Cat," *EQMM*, May 1972. Collected in *The Thefts of Nick Velvet*.
17. "The Theft from the Empty Room," *EQMM*, September 1972. Collected in *The Thefts of Nick Velvet*.
18. "The Theft of the Foggy Film," *EQMM*, November 1972.
19. "The Theft of the Crystal Crown," *Mike Shayne Mystery Magazine*, January 1973. Collected in *The Thefts of Nick Velvet*.
20. "The Theft of the Circus Poster," *EQMM*, May 1973. Collected in *The Thefts of Nick Velvet*.
21. "The Theft of the Cuckoo Clock," *EQMM*, September 1973.
22. "The Theft of Nick Velvet," *EQMM*, February 1974. Collected in *The Thefts of Nick Velvet*.
23. "The Theft of the General's Trash," *EQMM*, May 1974. Collected in *The Thefts of Nick Velvet*.
24. "The Theft of the Legal Eagle," *EQMM*, July 1974.
25. "The Theft of the Bermuda Penny," *EQMM*, June 1975. Collected in *The Thefts of Nick Velvet*.
26. "The Theft of the Venetian Window," *EQMM*, November 1975. Collected in *The Velvet Touch*.
27. "The Theft of the Admiral's Snow," *EQMM*, April 1976.
28. "The Theft of the Wooden Egg," *EQMM*, July 1976.
29. "The Theft of the Sherlockian Slipper," *EQMM*, February 1977. Collected as a separate pamphlet (under the title "The Theft of the Persian Slipper") in the limited edition of *The Thefts of Nick Velvet*, and (under the original title) in *The Velvet Touch*.
30. "The Theft of Nothing at All," *EQMM*, May 1977. Collected in *The Velvet Touch*.
31. "The Theft of the Child's Drawing," *EQMM*, October 1977.
32. "The Theft of the Family Portrait," *EQMM*, March 1978.
33. "The Theft of the Turquoise Telephone," *EQMM*, August 1978.
34. "The Theft of Yesterday's Newspaper," *EQMM*, March 1979.
35. "The Theft of the Firefighter's Hat," *EQMM*, June 1979.
36. "The Theft of Sahara's Water," *EQMM*, December 1979.

37. "The Theft of the Banker's Ashtray," *EQMM*, February 11, 1980.
38. "The Theft of the Four of Spades," *EQMM*, October 6, 1980. Collected in *The Velvet Touch*.
39. "The Theft of the Thanksgiving Turkey," *EQMM*, December 1, 1980.
40. "The Theft of the Lopsided Cobweb," *EQMM*, February 25, 1981.
41. "The Theft of the Red Balloon," *EQMM*, August 12, 1981.
42. "The Theft of the Picture Postcards," *EQMM*, December 2, 1981.
43. "The Theft of the Sliver of Soap," *EQMM*, May 1982.
44. "The Theft of the Used Teabag," *EQMM*, November 1982.
45. "The Theft of the White Queen's Menu," *EQMM*, March 1983. Collected in *The Velvet Touch*.
46. "The Theft of the Unsold Manuscript," *EQMM*, July 1983.
47. "The Theft of the Halloween Pumpkin," *EQMM*, October 1983.
48. "The Theft of the Overdue Library Book," *EQMM*, March 1984. Collected in *The Velvet Touch*.
49. "The Theft of the Dead Houseplant," *EQMM*, October 1984.
50. "The Theft of the Ball of Twine," *EQMM*, March 1985.
51. "The Theft of the Cardboard Castle," *EQMM*, November 1985. Collected in *The Velvet Touch*.
52. "The Theft of the Author's Eraser," *EQMM*, June 1986.
53. "The Theft of McGregor's Skunk," *EQMM*, November 1986.
54. "The Theft of Cinderella's Slipper," *EQMM* (as "The Theft of the Lost Slipper"), April 1987. Collected in *The Velvet Touch*.
55. "The Theft of the Matador's Cape," *EQMM*, September 1987.
56. "The Theft of the Birthday Cake," *EQMM*, May 1988.
57. "The Theft of the Faded Flag," *EQMM*, September 1988. Collected in *The Velvet Touch*.
58. "The Theft of the Doctor's Chopsticks," *EQMM*, February 1989.
59. "The Theft of the Empty Birdcage," *EQMM*, July 1989.
60. "The Theft of the Christmas Stocking," *EQMM*, Mid-December 1989.
61. "The Theft of the Mannequin's Wig," *EQMM*, June 1990.
62. "The Theft of the Bingo Card," *EQMM*, November 1990.
63. "The Theft of Leopold's Badge," *EQMM*, March 1991. Collected in *The Velvet Touch*.
64. "The Theft of the Lucky Cigar," *EQMM*, September 1991.
65. "The Theft of the Barking Dog," *EQMM*, March 1992.
66. "The Theft of Santa's Beard, *EQMM*, Mid-December 1992.
67. "The Theft of the Bald Man's Comb," *EQMM*, July 1993. Collected in *The Velvet Touch*.
68. "The Theft of the Canceled Stamp," *EQMM*, January 1994.

69. "The Theft of Twenty-nine Minutes," *EQMM*, October 1994.
70. "The Theft of the Snake Charmer's Basket," *EQMM*, April 1995. Collected in *The Velvet Touch*.
71. "The Theft of the Campaign Poster," *EQMM*, November 1995.
72. "The Theft of the Rusty Bookmark," Mysterious Bookshop pamphlet, 1995; reprinted in *EQMM*, January 1998.
73. "The Theft of the Bogus Bandit," *EQMM*, July 1996.
74. "The Theft of Columbus's Head," *EQMM*, July 1997.
75. "The Theft of Gloria's Greatcoat," *EQMM*, May 1998. Collected in *The Velvet Touch*.
76. "The Theft of the Birthday Candles," *EQMM*, March 1999. Collected in *The Velvet Touch*.
77. "The Theft of the Parrot's Feather," *EQMM*, August 2000.

CRIPPEN & LANDRU, PUBLISHERS

P. O. Box 9315, Norfolk, VA 23505
E-mail: info@crippenlandru.com; toll-free & fax: 877 622-6656
Web: www.crippenlandru.com

Crippen & Landru publishes first edition short-story collections by important detective and mystery writers. The following books are currently (September 2006) in print in our regular series; see our website for full details:

The McCone Files by Marcia Muller. 1995. Trade softcover, $19.00.

Diagnosis: Impossible, The Problems of Dr. Sam Hawthorne by Edward D. Hoch. 1996. Trade softcover, $19.00.

Who Killed Father Christmas? by Patricia Moyes. 1996. Signed, unnumbered cloth overrun copies, $30.00.

My Mother, The Detective by James Yaffe. 1997. Trade softcover, $15.00.

In Kensington Gardens Once by H.R.F. Keating. 1997. Trade softcover, $12.00.

Shoveling Smoke by Margaret Maron. 1997. Trade softcover, $19.00.

The Ripper of Storyville and Other Tales of Ben Snow by Edward D. Hoch. 1997. Trade softcover. $19.00.

Renowned Be Thy Grave by P.M. Carlson. 1998. Trade softcover, $16.00.

Carpenter and Quincannon by Bill Pronzini. 1998. Trade softcover, $16.00.

Famous Blue Raincoat by Ed Gorman. 1999. Signed, unnumbered cloth overrun copies, $30.00. Trade softcover, $17.00.

The Tragedy of Errors and Others by Ellery Queen. 1999. Trade softcover, $19.00.

McCone and Friends by Marcia Muller. 2000. Trade softcover, $19.00.

Challenge the Widow Maker by Clark Howard. 2000. Trade softcover, $16.00.

Fortune's World by Michael Collins. 2000. Trade softcover, $16.00.

The Velvet Touch: Nick Velvet Stories by Edward D.. Hoch. 2000. Trade softcover, 19.00.

Long Live the Dead: Tales from Black Mask by Hugh B. Cave. 2000. Trade softcover, $16.00.

Tales Out of School by Carolyn Wheat. 2000. Trade softcover, $16.00.

Stakeout on Page Street and Other DKA Files by Joe Gores. 2000. Trade softcover, $16.00.

The Celestial Buffet by Susan Dunlap. 2001. Trade softcover, $16.00.

Kisses of Death: A Nathan Heller Casebook by Max Allan Collins. 2001. Trade softcover, $19.00.

The Old Spies Club and Other Intrigues of Rand by Edward D. Hoch. 2001. Signed, unnumbered cloth overrun copies, $32.00. Trade softcover, $17.00.

Adam and Eve on a Raft by Ron Goulart. 2001. Signed, unnumbered cloth overrun copies, $32.00. Trade softcover, $17.00.

The Sedgemoor Strangler by Peter Lovesey. 2001. Trade softcover, $17.00.

The Reluctant Detective by Michael Z. Lewin. 2001. Signed, numbered clothbound, $42.00. Trade softcover, $17.00.

Nine Sons by Wendy Hornsby. 2002. Trade softcover, $16.00.

The Curious Conspiracy by Michael Gilbert. 2002. Signed, numbered clothbound, $42.00. Trade softcover, $17.00.

The 13 Culprits by Georges Simenon, translated by Peter Schulman. 2002. Trade softcover, $16.00.

The Dark Snow by Brendan DuBois. 2002. Signed, unnumbered cloth overrun copies, $32.00. Trade softcover, $17.00.

Come Into My Parlor: Tales from Detective Fiction Weekly by Hugh B. Cave. 2002. Trade softcover, $17.00.

The Iron Angel and Other Tales of the Gypsy Sleuth by Edward D. Hoch. 2003. Signed, numbered clothbound, $42.00. Trade softcover, $17.00.

Cuddy – Plus One by Jeremiah Healy. 2003. Trade softcover, $18.00.

Problems Solved by Bill Pronzini and Barry N. Malzberg. 2003. Signed, numbered clothbound, $42.00. Trade softcover, $16.00.

A Killing Climate by Eric Wright. 2003. Signed, numbered clothbound, $42.00. Trade softcover, $17.00.

Lucky Dip by Liza Cody. 2003. Signed, numbered clothbound, $42.00. Trade softcover, $17.00.

Kill the Umpire: The Calls of Ed Gorgon by Jon L. Breen. 2003. Trade softcover, $17.00.

Suitable for Hanging by Margaret Maron. 2004. Trade softcover, $17.00.

Murders and Other Confusions by Kathy Lynn Emerson. 2004. Signed, numbered clothbound, $42.00. Trade softcover, $19.00.

Byline: Mickey Spillane by Mickey Spillane, edited by Lynn Myers and Max Allan Collins. 2004. Trade softcover, $20.00.

The Confessions of Owen Keane by Terence Faherty. 2005. Signed, numbered clothbound, $42.00. Trade softcover, $17.00.

The Adventure of the Murdered Moths and Other Radio Mysteries by Ellery Queen. 2005. Numbered clothbound, $45.00. Trade softcover, $20.00.

Murder, Ancient and Modern by Edward Marston. 2005. Signed, numbered clothbound, $43.00. Trade softcover, $18.00.

More Things Impossible: The Second Casebook of Dr. Sam Hawthorne by Edward D. Hoch. 2006. Signed, numbered clothbound, $43.00. Trade softcover, $18.00.

Murder, 'Orrible Murder! by Amy Myers. 2006. Signed, numbered clothbound, $43.00. Trade softcover, $18.00.

FORTHCOMING TITLES IN THE REGULAR SERIES

Thirteen to the Gallows by John Dickson Carr and Val Gielgud

The Mankiller of Poojeegai and Other Mysteries by Walter Satterthwait

A Pocketful of Noses: Stories of One Ganelon or Another by James Powell

The Archer Files: The Complete Short Stories of Lew Archer, Private Investigator, Including Newly-Discovered Case-Notes by Ross Macdonald, edited by Tom Nolan

Quintet: The Cases of Chase and Delacroix, by Richard A. Lupoff

A Little Intelligence by Robert Silverberg and Randall Garrett (writing as "Robert Randall")

Attitude and Other Stories of Suspense by Loren D. Estleman

Suspense – His and Hers by Barbara and Max Allan Collins

[Currently untitled collection] by S.J. Rozan

Hoch's Ladies by Edward D. Hoch

14 Slayers by Paul Cain, edited by Max Allan Collins and Lynn F. Myers, Jr. Published with Black Mask Press

Tough As Nails by Frederick Nebel, edited by Rob Preston. Published with Black Mask Press

You'll Die Laughing by Norbert Davis, edited by Bill Pronzini. Published with Black Mask Press

CRIPPEN & LANDRU LOST CLASSICS

Crippen & Landru is proud to publish a series of *new* short-story collections by great authors who specialized in traditional mysteries:

The Newtonian Egg and Other Cases of Rolf le Roux by Peter Godfrey, introduction by Ronald Godfrey. 2002. Trade softcover, $15.00.

Murder, Mystery and Malone by Craig Rice, edited by Jeffrey A. Marks. 2002. Trade softcover, $19.00.

The Sleuth of Baghdad: The Inspector Chafik Stories, by Charles B. Child. 2002. Cloth, $27.00. Trade softcover, $17.00.

Hildegarde Withers: Uncollected Riddles by Stuart Palmer, introduction by Mrs. Stuart Palmer. 2002. Trade softcover, $19.00.

The Spotted Cat and Other Mysteries by Christianna Brand, edited by Tony Medawar. 2002. Cloth, $29.00. Trade softcover, $19.00.

Marksman by William Campbell Gault, edited by Bill Pronzini; afterword by Shelley Gault. 2003. Trade softcover, $19.00.

Karmesin: The World's Greatest Criminal — Or Most Outrageous Liar by Gerald Kersh, edited by Paul Duncan. 2003. Cloth, $27.00. Trade softcover, $17.00.

The Complete Curious Mr. Tarrant by C. Daly King, introduction by Edward D. Hoch. 2003. Cloth, $29.00. Trade softcover, $19.00.

The Pleasant Assassin and Other Cases of Dr. Basil Willing by Helen McCloy, introduction by B.A. Pike. 2003. Cloth, $27.00. Trade softcover, $18.00.

Murder – All Kinds by William L. DeAndrea, introduction by Jane Haddam. 2003. Cloth, $29.00. Trade softcover, $19.00.

The Avenging Chance and Other Mysteries from Roger Sheringham's Casebook by Anthony Berkeley, edited by Tony Medawar and Arthur Robinson. 2004. Cloth, $29.00. Trade softcover, $19.00.

Banner Deadlines: The Impossible Files of Senator Brooks U. Banner by Joseph Commings, edited by Robert Adey; memoir by Edward D. Hoch. 2004. Cloth, $29.00. Trade softcover, $19.00.

The Danger Zone and Other Stories by Erle Stanley Gardner, edited by Bill Pronzini. 2004. Cloth, $29.00. Trade softcover, $19.00.

Dr. Poggioli: Criminologist by T.S. Stribling, edited by Arthur Vidro. 2004. Cloth, $29.00. Trade softcover, $19.00.

The Couple Next Door: Collected Short Mysteries by Margaret Millar, edited by Tom Nolan. 2004. Trade softcover, $19.00.

Sleuth's Alchemy: Cases of Mrs. Bradley and Others by Gladys Mitchell, edited by Nicholas Fuller. 2005. Trade softcover, $19.00.

Who Was Guilty? Two Dime Novels by Philip S. Warne/Howard W. Macy, edited by Marlena E. Bremseth. 2005. Cloth, $29.00. Trade softcover, $19.00.

Slot-Machine Kelly by Dennis Lynds writing as Michael Collins, introduction by Robert J. Randisi. 2005. Cloth, $29.00. Trade softcover, $19.00.

The Detections of Francis Quarles by Julian Symons, edited by John Cooper; afterword by Kathleen Symons. 2006. Cloth, $29.00. Trade softcover, $19.00.

The Evidence of the Sword by Rafael Sabatini, edited by Jesse F. Knight. 2006. Cloth, $29.00. Trade softcover, $19.00.

The Casebook of Sidney Zoom by Erle Stanley Gardner, edited by Bill Pronzini. 2006. Cloth, $29.00. Trade softcover, $19.00.

The Trinity Cat by Ellis Peters (Edith Pargeter), edited by Martin Edwards and Sue Feder. 2006. Cloth, $29.00. Trade softcover, $19.00.

The Grandfather Rastin Mysteries Lloyd Biggle, Jr., introduction by Kenneth Biggle and Donna Biggle Emerson. 2006. Cloth, $29.00. Trade softcover, $19.00.

FORTHCOMING LOST CLASSICS

Masquerade: Nine Crime Stories by Max Brand, edited by William F. Nolan, Jr.

The Battles of Jericho by Hugh Pentecost, introduction by S.T. Karnick

Dead Yesterday and Other Mysteries by Mignon G. Eberhart, edited by Rick Cypert and Kirby McCauley

The Minerva Club, The Department of Patterns and Other Stories by Victor Canning, edited by John Higgins

The Casebook of Jonas P. Jonas and Others by Elizabeth Ferrars, edited by John Cooper

The Casebook of Gregory Hood by Anthony Boucher and Denis Green, edited by Joe R. Christopher

Ten Thousand Blunt Instruments by Philip Wylie, edited by Bill Pronzini

The Adventures of Señor Lobo by Erle Stanley Gardner, edited by Bill Pronzini

SUBSCRIPTIONS

Crippen & Landru offers discounts to individuals and institutions who place Standing Order Subscriptions for its forthcoming publications, either all the Regular Series or all the Lost Classics or (preferably) both. Collectors can thereby guarantee receiving limited editions, and readers won't miss any favorite stories. Standing Order Subscribers receive a specially commissioned story in a deluxe edition as a gift at the end of the year. Please write or e-mail for more details.

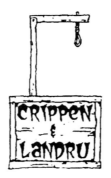

Printed in the United States
201164BV00003B/244-291/A